CAST A BRIGHT SHADOW

Tanith Lee has been a writer from the early age of nine, and her first adult fantasy novel, *The Birthgrave*, was published in 1975. Since then her highly individualistic and multi-hued style has inspired whole new generations of fantasy writers throughout the world. Born and brought up in London, she now lives in the south of England.

TANITH LEE

CAST A
BRIGHT SHADOW

Book 1 of the Lionwolf Trilogy

TOR

First published 2004 by Tor

This edition published 2005 by Tor
an imprint of Pan Macmillan Ltd
Pan Macmillan, 20 New Wharf Road, London N1 9RR
Basingstoke and Oxford
Associated companies throughout the world
www.panmacmillan.com

ISBN 0 330 41309 0

1 3 5 7 9 8 6 4 2

A CIP catalogue record for this book is available from
the British Library.

Typeset by IntypeLibra, London
Printed and bound in Great Britain by
Mackays of Chatham plc, Chatham, Kent

Firstly this book is for Jean Holden – who told me I would write it long before I knew, myself.

Also it is for the wonderful writers Cecilia Dart-Thornton and Liz Williams, whose work has given me such pleasure, and hope for the future of Fantasy and Science Fiction.

And, too, it is, as so often, for my husband and partner, John Kaiine.

Last but not least, a special thank you to *Wolfshead and Vixen* Morris.

Translator's Note

This text has been translated not only into English, but into the English of recent times. It therefore includes, where appropriate, 'contemporary' words such as *schizophrenic*, or even 'foreign' words and phrases such as *faux pas*. This method is employed in order to correspond with the syntax of the original scrolls, which themselves are written in a style of their own period, and include expressions and phrases from many areas and other tongues.

As with the main text, names, where they are exactly translatable, are rendered in English – for example, the name/title, *Lionwolf*. Occasionally names are given in a combination of exactly equivalent English plus part of the original name where it is basically untranslatable, as with the Rukarian Phoenix, the *Firefex*.

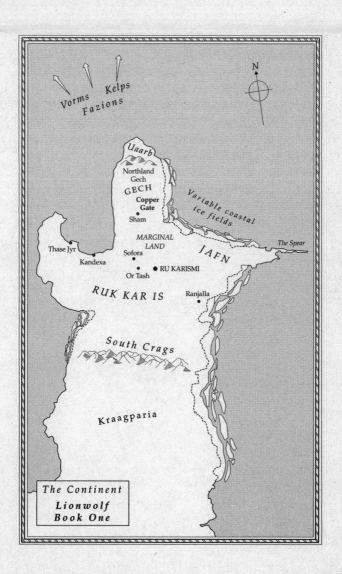

The Continent
Lionwolf
Book One

In what distant deeps or skies
Burnt the fire of thine eyes?
On what wings dare he aspire?
What the hand dare seize the fire?

William Blake
Songs of Experience. The Tyger

First Volume

FIRE JEWEL AND HEART OF ICE

The future is always more clearly to be seen than either past or present.

Magikoy saying: Ruk Kar Is

ONE

Red sky met white land. Between the two lay the city.

As he drove along Kings Mile, the great ice road that approached Ru Karismi from the south, the magician stared unblinking with his eagle's eyes. In the sunset, the city had that look it always had, and was intended always to have perhaps. Every wall and tower, every terrace and roof that showed above, seemed razor-carved from the surrounding snow.

Thryfe stood bracing his tallness against the onrush of the sleekar. The team of horned lashdeer appeared to fly, and the vehicle's runners barely touched the road's surface. If any had been out so late, they would have turned and gaped, knowing this smooth-streaming thing at once for the chariot of lord or Magikoy; few others could command such power. But the snowfields were empty by now, while only the occasional bank of smog or speed-smeared light revealed the steads that littered the city's outskirts.

The sun flashed and was suddenly down. Tinted glass parasols on the heights winked ruby and diamond, and went out. Half a minute more, and Thryfe had reached the outer wall.

Over Southgate the torches blazed. The gate stood open wide – they had seen him arriving. There was, of course, no challenge, and if he glimpsed the salutes of the guards,

Thryfe did not acknowledge them. He raced through the gate and on up the streeted slopes of the city, to the Stair. Here he paused only to halt the chariot and dismount. Most men took breath before they climbed, and again later. But Thryfe, ascending the thousand-stepped staircase of white marble, between its diagonally set thousand statues of steel, did not stop once either to breathe or to admire the view.

At the top, far above the city, the Gargolem came from its alcove in a high and shadowy door.

'Greetings and welcome, Highness Thryfe.'

The Gargolem was mechanical. The Magikoy had made it centuries before. Its metallic body was like that of a human male, though far larger in height and somewhat in girth. Its head was that of an unknown beast, maned and fanged, yet it spoke like a man. It was always addressed in turn.

'Good evening, Gargo. I'm here for the kings.'

'They do not know. Did you send no word?'

'No, Gargo.'

'I will do it now. Proceed.'

The door opened as night strode over the sky. Beyond, in amber air, lay the lanterned garden terraces of uppermost Ru Karismi, starred with palaces, whose complacence Thryfe had come to spoil.

Ruk Kar Is had at present three kings. The mightiest of these, Sallusdon, King Paramount, was currently in the west. Now the two Kings Accessorate waited on their balcony, looking at Thryfe.

By Ruk law, both these kings were of equal importance.

But, as with their build, they differed in the extreme. Bhorth was blond, a heavily muscled man run to fat, often argumentative, but weak. The other, Vuldir, sombre and slender, had an elegance of person and mind that were pitiless: the skins and tails of eighty black and white icenvels lined his exquisite mantle. He was known to dispatch humans with the same uneconomy.

The balcony jutted from the Kings Hall, out over the abyss of city night, which fell through a glitter of lighted windows and lamps to the Palest River three miles below. Dwarfed by distance, frozen, the Palest made another roadway, gleaming with torches. At this Thryfe gazed down. He ignored the kings, letting them loiter, for he was more powerful than they, and Vuldir at least needed reminding.

But it was Vuldir who spoke.

'What is this about, Magus? You've called us from dinner. My brother's belly will certainly never forgive you.'

His voice was acid. Brother Bhorth scowled.

Thryfe removed his gaze from the river, and met Vuldir's narrow eyes.

'The augurs that were taken, Vuldir, have changed aspect.'

Bhorth, the slow one, was still the one who swore.

Vuldir said, 'Which augurs, precisely?'

'Those that relate to the marriage of your daughter.'

'My daughter. You mean Saphay? But she sets out tomorrow, at first light.' Vuldir sounded bored. 'It's a minor affair, but may be useful. I believe you understand its relevance?'

'She is to wed into the Jafn Klow.'

'Exactly. Once our enemies, the Jafn are now our dear friends. This first marriage is tentative, naturally. If it blossoms, Sallusdon will consider a stronger match, one from his own and his queen's royal loins.'

'I am aware of that. I'm here to tell you something new. The augurs were taken at the betrothal and seemed sound. But today, gentlemen, I saw something else.'

'What? How? Did you go searching for it?' demanded Vuldir. Rings brightened on his hand as he made, inadvertently perhaps, a gesture of dismissal. With a lesser man than Thryfe it must have sent him from the room, but no king could order one of the Magikoy. They were the servants of common men, but the superiors of princes.

However, Thryfe answered, looking from Vuldir to Bhorth and back again.

'I don't have to tell you what I have seen, or how I have seen it, nor if I searched for it – although I did not. If I say to you it *is*, then you know I speak the truth.'

'You're too volatile, maybe,' said Vuldir.

Bhorth enquired, 'What's the nature of the possible harm?'

'The death of Vuldir's daughter. Or worse than her death – though further than her death I was unable to see for her, as is often the case. There is a massing of envy and darkness. Old foes, or fresh ones, in secret. If you send Saphay out of Ruk Kar Is, she'll be lost. And much will be lost with her. I'll tell you plainly, you will be accommodating some force which will eventually destroy you.'

'*I?*' Vuldir was amazed.

'You and all your line. All the line of the Ruk. The land, the people. It will set the world on its ear.'

'Unending Winter has done that,' grumbled Bhorth, 'five hundred years and more.'

'To this, Bhorth, Unending Winter will be Summertime.'

Far back beyond the balcony and its fretted screens, music played and candles fluttered like gold butterflies.

Bhorth turned uneasily, peering through frets at the warm world that was apparently threatened.

But Vuldir said, 'Well, you've aired your fears, Magus. Our thanks.'

Bhorth spluttered in alarm. Thryfe merely turned away. He had done what he must, with proper haste and authority. No more was asked of him.

Without offering any token of respect, he walked from the balcony, and back through the sunny candlelight of the Hall. He was bowed to on every side by men and women clad in silks and jewels. He paid them no attention, and said nothing else. Like many of the Magikoy, he believed himself a fatalist. To Thryfe's pitilessness, therefore, the small blind malice of a Vuldir was nothing.

On the east and coldest side of the Womens Pavilions, King Vuldir's fifteenth daughter had her apartments. The winds, when they woke, whistled and gnawed at the shutters and glazing, which were not always in repair. Let through, they gushed along the floors like waves of ice.

Tonight the evening was windless. Yet everything else here was in motion.

Women ran back and forth through the rose-lit rooms, their anklets jangling, voices calling, their arms full of clothing, bedding and other stuff selected for a journey.

Within the central room, Saphay, the fifteenth daughter, sat contrastingly still as stone in a chair, while her old nurse wept at her side.

'I shall never see her again,' wailed the nurse, 'never, never.'

'Yes, I shall send for you,' said the princess wearily. She had declared this many times, but neither she nor the old woman believed it.

'I am thought too shabby for this court of barbarians,' bitterly wept the nurse.

'No, you're thought too fine for it.'

'And too old – I'm too old. Oh, if she leaves me, I shall die. What else will be left for me?'

Saphay said nothing. She moved only a little, nodding as another woman asked her about some garment, who then ran busily away, bawling to others.

No dinner had been served them. Probably Saphay's apartment was forgotten, for a fifteenth female child, got by a secondary king on a much lesser concubina, was low in standing. Generally she ate in the Hall, in the place reserved for such persons.

Saphay had wondered if she would miss these chilly and unluxurious rooms, miss the grandeur of the palaces, the gardens with their frost-trees, glass parasols and statuary of steel and serpentine and ice; or the city itself spread always below. But she had lived since birth on the cold-shouldered east of the terraces, and so to be sent further eastward, to the land of the Jafn Klow, had an ironic rightness.

In her childhood another nurse, not this one, had told Saphay that the Jafn ate young girls, having first roasted them alive. But she had been told many things in childhood that were lies, and was still lied to, but now knew it.

Vuldir had bothered to come himself and tell her the facts of her impending use. She was to uphold the honour of the Ruk by marrying a Chaiord, a chieftain of the Jafn peoples.

Her father, whom mostly Saphay had seen only far off, while often hearing tales of his harshness and sense of fashion, looked her over that day, properly noticing her for the first time. 'Yes,' he remarked, 'you will do. Indeed, you're too good for this. Always remember that, girl. You're too good for the Jafn.'

Two of the apartment's little cluster of god-aspects were borne through. A violet mask glared at Saphay over a running shoulder. Then, as a mirror was hurried by, the young woman more strangely saw her own face rush past her. The glimpsed face was clouded round by topaz hair, its eyes dark as her father's, but of a different shape. Her skin, as in songs sung to others, was white as unmarked snow. But already the mirror had carried her face away.

A woman burst in at another door, bringing with her a blast of cold from the night outside. She stood, shaking off the coldness from her, wringing her hands and crying out, so all the other women stopped their activity, turning to look at her. Even the nurse did so.

'The High Magus Thryfe came to the Hall,' cried the woman who had entered. 'He took the Kings Accessorate aside. No one knows but they what he said, but he came out like an eagle, cloaked in storm. They say' – she stared at Saphay, who was not her mistress, only one more nobody the woman must serve – 'that the omens have changed. This marriage in the east is rotten and will bring only bad luck.'

Someone screamed. It was not Saphay herself. In the silence, Saphay stood up. 'Go about your duties,' she said to the woman who had come in. 'What do you know, you

9

insect, of the mind of a Magikoy? And the rest of you, get on with your work. Or I'll send to my father to have you whipped.'

She was only a girl, not yet seventeen years of age, yet she had learned things in Ru Karismi. Inevitably, to be harsh was one of them – she was Vuldir's daughter. And now she was obeyed.

But in her heart, Saphay thought, *It is true, I know it. It is darkness I go towards in the east, when the sun rises.*

Thryfe rode back from Ru Karismi, out of the yawning gate, along the glacial highway of ice. One of his houses lay to the south, but few would find it save he or another of his Order.

Beyond the limits of the road, the velocitous sleekar took to the snow-hills without apparent effort.

Above, the first moon rose. It was white as the snow or a girl's pure skin. Thryfe did not bother with it.

After an hour or two, he drove up into the forests. The trees, runnelled pillars resembling black glass, canopied with snow and spears of ice, were busy with ice-spiders brought out by the moon. They glided, winking like opals, under its rays, spinning webs like thin steel. Yet the passage of the sleekar broke through hundreds of these webs, leaving them behind in tatters.

The second moon was rising, a quarter like a piece of a coin, when the mansion came in sight for Thryfe.

He saw the windows shone blue, a sign of his long absence and that nothing unlooked-for had occurred.

Unhuman grooms, a lesser type of gargolem, emerged to take charge of chariot and team in the courtyard. As he mounted the shallow steps, the torches on either side sprang alight, and the blue windows above altered with lamp flames. He touched the door only with his glance, and it opened as it would do for him alone.

So many hours had been wasted. Was it only time that was spilled away? After he had gone up into the towery, Thryfe began after all to feel anger.

The third moon rose on Ruk Kar Is.

By this brilliant triple light, bright now as the most freezing, whitest day, Thryfe cancelled his lamps and stood before the eye of the mansion's oculum. It was blank, demonstrating none of the disturbance he had witnessed earlier.

He was dissatisfied. For once he felt his youth and its passion of rage, although he was no longer quite young, and was a fatalist.

To the serene chamber, Thryfe said this: 'I shall regret not doing more. I notice the shadow of regret before me now.' He thought, *And it outshines the night.*

He had seen Saphay now and then, over recent years, in the Kings Hall. She was lovely and childish, finally almost fullgrown. Unbound, her hair hung to the backs of her knees. Yet once he had beheld her slapping a waiting-woman who annoyed her, and how the ring on her hand had caught the woman's mouth, which bled. He had not been so charmed by Saphay after that. Like her father – yes, surely. Was it for this Thryfe had let her go so readily?

But her destiny was less than the land's, and the land too he had let go.

The globe of the oculum continued to give nothing. Only the moons drifted, a three-dropped necklet of porcelain, in the windows. Then the wind began to lift its wing across the plains.

I have done enough. Be damned to them all.

Eastward, where the moons and the wind had risen, there was a smell of burning on the air that night.

A considerable distance from the city of Ru Karismi spread an area known as the Marginal Land. It was located above the north borders of the Ruk, and cut into on the east side by the sea, which, frozen solid, extended the terrain on for miles of fluctuating, treacherous ice field. The place of burning was a day's ride inland from the ocean. Here, deep in the Marginal, ice-jungles matted the landscape, frigid tangles of obsidian and crystal, sometimes undone in clearings. In one of these lay the charcoaled embers of a large village, from which smoke yet poured.

Peb Yuve scrutinized, from the back of his flaxen transport, the sorry coffle of slaves driven off from the ruins by his men. Beside him, one of his seconds, Guri, also astride an ice-mammoth, counted gemstones, coins and bits of metal.

They were men of Olchibe, their dark yellow skin the shade of leopards in the dying arson-glow.

'Look at them, such weaklings. They'll fetch nothing in the markets of Sham.' This regretful remark was Guri's, as some of the coffle, mewling and whipped, fell down.

'No matter. This shows them, the lords in Rukar, what we may do. It's a symbol. As that it has worth for us to destroy these hovels and collect this rubbish for sale.' Peb Yuve nodded. 'Great Gods witness I have spoken.'

'Amen,' added Guri piously.

He put the cache of jewels and money into a pouch; then, like his prince, sat watching their raid's aftermath.

All about, under the static boughs of frozen figs, the Olchibe mammoths stirred like ghosts.

'The gods of these Rukar, they trouble me,' said Guri. He pushed back his fur cap, scratching at his braids.

'Why? They're false gods.'

'That's so, but nevertheless . . . Each god of the Rukar is doubled, split in two – one cruel and one fair aspect – but is still the same god. Does that give them strength, or lessen them?'

Peb Yuve did not reply.

A war leader, he was also the priest of his band, which approximated five hundred men. He thought carefully, and Guri waited in humility.

'Their gods are nothing – weak, as they themselves are. Once I knew a man among the sluhtins of Olchibe. His brain was this way, too. One hour he would be brave and glorious. Then the next he would turn, like milk, and was insolent, and vicious as a fleer-wolf.'

'Ah?'

'I shot him,' said Peb Yuve, 'with my woman bow, and with arrows for women.' He nodded again. 'I have no fear of the crack-brained gods of the Ruk.'

The coffle was upright once more. As it was dragged off, Guri visually selected for himself a woman he fancied. He knew Peb Yuve would have no interest in her. The Olchibe leader was saving his rapist skills for the near future, when they had taken the east-travelling caravan with the Rukar's princess. She was only minor royalty but, like the village they had burned tonight, she was a symbol. She would have her worth.

In the pink dawn, the procession wound down from the city heights along the huge ramps beside the Stair. Sleekars and carriage-slees, with their teams of deer, moved under banners that ribboned scarlet and silver for the royal houses of Ruk Kar Is. On the wide avenues below, crowds came out to applaud. From balconies there dropped a few hothouse flowers, past their best, left over from the previous night.

This exodus was of small importance. It was the show of a minute. If any dedicatedly craned for a sight of the girl from the palace, sent off now to barbarians in the east, they were disappointed. Sheltered by the red silk half-shell of her slee, she was also concealed by furs. But she could mean very little to them. They had never seen her before, and probably never would again.

For herself, Saphay gazed about her through her mufflings. Ru Karismi, jewel of the ice plains, was almost as unknown to her as she to it. She saw it now for virtually the first time as she left it. Its glamour was already redundant.

The caravan departed from Kings Mile at the East Pillar. Passing the solitary pylon, it coursed away into the ice fields.

Already steaders were abroad, among the man-high channels and runnels in the packed snow, labouring on those crops which survived here. The lesser road took the caravan through plantations of dormant grain and dilf, past isolate brewing and smoking-towers, each with its plume of steam or smoulder, hothouses and wind-strafed cots. Stooping apple groves covered the country beyond, and vine trees, their fruit packed tight within deformed trunks.

Once they emerged on to the open plains, the road became less pleasant, cratered in parts or covered by old snowdrifts hard as rock. Only their accompanying mageia could deal with these. Meanwhile freezing wind gusts slashed at their faces. Visors were snapped down from helmets; masks with glass eye shields were raised. The teams of lashdeer had covered their eyes at once with their natural blinders of transparent membrane.

The two women who attended Saphay sat grumbling nervously among the cushions of the half-shell. They had not wanted to come but had no choice, just as Saphay had not. They were afraid of the Winter, the plains, their destination. Not wishing to talk to them, and eventually not to listen to them any more, she finally told them to be quiet. Then their scarcely veiled expressions of hate and fright were familiar, all now that was.

At midday there was a halt, and the mageia called fire. She was a tall woman from a town to the west of the city, with indigo hair woven with charms. Fire arrived and hot food and wine were served. In the evening, after a raw sunset, this procedure was repeated.

The party then slept, distributed among the bulbs of tents lit and heated by the arts of magic. Outside the wind yowled, or else eerie echoing silences, often filled with imagined sounds, rang over the sheet of the snow.

Saphay could not sleep. She heard one of her women weeping like the nurse, if for the opposite reason.

*Why has anyone been sent with me? I never wanted them.
I would rather be alone.*

She thought, *I am alone in any case.*

They travelled in this way for an endless while. Nothing
varied, even the weather very little. It was always Winter.
There were ice-forests, ice-lakes, ice-hills and once, in the
distance, a white volcano with a cloud on it. Usually the
sky was overcast, and at night starless, the occluded moons
like dirty lamps.

Sometimes a town or village appeared. Twice they dined
and slept not in the tents, but in a rambling inn built of
whole black trees smooth as polished coal, and then an inn
paved with ice-bricks.

They saw a few animals, deer of several sorts, snow-
hares, woolly elephant, and an enormous bear far off, itself
like moving snow.

'It isn't lion country,' the captain of the soldiers said to
one of Saphay's women. 'Nothing like that here. In the east
it's different, but they have their ways of dealing with them
there.'

There were thirteen guards, the auspicious number
selected by a mage of Vuldir's. Altogether, the caravan
numbered only thirty-three persons, including the essential
mageia and Saphay.

Saphay stopped telling her women to be quiet. She was
learning more now of where she was going from their
chatter, for they consorted with the drivers and guards at
every possible juncture. So Saphay heard improbable
things she assumed to be true: of the lion sleekar teams of
the Jafn Klow, of their single God who lived beyond the
world, and their plethora of sprites and spirits who lived *in*
it; of their codes of honour and feud. She had been told

already her husband was white-haired, but had never seen him nor anyone like that, except the elderly, yet it seemed white hair was common in the east.

The road finished at the town of Freyiz. This was civilization's finish too. After Freyiz, the mageia stood in the caravan's front chariot, constantly employed in the shifting of obstacles.

'We move at a sen-snail's pace,' whined the women.

Saphay was glad of that, not wanting to reach journey's end.

Next day, the sun smashed open the sky. A dome of coolest blue overhung the plains, unmarked by anything.

The terrain offered better going. Ice-jungles appeared to the north, and the wind had dropped. They made excellent speed.

At the noon halt, the captain of the guard came over to the fire. He addressed Saphay directly.

'Madam, the mageia must have a word with you.'

Saphay stood up. When the mageia approached, Saphay bowed to her, as was customary. Behind her, the captain stood poised, unreadable. The woman nodded her charm-clinking head.

'I've seen signs, unmistakable. Trouble is coming. From the north.'

'Of what sort? Bad weather?'

'No, Saphay. Men intent on harm. They were shown to me as a wolf-pack running – but aren't wolves. Their muzzles were wet with blood.'

Saphay felt her heart stop. The captain stepped forward.

'The mageia says they're well over three hundred in number. A vandal band I'd guess, from Gech, or the Olchibe, though it's far south for them. Filthy brutes.'

Even Saphay had heard of the hordes of Gech and Olchibe and their atrocities. Her heart leapt up again and began to race – but it had nowhere to go.

'We are thirteen, and your drivers and grooms armed only with knives. Our best course is to turn back,' the captain said. His face now was grim enough. 'There was a village we passed. It offers our nicest chance.'

Saphay was aware the village had been small and pitiful, and was anyway more than a day's ride behind them.

Besides, the mageia shook her head.

'You can't outrun them. They are Fate.'

'With respect, lady,' said the captain, 'we must try. And I hope you'll help us.'

'I'll do all I can.'

She quenched the fire with a word. As it crumbled instantly into nothing, Saphay was appalled by the omen.

With the rest, she bolted to her vehicle. The whips cracked over the backs of the lashdeer, and they rushed towards the west.

Less than an hour later, the vandal band appeared from the jungle now to their right. The mageia had been dilatory or incompetent, but then she was not one of the Magikoy, only a witch from some town.

The vandals, spilling from the static dark of the jungle, were at first only a mobile dark, as if the trees had found legs. Then you saw the glint of mail, harness, weapons, and the wink of their yellow banners. They were Olchibe, and the top of every banner-staff would be crowned with a severed head – even Saphay knew this – in discrepant stages of freshness, decay or bare bone.

She was so afraid, she had no thoughts, but her women shrieked and screamed, writhing and clinging to the slee's rail. The other slees and chariots tore forward. Where the emerging Olchibe horde looked dark to them, to the Olchibe *they* would be as clearly marked by a frenzy of thrown-up snow-spume.

The cursing of the drivers, Saphay's among them, vied with the slap of whips and sluice of ice.

Yet, even running at full stretch, Saphay noted how that dark still oozed from the jungles alongside. The horde, as warned, comprised many hundred men, who all the while lurched nearer. Once free of the shadow of the trees, Saphay could see what they rode. Mammoths moved fast when trained to it. Larger in size even than the wild elephant herds, they would also trample men underfoot, or lift them in their trunks to spit on their curving tusks.

To try to escape was futile. There was not one of the Rukarians who did not understand this, but there was no other choice. Olchibe took few prisoners, and those only as slaves.

Soon Saphay could make out individual patterns and savage images on the banners. Presently flaming arrows rained down on the vehicles.

Sleekar after sleekar skidded to avoid the started fires. Some two or three chariots had caught alight at once. The deer were screaming, and Saphay's women, too, in a dreadful harmony.

The mageia, who had tied herself to her sleekar's rail, howled her phrases to put out fire. But the Olchibe too, of course, had their witches, the eldritch Crarrowin of their sluht-camps, and these had evidently put on a preserving magic more effective than the mageia's quenching. The burning vehicles burned on.

There was no more order. Saphay found herself trapped

in a whirling wheel of fire and collision, where suddenly her driver must veer to the right to miss a tumbling chariot. Her women fell; she too was shaken to the floor. Next second, through spume and smoke and flame, the girl beheld the Olchibe looming up on their mammoths, high as stampeding towers, and so close she smelled the stench of them: men and beasts and dank wool.

Her driver plunged back nearly on top of her. She was soaked and covered in his blood. His throat was cut. She saw one of her women hauled bodily up from the half-shell by a trunk like a hairy corded serpent – screeching, she was gone suddenly into the air. The other woman, in her terror, threw herself from the slee. She landed beyond sight, among the spinning runners.

The Olchibe who had killed the driver sat backwards on the rump of one of the still-running lashdeer. He faced Saphay grinning, and she had space to study him. All the tales were exact: his skin was yellow as the banners, his teeth painted, his hair mammoth-colour whitish – perhaps as her eastern husband's was. The husband that now she would never live to wed.

The Olchibe spoke, friendly, to her. Saphay did not know his language, as she knew so little. When he swung forward to take hold of her, she pulled the lifeless driver's dagger from his belt and thrust upward.

It was a fluke. She did not, either, know enough to have grasped how to kill a man. But the blade, maybe assisted by the jolts of the slee, went straight through his wind-pipe. His look was one of shock as he crashed headfirst from the car.

Saphay remained crouched on the floor. The dead driver bounced against her. Everywhere around, the world heaved with the huge phantasmal jostle of blundering mammoths. Driverless and beyond control, the lashdeer galloped headlong. Any moment, the slee must hit something, overturn, and be taken. Then they would have her. Saphay shut her eyes.

It had not occurred to her that the driver's body now hid her from the rampage. The Olchibe, tickled at such an easy conquest, for even with a minor princess a bigger retinue had been expected, paid no heed to the one runaway carriage, apparently empty save for a corpse. For the lashdeer, they had only contempt – the Olchibe scorned even to eat them.

Finally it was Peb Yuve himself, surveying the dead soldiers and frightened remains of the caravan, who turned and struck Guri across the face. 'Where is she gone?'

'The princess? *There*, Great One.'

'No, that's only some whore. *She* has gaudy hair, the Rukar royal.'

Distressed by his failure, Guri stared desperately about. Across milling mammoths, he spotted the now distant snowspray of the slee. Oddly, it raced back towards the ice-jungle.

'*There*, Great One,' Guri announced again.

Peb Yuve did not even watch Guri and his group set out. Yuve was, for that moment, more interested in the Rukar witch who, having sealed herself in a globe of force, stood glaring, as Olchibe warriors took turns in trying to pry her loose. They were electrically flung several yards each time for their pains, which vastly amused the rest, Yuve with them.

*

21

The slee was well in under the noiseless caves of frozen jungle before Saphay heard the thunder of pursuit begin again.

She recognized the heavy tread of the ice-mammoths.

Nevertheless, as the mageia had said, it had the note of Fate. She knew she was not strong or heavy enough to secure and manage the reins of the deer. Already their jolting progress had shaken out the corpse of the driver. As they rushed through the jungle's knittings, the horns of the team dislodged the more brittle boughs. Creeper and cascades of black splinters showered the slee.

Saphay rose from the floor of the carriage. She gripped the rail. She had killed a man – was changed.

To her left she glimpsed an unexpected vista, a bizarrely wide and unimpeded stretch of ice bisecting the jungle like a city street. Though unable to hold the team, she knew the cry for a leftward turn, and gave it. The deer obeyed, careering across thickets and out on to the nature-built boulevard.

Their hoofs drummed on packed snow. But, at her back, the thunder of the mammoths rocked the ground. The Olchibe would not give her up. Should she, like her woman, jump out of the slee? But driverless and panicked, the deer went too fast, refused to slow, and would not maybe for an hour or more.

Ahead lay the Marginal Land, and at last the awful glass of the sea.

Saphay prayed, but her gods had been left behind.

Only the sky saw how the slee surged on, mile on mile along the open track. The sky saw also how Guri and his cohort of twenty men discovered the track, and thudded after. Their speed was less, but enduring. Guri even laughed. 'She wants to warm us up for her!' He knew, when Peb Yuve had had his fill, the favourite seconds would get their turn.

Then the sky above the open track began to purple. Inflamed claw marks went up it from the jungles to the left, where the sun would sink.

The Olchibe shouted to the girl to give in. 'Let's take you home,' they cried, jocular. But the bitch could not speak their tongue.

Well into the Marginal now, even so none of them anticipated the sea. But the sea had drawn near. The blue day had changed the nature of the snow a little, which other blue days had also done, unlidding an inner pocket of ocean. It was not liquid; it only shone like a mauve mirror fallen on its back. As the jungles broke away and the snow lay upheaved in chunks along the sides of the track, whose openness might have warned them, all at once they were on it.

The deer shot out on the rippled ice, their hoofs going from under them, the slee-runners spitting sparks. The pursuing twenty-one men and beasts had scarcely more time to judge their path. They were already skidding at the approach to the pocket of glass water before they knew it, coping far worse than deer trained to roads of ice.

A curious dance ensued: the sliding slee, the cavorting mammoths skating over the sea lake. Shouts hit the sunset, then came precarious stasis. Everything was stilled.

The first and second moons, rising tonight together, brilliantly showed the slee lying on its side, one runner broken, the silk half-shell dislodged, the lashdeer petrified. Closer to solid ground clustered the twenty-one mammoths, some kneeling, three fallen, wrecked and grunting. Men stood scattered on the ice.

The pursuers did not pound towards their quarry now. She did not fly, either. None of them dared *move*.

But something else was in motion.

As the white moons climbed the twilight, they began to reveal an unfathomable blackness deep down in the sea-pocket.

'What's that shadow, Guri?'

Guri looked. He dismissed it. 'Ours, our shadow, from the moons.'

The whitened ice darkened further. The shadow spread like ink beneath their feet. Something black as moonless night was gliding by beneath.

Guri caught his breath. 'Great Gods – Great Gods—'

Perched in the tilted slee, Saphay gazed, without Guri's education, at the shadow-cloud under the ice. But she did not require tuition to know it.

Horror is infinite, and needs no time. There *was* no time. A roaring and groaning split both the quiet and the ice together. Dislocated walls of ice exploded through the air, moon-sparkling. A black crack commenced, displayed an artery of liquid blacker still, and then the liquid was obscured, and something filled the channel, filled and filled it to bursting, *burst* it – pure darkness came thrusting upward from the depths, behind a sallow pointing lance. It was an ice-whale, breaching.

Sleek as jet, erupting blazing water from its blowhole. It was horned with one single, whorled tapering tower, which had at its base a series of ivory spurs, each bigger than a wagon. Tenacious, deceptively slender forelimbs clutched the edge of the ice-pocket, and broke it in pieces.

The whale had strayed far inland. It was not yet nearly fullgrown, yet it was the size of the ice-lake, which it had smitten, indifferently, in two.

Bellowing, men and mammoths were showered off its launching back. They went into the sea below the ice, and vanished. Only Guri, freakishly positioned by some anomaly of its trajectory, sprawled face-down on the whale's spine, and kept hold. More, he began to scale the slope.

He had drawn his knife in the second of awareness, and in his other hand was a hook of honed steel he had from the burnt village. These he drove into the whale's unfeeling carapace, forcing his way up the monster's length, towards its bulbous head.

Reason had gone from Guri now. All he recalled was that Peb Yuve wanted the Rukar princess – and there she was. Unlike the others who had perished, the girl, the slee and its team were somehow caught and knotted about the whale's tree-high horn. The spurs had meshed them. The deer were dead, the slee smashed, but he could see the girl was still alive. He pulled himself on towards the beacons of her fear-bright eyes.

Saphay felt herself screaming, but could not hear it over the grinding of the ice. She saw the tiny Olchibe clawing, knife and hook, towards her. Yet he did not matter.

The whale, still breaching, hurled itself ever upward.

Guri made no sound as he was shaken loose. He dived, an involuntary acrobat somersaulting over the whale's back, cast towards the moons. Then in mid-air, perhaps not even meaning to, the whale met him again. This time it impaled him with the tip of the horn. It had repayed the unnoticed little spikings of the knife and hook with interest.

The monster arched over like a bow, downward now. It plummeted, its double leap ended, into the channel it had made, back to the familiar darkness – carrying its cargo with it.

Midnight beyond all nights shut Saphay's eyes, cold beyond all Winters covered her.

Above, the rift in the ice healed over in an hour. By then the adolescent whale was halfway to open sea.

Vuldir, King Accessorate, lifted his eyes from the pelts he was examining. Instead he observed carefully the man who had entered. Presently Vuldir drew him aside.

He and the man stood in the deep embrasure of a window glazed crimson.

'You have news, then?'

'Yes, lord king. The tidings should reach Ru Karismi officially tonight.'

Vuldir sighed. 'The wicked Olchibe, so easily tempted and misled. Tell it all.'

'The caravan was overtaken and wiped from the face of the earth. The guard was inadequate, as planned. No one survived except for the witch – *that* the Crarrowin will no doubt see to – and a couple of women nonentities the Olchibe have kept to sell as slaves in the dunghills of Sham.'

'Excellent. And my daughter?'

'Reports contain no evidence of her being among the Olchibe. They wouldn't sell her, not a royal woman. They'd rape her to death or simply kill her. They hate all the lords of the Ruk so much, their honour would be at stake if they let her live.'

'Yes,' agreed Vuldir. He looked from the coloured window down at a crimson city. He thought of the Magician Thryfe, who had come to caution them, dressing the prognostication in all kinds of absurd direness – Thryfe who was so wise and yet had not seen the hand of Vuldir himself in this calamity. Thryfe was not usually obtuse. The gods themselves, Vuldir thought idly, their fouler aspects that was, must have muddied the mage's oculum.

The Jafn Klow, a rabble worth hardly more themselves than the Olchibe or similar scum, had grown powerful in their eastern fastnesses. Sallusdon, King Paramount of Ru Kar Is, had deemed it necessary to placate their war leaders with a small marriage. Therefore the Ruk had sent the girl. Alas, the filth of Olchibe had intercepted her. Was that the fault of the Ruk?

Fastidiously, Vuldir had made certain nothing of his, even such a slight thing as a fifteenth daughter, entered Jafn possession. The thick-brained barbarians would never guess they had been cheated. Still they must hold to the pact. Indeed, the girl's loss might even be partly blamed on the Jafn. It could be said that, if they had come out to meet her, she would have lived and been theirs.

Vuldir struck a bell – the man with news was gone. The king's servants brought in the furrier. 'I will take these pelts,' said Vuldir, 'but they are not enough. Are your men lazy? Get them to shoot more.'

No thought, no sight, no breath. No self.

Unravelled and adrift, cold as diamond, silently.

There came to be a hollow in the black. And in the hollow, after all, a radiance. A lamp was burning there, deep in the water, like the jewelled egg of that mythic bird her nurse had told her of once long ago, the Firefex . . .

Thoughtless and unbreathing still, dead still, nameless and forgetting, she must allow the current, which had washed her from the back of the whale, to bear her on through gargantuan colonnades of night towards the jewel of fire.

TWO

Over the petrified fields of the sea the lion-drawn chariots came flying, winged with ice-spume. Torches spat green against a night long emptied of its moons. Far out, miles away and invisible, liquid waves moved with a sullen sound. The riders, used to ocean in both its forms, paid neither any heed. The grey, densely furred lions, their black manes plaited with coloured beads and metal, were as indifferent as their masters.

Along that bleak coast stood the Thing Place. It was an area of truce, and here the Jafn – those of their peoples allied or otherwise – would meet, summoned by magical sendings. Five allied groups would be there tonight, in the dead of the moons.

The marble shoreline curved.

The Thing appeared. It was ancient and curious, a huge, seventeen-masted ship changed to ice and buried up to its waterline in the shore. It gleamed, spectral, strung with crystal cryotites.

Athluan knew it well. He had been brought here to Thing meetings since the age of nine, then the Chaiord's second son. Now, father and elder brother dead in war, Athluan himself was Chaiord.

The chariots slowed, their runners squealing.

'All already here,' commented brown Rothger, the

29

charioteer, Athluan's younger brother. 'Regard them: banners of the Shaiy and the Irhon too. When did *those* peoples last bother themselves with a Thing meet? We're honoured.' His voice was smooth with sarcasm. Athluan took no notice; his mind was on other matters.

At the edges of the Place ran pillar-markers of black spar, dragged there centuries before and washed only once in two lifetimes by the sea, perhaps. Rothger reined in. Athluan leapt, dismounting from his chariot, and went forward on foot, as Jafn law decreed – presently followed by his brother and nineteen picked men.

Similarly equipped, the other Jafn Chaiords stood attentively. They had been kept waiting on the Klow, for the weather had been variable. Ice floes on the move, cracks cutting the frozen shore, had delayed Athluan's excursion.

Allies then, these five leaders, but also enemies once, and quite likely to be so again soon. All Jafn peoples fought against each other. That was necessary, for their lands were harsh and every advantage coveted.

Rothger, behind his brother, ran his cool eyes over the assembly. The Jafn Shaiy were restless, both those staying outside the markers of the Thing Place and those within. The Irhon and Vantry faces were blank as the riding masks they had removed. Under his banner of a snow-ox, the aged Chaiord of the Kree, Lokinda, was the only man whose expression openly showed grievance.

'Well,' he said, as Athluan strode to the centre of the Place, 'I'm big in years to be out of my House tonight. What's so urgent, eh?' He had the face of a toad.

'I'll tell you,' Athluan said, meeting their eyes, gaze to gaze. His were grey as lions under his pelt of hair that was whiter than old Lokinda's own. 'As you know, the Rukar made a pact with the Klow, and therefore with you, Klow's allies. A royal daughter was to be sent to wed me – or Conas my elder, if he'd lived. As you know too, the Rukar lords hesitated. Then came word the girl was on her way. *Now* there's other news sent us from her city.' All the Jafn in the Thing Place listened now. Somewhere a lion growled softly and they heard, in the great silence, the charioteer's rod striking on its flank. 'Olchibe attacked the caravan. The girl was killed.'

After a moment, it was Lokinda again who spoke.

'So, one more to feed the snows. They must send you another bride.'

'Chaiord Lokinda is playful. Does he truly believe they will? They've offered us friendship by *intention*. By our own law, *we* must keep faith with them, but now *they* need pay nothing.'

'The point is, sir Chaiords,' said Rothger silkenly, 'they reckon us all too stupid to object. We had the betrothal, which makes us their kin. Soon they'll be busy at one of their own wars. And though we, without the woman, will never have any claim on *them*, they'll expect things of us, since we are allied through our own law to them – even if my brother must bed and cutch a ghost.'

One or two glowered at Rothger's foul language. In a Thing Place neither blasphemy nor coarseness should be uttered.

But Lokinda let out a laugh. 'By the Face of God, they've been clever. Do you think they companionably helped the Olchibe kill the girl?'

'Most probably,' said Athluan. 'All that was needed was

31

to let Olchibe scouts get wind of a special caravan. But now there's another happening.'

'Say it.'

'A wise-woman of a whaler village downcoast has sent to me. Her message was brought in the hour after the death-news came from the Magikoy lords at Karismi.' Athluan paused, then said, 'A wonder was shown the whalers. A pyramid of ice came up out of the open sea, and drifted inland. Such things, of course, occur. Sometimes these floating ice-hills even ground on shore, and this one did so. The village went to see because, as we know, occasionally such hills contain riches: birds, fish or grain, or seeds that can be used.'

Lokinda said, 'So they do. One time in my youth, a whole fruit forest came in a hill of ice to a village of my father's. At the Kree House we ate apples and peaches for half a year.'

No one else added anything.

Athluan went on, 'The whalers, when they reached the icehill, were afraid of it. It was of too regular a shape; it had no look of anything natural. Yet something was inside it. The Rukar princess lay there, in the ice.'

Used to weird miracles of the ocean, in the green torchlight men nodded their heads.

Only Lokinda said, 'But is it so? Or was it just some vision the whaler witch had?'

'No vision. Look, here's a piece of the ice she sent me.'

From the rimed bag at his belt, Athluan removed a shard. He gave it to Rothger to take in his gloved hands and show them.

One by one, they stared down into the milky ice, at the

tiny scarlet gem which glittered there inside, cut and perfect.

'How did the girl get into the sea?' Lokinda finally asked.

'Perhaps the Olchibe dirt threw her there when they were done. Or else, even dying, she escaped from them. The Ruk deer-teams run fast and far – perhaps even to the sea,' Athluan mused, his eyes burning cold, 'and then the ice gave way, as recently it does.'

'And she is in the ice-hill? It's *her*?'

'We were told her hair was yellow as lamp oil. Or we were told it was like gold . . . The one in the ice is royally dressed, and has such yellow hair. It's her.'

It was Rothger who ended the pronouncements: 'Give the Klow leave to ride on over your lands. The village is downcoast to the west of here, three days and two nights' journey. Come with us if you will. She's dead, but ours. The Ruk hasn't cheated us of everything.'

Jafn law had been old, time out of mind. There were supposed reasons for all of it, or most of it. That a chieftain who had lost his wife to sickness or childbirth might not call out her kindred as allies, while he himself – and his – stayed bound to assist these same kin in any fight, thus prevented, they claimed, his making too light of a wedding. For that cause, too, a wife who vanished left him no rights at all. However, should his spouse continue to receive honour after her demise, her bones locatable and wholesome, and offerings made her in a proper tomb, certain other claims could be advanced by the grieving widower. To this, through the betrothal, the Ruk had made themselves party.

Athluan pondered this law as they rode on along the coast, westward.

He had, he thought, no illusions. To wed some garish-haired female of the Rukar had never appealed to him, in itself; but to be friends with the Rukar nation was no bad thing. Everywhere the frigid world was at war – Jafn with Jafn, with Olchibe and their ilk, and with any greater inland power that chose to stir; while from the black outer ocean there came, now and then, tides of water-reivers such as Vorms, Kelps, Blue Fazions – raiders whose ships were made of whalehide and whale ivory, lean and deadly as the snakes they carved on them, and whose minds were more blindly benighted than the open sea.

'Surely not still dreaming of your bride?' Rothger annoyed him always, but protocol demanded his position in the chariot now. Third son, he must be groomsman at any marriage Athluan made. 'Ice preserves, of course, so perhaps . . . like Lokinda's peaches and apples . . .?'

They drove all night, the Klow and the other Jafn who chose to go with them. At dawn, they rested the lion-teams, ate, stretched their legs, ran races and wrestled round the fires the mage had made. The Jafn took pride in their physical skills, also in their ability to do without sleep. On this rush down the coast, they would slumber only two hours in the second night.

Inland, gloomy ice-forests and jungles went by, some-times flowered after sunfall with village lights. Low mountains showed too, now and then, but these lay out towards the sea – other ice-hills which had stuck.

Early on the afternoon of the third day, they reached the

whaler village. This land was theoretically no one's; it belonged to the sea. But the Shaiy were the nearest land-holders, and no doubt they were not best pleased that the wise-woman had not sent also to inform them of the wonder. Or perhaps, prudently, she had, for they had not seemed at all surprised, and only four of their number accompanied the Klow.

From the village up the shore, the men came in their tough fish-skin clothes. The wise-woman was the only female, but she stalked at their head. When she was twenty paces from Athluan's chariot, she raised her skinny arms. A small wind blew at her bidding, circling round her then approaching the Chaiord. It contained a silvery, translucent hovor, one of the lesser spirits of the upper air. Bound by the witch, the creature bowed low before Athluan. On the ice it deposited one flawless amber glass leaf, torn from some tree – a gift – then leered and dissolved. Rothger got out and fetched the leaf, turning and admiring it.

'Greetings, lady,' said Athluan. The witch wore a mask that hid all her face but for one pale wild eye. He continued, 'I thank you. How far is the ice-hill?'

'Curb impatience,' she said. 'You're only a boy.'

'I am three decades.'

'A boy. Listen, no hill of ice, but a *building* of ice.'

'So you've told me in your sending. Is that possible?'

'All things are.'

'Who then built the building of ice?'

The witch said nothing.

Not to offend her, Athluan left the chariot and stood quietly beside her, looking out along the near shore, which was devoid of any ice-hill. But the vista beyond the village sloped and swelled concealingly.

'Behold,' said the whalers' witch, 'this eye you see, sees you. The other eye is hidden. That sees elsewhere.'

Athluan said, 'I've brought you apricots from the hothouse tree, and jars of white wine.'

'You bargain well,' said the witch.

'There are other things.'

'That will do. I'll take you now to the place of the ice-pyramid. But you must come with me alone.'

At that, the Jafn men made a protest. Catching their disturbance, Athluan's pair of chariot lions, too, roved forward, pulling the vehicle, snarling, until Rothger sharply ordered them back.

'I've nothing to fear,' Athluan said.

One of the Vantry shouted, 'Yes you have, Chaiord. She's a *Shaiy* witch.' And now the Shaiy snarled.

'Hush,' said Athluan. 'We're here for profit not fight. Please to go on, lady,' he said firmly to the witch.

She chuckled, in her flat pale mask. '*Boys.*'

He followed her up the shore between the knots of staring whalermen, and along the single street of their black narrow sheds.

Some way beyond, the rising ground dropped suddenly, shelf on shelf of ice layered with stone, to an area of the ice fields some hundred feet below. Down there was a bay scooped into the ice, and in it a basin of blue-black liquid. On this, borne in from the further water, stood the thing from the sea.

As she had told them all, it was an exact pyramid. Regularly constructed, coloured like emerald at its base, but higher up cloudily transparent as polished vitreous, it was like an artefact made in some city.

First he climbed down the cliff. He was used to such exercise or he might have fallen. The witch stayed where she was. Alone, he walked out towards the hill in the bay.

The shape was tall as the Klow House, two high storeys, seven times the height of a man. It stayed opaque to far up beyond his eyeline.

So then Athluan waded out through the shallow edge of liquid water, and climbed the pyramid. This sort of climb too he had often done in his youth. But if the witch thought him still a boy, perhaps it was appropriate.

As he climbed, by means of boots and gauntleted hands, and both his knives pushed into more porous material yet sometimes slipping, the glinting of the distant sea confused his eyes. His ears began to sing: he seemed to hear voices which might be spirits or demons, or nothing.

And then, his face was pressed over a pane like clearest glass. He looked through the window – and saw.

The whalers had done this too, some of them. The wisewoman had not climbed, of course, or maybe one of her servant winds had carried her up. They had chipped out the ice shard as proof.

'Face of God.'

But it was not the face of God, in the ice. It was a woman's face, young, beautiful and deathly, framed in hair like the wine he had brought for the witch. And in that hair were a thousand flaming sparks, more of the jewels he had been sent. But they were not cut rubies; they were a rainstorm of blood. And each drop *burned*.

Her eyes were open. She had looked on death. Athluan stared, expecting to see death's signature painted on the irises. He saw only his own reflection.

Something was happening, for a moment he did not know what it was. Too late he tried to shift, but she had mesmerized him and made him careless.

The slab of ice beneath him slid, and *dropped*.

Athluan threw himself sidelong, grasping for purchase.

The bodyheat of a man was not enough to melt such a thickness of pure ice – and yet it seemed that his had done so.

He was slipping, slipping down forty odd feet, he thought, to smash hard as iron on the steel surfaces just below the water. Instead he sank forward, down but *inside* the gut of the ice. The pyramid was sheering and splintering everywhere, bursting off sunlit needles, till he shut his eyes to save his sight. And then he found himself at anchor.

He had swum, more than fallen, in upon the body of the frozen girl. In a cruel parody of couching, he lay breast to breast with her. His mouth was on her mouth.

Athluan shuddered. She had a taste of scented lip-paint. She was – *warm*.

That appalling astonishing kiss had lasted less than a second. But, as Athluan pulled back his head, he saw her open eyes swirling with some organism that could only be consciousness. They focused on him entirely.

He had heard of such events: animals, men, frozen in the floes, brought out with a flash of seeming life, gone in a breath – or, if living, a mindless shrieking lunacy.

'Where—?' she said. Her voice was a whisper. 'Where . . . where—?'

'Here,' he said. 'You're here.' He thought of the tales and added slowly, 'Tell me your name.'

'*Saphay.*'

The Chaiord brought his bride home at sunset.

Under the closing sky, the entire Klowan-garth blazed with torchlight. The people there, in the wide wandering streets that had formed between the dwellings, looked long and in utter stillness at their chieftain's consort-to-be. More than just an alien from Ruk Kar Is, she had come back from the dead.

To Saphay the strangeness of this Jafn town, raised on its platform and surrounded by snow-locked walls and moats, meant little. She glanced randomly at the squat houses. They were clung with vines, their tallow-lit windows dulled by shutters of membrane. Everywhere totems stood on poles, among them the images of ice-devils, spirits, elementals. The Jafn did not worship these, she knew, for she could recall the chatter of her women on the journey – how long ago had that been, surely months? Once her memory reached the moments of the glass lake – the sliding, tumbling slee, the shudder of the ice as the pursuing mammoths went down – a curtain dropped across her brain.

Yet memory began again with startling immediacy. It contained a face which stared at her, inches from her own. A white-haired man, with eyes hardly much darker, his wind-tanned skin tasting of heat and cold. For he had kissed her, and left the impression on her lips.

Now he stood beside her in the chariot, their two hands, his left and her right, bound together with a cord at the wrist. They did not speak – altogether he had told her not much.

The lions padded on through the streets, up towards the garth's summit, the Klow House. She thought, *If it were not for what has already happened to me, should I be frightened now?*

Athluan lifted her from the chariot, at the arched door. A great steel sword was fixed above it, kept always bright for the Chaiord's honour. It lay sidelong, to indicate peace.

It was Rothger, the brown-haired brother, who cut the magetied cord that bound bride and groom, freeing them for each other. Then they went into the House.

'My father,' he said, 'could heft and swing the door-sword one-handed. So could my elder brother, Conas. It weighs heavy as a man of fifteen years, and I can only lift it with both hands. Do you like me less, now you know I'm a weakling?'

Amazed, Saphay looked at her husband across the narrow bedchamber, where other weapons hung on the walls. Having kept silent till now, suddenly he talked as if they had known each other, were friends, had agreed to this wedding long since, and to what came next. Furthermore, as if he had chosen her, and she him. She lowered her eyes. 'It isn't needed that I . . . *like* you.'

'Then you don't? Or are you afraid of me?'

'Yes,' she said.

She had learned, from everything yet seen, a man did not mind making others afraid. Partly she said it to flatter. Though it might be true; she did not know.

Below, in the joyhall of the House, the Jafn Klow had earlier feasted on roast venison, shark and deer-seal, and on alcohol of various kinds. The thick pillars in this hall were painted and carved, and held up a roof that partially comprised rafters, where the Jafn's striped ice-hawks perched. Shaggy hounds patrolled the floor between the benches. There were lions too, the best trained and most favoured. Of these both males and females were maned. Athluan's pair of beasts had sat by his table, in gold House collars, where he fed them meat and fruit. The chamber was full of smoke and noise. When the women came to take her up, Saphay was glad. Athluan had not exchanged a single word with her there.

Now he swore, but the oath was beyond her, for Jafn speech combined two or three languages, one sufficiently like that of the Ruk to be comprehended, but of the other two was this one, which was not.

'Saphay,' he now said. He lingered on the name, then said it again. 'Saphay, I think your people never told you of our customs.' She waited, eyes down. 'A man mustn't converse with his wife on the day of the wedding, not all day, until they're alone. Then, and thereafter, he can.'

She felt foolish, childish, frightened after all. 'They didn't tell me.'

He sat in the chair across the room, and she in the vast stonewood bed, among its furs and dyed, chequered coverlets. The lamp burned low. From the shadow he said, 'Let me tell you then why. Long ago, the hero Star Black brought his wife to his House. He was so taken with her that he spoke only to her, neglecting his guests. Most excused him, but one was a gler, a thing of outer darkness which had got in disguised as Star Black's uncle. This devil then followed Star Black up to the bedroom. It stood outside, and no sooner had Star Black laid hands on his wife than the gler spat out its bane. The muck ran in under the door like the venom of a snake, and touching the girl's bare feet, killed her. And for that reason, Saphay, to protect his bride, no man gives her a word until they meet in the upper chamber.'

Saphay did not know if she should laugh or shiver. To the Jafn, as she had already noted, the supernatural was real and ever-present. On the way here from downcoast, after Athluan and his men had brought her out of the ice, she had seen them sometimes talk to beings in the snows and in the winds, even leaving them out placatory food. To her, these creatures were invisible, but she did not necessarily doubt them.

'Why do you call the hero Star Black?' she asked lamely.

'His hair and skin were black as coal.'

The lamp flame fluttered. Outside a wind was rising from the ice fields of the sea. This was a bleak and deadly place, and they had wed her to a barbarian.

She did not really believe, even though she remembered it, that she had been found in an ice floe, scattered by frozen jewels of a blood not her own.

He, this man, reckoned his God had saved her, and the jewellery blood was therefore His sign. Saphay must herself accept that the barbarian had rescued her from living death.

Athluan stood by the bed. Under the robe of fur he would be naked, as the Jafn women had made her for him. The wedding ceremony was nothing, a word or two, and the binding cord. *This* was the wedding, how a man and woman became married.

'Saphay,' he said again.

'Yes,' she said, 'I'm afraid. Please do to me quickly what you must.'

He turned the lamp round to its darker side. She thought of what he had said about the door-sword, and wondered if he indicated something else, some sexual failing. Then his hands were on her, and his mouth on hers.

Memory remembered, too, his mouth. It was this very act, the pressure of his body, his hands, his lips, which had brought her out of the ice-sleep, melting to warmth.

She clung to him, crying. He held her. It was not his comfort she wanted. She remembered *him*, and it was she herself, all at once, insisting, urging. And Athluan abruptly who hesitated.

'Please,' she said, 'I'm willing, yes—'

At the brink of her, unbearably he paused, apparently undecided. His face was stern and remote, and she laughed at this face and drew it to her breasts.

Saphay did not guess how she knew so much. In turn she had put her hands on him. Her body tingled with desire, yawning open like a flower, and fully aware of its moves.

'Surrender to me,' she said, as if she were the warrior.

They came together under the furs and colours and checks, which presently poured off onto the floor.

Before the statue of God, below the cellars of the House, Athluan, Chaiord of the Klow, waited in silence and bitter cold.

The statue had no face, for the Face of God might be seen only before birth and after death. The form of God

43

was without limbs, glassy in texture, inert yet animate. Through the edges of it, which he had grasped, Athluan felt the pulse of eternity.

'I swear this to You, no other shall know but myself. Nor will I exact any penalty from her. She recalls nothing of it, or she could not be as she was with me. She's suffered enough. I will cherish her. She'll make a wife for me better than any other. I shall come to love her.'

This secret must otherwise be strictly kept, to save her further shame or peril. Its substance: Saphay had come to her husband unvirgin. She had been broken into, and recently. The Olchibe would have done it, before she fled, a couple of them – not more, he thought. They had not destroyed her, or her body's beauty.

That those scornful and lying murderers in Karismi could have sent her to him already breached was also possible, but he doubted it. She might, despite their plots, still have reached him – as she had *done* so – and the insult then begun by a previous deflowerment would have led not only to the cancelling of any pact, but to blood-feud or war. Besides, the evidence of her unsealing was fresh, enough so to ensure she had tonight bled again, which would make glad the chamber-women in the morning.

Her rape plainly she did not recollect. She was innocent of it. She must be, or could not have behaved as she had – tense and timid, and then a spirit of the fire. God would know. God also perhaps knew that Athluan, from the instant he saw Saphay in the ice heart, had taken her into his own.

Up above, in the House, the Chaiord faintly heard laughter in the joyhall. Rothger would be clowning to amuse them, maybe walking round the benches, one foot each on a separate lion's back. They were in fact the lions of Athluan's own chariot, but Athluan did not see this as he climbed again up the private ladder, to his wife at the top of the House.

THREE

A face, a kiss, had woken her out of death. Now, again, the black of nowhere flooded with light.

Curling and rushing, it came like fire, and with it an incandescence of heat. It was a wave, deep in the sea, a giant comber of gold, and from it something golden gazed in at her, trapped there in her globe of ice.

Athluan, as he himself had learned, had been second with her.

She remembered now, almost remembered . . . golden eyes, a force that raised her like a vast hand, and scorched the length and depth of her body.

Asleep, her awareness far away from the stonewood bed in Jafn, Saphay twisted in terror and pleasure.

Yes, she remembered. Among the blind caves which had grown up between the skidding of the slee and her awakening under the ice-hill, memory still survived, though fragmented to a tribe of shining beasts.

She *saw*, as she had *seen*, the colossal columns that held up a roof of frozen water like clouds of cut pearl. Around her, in midnight liquid which could flow, entities and bubbles of life revolved. Through the black ran veins of floating ice, cold blue, and streams of fish that, with scales thickened to armour, could outwit the temperature. But these extraordinary sights, granted normally only to those who drowned, were lost on Saphay. She had begun to see, instead, the god.

Dreaming now, she felt the weight and heat of him. Her flesh burned at his flesh, under the showering laval silver of his hair.

Did she know him? Partly she did. He was a god of the Ruk there beneath the ice of the Marginal Land, one she had made offerings to, even feared as a child. This of course was his predisposed and genial aspect: he was amorous. If he had been in malign mode – his other aspect – his mood alone could have torn her apart.

The bloom of such lust was a glory. Orgasmic tumult eviscerated her. Nothing mortal could have induced this ecstasy.

But in her sleep she made no sound. She did not move. She had in fact grown stiff as a corpse, if anyone had been there to observe or touch. But the Jafn spurned sleep. Athluan had left her after another hour of love – gone hunting. So she lay alone, if not quite alone, coupling in her dream over and over with that power which had taken her virginity under the sea.

That was the first memory, and in the morning Saphay again did not recall it.

She woke in the bed when the women came to wash and dress her. Saphay felt ashamed – she did not know why. The ones who waited on her, two of them old and seasoned, and finding the blood-marks in the bed, took her reticence as proper.

Before she left the chamber, expected below as the Chaiord's new wife, Saphay sent the women out. She had lost, during the Olchibe attack, the gilded box which contained her personal gods, those three allotted her at birth in Ru Karismi. Although respectful to gods, she had not thought very much about them, save when made to as a child. Now, however, she offered to them wine and a blossom pulled from the vine across the window, which flowered only where it came inside the room.

She sensed their presence then. She uttered a prayer, and began to name them carefully, in a low voice not to be heard outside the door. 'Yyrot, *Winter's* Lover. Ddir, Placer of Stars,' Saphay stammered. A gush of feeling, between horror and sweetness, caught at her insides. Her cheeks flamed, and she spoke the last name haltingly. 'Zezeth . . . Sun Wolf.'

Shadows flickered across the room, then were gone. But, above the Klowan-garth, four or five hawks were flying, visible through the window. It would be that.

Out on the ice fields, other Klow hawks had brought down several white-kadi from a flock that had been fishing in thin, thawed cracks and channels. The hunters had seen a trio of bear too, and given chase, their lion chariots bolting. But the bears vanished into the snow – perhaps they had been demon things.

The party paused to eat and play games of skill, shooting at sticks stuck in the ice, with horn bows.

'The Chaiord's eye is out this morning.'

The men laughed. To be a poor shot after a night of bliss with a bride was as correct as her virginal blood on the sheets.

'Soon it'll be Roth's turn. What do you say, Rothger? Do you pine for a wife?'

'I?' Rothger squinted down the bowstring at the marks.

He let the light arrow loose without a hitch, and it struck full-square. 'When I go courting, God spare me a bitch of the Rukar.'

'But she's a pretty face.'

'And clever too,' Rothger added gently. 'She can lie packed up in ice and come out whole.'

The group of Klow about Rothger fell to brooding. They had been trying, in their own way, to mislay the bride's uncanny adventure.

'She was meant to be ours,' one of them said at last, 'and so endured.'

'Maybe she was. Do you call to mind the story of the Crarrow?' said Rothger, who had entertained them all so well at the feast the night before, playing the fool or performing cunning tricks and bizarre magics that made even the House Mage start. Rothger had joined in the telling of tales also. Now it seemed he had another.

They knew this one, most of them, but they waited, attentive. For the recounting of stories out-hall was always laden with presage.

Rothger spoke. 'She was a Gech witch, one of the Crarrowin. The Jafn hero Kind Heart, when hunting, found her lying in the snow, bleeding from the attentions of fleer-wolves. She hadn't died, but he put this down to her arts. In the night she set a spell on him and he was seduced. He cutched her for seven hours, never taking a rest, so greatly did she inspire him, despite her nasty ochre skin. Then he took her home and wed her. The Crarrow was the best wife in the world to him, for half a month. Then came the night of triple moonrise. That night the Crarrow rose up on their bed and herself turned into a fleer. She tore out Kind Heart's kind heart, and ate it smoking hot. Then she did for as many of the garth as she could, before its warriors killed her. Nor did she stay quiet in the grave, after. Every triple-white night she would be up again at her business. Not till they burned her, and closed the ashes in a silver-lead casket and flung it in open sea, were they free of this devil.'

The men considered this, silent. Down the shore, their Chaiord took aim again, missed again, and himself laughed.

Now, to the watchers, this had an ominous look. But Rothger shouted for more of the black wine.

Cup in hand, he strolled to companion his elder brother.

'Have the mages sent yet, Athluan, to the Magikoy in Karismi?'

'Tonight they'll do it. They need Saphay for that, and I left her sleeping.'

'Yes, they're fond of their sleep, the western peoples.'

'Try this bow,' said Athluan. 'It won't oblige me.'

Rothger smiled and thanked him. For any other man to be allowed use of the bow of a Chaiord was a vast compliment. Rothger took an arrow and set it swiftly to the string, drew and shot. Perfect: the marker was split in two. A cheer bounced up the shore and made the ice-hawks jatter.

That night the Jafn Klow sent tidings to the Ruk of Saphay's survival. The distance was great, and the image must be clear. Sixteen garth mages came into the House to do it, to the Thaumary behind the joyhall.

The room was built with three sides only, and the wooden panels of the walls were drawn with scenes of ritual and magic, blurred and centuries old. There were no windows. At the core of the place squatted an iron basket filled by pine cones and coals. This the Mage of the House fired with a word. The flames the Jafn used at such times, as with their torches at an allied Thing meet, were green.

Saphay stood in her Jafn royal robe, trimmed and belted with silver. The atmosphere was quickly heavy and prickled by energies, and she felt the hair bristle along her scalp, even at her groin. She sensed she had displeased her new husband, despite the fact he had spoken to her courteously on his return from the hunt, and kissed her lovingly before the crowd to show he valued her. She did not know what it was – perhaps he had not liked her sexual hunger. She had been startled at it herself. Besides, how could she understand Athluan? For she was among a strange people. Even so, and even though uneasy, she longed to meet this man again in the bed upstairs.

Now the mages chanted and made gestures of summons and arrangement. Peculiar rays and specks of light whirled round the chamber. Then Saphay saw a door open in the air. In distaste, she found herself glaring along a spinning tunnel, and it seemed to her she must be sucked into it. She shut her eyes, as she had done in the escaping slee. The older nurse had once told her a basic trick of lower witchcraft – deliberately not to see might render you yourself invisible.

Saphay knew, however, that the mages were pressing her likeness on the tunnel, pushing the facsimile away towards Ru Karismi, to prove she was alive and in the east.

Although she had been told nothing of the thoughts of these people, or their suspicion of a Ruk plot to kill her and so deprive the Klow of her pact-worth, Saphay wondered what the lords in the city would think on discovering she had not perished. Her father, she believed, would be indifferent either way. For the rest, they scarcely knew who she was. The other King Accessorate, Bhorth, on the two occasions he had spoken to her, mistook her for another of the minor daughters. The King Paramount, Sallusdon, had never spoken to her at all, or probably even physically noticed her.

Something shook and tugged at Saphay. Her hair was blowing round her, and her robe billowing about her legs, as if she poised at the heart of a gale.

She opened her eyes after all. Appalled but resigned, she saw her mirrored image arrowing like a fish away through the tunnel. Then it was gone. The wind dropped. Her hair settled. She thought, *But when have I ever seen a fish which moved?*

The room was cold, and the green fire had, in the second before it too disappeared, adopted a curious shape like that of two lions, or perhaps a lion and some other animal, fighting.

The mages did not speak to Saphay. Task completed, they walked straight past her out of the chamber. Here, too, she was apparently beneath notice.

Saphay leant towards the fire-basket. It was heatless and dead, but none of the cones or coals had been consumed.

'Chaiord's Wife! Chiaord's Wife!' called a woman from the doorway. She waved her hands at Saphay, entreating her to come out.

She dares not enter, and I myself must leave.

Some impulse made Saphay turn as if to glance back, and, as if tidying a fold of her skirt, snatch one of the dead coals off the magic hearth. Never before had she done such a thing as to interfere in thaumaturgic acts. Even these barbarian magicians had the craft – so she had surely been foolish, and risked danger. Concealing the coal in her sleeve, she did not know why she had done it.

The House Mage said, 'Athluan, your bride's candle is lit.'

Athluan's face did not alter. 'So soon. Are you sure?'

'Of course. The flame is lodged in her womb. It was clearly to be seen during the spell of sending.'

'And gender, could you see that too?'

'A son, Athluan. You're blessed.'

'Thank you for the news. I'll make an offering to God, and a placation to the relevant spirits – but without too much fuss. It's very soon to inform the House, let alone the garth. She's only just arrived.'

When the Mage was gone, Athluan walked about. He was in the small space a Chaiord kept for himself to the north of a joyhall, opposite the Thaumary. It was a study formed solely by wooden partitions. In the candlelight, the pelts stretched over these partitions, each with its glass stare, watched enviously his ability to live and move.

Tonight it seemed to him there were more spirits and presences abroad in the House than was usual. At the foot of the ladder-stair he had spotted a vrix lurking in the shadows. It was wan and tenuous but wicked-eyed. He muttered the formula to see it off, but it only pressed into the outer wall, and merged itself in an old carpet hung there, in the design of which parts of it were still easily to be seen. Athluan had sent one of the under-mages to deal with the creature, since it was beneath the attention of the House Mage. He hoped it would be gone by the time he went up to Saphay.

He paced, and thought, while the pelts watched. *She is*

quickly sown. Was it from me – or from that other one-of-how-many who had her before I did?

During the night, the ice cracked for a mile out along the extended shore, a barking terrible sound. This was to have been a House nocturnal of three or four hours' sleep. The hall had put aside its wine cups and skins of leaf ale, and the men, with their women, stretched along pallets in the semi-privacy behind the pillars. Children had been sent to their own house across the yard. The lions had lain down, and the dogs, too. Only the hawks amid the raftering, quickened by their day of hunting, preened and fought each other, so that barred feathers clattered to the floor. But when the bark of the ice came, all the House burst awake. And out in the Klowan-garth the torches flashed, and people ran along the streets.

Athluan swung out of the bed. 'I must go to see. Last time the ice gave with such a racket, the water came in as far as the lower walls.'

Saphay thought, *Why do they live so close to open water, only a few miles from it, if there is this peril?*

But she knew the ice seldom gave, only shifted or baulked a little. There had not been, in these lands, an episode of *Summer* in any living memory.

To her surprise again, he took her hand a moment. 'Stay here. We build high, so even if the sea comes, it can't breach the garth. You will be safe.'

'Thank you for your care of me.'

'Naturally I care for you. You're my wife.'

But he had cheated her, coming to bed with only a kiss.

A sleep night was not, it seemed, a night for anything else among the Jafn.

She watched them ride off in their chariots, from the window hidden in the vine. There were, as she had been told, so many white-haired persons among the Jafn Klow that in the dark she quickly mislaid him among his men.

She was not afraid. Let the sea come, what did she care. She had survived the sea, and the ice . . . Something had happened to her, something impossible. And yet, she now had nothing left of it.

Saphay went back to the bed. She lay down on her side. In the far corner she could see the chest that now was hers. Inside the chest, wrapped in one of her shifts, nested the coal from the sending fire.

Not thinking to sleep, suddenly she found herself lying in a cave of gold. Before even he was visible, she felt the god, his caresses, his mouth, felt his penetration of her. She knew him instantly in the *dream*. Bewildered, too, she thought, *But I forgot*— then forgot everything in the agony of delight that Zezeth Sun Wolf gave her.

As he drove towards the rift in the ice, Athluan might have heard or glimpsed something of this, but he did so without knowing what it was. He looked over his shoulder, back towards the garth, once, twice, as if alerted at a cry. But tonight he was his own charioteer, Rothger riding in another car. Needing to keep his eyes on the way, Athluan did not turn a third time.

When they reached the spot, it was far out along the ice fields. The moving sea was present at the horizon, tufted with its white spit under two moons.

The rift was not so bad as it had sounded, yet it was deep, a black channel riven down about a quarter mile into the ice-plates. The liquid water at its bottom was sluggish, however, and had not greatly risen.

They went along, checking for other flaws or fissures, and located none. On the chariot-sides the lion harness, little bells and discs, jinked in the towering silence of the Winter night.

The under-mage they had brought with them leant on a staff, staring down at surfaces. He said presently, 'The crack will heal over – but something has come out of it.'

'What?'

'A thing dead, yet alive in spirit.'

Athluan said, 'Must something be done to appease it?'

'No, Athluan. It's already gone.'

It was Rothger now who looked behind him, back towards the Klowan-garth, then up at the sky. A ghostly cloud appeared blowing by above, moonlit, without any wind to power it. Seeing him look, others looked and saw it too. Some even pointed. But the dead-and-alive came often from cracks in ice. They got out and blew around the world a while, before going to the Other Place outside.

On the ride back, the sky-cloud was ahead of the warriors but by the hour they reached their platformed town it had vanished away.

In the joyhall, drink was heated. There was only a pair of hours left before the dawn, and no one now was in a mood to sleep. When the Chaiord took the ladder door, presumably going up again to the bedroom, some of the men nudged each other and grinned. A few seemed less happy at the sight.

For himself, Athluan had noted previously that the vrix had left its partial concealment in the wall. Yet, reaching the laddertop, his whole body seemed laved in cold. He stepped off into the room.

The lamp had guttered out, but the sinking, vine-littered moonlight showed the bed. Athluan's wife lay sleeping stilly. Near her feet, and on the bed, crouched a wiry, ugly man. His skin was leopard-colour, his braided hair like murky milk and decorated with tiny beast skulls. An Olchibe!

Athluan knew this being was not fleshly-living. Though solid, he had no weight to him, left no imprint on the covers, cast no shadow. Nor did he glance about to see who had come in to disturb him. In his own tongue, which Athluan could speak, the Olchibe muttered, 'Bitch-whore, bitch-whore, through you I am this. I will curd you. I'll take your skin off for me, bitch of bitches.'

Is this the one who was before me with her?

Athluan spoke, in the language of Olchibe. 'How did you die?'

A Chaiord, who dealt often with his mages, learned certain lessons. This was how one must address the dead, especially the savage, angry dead. It was usually their main bone of contention, and centred them upon their state.

The ghost looked round, peering through its braids at Athluan. 'I'm not dead.'

'Yes, you are dead. Where's your shadow?'

'I left it with a friend, for safety.'

Athluan took a new tack. 'What is your name?'

'Why should I tell you?'

'Because this is my House, and that is my bed, and she in it is my woman.'

'Ah?' The ghost seemed pensive. 'I shall kill her. She was *mine* – my prize for my leader. But she got away from

57

me. The wind came out of the water. It was black and had a crown of ivory spikes. *Whale* – it was a horned whale. She and I, we rode the whale. Then it went down.'

'And your name, rider of a whale?'

'Guri.'

'Off my bed, Guri.'

The ghost slipped round, and then, weightless, fleshless, boneless, sprang right at Athluan. It was the kind of leap a cat would make, teeth jutting to bite, and nails better than daggers.

Athluan stood, unmoving, and spoke a word. Guri sprang over and through him. Without substance, the ghost, yet Athluan *felt* it pass through his own body, like scalds of water, in at the front and out through his back.

When Athluan looked, no one was behind him, no Guri now was anywhere to be seen. Athluan coughed and spat. He would need the Mage to clear him of Guri's taint, but that could wait. In the bed, Saphay was stirring. Athluan regarded her, tousled and lovely, rosy from the warmth of sleep, blameless in all of this.

She must be protected. The Olchibe had come back from death to harm her – his reason muddled, as the reason of ghosts frequently was, when they had been meshed in the world.

'Come to me,' said the girl in the bed.

Who is she seeing?

The urge to tell her she had been visited by a vengeful undead was strong, to try if it would release some memory in her of her rape. Athluan perceived he required to hear from her how much she had suffered. He was growing convinced she had *not* suffered. That what she had forgotten had been her pleasure, not her pain. For the room, soiled by

Guri's ghost, had also a glow about it, and she, over whom the ghost had shed his aura, was like a woman who had been dreaming of her lover.

Nights came and went, and days beside them, over the Klowangarth. Blocks of eleven days and nights, which the Jafn named an Endhlefon, absorbed the single days and nights. A month had passed, and then another.

Saphay sat in the upper room, by the window. She had been filled with loose, warm lead.

As the lead weighted her to the chair, she stared on and on at the pale blossoms opening inside the window embrasure.

'Is it like that?' she asked the vine.

They had told her, yesterday, she was with child. She had of course strongly suspected, knowing about such things, but Saphay found the idea absurd. It was what a woman was meant to do with her body, and yet she had not, somehow, even through the most avid nights with Athluan, anticipated its occurring. It had nothing to do with her, but was now a fact.

Her sense of growing enervation, too, was explained, and the nausea she sometimes experienced on getting up or lying down.

Saphay was removed from herself. She felt muddy, and strangely old, crippled almost. She spoke aloud to objects, and said nothing much to human things.

At the start of the two months, before she had realized or been informed of her condition, the bedchamber was cleansed by magic. Athluan mentioned that the cleansing, and the hanging of garlands of flylarch and weed-of-light, were to protect her during a future carrying and parturition – but even that had not alerted her at the time. The weed-of-light, which threaded the ice-forests with dim bluish flowers, stayed crabbed and did not burgeon in the room. The flylarch opened green needles and long red berries. They did not fall or fade. Had Athluan been so sure she would conceive? She half wondered now if the greenery itself had primed her to be pregnant.

No one told Saphay these plants, along with the amulets and charms mingled among them, were actually an extreme protection from ghosts.

Beyond the window, the garth today was busy. Vehicles came and went. Anvils rang and sparks and smitches rose. A seller of smoked fish walked into the yard, and another bearing slings of oranges from the hothouses.

Then Rothger arrived, driving his chariot up through the lower houses, among the icons of vrixes and sprites.

Rothger she did not like. She did not know why; he had little to do with her. Besides, it was irrelevant for a woman to dislike a powerful man with whom she had no close connection. Even so, she believed she had had a dream recently, remembering how he cut the wedding cord at her wrist, and in the dream he had cut her hand, too.

There were other dreams but she could never recall them; they ran along the outskirts of her awareness. They had been like honey once, something kind and marvellous, though then forgotten. Now this was no longer the case: often she woke with her heart crashing under her breast. Probably this child in her belly was responsible for that.

Her head sank back. Saphay found herself in a hollow of darkness. She knew she had fallen asleep, and that she was afraid.

The darkness moved. It was full of the jewels of gliding fish, although nearby lay several fish which had frozen.

The water – it *was* water – parted. A wave was coming. It was a roil of ink streaked with blood.

The chariot, as it breasted through the sea, was of agate, and drawn by wolves of ice that bounded along the floor of the ocean.

Saphay knew utter fear. She dropped to her knees.

The schizophrenic god had changed his aspect: there in the chariot he stood, his face stained to a violet mask and his hair the grey of ashes. His eyes too were agates, devastating with his own blasting contempt – and the violent madness it provoked in him.

As he raced by her, he did not even glance her way. And yet the chariot veered, deliberately, so the near runner smacked into her body. In waking life, this would have been enough to break her arm and splinter her shoulder joint. In the dream she was only thrown, hurt and frantic, slung away. The sea rumbled. Somewhere fire spouted from the basement of the earth.

What had she done to bring this aspect of disgust and malevolence on him, the god who had loved and lain with her? But Saphay knew, although he had not deigned to tell her. She had conceived his child.

Athluan came up to the bedchamber to fetch his second bow, which hung on the wall with other secondary weapons. By day now, unless he chanced to come here, he seldom saw his wife. Nor did they meet at night very much, for while she slept he was awake and at the work and acts of a Chaiord. Athluan's master bow had something wrong with it. Since that day's hunting on the ice, it had turned against him. The House Mage had told him a corrit had got into it; it must be purged, and even so he might now need another.

Disconcerted a moment, he had warned himself from his own dismay. These things happened. But when he stepped off the ladder-stair into the bedroom, Athluan changed to stone.

Without telling her, he had asked the Mage to put up protections for Saphay, from the Olchibe phantom. And since that was done, so far as Athluan knew they were free of it.

Now, despite that precaution, something else was there in the room.

Athluan stared.

Saphay, sleeping as so frequently she did, lay in the carved chair. Her belly, even this early, had begun to round, sticking up like a small knoll from the slenderness of her frame. Something . . . *spilled* from her there. It was not anything coherent, but a kind of line formed of red light, thin as a scavenger snake. It emerged from her belly and her gown, and dropped and coiled along the floor. At its end lay a heap of the blood jewels, bright as fire, which had spangled all about her in the ice-hill.

When he and his men had struck the splintering ice with axes, to get her free, these jewels had hailed out in all directions.

Where they fell in the bay, they sizzled and, sinking, shone for maybe a minute. Those that hit the snow and ice stayed longer in it. The Jafn were puzzled. They had prudently made protective gestures against the gems, but not against the woken girl. Later, by the time they let her out, all the jewels had faded into the shore or into the water.

Now here they were again, a cache of thousands, like the hoard of a dragon. At first Athluan did not see what sat on them – because at first it was unclear. But the instant he started to notice it, it hardened, gained colour, and began to move. It was a naked child.

The child did not look at him, but only sat there, holding its face in its hands, hiding its eyes, obviously frightened by the physical world in which it found itself.

A boy, Athluan could see presently – a boy-child of about three years, long-limbed, wind-tanned, his hair a burning shade like new copper.

Is this my son, come out in spirit from her womb? The soul grows quicker then than the flesh.

Something surged under Athluan's ribs. His unlegal pairings with women in the garth had seldom produced progeny – and those that appeared were girls.

Just then he thought the boy was turning to look at him, but the eyes – they were blue – stared right past Athluan, behind him. Athluan felt a second presence, at his left shoulder.

Then something moved *through* him. He recognized it: it had done this two months before, but going in the opposite direction.

The sensation made him ill a moment. A sick blurring of vision, a ringing in his skull, bowed him over. As the faint-ness went off and he was able to straighten, he beheld plainly the ghost, Guri, standing there peering down at the seated child.

Athluan tensed, meaning to move forward and, as he did so, bellow for the mage down in the hall. But he discovered he could neither utilize his limbs nor release his voice. He was unable even to croak out magical words to offset the spell. Powerless, reduced to an onlooker, he could only gaze and wait. And listen, too, for they spoke now and he heard them.

'Whose kiddling are you?' asked Guri, and continued, 'The women ought to keep you by.'

The child turned and pointed back at Saphay, still asleep. To Athluan the gesture was evident enough: *The woman there has kept me by her.* But the ghost seemed unaware of any others in the room. Perhaps, being still partly etheric, like the ghost itself, the soul of the child cancelled out more physical things for discorporeal Guri. Either that, or the protections hid them from him.

Guri sat down before the child and began to unbraid and rebraid his hair. The child watched him.

'I have seen some things,' said Guri. 'I've been to the bottom of the sea.' The child shuddered – this was very clear to the other watcher – and Guri reacted to the shudder. 'What?'

The child spoke. '*He* is there.'

'He? Who?'

'*He – he* is.'

Guri shrugged.

The child said, 'He's fire, sun under the sea, and now he rages.'

Guri paused. 'A demon?'

'He has two faces.'

'Ah?' Guri braided conscientiously. Then: 'A god of the Rukar.'

'I ran away,' said the child. 'I ran here.'

'Out of her womb. I see it – but it's not yet your time to do that.'

'I never yet live in her body. What I *shall* be – *that* lives there. It binds me close, but not there inside.'

Athluan thought how the child seemed growing progressively coherent, in a disproportionately adult way. He tried again to move. What they said, the ghost and the out-womb soul, troubled him, but still he could not shift the spell that held him like stone.

'Yes,' said Guri, 'I never liked the gods of the Rukar. Let me tell you of the whale. He had a snow-white horn far longer than my body, but he was black as night – as the sea-depths where he took me. There was a woman too—' Guri checked. He gazed over at Saphay and now saw her, but imperfectly it seemed. He ground his teeth slowly, then looked back at the soul-child. 'Come here,' he said, kindly. 'Get the knot out of this braid for me.'

Athluan writhed in stasis. He watched the child – *his* child – get up and go over to the vengeful ghost.

In the back of his brain, Athluan began to pray to God for help. Either God sent it, or more likely it was unneeded. Guri leant over so the child could pluck at his tangles. Carefully the boy unpicked the matted hair, then Guri grinned in his face. 'Not feared of me, are you?'

'You?' asked the child wonderingly. 'No, not of you.'

'You needn't fear Guri, your old Olchibe uncle. I've fifty, sixty kiddles among the sluhtins. I like them all finely, and they me. I bring them gifts from my wars. I'll bring *you* something, too.' Then he reached out and ruffled the boy's hair in turn. 'Listen to me, any time that he comes after you, that Rukar god in her insides, you call out for me. Call by my name, which is—'

'Guri.'

'Guri, yes. Olchibe Uncle Guri. I can't fight a god, but I know a trick or two. I've been under the sea. There are ways to hide.'

'Guri,' said the child again. He lowered his coppery head against the chest of the ghost, and Athluan felt a stab of most inappropriate and extraordinary jealousy.

It was at this second that a step sounded on the ladder-stair, coming up from the joyhall.

The Chaiord recognized the step. It was his brother Rothger's.

Guri also heard it. He got up, and lifted the boy in his arms. Athluan knew the Olchibe were a rancid, murderous people, less mild even than ravening beasts. But where they would rape, torture and kill, laughing, they had a good-heartedness towards the very young of any race. *Too new to spoil*, was their saying for a baby – or a child up to the age of twelve. Their punishments for any of their own who transgressed against this law were very dire. Athluan's alarm had been misplaced. Now the ghost stood there, holding the child well, as only a man can who has held children often and become willingly used to it.

'Let's be going,' said Guri. 'The cold is coming in.'

Where they went Athluan did not see. In the moment they vanished, Rothger was there, striking him hard between the shoulders, shouting, in his light metallic tones, an uncharm common to any educated Jafn who could use his voice.

'Face of God,' said Rothger, 'this room stinks of summonings, of witchery. I could smell it on the stair.'

Dizzy and sickened, Athluan leaned on the wall. The spell in the room had drained his energy. He saw Rothger

stride about, in perfect command of himself and everything, clapping his hands, flinging open window shutters
to let in cleansing air.

'Did you see?' Athluan asked. His voice came out
unsoundly.

'See? Yes, a flick of something red. It's gone. What was
it?'

'A vrix,' Athluan lied. 'It's been haunting this area of the
House.'

'A vrix with such power? You couldn't move, brother,
I could see that from the steps.'

'What made you come up here?' Athluan asked.

'Luck, maybe. And you were a long while gone.'

Athluan thought woodenly, *You sensed something awry –
but did not necessarily come up to assist me. To spy, that was the
reason you came up here.* In the past, especially in their youth,
when Conas had been Chaiord, Rothger had spied on
Athluan a great deal, particularly when he went with
women. Perhaps it was that again. Rothger himself, though
he had lain with occasional females among the Klow, did
not often indulge. They said his heart was cold.

How cold Rothger's heart was, only Rothger could truly
be aware.

He went to the table and poured wine for Athluan,
bringing it to him in the black jade cup. As he did so he
glanced at Saphay. 'Still asleep. Always asleep. And slept
even through *that*.' He gave the cup to Athluan, who drank
it down. Rothger said, 'That was no vrix, my brother. It
came from *her*, didn't it? Some *thing* from the night-behind-
the-day. Don't shield her. Does she know about it? Is she
some filthy conjuror of elementals this woman they sent
you from the Ruk?'

'Quiet.' Athluan was himself again and glared into Rothger's face. 'Do you think I'd protect her if she was that? I told you, it was a vrix. Sometimes they gain in power. I must talk to the House Mage.'

'Talk to me first.'

'Who are you? Merely the Chaiord's brother. It is *I* who tell *you* how I proceed, not the other way about.'

'Pardon me, then,' said Rothger. His tone was offhand, neither rebuked nor sorry.

'We will go down. After you, Roth, on the stair.'

A minute after they were gone, Saphay woke. As can happen, she knew the area had recently been full of activity, of people, but no one was there now. Only the jade cup stood on the floor, its lip wet from drunk wine.

There had been another bad dream, but she could not recall it. Something had thrown her down, or she had fallen . . . It had lasted on and on, happening over and over. A feeling hollowed her heart, echoing with distress and darkness like a dungeon, but its contents were unseen.

Just then, one of the women attendants came up the stair and into her room. It was old Rowah, the eldest of the older women, her hair white as any Jafn maiden's.

'You're to shift quarters, lady,' said Rowah pragmatic-ally. 'The Chaiord says I'm to help you gather your things, and the girl is coming to help too.'

'Why?'

'A fault with the shutters. Look, they've flown open again while you rested. The ice-wind has left its footprints all over the floor.'

FOUR

He climbed now only a hundred stairs.

For a towery of the Ruk, this was not high, but the western quintul house ran also below ground; he had negotiated several previous flights from the subtor. Here, in a room at the centre of the towers, the oculum blazed, exactly as he had felt it doing from the depths of the house.

Thryfe crossed to the oculum.

Its black globe had become a vortex of spinning lights. Thryfe raised his left hand, only that. Like a panicky animal responding to a known and welcomed touch, the globe composed itself.

Now it grew opaque, and then its internal mirror began to appear. Within that might be glimpsed virtually anything a magician of Thryfe's mental stature could demand. But also it was, like all the greatest of its type, autonomous. It had signalled to him. Next it would reveal its message.

The image came. It surprised, nearly startled him. An oval ruby burned in the mirror, throbbing with heat and radiance. All about lay walls and spires of ice. They were unaffected by the jewel, nor did they have on *it* any effect that was apparent. Thryfe waited.

Since the sending had come so vehemently from the Jafn, assuring the Ruk that Saphay had survived, Thryfe had anticipated further tidings. The kings in Ru Karismi, he was aware – they had told him – did not believe in the Jafn sending. The girl who *one* king at least had dispatched to her death, was *meant* to be dead and could not therefore be alive.

Thryfe, along with others of the Magikoy, had seen the sending. Though patchy in detail, it had carried Saphay's individual and unmistakable physical print. Thryfe and his fellowship knew that rarely, if ever, could such pictures be faked to so absolute an extent. But additionally Thryfe held his own doubts. For he had at first failed to see the vile little plot Vuldir had made, sacrificing his own daughter in order to cheat the Jafn. Whether Sallusdon had had a part in the scheme Thryfe did not bother to investigate. Blameless or a villain, the King Paramount was a fool worse even than Bhorth.

Yet Thryfe had no excuse for his original lapse of vision and deduction. *Why* had he lapsed? Vuldir's game should have been as clear to him from the first as presently it became – clear as a drop of blood running on the face of a moon. But he had missed it. Of all the Magikoy – sensing, as most now did, the impending obscure doom which threatened to push the world out of kilter – none had noted Vuldir's hand in the pot. It seemed to Thryfe that they had been meant to miss it. Such was the psychic muscle of the doom which flaunted itself, yet simultaneously *veiled* its nature entirely. The thought was very terrible. If Fate chose to conceal its path – as, for ordinary men, usually it did – from those of the calibre of the Magikoy, what hope could there be?

Partly to brood on that, Thryfe had come far west to the quintul house.

The jewel in the oculum began to crack open. Thryfe

stared, seeing now for sure that it was an egg. From the tissues of it poured shining streams, and then something burst out of its core.

It was a Firefex, the bird of fire, mythical yet possible, always credited.

The huge smooth body fully formed, the long neck and crested head all red as blood, the beak like hammered gold, and trailing feet like molten brass, were nothing to the outspread wings. They seemed wide as the sky, made of cinnabar and lightning. Upon them it rose instantly from the earth. The mirror tracked it, up through the temple of the ice, into a black heaven. Where, not like a drop but like a *river* of flame and blood, the Firefex passed over the masks of all the frightened moons.

The Fazion ships, low and lean, nosed from a night of wind and light-blowing snow.

There were, as they said in Fazion lands, a jalee of them: thirteen. Behind them, out on the deeper open water, wallowed the Mother Ship, fat and bottom-heavy, driven by witchcraft and her nine crowded sails.

Along the sides of the slighter vessels hung weird shields, and at the prows were the horns of sharks and land cattle, used for rams. But the Mother Ship was decorated with the skulls of men. They somewhat resembled habits of Olchibe in that.

Twenty further Endhlefons crossed the garth. Nothing altered very much, until the soft snow fell in a rain of dull stars.

The riders were mounted on hnowas, bulky beasts that could support the full weight of a man, caparisoned in rainbow fringes and colours. Having ridden far, they poured loudly into yard and House. They were messengers, necessary because no sending had been feasible.

'Their shamans barred our witches with a wall of sorcery – as before.'

Saphay, balanced in the door of the room they had made for her, to the east of the joyhall, heard these words.

Life had stopped in the hall. Athluan, standing with the messenger's leader, the other men, having also stood up, also immobile, and the women in the middle of various tasks at the hearth, the looms, were like statues. Light glinted on eyes bright with alert alarmed concentration. Well schooled, no child began to cry.

The raid had happened along the coast east and north, near the area of narrowed land that stuck out in the sea, and which the Jafn called The Spear. Raiders often began there. Last year it had been the Kelps who came and burned the steads and villages, as now the Fazions would be doing.

Life in the hall resumed. The men started to shout, to charge about. Dogs leapt and barked, and those lions which lived in the House growled. Two turned on each other, and their masters hauled them back, striking them with the flats of their hands. From the walls the great swords and axes were being unslung, a rain now of steel not stars. Carapaces of metal and hardened leather were brought out. The women were running to unfold Klow lion banners from the chests at the hall's back. And the House Mage was striding in, followed by all his lesser counterparts.

Beyond high shuttered windows, Saphay heard more noise in the streets, and out of the door the rumble of assembling chariots.

Hate or like it, they were used to war here. In Ru Karismi, Saphay had never seen any skirmish worse than that of a pair of nobles duelling in the terraced gardens, under sculptures of ice.

Weighed down by her physical occupant, she returned slowly into her room. It was not horror or fear that pushed her back there. She could not, herself so leaden and without energy as she was, comprehend or bear the activity. In fact the raiders did not seem to her at all real. For these last three months, nothing beyond herself had seemed so.

The room was simple enough, constructed of high wood screens and with a tent roof. It had another bed, rather smaller, but ample since Athluan did not often share it with her – and then never to join her in sexual love. The Jafn were abstemious during the last months of pregnancy, and she was by now too big. Saphay sat down in the chair brought from the upper bedchamber. She had never been told, or reasoned, why neither she nor Athluan had gone back to that upper room. Surely, in a space of seven months, they could have mended the shutters?

A fire splashed in its basket. Saphay warmed her hands.

An hour later, Athluan came into the room.

'You'll have heard.'

'Yes,' she said.

'Don't be afraid. We've dealt with this outland dirt many times. They stain their faces blue and wear jewels fashioned with eyes, and fight like butchers. They ride monstrosities another man would scorn. And yet they are nothing. The Kree and Shaiy will come with us, too.

We've sent to them. The Fazions can't blot out our spells here; we're too far off and our mages too vital.'

Saphay smiled. She wished he would go, he was tiring her so with his own vitality, and the weapons he had put on, the cloak of bear fur, his warrior-strategist's eyes.

Yet she heard herself say, 'I saw a man once, he stained his face blue when he was angry.' She thought, *No, I have never seen a man like that.*

Chanting made a sea-sound from the Thaumary. Not bellicose, but hypnotic. Somehow she had closed her eyes. Athluan bent over her. 'I'll be gone at least two Endhlefons. Rothger of course goes with me. Erdif holds the House and garth during my absence. Take care with yourself. You're near your time.'

I know, she thought. She thought, *He tries to be kind and courteous, and to want me as his wife still. But I believe he has no true interest in me. He says it is a boy I carry – his mages say so. Does he want the boy, then? Or loathe him?*

Athluan kissed her, not her mouth but her forehead. She was too pregnant, it seemed, to be kissed on the mouth. She remembered the passionate acts they had played out in the upper bed. Those seemed like madness now, but the madness had brought her to this.

Athluan noted Saphay was again asleep. He could not help considering Jafn women who, even when massively with child, only slept three or four hours every third night. But Saphay was a westerner.

As he crossed back through the busy hall, one of his hawks flew off from the rafters and came to his arm unbidden. People stared at this. Hawks were seldom taken into war.

Athluan said mildly. 'He's come to wish me luck.'

He stroked the creature's head, and tossed it up again into the roof, where it settled instantly.

It was Rothger who said to those men near him, 'What was that? There was a hero once whose hawk flew down to him when he was going to kill a dragon—' Then he broke off. The story nevertheless, known to all of them, continued in every head. The dragon had done for the hero. His hawk, foreknowing, had flown down to say farewell. The men murmured.

Rothger shook his head. He spoke a word to unsay an accidental omen. 'Forgive my loose tongue. I'm prattling like some girl at the washing.' He took his sword from the servant who held it ready, and touched the blade with his lips. 'God guard us. May the snow cover deep all our enemies.'

In other weather it might have been a journey of a handful of days. It took more than seven. At first the snowfall thickened. Then came a light freeze which made the land surfaces treacherous, like slippery brittle sugar with a soft quag of uncohered snow beneath. After that the winds picked up, scything across the ice-sheets. The lions bounded, relentless, strong, their eyes covered by crystalline visors. Now and again, a chariot sloughed, swerved. One foundered and was consumed up past its runners. Another chariot stayed back, with grooms and an under-mage to get it free. The days were dark nearly as the nights. Then, when the wind and snow eased, a night's brilliant stars seemed to hang in nothingness, between earth and some other thing, neither sky nor heaven.

On the eighth day they gained the upland plain which

looked out along The Spear. Here there was a cliff range jutting from the snow, furred with ice-woods. As they roared up to this place, white bats, which made their caves beneath the top-ice, burst from the ground in cascades like water.

A kind of twilight came, late afternoon but overcast, with two early moons, one full and one a crescent. Assembled in the lea of the woods, the Klow men could look for miles towards the east. Out along that shore, where the deep sea lay liquid and black, there was still a fog of smoking and burning. It was too distant to make out the flames, the ships, the carnage and death. Some hours more of travelling, and they would reach them.

'They're lazy, these Fazions, don't shift themselves from where they got in.'

'But, again, there are rich villages there: huge stores of fish and whale meat, and hothouses packed with fruit and vats of wine. They can feast and thrive.'

Above, the bats still circled.

Athluan thought of the hawk which had flown down to him. The House Mage kept to the garth, as he must in wartime. The mages who accompanied the war band were trained to operate in battle, but he had not consulted any of them. There was enough to do.

Rothger was suddenly just behind him, having approached soundlessly over the snow.

Rothger said, 'Am I with you in your chariot tomorrow?'

It was tradition in war, as at betrothal and marriage, that the nearest brother of the Chaiord be his charioteer. In the past, Athluan had done the service often for

Conas; in recent years Rothger often for Athluan. So why ask?

Athluan looked round. Several men had come with Rothger. They stayed still and quiet, as if to support him in some claim.

'Why ask me? It's how it's done.'

'So long as it suits you.'

'Why would it not?'

'Well,' Rothger said. He dropped his voice. It was still Rothger's clear voice, one that carried even when muted. 'We've had words already about certain worries of mine to do with the woman you have to wife.'

'Months back.'

'I don't forget them. I was hurt, I confess.' As Rothger paused, Athluan considered Rothger, hurt. 'But I meant no dishonour to you. Only . . .' Athluan waited. The men, too, also waited at Rothger's back. 'It would shame me if you didn't want me for your charioteer, brother.'

'I have never doubted your courage and wisdom in battle.'

The men with Rothger produced a little approving noise.

But Rothger said, 'Yet, if I displease you . . .'

Athluan saw that more than this small group now paid attention. Among the listeners were some of the Shaiy and Kree allies who had ridden ahead and already caught them up. The son of the Kree Chaiord, Lokinda, was there, a burly young man with big ears.

Athluan stepped forward. He clasped Rothger in his embrace. 'The Fazions *displease* me, and you are my kinsman. We go to fight together.'

*

Some time after full night had come down, something stood up on the cliffs, gazing over curiously at the war camp of the Jafn.

Guri was accustomed to war camps of Olchibe, which did not create large camp fires but kept tiny personal fires in vessels for carrying. Their banners were superior too, with the severed heads on the staves, and depictions of fiends and unknown, scarifying animals.

Nevertheless, he took an interest. Now he was, as he supposed, a ghost, he had access to many formerly unrealized activities.

Down in the Klow camp was that man who believed he had fathered the red-haired child. Or possibly he did *not* believe it. Guri had figured everything out: the woman's Rukar god was the father. Maybe the Klow chieftain had grasped this also, for as time passed he had certainly grown less and less fond of the woman. Guri had seen this happen, because he kept an eye on them. Even so, the Klow chief was not cruel. He appeared even sorry.

But it was the child Guri liked. Children were the future of all men. You could see the future *through* them: an easy enchanting sort of magic given only by the Great Gods, therefore special. They had met, he and the child, twice more on the edge of physicality, although the child had not been calling him: it seemed the god had, for now, withdrawn his animosity to him, as the Klow chief had done with his love.

Where Guri went, when not in the world, he himself did not know, nor did he care. But somewhere, on the shores between there and here, having again met the child, Guri had found too a gift to take him. It was a beautiful little carved mammoth, every hair delineated and the tusks of ivory. Mounted on runners, it could be ordered into move-ment by three simple if sorcerous words of command. Guri vaguely recalled finding and giving something similar to one of his sons among the sluhtins, but never mind. The best gifts might be repeated.

The stars were stretched tonight – twice their normal size, Guri thought. He missed riding his own mammoth, and thumping into his own Olchibe wars behind Feb Yuve. On the other hand, he could now run for miles above the ice, spring across frozen channels wider than vision could span. If he wanted, Guri guessed, he could spring *upwards* and seize the dazzling stars with his hands.

Rothger entered the cave under the ice.

He had come up here to the cliff base, through the woods, and no one had seen or heard him. In his tent behind the fires, his copy lay seeming to sleep its three allotted hours. The copy was not very exact, but enough to convince anyone who did not look too closely. Having grown up privy to magecraft, Rothger also had learned some of it, perhaps a fraction more than was usual.

Bats hung in the cave whose walls glowed mauvely green from outer moonlight. At its furthest end, against the cliff, was darkness.

Rothger walked on into the dark.

Here he threw down the powder he had brought. Where it dropped, it smouldered and smelled of cooling metal and of other things.

In blackness, a presence began to be.

'Is it you?' enquired the presence.

'Who else?'

'Who else but you would dare?' said the presence. Its voice, strangely, was the same as Rothger's own.

'Oh, I dare.'

'What do you have for me?'

'First, what do you have for *me*?'

Then it emerged.

He had seen it before, more than once – unsurprisingly since he had summoned it in the beginning. With familiarity, it had taken on not only Rothger's tones but something of his looks. Yet it was white and partly transparent, and its eyes burned yellow. It was a seef, a type of ice-devil.

'Well,' said the seef, 'I can give you what you wish.'

'So you say.'

'Give me a small present,' said the seef, coaxing and reasonable. 'It will make me vigorous, so I can slave the better for you.'

Rothger grimaced, then he sliced his dagger, already drawn, across the back of his left forearm – already bared for the assault. Blood welled, in the dark almost invisible, but not to the seef.

'Give me—' it wailed, frenzied and wriggling with greed. 'Give – give—'

Watching it the while, Rothger raised his cut flesh to his lips, and slowly drank his own hot blood. As he did this, the seef rocked with ecstasy. Its cat's eyes shut, it held itself in its own arms, trembling, and gradually its pallor was suffused with the faint pink of earliest dawn.

'Now,' said Rothger.

'Yes, you shall have it. You know I am able. I showed you that day with the deer.'

'True,' said Rothger, 'but swear it.'

'Why must I swear it? You and I are kin now.'

'So says my brother, too. *Swear.*'

'I swear by all the gods—'

'No,' said Rothger haughtily, binding his arm with the strip of cloth he had brought for the purpose. 'Make the only oath to me I know you'll keep.'

The seef spat. Its spit was visible like a struck flame, but where the spit landed on the cave floor it chimed like a silver bell. 'By that, then. I swear by the blood in me and the blood to come. By that I swear I will do all you want, providing I am fed after.'

'I always feed you. How else do I retain your charming loyalty?'

Miles off, beyond the cave and the obdurate-icicled woods, came the awful cries of lost children and agonized young girls weeping and shrieking, echoing over the plains and rocks of The Spear.

'Listen,' said Rothger, 'the song of fleer-wolves, out mourning and dining on the remains of the Fazions' war.'

'Yesss . . .' said the seef. Its eyes twinkled. It shape-shifted suddenly, was now a glistening cryomite, and then was gone, away along the night to feed on the feeding of the fleers.

Above the House door, the horizontal sword had been set upright and anointed with the blood of a herd animal.

Saphay saw this: it meant the Klow were at war. And to Saphay it meant *nothing*.

Rowah led her back to her room. It was fitting for a Chaiord's wife to view the sword. But, though Erdif the steward had requested this, Rowah did not approve.

The Rukar princess was near her time. Rowah felt the tension in the air of the room, the tension of Saphay's womb preparing to give up the child. 'I could count the hours left before she starts,' Rowah murmured to God, in whom she often confided, 'count them on the fingers of one hand.'

Both Rowah's hands were missing a finger each.

She was right. Three more fingers-count after witnessing the war sword, Saphay's pains began.

Before the sun came up, the Jafn mages performed pre-battle rites.

Every man received his drop from the sacred cups. Around him was woven a protection which, if it did not keep him alive, would still guide him safely into the afterlife, the Other Place beyond the world.

The Kree and Shaiy, who had been arriving all night, their chariot runners thick with snow, had among them too a wisewoman originally from the far north. She prowled down the lines. Where she touched the lion-teams, their manes crackled with lightning, and they bellowed and pawed the ice. The swords of leaders, drawn and given her to handle, she made into flames and handed back. These incendiary lights faded only slightly in the scabbards.

When the magic was completed, shouting, and high as the hidden stars, the men rampaged into their vehicles. Like a tidal wave, the Jafn army whirled across the plains towards the shores below. After a while, as they went, the day rose up to meet them from the sea.

Already out and about in the morning, invading Fazions glanced from their toil among the ruins.

Along the shoreline, the jalee of smaller vessels lay at

anchor, as if they suckled at the land. The Mother Ship had slunk far in, her sails part-reefed, black on sunlight.

Of the fat rich villages of the coast, not much was left. Mile on mile they had been calcined, their goods, treasures, cattle, women and boys boarded on the Mother. But the Fazions were still searching for anything valuable, or even usefully alive, among the wreck they had constructed. Thrifty, the Faz. Like the Jafn peoples they rationed sleep, but to a greater extent. A Faz warrior who could not go seven days and nights awake and functional they would themselves kill, slinging him to the sharks and spine-rays. Awake, needless to say, they had been drinking and eating heartily, singing all the past night and telling tales of their victories, historical or to come. Their faces were freshly blued, which they did every evening before supper, during raids. On hands, around necks and arms and booted ankles, were polished quartzes with, fitted inside, the once living eyes of those they had slaughtered. The more jewellery a Fazion possessed, the more men he had slain.

But now they beheld the sunlit roller of the chariots coming down on them.

Then you saw what else the Mother Ship could do.

Ramps slid out of her between the oar banks. Along these there soon stampeded something which gushed straight off into the water, then raced for the shore.

'They have their bloody demon horses with them!' The Jafn shouted the report to and fro. No one was astonished. Most of the reivers who used the open seas had acquired similar steeds. Yet some of the Jafn's younger men, new to fighting, had never seen these things before – except with the inner eye at story times.

As the beasts landed, they shook icy liquid carelessly

from them. Such horses, which the Faz called *horsazin*, loved the sea. They travelled easily inside the guts of a Mother Ship, let out every day to swim alongside her, sporting in the death-cold water. It was true they had each the body of a horse, an animal otherwise seldom come on in northern climes. Also, like deer, they were horned, although the horn was singular, and jutted centrally from the forehead. But their main characteristic was that their skins were scaled like those of huge fish. Grey as ice-bass, with round pale uncanny eyes, they flexed themselves on the shore, tossing thin wiry manes and tails the greenish shade of the sides of glass. They were covered too with barnacles, sea-parasites, seaweeds from the farthest outer depths.

The Fazions sprinted to them and careered up on to their bare backs. Only one other procedure was observed. Slinging a piece of cord about the long neck of his mount and through a kind of halter there, every rider then tied this rein swiftly at his belt, leaving his hands free for the trade of war. Howling, they rode inland.

One wave hurtled towards another now. Down from the plains the Jafn chariots came, up from the sea the Fazions on their fish-horses.

They met above the shore. The clash shattered the day. The symmetry of either charge was lost in a maelstrom of exploding lights, buckling vehicles, sunny red columns of blood.

'Lady, you must work harder.'

Saphay stared in disbelief at the faceless women clustered around. Who had spoken so insanely?

Another spoke, also unseen: 'Men fight with swords. This is the woman's war.'

Then pain, enormous and unthinkable, drove for the millionth time through Saphay's body.

She had tried not to scream; it was some vestige of pride, of anger really. She did not want the barbarian hall to hear her screaming. Nevertheless soon enough she had begun to scream. Now the cry burst from her, and she heard it far off as the stinking makeshift room receded.

She would die here. She would die and it had not been fair on her. But to escape this horror – oh, death would be so good.

Falling then – down, inwards, away – Saphay glimpsed great pillars and vast darkness. In the dark a violet flame bloomed like a blossom. Seeing it, a different terror clutched her. *He* was there – *he*. Within herself also now, Saphay screamed out – not to the gods, for *he* was a god – but to nothingness, to *everything*. And, as she did so, she heard a second voice raised with hers.

Swinging the axe one-handed, Athluan watched men fall, headless or otherwise apart, under the runners of the chariots. The evil horsazin reared all about, kicking with steel shoes. They reeked like curing mackerel. One thrust close to him, snapping shark-like. With the sword in his left hand, Athluan sliced through its fish-snake's neck. Witchfire danced on both blade and corpse. As the monstrosity went over, Athluan sheered undone its Faz rider – a filet off the bone.

Rothger laughed. He yelled wordlessly back at the dying Faz, an enemy strung with fifteen necklets of eyes, all of them agog at his collapse. Though controlling the reins of the lion-team, Rothger had secured them around his waist, as in a war chariot it was done. He shot with the Chaiord's own bow, the one Athluan had given over to him, bringing man after man from his horsaz. Rothger quilled the sea-beasts with arrows too, because it amused him.

To the south of the field of conflict bulked a row of stationary chariots, where stood the war mages. Guarded by Jafn warriors and beset by Faz, they cast thaumaturgic energies along the lines. Out at sea, in turn, the reiver shamans were also busy on the Mother Ship. Rays of psychic fission lanced and crossed, until the battlefield below bubbled under an iridescent spider's web. Raw concussions rocked the sky.

Another foe had evolved, more personally: not the first to try, he was climbing into Athluan's chariot. The Fazion axe flapped, and the long knife, deceptively weightless. Athluan deflected them and carved the Faz free of his body.

A former would-be invader, before he was repelled, had slashed Rothger across the back. It had been a light blow like a razor's, letting blood, but as yet unfelt, unheeded. Athluan too had been marked. Against the three-year scar lying along his upper arm was now added a sibling stroke. Meanwhile a Faz knife-hilt had opened his cheekbone and bruised it black. Both brothers were covered in blood, mostly not their own.

A streamer of mage-fire dropped through the turmoil. It appeared to do no actual physical harm.

A reiver leapt from his dying horsaz towards them, and Rothger shot the Fazion through one of the non-jewellery eyes in his head.

The day's brightness was now entirely gone. Gradually, beyond the net of sorcery, the sky congealed. Specks of cold touched the heat of faces.

As snow again began to fall, Lokinda's big-eared son manifested by Athluan's chariot.

The Kree had lost his own charioteer – his bastard brother. Handling the car himself, his weapons all blood, he grinned. He was drunk on murder. 'God snow them in deep where they lie.' He spoke the ritual phrase with relish.

Athluan nodded. 'Deep on deep.'

He noticed a sort of lull had formed about them here. Through the snowfall he saw Klow, Kree, Shaiy and Fazions hacking and hammering down the shore. Fewer blue faces, however, were visible.

Was Lokinda's boy distressed his kinsman was dead? Or had he always distrusted and disliked him, as Athluan did Rothger? In battle things were sometimes arranged . . . Something nudged Athluan low down in his mind. *You too could have arranged it. You may regret you did not.*

He would not glance at this thought; he had never countenanced it for long.

'Some of the outland muck broke for the plain,' said Lokinda's son.

'Yes,' said Rothger, 'look there – twenty Jafn chariots in pursuit of them.'

In the snow, Athluan was not so certain of numbers. But other holds and villages dotted the plains, and the Fazions were equally vicious in triumph or defeat. They must be followed, eradicated.

Elsewhere here, the Jafn victory was spreading. At the sea's wet edge, Klow and Kree fired flaming shafts at the

Faz Mother. Several had struck. Two masts burned and smoke rushed from her. Her magic rays diminished.

Athluan turned to Lokinda's son, whose name he had abruptly forgotten. 'Sir, will you oversee the taking of the Mother Ship?' The boy seemed pleased: it was an honour, but not a taxing one now the shamans were waning. Otherwise such vessels were crewed by slaves eager to rebel.

'Trust me. The Jafn captives will be brought ashore.'

'I'll go inland after the dregs,' Athluan said.

Lokinda's nameless son saluted him. He signalled to the northern wise-woman. Her chariot was pulled by men, who brought it forward now.

Athluan, as Rothger spun the chariot, saw her slender and upright, green hair blowing back in a wind of supernatural power. For some reason, it made him think of Saphay. But his feeling for Saphay was poisoned, and he dreaded the coming of the child which was not his. Tonight, when the fight was done, he might take the wise-woman aside. She was young, and had smiled at him when she fired his sword. She might well be willing.

Guri had left the Jafn war camp last night before any moonrise. He had sped over the land, fleeter than a deer, bounding and cackling. Once he noticed bears and paused to annoy them, for they suspected his presence even if they could not properly see him. When he was tired of that, he went away into that region he could not afterwards recollect. It was actually only like falling asleep for an hour or so. The Olchibe favoured ordinary sleep;

it refreshed him. Then he made on towards the Klowan-garth, where the child would be.

The child was now always there, attracted increasingly to its fleshly self since the woman was close to birthing. It seemed all spirits did this. Even he, Guri, must have done it twenty-eight years before, when his mother was lugging him about in her womb.

Of course, he did not need to run there, even if running so fast and far was exhilarating. For now Guri had found he could be anywhere he wanted in the blink of an eye.

Up on the snow plains, then, he stopped, to watch two moons rising hand in hand. The third moon, thin and wan tonight, had already slipped embarrassedly away.

As Guri watched, he became aware – as he believed, for the first time – of some wonderful and perfect *other* thing. Exciting to him, yet calm to him, this thing was nothing he could identify – and yet he *knew* it, and knew that he did. Guri, when physical, would never have observed in himself such a feeling. Now, however, he began to think he understood what it was. It was the *There* calling to him. *There* which Olchibe and Gech titled the World Behind the Moons, and the Jafn called the Other Place – and which in Ruk Kar Is they luxuriously named Paradise.

Guri stared at the sky, thinking he saw the route now which led into the second world, the world of *There*. And he was infatuated with it. For all the enjoyments he had been having here recently, they could not begin to compare, he sensed, with an afterlife. He *knew* they could not. They were flimsy beside its potency, inspiration and splendour.

For a pivotal instant, forgetting everything else, Guri lifted his arms, preparing to fly upward into eternity.

But sweetness fractured in irrecoverable pieces.

'*Guri – Uncle Guri – Uncle Guri—*'

The child's shrill voice had smashed the dream of else-where. Mislaying elsewhere at once, Guri turned his back on limitless joy. He had given his word, and he dived headlong from the night – into the country of Saphay's unconsciousness.

They were themselves running.

Bent forward as she ran, the woman held the child in her arms.

It was beneath a sea, beneath a roof of frozenness, like clouds, supported by columns made of midnight. Comets and stars that were fish sped by.

Her hair blew behind her, gone a sour shade in the water. The child's hair blew also, dark like blood.

Guri knew them both quite well by now. He stepped into their path. With a pang of uneasy relief, he saw how the boy at once reached out to him. But the woman gazed at Guri with insane wild eyes. Did she recall they had already met?

He knew her name, having heard it spoken about the Klow House.

'Saphay – wait, girl. Is it him, that stink-god, comes after you?'

She had halted. She panted, thinking she had run far, although in this present form she did not need to pant or even breathe. She could say nothing.

The child now struggled away from her. He propelled himself through the water at Guri.

'Up on my back, my lion.' Guri turned again to Saphay.

'*He* hates the baby. There are animals like that: they kill their cubs.'

Behind the woman, in the core of the liquid night, some great advent was approaching. Flares and redness spurled before it, as if from a volcano erupting under the sea.

Guri thought the girl was a dunce and useless, but he said, 'You're caught in your dream. He's caught with you, this one. And that other gets in as he pleases. Wake yourself up. Go back to the world. You're safer out there. I'll take care of the boy.'

'I can't wake,' she said. 'They smoked an incense to ease the pain – a drug. It makes them happy, but makes me sleep. I am . . .' she hesitated, he saw her face grow savage with female scorn, 'in labour, half dead. If I die, then he—'

'Don't die then, silly bitch. Go on, go *back*. I'll help you.'

The sea behind her was sprawling wide in a laval labour of its own.

Guri glimpsed a vehicle, pale racing animals with horrible eyes, and a violet face, almost a man's, whose eyes were Hell itself.

Then he slapped Saphay so hard she folded up like a city book, closing all together, becoming two-dimensional, half transparent, fading . . . *going back*.

The sea trumpeted.

Like a crashing meteor, the chariot came.

Guri had never faced a god before. He put this down to his own infinite good sense.

He dropped on his knees, and from his etheric person pulled a cloak of disguise across the child who clung to him. Saphay had vanished.

The chariot stilled. It idled there, and the white

wolf-things shimmered, black saliva beading out of their mouths.

Guri, eyes downcast, gripping the boy's feet in hands of iron, prayed. He prayed to Saphay, that she should wake up.

The god spoke. 'Have you seen a woman with a child?'

It was what any *man* might say on the earth outside. Guri supposed his brain translated what the god said, for doubtless this Rukar deity of double aspect did not even speak to Guri in any known language.

'I see nothing much, lord. I'm only dreaming: about me and my little brother that died of a fever.'

'He you have hold of?'

'Yes, lord. An ugly little wretch' – Guri had made sure he altered the child to look ugly and much older, five or six years, caked with sluhtin mud and fire-smoke and fleas – 'but I loved him well.'

'You are lying,' said the god. 'Yet I cannot now go past your lie. We shall meet again. *Then* let us see what you will do.'

Guri felt an alarming wrenching. The sea fragmented, he tumbled upward, thrown away. Guri knew what this was: not the god's fury, which had been withheld coyly until another time, but the final spasms of birth.

The Olchibe warrior regained the natural world. He landed smack in a corner of a room of women, among screeches and smell and showering blood. He saw one old dame holding up, on a silken serpent of birth-cord, a baby made of noonday. Still joined, Saphay on her back lay staring at what had been dragged from her.

Unseen by any adult eye, Guri took out and displayed

the little toy mammoth, showing the newborn child what delights were in store; that life *was* worth living.

Wind and snow drove thickly across the plains, and had brought down the dusk. Through this twilight and storm, the Jafn chariots pursued the last of the Fazions.

Now and then the Jafn signalled to one another with shouts, and mage-lights still lingering on swords. Now and then they came up with and killed more Fazions. But generally the Faz were scattered. Despite, perhaps even because of their repugnant scaley steeds, the reivers preferred sea travel and the hem of the ocean. Gradually, too, the hunt being so widespread and successful, regardless of their signals the Jafn became separated.

Athluan had lost track of time and of locality. The sidelong snow had begun to hypnotize him, a thing he had heard of, yet never before himself experienced. He thought maybe the wound in his arm had been caused by a weapon with a bane on it. He would need to consult a mage.

For now, he did what he must. He was a Chaiord, a warrior. It was later he started to think that, along with himself and Rothger his charioteer, something else rode with them in the chariot.

The being was pallid and semi-impermanent – here, then *not* here. Three times only he caught the smeary gleam of its eyes.

He said nothing to Rothger. Athluan was not entirely sure the being – a seef of the waste, most likely – was really present. He felt ill, and might be imagining it.

In any event, he did not trust Rothger.

Rothger, like the Fazions, was his enemy, though he hid it more ably than they.

He wants my place. Oh, I always knew. In his way he has always shown me. Why do I bother with this now?

The wind cantered off. Like a gigantic beast made of freezing flaking sky, it reversed itself, then came galloping back towards them.

On either side, the three or four accompanying chariots responded with calls, and the snarls of their lions. Then all company was gone.

Athluan found he was alone with his brother. As they drove forward, the vehicle lurched, the runners struck against some obstacle obscured in the malicious top-snow. With a disintegrating sound, a metal shriek, the chariot juddered to a halt. The lions were punched upward, one falling, then scrambling to its feet again.

In their sudden immobility, the ravening beast of the wind slammed against them all. They stooped beneath it. The gust surged over, and Athluan saw how the lions and Rothger lifted up their heads, masked and bearded in dead white. He shook the whiteness from his own face, and beheld the seef with utter clarity. It smiled at him like a co-conspirator, and melted away.

'Do you note,' said Rothger, 'what lamed the chariot?'

Athluan glanced down. He saw a man's arm and shoulder poked up from snow, among the breakage of the left runner. From its jewellery, a Fazion.

Rothger swung over the rail, to land beside the Faz.

'What in God's Night are you doing?'

Athluan heard his own voice, which was abruptly unsteady like a boy's.

He watched Rothger kneeling in the snow, slitting the

dead Fazion with his knife, letting the blood gush up, drinking the blood, on and on. Presently, as the flow clotted and ceased, Rothger heaved more of the Fazion from the snow, found his neck and cut it open and, bending his head again, drank from that.

Why does he do this in front of me? Before, I have suspected he has done it, but never seen.

Athluan felt adrift inside his own body. He clutched after the sword the wise-woman had enflamed with magic, but it had stuck fast in the scabbard, and no longer gave light.

Rothger stood up again. His mouth was bloody, but he wiped it carefully on his sleeve. Now it was only more blood spilt in legitimate battle.

'Get out of the chariot, brother,' said Rothger.

The lions, Athluan's own, dressed in their war collars, glared at Athluan, unblinking. Only last night he had fed them from his own hands. He realized now they were changed towards him. They did not know him.

He left the chariot. He saw he and all things had sunk beneath some deathly spell.

Rothger moved off a little way. Then he stopped and beckoned. Athluan found he must go to him.

'You thought you could be Chaiord for ever,' said Rothger, 'and I would be your little faint echo, while you got your alien slut with sons to rule after you. I saw it, that child in the room upstairs. Where did that red hair come from, Athluan? *Her* tribe? I seldom heard yet of any of the Ruk who get red hair. And among the Jafn, never.'

Athluan turned away. The storm was solid as a wall, but after the one great gust had passed, no wind blew. The snow hung motionless in air.

'You've worked magic,' he said.

'Have I? Someone has. My lovesome friend the seef. He needs me to drink blood for him. I've grown to like it. We suit each other well. He's been a better kinsman to me than you, Athluan. He gives me things: nicer than a knife or a bow I'd already spoilt for you.'

'Whatever you plan,' said Athluan, 'will be discovered.'

'No. This very minute, you and I are riding still in our chariot out there, seen by all our companions. We're after the last of the Fazions.'

'An illusion.'

'No, dearest brother. *This* is the illusion.'

Athluan stared. He stared at the lions. He saw they were not real. The half-visible seef had been more real than they. He longed to find himself, but knew he could not and despaired.

'Tell me the rest.'

'Soon told. Out there, a Fazion arrow, flighted black with raven feathers, will pierce your heart. We will all see you die, quickly and nobly as the leader should. First I must make you die here.'

'How could you and a *seef* manage all this—?'

'I've also human friends: Lokinda's unhandsome son, and a green-haired witch from the north, too, who assisted me.'

Then the bane had come from *her*. How curious, Athluan thought, and he had fancied her afterwards.

Out of his body, this vestige of his physical persona, this totally diluted disarmed spirit of Athluan, waited now in silence.

There were legends that related such things. Two

deaths: the intelligence and *life* killed first, to make the killing of the body simpler.

Yet how strong Rothger had made himself. All those years endeavouring, while he had seemed only so shallowly to exist. *I never saw it, I never looked to see.*

Then the wind returned. It came seething low across the white plain, which now was empty of all other things, even of the chariot, the lions, his brother Rothger.

Looking into the wind, Athluan remembered Saphay, the child, after all with regret and sorrow. He would at least have protected them.

But among men, only the dead see the wind.

It smote him: a thousand dagger-points bit him through. Creatures were *in* the wind, gelid ice-creatures, winged and fanged. He saw his flesh – not of the body but of the *inner* body, which is wounded often first – saw it torn off in chunks. His atoms flared all around him, devoured in the mouths of vampire-fish that flew.

As Saphay had done, Athluan shut his eyes.

Out beyond the area of sorcery, where the Jafn tackled the last of their foes, a Fazion shaft, recognizable by its flight feathers, skimmed from the tussle. It buried itself in the physical heart of Athluan. Many witnessed it. Rothger alone was aware of the hand which had guided it, translucent, just flushed with nourishment, lost in the falling snow.

When the fight was quickly finished, anger at a Chaiord slain lending the Jafn vigour, the men from the five allied chariots stood above Athluan's body.

'Battle-death is always best. No man can avoid his bed for ever. Even the stars are only dogs in the hand of night.'

FIVE

Saphay had been flung from an abyss of nightmares into a bath of excruciation. Then, discarded on some mindless plateau, she saw what had caused all this, now elevated in front of her.

With the going of the pain, *so* she saw him: a golden child on a platinum cord. She had given birth to the sun.

'Here, lady, here you are. Here's your boy – flawless.'

He was *hers*.

Never had anything been hers. Even those things they had informed her were hers – her tiny royalty, her barbarian husband – she had never chosen them.

She had not chosen this one either.

But, oh – oh, if she had been given to choose, *this* one she *would* have chosen over all others.

Hers.

As they pressed the last debris from her body, and washed her, he lay on her breast. Miraculously, the eager milk came in a stream.

The attendants nodded. At last, this unJafn woman was behaving as a true woman should.

But how else? He was such a comely child, and a boy.

*

As Athluan had promised her, two Endhlefons went by. The people in the House remarked that their warriors must be chasing Fazions still. After the fight, they and their allies would feast; there was help necessary for the rescued villagers, too, who had been robbed of everything.

Erdif the steward stalked about the House. He was a man late in years, over-temperate and stern, who prided himself that he took less sleep than a Faz reiver. Erdif also rated his position highly. He fretted that no news had been sent him.

The House Mage declared that severe snowstorms raged along The Spear, and such things could deflect sendings.

On the twenty-third day, a sentry posted on the upper walls saw the men of the Klow returning over the ice.

Rowah came to Saphay in the makeshift room. The young woman was nursing her child, with every appropriate look of absorption and serenity.

When Rowah gave her announcement, Saphay seemed bewildered.

'You must come out, lady, to welcome your husband. That's how it's done in a garth.'

Saphay frowned. She let the child finish his drink – he was at once asleep. She laid him down in the wooden cradle, not wanting to let him go. When she had done so, as always she felt out of balance, fragile and bereft, as if he were still attached to her and to put him down meant pulling away part of her own body. Normally she held him on her lap or walked about with him in her arms, all day and sections of every night. She too had now learned to go without much slumber, in the Jafn manner. The child had taught her with his demands, his sudden loud cries or slight stirrings. When she slept in the bed, he lay with her on the pillows. The women did not like this. They said she would roll on him – like some cow in a byre, she thought – and suffocate him. Saphay paid no attention to them.

Her love for this creature, barely alive but not yet human, not yet anything she comprehended, was blinding and total. She knew she would no more *roll on him* in unaware sleep than she would cut her own throat.

She must not take him into the cold – he was too new for the severity of the outdoors – so Saphay went out alone, already aching for her missing, intrinsic part. Insecure, she waited on the garth wall among the people and banners, swathed in her furs. And in this way she saw them bring back Athluan, and that Rothger now was Chaiord of the Klow.

Rothger entered the Klowan-garth, driving the chariot which had been his brother's. The lions knew him. He had been their frequent charioteer for several years. Athluan stood in the chariot's back as usual. Frozen solid, the corpse was strapped to the vehicle's side. It was Jafn tradition, when such war-deaths occurred, that if possible a lord returned to his hearth standing.

In garth and House the period of mourning commenced. White clothing was donned to signify the snows that finally devoured all things. The mages visited the fires of every dwelling, turning them, by magic, black to demonstrate the starless night of a king's overthrow.

Saphay, walking up and down in her prison-like chamber of screens, the child resting on her breast, wondered what she would have to do next. Rowah had mentioned the cropping of hair, an offering to go down into the grave with her husband – also days of fasting. For a long while the morning and evening meal had been the only times, aside from her ascent of the wall to see the dead brought in, that Saphay had left this awful little room. She was a foreigner among them and, though they had tolerated her while Athluan lived, the women intimated it was now her station to be circumspect.

What did she feel anyway about Athluan's death? She had despised and feared him, lusted after him, begun to doubt him again. He had never been unkind to her – she thought of his efforts to explain and amuse her before their bedding on the marriage night, his tale of the hero Star Black. Yet he had distrusted her too. They had gained no enduring intimacy; sex had not unified but rather separated further, for it had brought the child.

She had been concerned how he would greet her son. She had worried over it. Surely he should have been glad? Somehow she knew he would not. Yes, even though with the Jafn a son especially was prized. But something had interposed between them. Now death concluded all.

For Rothger, she grasped he hated her, found her perhaps actually repulsive. She was an outlander, effete and nearly worthless. She sensed already what would happen next, although in her conscious mind it was unthinkable.

When Rowah entered, five days after the warriors' homecoming, Saphay turned, holding the child firmly in her arms. He had no name: only the father could name a male child. As the father was dead, the child stayed nameless.

'The Chaiord says you're to go to hall.'

Rowah seemed troubled. She, too, perhaps found it difficult to call Rothger *lord*.

'Then I must.'

'He is still . . . in his chair. You know the custom, lady.'

Saphay nodded. For nine days and nights, Athluan would remain seated in his carved chair in the coldest area of the joyhall. Despite the cold, it was warmer indoors. Already he had begun to thaw, and to reek. The smell of it, and the camouflaging perfumes, stole into the room of screens.

She walked out into the hall, and Rowah followed. No other women attended her.

Rothger sat in the Chaiord's place, but on an ordinary bench – his nobles, such as they were, grouped about him. There had been drinking, and some games to entertain the dead – another outlandish custom. Along the room the mages sat, twenty-five of them today. Now all eyes fixed on Saphay.

Never, in the term of her lonely life, had she felt more solitary, more unsafe. But the child shone on her breast like a live coal.

'Now,' said Rothger. He held out his cup, the one which was black jade, and it was filled for him. 'This woman of the Rukar country.'

Saphay accepted they would speak of but not to her. That was what they did. They began to discuss her merit among themselves, any value she might have. That she be present was not, she thought, in order that she might hear or speak out in her own defence, but that assessing her might be made more easy for them.

'She's young,' one of them said grudgingly, 'and she can bear. Another could wed her. The law says that's the best way. Even the next Chaiord sometimes takes on his brother's woman. Then he may choose again elsewhere: two wives offer some advantages.'

'Do you mean me?' asked Rothger.

The other looked abashed.

A second man said, 'Or she can stay a widow among us.'

'So she can,' said Rothger. 'There are the alliance rights we have from her people.' The men assented. All cups were refilled. Smoke and stench and scent bothered the child, who raised his head and gazed around.

At this, some of the men took note of him.

'He's a fine-looking boy.'

'His father was of the finest.'

'Ah,' said Rothger. 'Yes. There it is.'

Silence clamoured. Just the fire made a noise, like teeth crunching bones.

Not meaning to, Saphay turned to see Athluan's corpse. His face was changing in decay to a blue mask—

Rothger had got up. He poised, playing with the precious cup.

'My father,' said Rothger, 'made three legal sons: there was Conas, there was Athluan, there was myself. Down through our line there was no man, not even in a story, and there is no man now, who has hair the colour of the hair of that child, nor skin like the colour of that child's skin. He looks as if he's been tanned at a fire. Red hair? A brown skin? Now, to my mind comes the idea of Olchibe.'

'They're yellow!'

'Yes, true, yellow like this woman's fleece. Perhaps *her* hair and *their* skin produced such a boy.'

'His hair may alter. He's not so many days old.'

'Well,' said Rothger, 'I'll tell you something now. You

recall Athluan moved this woman's bedchamber out of the upper room. Why? Because ghosts and vrixes haunted it. Once I went up there to find my brother, and I came on him struck to stone, unable to stir hand or foot. And this woman, she sat talking to this very child we see here, which was then *inside* her – but its spirit was *out*. It was older in appearance than now it is. The hair of it was red as copper.'

Down the hall swept the House Mage. He was grave, and the uproar fell away before him.

'This I will confirm,' said the Mage. 'Rothger told me of it that very day. And the room where this woman slept, hour on hour, was so choked by foul magics that we took her out of it. Even Athluan, we all remember, thereafter slept mostly in hall.'

'She's not a witch,' said Rothger, 'to deal with supernatural things. It isn't her calling. No, she is instead a magnet for such mucky stuff. And look what it's produced. Let go the rights of alliance, I say. Do you think the Ruk will honour them? They sent us tainted goods and, as Athluan himself suspected, tried to lose her on the way in case we learned as much. Remember how my brother found this whore, sealed up in ice and yet alive. She is herself some kind of demon. She arrived here with that thing already in her belly – it's no sowing of my brother's. You've seen his children: there are only girls, and white as snow.'

Over a blurring vortex – the hall itself – Saphay saw the rotting violet face looking at her with eyes of nothingness.

Without warning or prelude, she remembered.

She remembered the sea, the dreams, the fire, the blueness of horror – *everything.* She remembered the god.

If she had been in some other spot, she would have

screamed worse than at the birth of her child. Here, blasted into bits, she was rigid and noiseless as her husband had been in his death chariot.

Rothger was quite right: she had attracted to her something terrible. It had done with her as it wished, and she had gloried in her use. And here she was, clutching the fruit of the horror and hell and lighted darkness. Athluan had seen what she would not. No surprise he had ceased to like her. She stared at the baby in her arms.

All about her, the men shouted and argued, saying the Ruk alliance was worth something, saying it was not, talking of wickedness and evil craft. None of this meant anything.

She stared on into the face of the child. 'Oh, you . . .' she whispered.

The heart of Saphay broke in her breast and instantly fused together again, hard as granite, cold as ice. She put her hand over the child's head, with its down of faintest hair, and bowed her own head to shield it. In some other universe she stood then, and waited now, with her one love, for the judgement of a paltry world.

It was night. No female had come near her; now one did. A green-haired witch, like a Jafn torch of meeting and sending, slid into the lamplight.

'He's merciful. He lets you keep your life.'

To Saphay these words were idiocy. She sat and still held the child.

'However,' said the torch-witch, 'they will sling you out of their clean garth. I'm to make them safe for that – from you and your get.' She meant, presumably, the child.

'Behold,' said the witch, 'I see its shadow on the wall. Never have I seen such a shadow cast by a human thing, not even a Magikoy of the Ruk.'

Saphay glanced. She detected nothing unusual.

The witch began her work. Hurricanes and tintinnabulation filled the screened room. Saphay believed that otherwise no one had stayed inside the whole House. They were out in the yard and the streets. Even the corpse of her husband would be there.

What the witch did was exhausting, indecipherable, and it took away all energy or any scrap of optimism that might have been left to her. Saphay felt herself drift asleep, as the child had, from boredom and enervation.

When she opened her eyes, Green-hair was gone. Some men were there. They were Jafn, she deduced, but they had covered themselves in the pelts and heads of animals.

They instructed her to get up. One dropped her cloak of fur across her shoulders. Another thrust against her a flask that slopped with some liquid and a small bag that contained something. It was awkward for her to take these, supporting the child as she was.

After this she had to go out.

The night was black and starless like the mourning fires. One narrow moon had been dropped like litter on the horizon.

A man in a bear's mask spoke, and she recognized the tones of the House Mage.

'Keep your life. We're blameless of your death. Leave this House and these walls. Go from our habitation and let your own familiars care for you.'

Saphay looked up. It came to her at last – they were going to exile her, not only from the House but from the walled garth. They were going to push her out into the ice waste.

They hustled her now through the yard gate, down through the wending streets, among the spirit icons and white-clad silence of snow and humanity. It was businesslike; no one spoke again.

For a moment, Saphay wanted to shriek out, not only from panic but with frustration and boiling anger. But then she seemed to see back along her life, and how she had been always at the command of others, how her life had never been her own. She had a memory of how she was brought here. Her exodus was more swift.

Over the door of the House, the sword lay peacefully horizontal once more. On the platform above the ice plain, outside the walls of the garth, Saphay gazed back at this and, though far off, she noted every detail.

The high wall-gate was by that time barred from within against her. The people had withdrawn, not merely into the garth but into their houses. One by one all the lights inside the wall went out. They filled their savage town with darkness including even the House, which also doused its torches and upper windows one by one. It was as if they concealed themselves from her, to show her – and God – the settlement was now empty, and therefore had no one in it who might assist her.

At a loss, Saphay looked in the only other direction. The snowscape was bleak and featureless, the sky almost featureless. Then even the sliver of moon slipped away. Heaven too had put out its lights against her.

Because there was nowhere to go, for a while she loitered outside the garth. But eventually, and for that same reason, Saphay moved down the platform by one of its treacherous ramps.

In the flask they had given her she was to find watered beer, and in the bag a burnt loaf. Thus they had guiltlessly provided her with covering, food and drink.

At first she walked not uncomfortably and not slowly on the packed snow. She might have been going somewhere – that was how she walked, and the child peered from his shawl, quiet in this vast and ringing shell of cold.

But the garth grew small and the waste grew enormous. It was an alabaster desert vacant of everything but herself and the nameless child.

Saphay wept, the tears freezing to her face. She ripped them away. Only the child gave her warmth. All courage, all terror, all anger, were gone. All things were gone. She walked.

'She doesn't see me at all,' said Guri, trotting in mortal mode to keep up, for the woman was fierce as she strode along in her boots, her eyes blank. 'But you do, my lion, don't you? You see your Olchibe uncle?' Guri, who had for now shelved his plans to harm her, quite admired Saphay at this point. She was not whining: she got on with her fate. She would, he thought, after all have made a fine consort for Peb Yuve, albeit a minor one. But Guri had not been able to see to that, and the time was past. Peb though would have valued her, once she proved herself worthy of not being killed. He would have valued her more than the Jafn did. Besides, Guri perceived how well she guarded her child. And one further thing there was: though she had no psychic vision, plainly the child still did, even now it was born and in the flesh. He made signs to Guri, this baby, in some non-physical manner. But you should expect nothing less. Certainly the child was more than mortal. 'You see your uncle and he sees you. And he sees that *shadow* of yours too. On the wall, in the lamplight, when that green trull was at her ravings. And from the moon before it went down. But in sunlight it's best of all, your shadow. All those sparkles in it, my lion. All those sparkles like fire.'

First Intervolumen

The barrier between reality and the unreal is thin as light, denser than a mountain; less penetrable than diamond, more easily shattered than a glass; the most absolute Truth, the first and final Lie.

Kraag saying: Southlands

For a time there was only day and night and elongate snow. Then there came to be weather also. The winds churned along the waste, empty of any matter but powerful as elephants. The woman, as she walked, fought them with every step she took. Before the winds, she had not stopped very often, only now and then, leaning perhaps against an upright drift, sleeping a few minutes as the child fed. She was still able to feed the child, but the flat ale and bread for herself were gone. Sometimes she put a pebble of snow into her mouth; that was by now her food and drink. The child had ceased to feel heavy, although briefly he had weighed like a heavy stone. Yet, in some way, out here he and she had grown back together, and he was now once more a joined part of her body. When the winds came, every hour or so, they threw her over. Then she must kneel, crouching across the baby, her back to the onslaught, letting her own frame take all the force of the wind's fists and knives. She did not cry; she was too cold for tears, and soon she felt nothing. She was burning down into the snow plains. She had ceased to care, and would next cease to exist.

Somewhere in the core of her skull jumped a howling rage. She noticed it vaguely.

The child was still warm. She noticed he did not sleep

now very much. He seemed more intrigued by something on the landscape she could never see.

'Jafn baby,' she said, surprised. Or tried to say; her lips would not really move. 'But I come from the Rukararian city westwards. And I have to sleep, . . . the sprites are invisible to me.'

The winds sounded distant. The numbness they had eventually brought was not unpleasant. It was not she believed she would die. After all, she had died and *not* died, previously.

As the sound and sensation of the world began to go, Saphay saw instead an object catapulting along the top-snow. Against the luminous gem of dusk, it turned cartwheels. What was it? The child laughed.

There, before Saphay's open, nearly sightless eyes, Guri performed a somersault which escalated into flight. Re-arriving on the ground, he peered in the woman's face, shrugged and spoke.

'This isn't any use. Hey, girl, can't you see me yet?'

Saphay yawned. Her eyes lidded over.

Guri himself seemed to see a diaphanous half-thing that floated round her – part of her soul coming adrift? He pushed it back, or tried to. He gave her this, she had done her best. Now he thought he had better save her, for without her, or someone similar, the boy-cub would not survive. It was not his time to die – and not hers. She was contaminated by a god, would have to use up and jettison all that before she could go properly elsewhere. Guri wondered, dissatisfied, if that also applied to himself.

Guri the ghost, whose undead magic proved an endless source of fascination to him, reached inside his being and brought up sheer physical strength. He leaned over and dragged the girl off the snow. Her head lolled. She said, 'Let me alone.'

'Shut your noise.'

The child climbed partially away from her, until some of its aura was sitting astride Guri's shoulders – with all the appearance of a boy of about two years. The baby, though, stayed curled in Saphay's locked arms and went to sleep.

Guri hauled Saphay and the double child up in the air. He scudded backwards over the plains towards the sky, holding her insolently around the ribs. As he did this, she began to swear and curse him. He was impressed a little by many of the phrases she knew, a mix of Jafn lewdness and Rukar profanity. How had she ever heard them? In a sane and conscious state of mind would she even remember such words?

The turquoise sky turned indigo. A moon rose through the darkness in a lurid white-gold cloud.

They splashed down into soft drifts.

'Sit there.'

'Cutch-gop, you soint.'

'*Yes*, ladyness.'

Guri put down the aura-child, who at once discovered Guri's gifted toy mammoth and began to play with it.

In turn, Guri released more of his own magery. In life, he had seen the Crarrowin make fire. *Then* he had not had any true talent for witchcraft. Now was different of course. He did it, however, as they did: not calling the flames out of nowhere, as for example the Rukar and Jafn did, but pulling them out in drops from the centre of his abdomen. The fire-drops landed on the snow and began to blaze, needing neither kindling nor hearth. The heat was good: it tempted even Guri, who did not need it. But he had other things to do.

Saphay was stirring as he left. Since she had seen him, through being half dead herself, he fancied now he might be fairly obvious to her, sometimes.

He leapt upward. The child watched appreciatively until Guri was out of sight.

Guri raced over the air, his own psychic speed pleasing him. He had reached the borders of the sea in moments, and next dived out across it.

Moon, stars, Guri rushed by each other. He could already smell – having snuffed after them – his quarries.

The ice-hill berg lay maybe seven miles offshore in liquid water. It was one of an army of bergs that still glimmered greenly blue, having trapped, it seemed, the ended dusk inside themselves.

But at least one of their number – the one he wanted – contained better things than mere light.

Guri put down on the berg. He paused there a second to take in the swinging view of sea and heaven, before plunging straight in through the granite thickness of the ice.

He struck home in a sort of wonderland. There, frozen in the innards of the ice, were weird-lit orchards of fruit and avenues of luminescent grain, ancient as the lost *Summers* which had formed them, potentially succulent as if ripened yesterday.

Channels were chopped slenderly through the ice as Guri went harvesting. He ravished the berg, ripping out sheaves of dilf and wheat, snapping away boughs, the improbable green of verdigris, massed with rouged plums and apples, vine-grapes black as the evening.

After the berg, Guri soared back inshore. He found the

herd of deer at the perimeter of an ice-forest which, unlike the trees in the berg, had no colour at all.

Guri tried to kill one of the deer. This proved impossible, to his irritation. Yet he managed to extract several handfuls of blood from three or four of the sprinting beasts, nipping their arteries open then quickly shut, as he had once seen a Crarrow do. It would be a while before he would question himself as to why he had not let the deer he could not otherwise bring down simply fall from blood-loss.

The bounty anyway was not so bad.

Proud of his ingenuity, heavy-laden and jolly, Guri galloped back towards the woman and child.

Waking by the fire, Saphay had no instant of confusion. She knew she was not in the garth, nor in a city. She recalled precisely what had happened.

Oddly, however, she recalled also another thing, which all this time she had forgotten.

There was something in one of the deep pouches of the cloak she wore. She had clandestinely put it there, taken out of the chest, on the day she was moved from the upper chamber to the room of screens. She had never considered why she did this, but it was, after all, a sorcerous object. Perhaps now the vivid flames reminded her.

Saphay slipped her hand, which had felt cold and wooden but was now pliant and helpful again, into the lining of the cloak. No one, it seemed, had thought to search Saphay's garments.

She brought out her trophy from the Klow sending fire, and held it in her available hand.

The coal was black and inanimate, just as it had been when she stole it from the fire-basket.

She sat against the snow-bank, looking at the coal in the firelight.

The baby slept in her arm. She could feel his even, healthy breaths against her heart. Somehow, too, she seemed to see into his dreams, and beheld him there running and playing with some toy that moved independently on runners at his side. She smiled at this, charmed by her own fantasy.

The fire that burned here was magical, and everything would now be well, for evidently some kind itinerant had found her or she them. It was only a matter of awaiting their return.

Feeling comfortably rational, Saphay did not probe this fuddled madness.

Instead, while she waited drowsily, she turned the coal in her hand. Then she threw it into Guri's mage-fire – perhaps because it seemed some sort of combustible.

As Guri then came soaring in down the sky with his lawless shopping, he was greeted by a display of lights all across the lower horizon.

Far, far north of this land and sea were the barren countries of such boors as the Vormish peoples. There lightnings constantly wheeled about the night skies, so Guri had been told. He had never wished to view either those lands or their illuminations.

He checked in mid-air, frowning. Then he saw what it was that dazzled in the sky.

No one had said the Vormish lights made *pictures*, or *images*. Yet here a lion and a wolf, both scarlet-red and jade-green, were engaged in a dance of war. One leapt at the other, both leapt, both fell and rolled together over the sky. The moon was caught in their mouths, in their pelts and manes. They coloured it and let it go, wanting only to maul each other. And either the lion was of a lesser size, or the wolf a giant of his kind, for they were evenly matched.

In his brain, this second brain of his earthly spirit, Guri heard the child. He was not calling in fear: he was *laughing* with enjoyment. The antics of the pair of fire-animals entertained him.

Uncle Guri, do you see?

'I see,' said Guri.

He shot forward down the night. You could not leave, as his own father had said, a woman alone for five seconds without she would be up to mischief.

It was as he sprang over and came down beside them that Guri took in two further items. For one, Saphay was alarmed, sitting up and properly protecting the baby with her arms, even as he struggled not to lose the gorgeous sight of the scene above the fire – and he laughed still, the baby, as he had inside Guri's head. The second thing was that now the wolf had pinned the lion to some invisible surface overhead. The wolf was mounting the lion, holding the back of the great cat's neck in his jaws. Guri conceded that the smallness of the lion's mane might indicate a female. That had not been battle, then, but foreplay.

Guri, despite himself, felt a surge of arousal. It was now plain that neither animal disliked their unusual sexual act.

Of course not, for Guri had heard of it. It was a legend among the Gech, if an old one and seldom mentioned, the mating of lion with wolf – which must then construct a creature both freakish and divine. In the ice swamps of Gech, now and then, so Guri's grandmother had said, they could point out to you the marks of lionish wolf-pads in the snow, prints of abnormal size which shone without need of sun or moon. *That* was the resultant hybrid: the lionwolf. But Guri had always thought this a story.

They were attaining their apex, the couple in the sky.

Guri felt the current of their climax stamp irresistibly through him. He turned away and quickly, unseen by woman or child, vented himself at the snow. That he could still do this did not astound him; he thought it his right, even after life. But psychic animal carnality was one thing; he who had raped countless women did not mean to offend this one, nor disturb her son.

Thunder rang over the sky. The wild flames flared. It was over. The lights went out. Guri tidied himself, turned round and walked sedately across the snow to the more traditional magic fire he had made.

'You can see me now, then?'

'Yes. Where does this food come from?'

'Out of an iceberg. Have you ever tasted better? Another day, I'll dive – get up fish for us.'

'None of this,' said Saphay, having come to a sudden conclusion, 'is real. I'm seeing supernatural events and apparitions, to which category *you* belong.'

'Great thanks, lady,' said Guri, sarcastic. He too slurped up the blood porridge he had heated on the fire in a bowl made of snow which neither melted nor restrained heat. The dish was thick with the rich dilf, nutty and salty and delicious.

'This won't sustain me,' said the woman.

Guri wished to slap her but he saw, dejectedly, that he

would never again be able to do this. Not after what he had witnessed.

'It *will* sustain you.'

Before, she had not been able to speak his language, but now anything he said and wanted heard was decipherable; and anything he listened to and wanted to grasp was the same. Might it have been easier if he and she could not communicate? If he *could* slap her? *Oh* yes. Well, no use lamenting sunrise, as Peb Yuve had been accustomed to say.

She nagged on, 'How can it? This food is all imagined. None of it's real.'

'Yes it's real, in its own fashion. Look at it this way. Part of *you* is not *real*, lady: your inner being – your physical soul. Feed that, and all of you gets fed – if you let it be.'

She looked haughty, the bitch. She *was* a bitch. No use lamenting . . .

'Pay heed,' said Guri harshly, 'the gods too are like all this. If you believe in them, they grow valid and help you. Or if you're frightened of them, they'll hunt and hurt.'

Her proud princess face, no longer ruined by the bite of the cold, the onset of death, sank on its bones. She lowered her eyes.

'Yes,' she said.

She and Guri sat thinking of the god under the ocean – this one's father.

This one.

'Lady,' said Guri, 'look there, do you see *that*?'

She glanced, warily. Apparently for the first time, as with himself she too now saw the true shadow of the baby, stretching down across her lap into the snow.

'Bright as the ruby-jewels of the Rukar,' said Guri, 'all those little spangles.'

'A child of fire,' said Saphay. She sounded complacent. Then suddenly she was asleep.

Guri hazarded, relieved, that as she grew stronger again, even on partly unsubstantiated foods, she would probably lose sight once more of the shadow's aspect, and – grant, oh Great Gods – of *himself*.

During the days, which was mostly when they travelled, Guri was often aggravated by their slow pace. Then he would take hold of Saphay and carry her, his arms fastened round her waist. Now, when he did this, he did not snatch her up, but suggested the portation first and took hold as politely as he could. To begin with she had protested, so he had had to explain the obvious to her.

'So we can go faster? Where are you leading us?'

'To safety.'

'Where?'

'Some settlement or town. Somewhere that Jafn Rothger and his curs won't harry you, or that he even knows exists.'

Guri thought the Jafn parochial and ignorant. He mislaid, blithely, the insular quality of Olchibe, which knew not much of anywhere beyond the back door.

He was not very interested, even now, in exploring this world. He took it for granted, as he always had, expecting of it nothing and everything.

She let him carry her, anyway. The child too loved it, coming out of his baby-shell and sitting astride Guri's back, while the baby-body slept.

He and Guri currently had conversations frequently, whether the baby was asleep or awake. They were childish talks, though intelligent. Occasionally something else was there, some brilliance. It manifested in a word or concept – Guri was never swift enough to catch or prolong these moments. But then, he had come across curiosities from the very young before. One of the kiddlings of the sluht-camp, four years old, had instructed Guri, with total accuracy, how to tie a particular knot of which the child had no knowledge. Even more oddly, one of his own kiddlings, only three, had told him frankly, 'When I was born before, I was a chief and I ate bearmeat.' Guri had thought that quaint and feyly believable. He saw now it had likely been prosaic fact.

They moved south, west of south, selecting plains between great forests, or flying over the forests with Guri in charge. Each evening Guri would find food. He went down through the crust of the earth into depths of black water, and brought up cryogenic fishes. But it was Saphay who had then to slaughter them. Guri had learned he could no longer do this, try as he might, his best blows passing through and through some animal, fish or bird, leaving it flummoxed but whole. He could only thieve a little blood. He remembered the Crarrowin said the dead could not kill any creature. Although he recollected also tales of how the dead could vex or *terrify* their own – living – kind into a grave.

Watching Saphay bash the fish over their heads, and then, the initial time, throw up on the snow and refuse to eat them, Guri pranced with frustration. But they improved: Saphay at her butchering, Guri at his patience.

Where they were going, Guri really was uncertain. He

guessed they would eventually arrive somewhere, some region that he might leave them to. He could not – though he did not acknowledge this – *visualize* leaving them; that meant leaving the child.

The boy had no name. In Ruk Kar Is, and among the Jafn, a father must name his offspring, thus proving his acceptance of it. Athluan had not, of course, done so. Saphay called the baby by love-words and pet names; Guri had called him *Lion*. After seeing the image of mating beasts, Guri thought it prudent to be less familiar. He was not afraid of the child; however there was more to this child *than* a child.

By then, too, Guri had begun to see other unhumans in the world. They were not exactly there, not in the world that Saphay and her son still inhabited. More, they were in a kind of 'tween-world which lingered always between the day of normalcy and the night of occult otherness. Guri, as he now was, could move in and out of this 'tween-world without a problem. He was becoming used to it. He saw the boy too, even when a baby, could see some of it as well. Saphay, despite continuing to see Guri, could *not* see the 'tween-world – except in bizarrre and random slices, as for example when they came out on to the shores of a great frozen lake plain, here and there cracked in mile-deep channels. Liquid water lined their floors, and there were meras sitting along the channel-sides. Mermaids, they were unearthly, yet *physical* enough, unlike Guri, to lay hold of fish and kill them – next eating them raw. Guri stood watching, envious and resentful. White-skinned, with pearly webbed hands and coiled pearly fishtails, their hair was formed of watery, weed-like tendrils, clear as glass.

But they too had the eyes of fish, lidless and pale. Their teeth were jagged as fishbones.

'What can you see?' Saphay asked, and then, 'What are those animals along the channels? Are they seals?'

'Meras,' said Guri. Why prevaricate?

Saphay stared, herself, then she put one hand to her mouth. 'Yes – yes I do see them. My nurse told me about them – they drown the ships. But no. No, they're seals.'

In a way he was not utterly sure the meras existed in her universe at all. They were more projections, *reflections* out of the 'tween-world. Even the fish they ate might therefore be reflected or illusory. Guri had glimpsed banquets in that place, and other things that could not be, yet were.

Saphay, after she had seen the meras which were seals, began to change. Her mind started to pull itself into a saner shape which rejected elementals and visions, even while intellectually crediting them. Her mind took a firm hand with her. Rather as Guri had yearned to, her mind slapped her. *Leave this alone*, said the slappy mind. *You are alive. The living of your race do not see such things unless gifted and trained by Magikoy. As for the Jafn, they are crazy, filthful and to be forgotten.*

Saphay determined to forget the Jafn. Her spite she kept aside for Rothger. Sometimes she thought, for a minute, of some man or animal attacking Rothger, tearing out his intestines. She had never known she could foster these kinds of thoughts – but she was Vuldir's daughter after all. Athluan haunted her in another way: she dreamed of him. Following the magic apparition the coal had caused, she dreamed of lovemaking with Athluan, and in sleep her body spasmed so violently it woke her. Saphay told herself, guided by her mind, that Athluan was of no consequence.

She could not find the coal that morning – Guri's fire had consumed it, as the sending flames had not. Athluan should be like that coal – all gone.

For the god – for all of that – she found another method. Maybe Guri's teaching had influenced her. No sooner did the bewildered limitless horror enter her awareness than she thrust shut some inner door against it. *I will not think of it.* How else could she survive? *I will not . . .* and did not. Vague as ashes he grew, shut out from her thoughts – the blazing Zezeth, Sun Wolf under the sea.

As for the child, she adored him. Naturally he was the best and most astonishing boy ever born.

Her eyes, though open, were closing again in self-defence against so much.

Even Guri grew less present to her. Sometimes she saw through him, then she reasoned ably: *He is some uncouth sorcerer of the wastes.*

The sky was often blue, as Guri the Wasteland Sorcerer carried her through it. Strange flying reptiles, scaled and with the wings of bats, flew over. Saphay decided these were birds – kadi or large ravens.

That night they followed, on foot now to accommodate Saphay, a wide avenue of snow that led up through an ice-forest of enormous height, width and depths. Ice-spiders spun through its upper tiers. Their nets dripped with tangled dying moths, out of which Saphay, with sudden uncanny sight, saw psyches escaping in misty streams.

Then the forest altered. It closed over and there was no exit upwards to the sky. Guri naturally would not be hampered by this, yet he was – for neither of the others could flash non-corporeally from one physical dimension to another. Even the clever child could not, being trapped now with his baby form.

Guri made fire. They did not eat. Guri had caught a fat white squirrelor, which Saphay adamantly refused to brain. There was an argument. The squirrelor made off up the nearest, hugest tree. Everyone sat sulking.

When dawn came, it barely penetrated the forest save in pockets. A dim half-light was all they had.

They went on.

Guri noted regretfully that the baby now seemed to be laying a firmer grip on its soul, forcing it more often to remain inside him. Coax as he would, Guri could not raise the auric child out of the flesh. Only sometimes it would manifest, tweaking his braids, scrambling up his shoulders – then be gone before Guri could even greet it. The toy mammoth, once so played with, had vanished somewhere.

Since the child did not converse with him now, Guri had no one to talk to. Women were not talking companions.

At evening, instead of darkness asserting itself, the forest began to glow. It was the snow itself, which was now more dense, filling up the majority of spaces between the trees, making snow-lanes between and frozen in plates across them, and across the roof of boughs, with only holes left like dully shining coins.

There was a colossal silence here, different from the outer silence of the plains. This was like deafness.

Contrary to all this, Guri sensed that for the first time on the journey they were approaching humankind.

Night came. The coin-holes went purple, and some glistened from moonlight, rays and needles running down the snow into the earth. All the trees were sheathed in ice and snow. The forest came fully internally alight, like a milky lamp.

Saphay sat down, with the baby, then she began to sob.

Again, from this very display, Guri felt they were near journey's end.

'Shush you now,' said Guri automatically.

But Saphay had already abandoned her weeping. She fed the child and so did he. Guri was always careful not to look at her breast – it might affect him, which could be dangerous. Even so, he guessed her milk was less abundant. The child, at first eager and involved, now tossed, dissatisfied and snivelling like all babies miserable at being in the world in such a wretched, helpless state.

'Stay here. I'll search around a bit.'

'No *squirrels*.'

Guri swore, and bounded off through the trees, using the lanes and gaps until out of her sight.

She had never entirely accepted his ghostliness. But then neither did Guri.

He went some distance before he found the statue.

It was of petrified wood, black amid the white. The image was of a hideous woman with lots of hands and claws and the carved coarse hair of a badger.

Guri made sure she was not supernatural, or alive in some way, before he genuflected to her courteously.

As he straightened up, some men came out of the heart of the trees.

They were heavy, their skins, visible between their furs, mottled greyish and brownish like a snake's.

Knowing himself now invisible, Guri observed them.

They passed within inches of him. They smelled to him nostalgically of unwashed bodies, fires and meals and the shut, smug indoors. Going by the statue, each man put something down at its foot without pausing. Guri looked to see what these things were. Then he looked again: there was nothing there. The men from the snow-forest had offered nothing to their goddess, each time in a measured handful.

Guri did not bother to track the men, nor to find their village. He went back to Saphay, and told her the good news.

She gazed at him as if afraid, then obscured her expression as he had seen her do before.

'Do you know this place?'

'No. Some heap, but it will do. You must have food, and the child must.'

The rill of fear went through her eyes again. She had been sent among barbarians once before, and look where it had got her.

They walked up through the trees, then the curious thing happened. Perhaps Guri should have predicted it. The ugly statue came into view. Saphay saw it and exclaimed in disgust. *Then*, turning to Guri, she glared right at him, her eyes widened, and she cried out in an awful scream: 'Where are you? Don't leave me here—'

Though *not* predicting it, he understood. He knew she could no longer see him, nor would she hear him. It was due to the potential for contact with her own species, he thought, with the living.

Guri shrugged. He hunkered down on the snow, watching Saphay screaming in fright and fury, watching her grow still and turn away, and go by the statue unerringly in the right direction.

*

The men stood staring at her. It was like the other time, in the joyhall. But contrary, for *these* were considering taking her on.

She fathomed their speech, she began to make out certain words, sentences. It was a little like one of the more glottal languages the Jafn spoke. As she had in the garth, Saphay started to comprehend.

They were saying she had come from nowhere – that was true enough. They were saying it was not believable, under such circumstances, that she was innocent. Either some party of travellers had thrown her out for some crime, or she was demonic in some form, and therefore went alone about the snow waste as she wanted, impervious to it, and causing trouble.

Apparently they had a test for demon qualities.

A woman came in and offered Saphay a bowl of something. When Saphay would not accept the bowl, the woman threw the contents over her.

Saphay, too startled to make a fuss, brushed the loose grains off herself and off the child. Hatred for these people, perhaps all people other than her son, filled Saphay in slow, steep waves.

But it transpired that she and the child had passed the test, the grains being magical, blessed by the village's witch-woman.

She had entered the village without quite knowing it at first. The dwellings and snow-walled corridors were all part of the trees, the forest, the Winter, it had seemed. Only the lights among them revealed gradually what they were, and by then men were on the thoroughfare. None of them touched her. Only the grain had done so.

Their mottled skins were disquieting, she thought; they

were worse than yellow Olchibe skins. The deserting sorcerer had also had a yellow skin – but had she therefore imagined him, like the fireworks in the sky, the mermaids . . . and the other thing, long ago, which must never be thought of.

A village man was saying something now. She abruptly understood most of the words, as if finally she had to.

'Nabnish have her. He not bother even if she felon. Nabnish can do with bit-girl keep house for him, since last bit died. Serve her right.'

Something dragged inside Saphay like a weighted chain.

Fifteen days Saphay was the property of Nabnish, there in the snow-forest.

She was not, at this period, Saphay – like her child, she had no name. Nabnish called her solely *Bit*. To these people this word represented three things: one, a possession; two, a congenital fool; three, something which had been created to work.

She beheld him first up in the top of his house. The building lay at the edge of the village. It was formed of trunks and snow, a sort of chimney, more to it upward than across, breached by wobbling ladders, rungs and steps, off which doorways opened like crevices in a hive. Nabnish sat in one of them.

He came out of his crevice in the end, and squeezed areas of her body. Guri at his most informal had never been so rough or graceless, but Nabnish was concerned to learn if she was fleshly. He said – and she grasped every word –

that he made sure too she would be worth broiling and eating, if ever he had the need.

The baby he dismissed.

Put it over there, on that shelf. It would die, then they could sling it out.

Saphay made a noise – for no purpose, it simply burst from her like vomit.

Nabnish struck her. Saphay went toppling backwards. She somehow kept the child pressed to her breast, herself taking all the slam of the floor, to which she plummeted from the ladder, onto her spine.

For a moment she thought she was dead. Then she recalled she did not die.

Nabnish snapped at her to get up. She obeyed, and found she had not been smashed in half. The child, also undamaged, gazed up at her with eyes like a wolf's, and also deep blue as the face of a god's wrath.

All those fifteen days and nights, something kept coming up to the windows, the lower and the high upper ones, and squinting in. It scowled, this something, enough to tear the membrane window panes in shreds.

Guri.

He spied on Nabnish, sleeping and eating, and having a game with coloured counters, usually by himself. And Guri spied on Saphay, toiling in the snow-house.

A large stove lurked on the lowest floor, like a spider, its looped metal arms reaching up the house, and around the ladders, to warm it. It was one of Saphay's tasks to keep the stove plied with wood from the store. When the store got low, another task for her was to go along to a communal woodpile in the street, lug off and break up more. She managed badly at this, her hands blistered and bleeding from the axe left by the pile, and from stove scorches. Soon her face was burned red, and all of her to some degree black with soot and dirt. Her greasy hair was the shade of badly smoked herring.

There were additional things she had to do. She must fetch Nabnish's food from the cookfire place. Here she was pushed and cursed by women, both village wives and even other bits who were more experienced and scorned her. In the house meanwhile there was always the sweeping away and mopping up of debris sloughed from the walls, the cleaning of floors, stairs, ladders and pipes. She must bring in snow and ice from the outer limit of the village, for water, and as a kind of plaster to shore everything up.

By the fifth day, when she had grown – as Guri supposed – dirty and unkempt enough to be alluring to Nabnish, he hauled her into his mattress room, a hole only large enough for the mattress and the man. He raped her twice, then thrust her out and went to sleep. Saphay, who had made no protest, sat on the ladder, shaking so vigor-ously that Guri saw it. Still she did not cry, and presently went to the baby, lifted it off the shelf and fed it. She did this whenever she could, Guri noted, even though now her milk seemed to have dried up.

Neglected perforce, the child did not die, as another must have done. Nor did it roll off the shelf. That was mainly due to Saphay's rearrangement of the rubbish left there, but also to Guri's vigilance.

After the fifth day, he came in sometimes, unseen by any of them, except perhaps the half-dead child. Guri stood over Saphay. He had never doubted an Olchibe man's right to possess a woman, but Nabnish was no Olchibe. 'Tackle him, girl.'

She answered under her breath, but evidently without realizing she heard any voice save in her own head. 'How can I do anything to *him*? The village is full of such as *he*. And where else can I go?'

But Guri had noticed a metallic hardness in her whisper, which might have come instead from her eyes.

Guri said, 'I shouldn't be here. I should be off.'

This she did not hear at all.

Guri went to the child. He stroked the child's forehead, and the boy turned in his fever-sleep, as if worried by an insect or a draught.

'You've forgotten your old uncle. Come out and let him give you a ride on his back. You'll feel well and finely out of that sickly body.'

But the baby now would not let its physical soul come out to play with Guri.

Where is the father? Guri asked himself, aggrieved at the mess. And he did not refer to Athluan. *If that one came, he could spin this turd-tip at the stars. A rotten god – brutal to his own.*

Guri went back to the outside of the snow-house. He took a stroll through the thoroughfares of the village which, he knew by now, the mottled people called a *city*.

Guri did a few things to upset them. He overturned standing thawed water, and pails of urine kept for bleach. He put out fires – and lit others where they were unwanted. Where they instabled their animals, Guri undid the gates and the grazing channels. Bucket-hipped cows shambled lowing through the lanes; the long-necked sheep ate fruit from house vines.

But all this was petty, and the fun soon levelled off. Leaving the village-city squealing, Guri returned to spy on Nabnish's house.

Nabnish was busy on Saphay again. Guri, even through the house steam, saw her eyes. If looks could kill . . . but she was no Crarrow. Nabnish was a big fat man – and besides, as she had said, after murder what would come next?

That night Guri went and milked one of the cows. He brought the milk back in a crock. The child was off the shelf, with his mother in the corner. He let Guri trickle the milk slowly into his mouth, then swallowed it and kept it down. Again, Guri did not think any ordinary child could, at this stage, have done that. The girl was more awkward. She ate most days from scraps Nabnish left her, but never much, not liking the village cuisine. Guri marvelled at her princessly spoiledness – admired it too. He left her a fruit, trusting she would have the sense to eat it secretly and without questions. She did so, but he could not read what went on in her mind. Each night then he brought them something, while the village snored and honked in stinking sleep. Yet even so he let their suffering go on, undecided, ten more days. He kept waiting for something else to happen and make the decision for him. And years after, when Guri, still loitering intently on the physical plane, reminisced on that, he could say, 'But you will see, I had been a second to Peb Yuve, never *leader* of a vandal band. I was waiting for *him*' – he meant the child – 'to settle it. That was my way.'

Of course, he had been wise, Guri. The child *did* settle it. The child who was to be the Leader.

*

135

An intense freezing marked that fifteenth night. Moonless, the snow-forest greyly shone, and Guri wandered under the stiff silver blades of palm trees, fretting and retying his braids.

When, at dawn, he dived straight into Nabnish's house through the wall, he saw this. Saphay was sitting by the stove. She had the baby in her lap. There was nothing new in that: she nursed him off and on, or simply kept him by her until morning when she could.

But the baby, which last night had refused to suck up the milk Guri brought, looked as rigid to Guri as the over-frozen snow.

A clutch of fear rattled round in Guri's a-physical blood. Also he felt guilty – to be dead was nothing, the boy would be better off. Had this made Guri give up on any proper action?

Exactly *then*, the other version of the child came into view. He was swinging hand over hand, back and forth across the chimney of the house, from the wooden ladders and the pipes. Though weightless, he looked happy and fit, and he was now at least twelve years of age – to Olchibe or Gech, a man.

'Great Gods' tails,' said Guri. 'Amen.'

The child cast him an ironic glance. He swung off into air, drifted and landed by Saphay.

'That's almost dead,' said the boy-man to Guri, pointing at the baby – himself – in Saphay's arms. Probably he had only got out for that reason.

'*Can* you die?' asked Guri, suddenly unsure.

'Why not? Because of my da, you mean, old sointy Blue-Face?' Guri was astounded not only by the boy's different use of syntax, but by this name-calling of a deity – worse than mere aggression, for you knew gods might forgive that sometimes, but never a rude name. *That* was blasphemy. But the boy continued, 'I'm half mortal. The mortal half can die. Without it what use would I be?'

He did indeed speak like a man, a very young one, slangy, arrogant, and fearless – and angry.

Guri gazed at him. He was spear-straight and already lightly muscular. He had long legs, and a long mane of reddest hair. Handsome, too, he was, as one must expect.

'And she'll cry,' the boy added. 'I writhe at it when she cries.'

'She never does much.'

'Oh, you don't hear it as I do. I hear her weeping on and on, inside herself, either that or shrieking for revenge. She'd kill that pig up there if she had the strength, or we had somewhere to go on to. Why didn't you take us elsewhere, Uncle?'

Hearing his avuncular title again, Guri was chastened.

'All these dumping-grounds are the same.'

'If you say so. How would I know? But look at what has happened to her. He porks her' – Guri grinned, shovelled the grin hastily off – 'and he slaps her. I can't do as you do, I can make no impression yet on this world. Guri, I don't want—' The handsome face was suddenly changed. It was the face of a lost child. 'Guri, don't let me die *here*.'

'Death's *good*.'

'No, not for me – not yet. Uncle, give me the world!'

Guri stared. He said quietly, although he knew *she* could not hear, 'The world hurts.' And he considered, too, why he said such things, even as a ghost – just as he had been slightly wondering when he had lessoned Saphay on the nature of gods. 'Maybe it's too late,' he added.

'No, look there.'

Guri looked. An unseen glimmer of something coiled off from the boy to his baby-self. And in the shadow, where the stove-light sent it down from the form of mother and child, there was a faint garnet flicker.

The child was not yet physically dead, but what to do? Before Guri could think another thought, he heard fat Nabnish creaking out on to the ladder above.

Saphay, too raised her head. Her eyes were knife-points.

All three stood watching Nabnish ponderously descend – only one of the three visible.

Saphay also had been over-frozen in the night, not by the cold but by a total collapse of her strength. As it died in her, another strength ran in. To herself she felt as if she had been encased in armour.

'Get up, lazy glob of a bit. Water not boiled – where's meal? Am I to house you and me go hungry? Is it you to go on fire to make my fast-breaking? Throw on baby, I'll eat that. Why alive still? I tell you, put baby out in cold to die.'

Saphay laid her son down on the floor. She did it with care, gently. Even so, as always, she seemed torn open wide with the letting go of him. In her hand she had a twig from the woodpile. She had been whittling it with a piece of a broken pan stolen from the village cooking-place. The wood was sharper than the dented metal.

As Saphay lifted up this home-made dagger, a wind knocked her aside. In it somewhere she glimpsed the leopard man with braids, and amazed she fell against the wall.

Guri drew up his psychic knack. He had never realized he could do what now he meant to, but like all the rest it came at the correct time.

Nabnish was nearing the foot of the ladder, his mottles flushing puce. His little eyes were on Saphay, and so an interruption of the vista surprised him.

What he saw was not Guri.

It was a bear, tall as the ladder, with flaring horns and gaping jaws.

The bear slashed Nabnish with its claws. Nabnish experienced the pain as they raked right through him, head to groin. There was no space for Nabnish to detect he had not been slaughtered. Instead the bear socked him in the belly, and Nabnish crashed through the ladder, disintegrating it. But where he tumbled, was against the scalding side of his own stove—

The house was at the hem of the village-city. If any heard a fellow citizen howling, they took it for a wolf out on the plains, or a woman being justifiably beaten. It was a high-pitched, shrill noise.

The boy danced about, laughing. He urged Saphay, 'There, Mother, do you like *that*?'

But Saphay had only picked up the baby again and pressed him to her breast, close as if to return him into her body.

Then Guri was before her. She *could* see him in a sort of fashion, translucent as the thinnest membrane pane.

'Sorcerer,' she disdainfully said.

Guri said, interested, 'Your milk's come back.'

Saphay looked down at herself. She saw the baby was awake and suckling. She felt the sore-sweet string of the milk pulled out of her.

Then she thought she saw a yellow bear go over and kick Nabnish in the testicles.

A short while later, having put the replete child down once more, Saphay too walked across to her master.

Nabnish was whimpering, burned, and throbbing from an assault that, though not corporeal, had *psychically* bruised him.

Saphay bent down. She stabbed Nabnish in the cheek with her twig. He yelped. She spat in his eye and twisted his hair around her hand and yanked on it.

'You are *my* bit now. Say it.'

Nabnish could say nothing.

Saphay poked the twig into his mouth and made his gums bleed. Then she stood up, leaving him at the bottom of his house in a puddle of his own wastes.

'Now,' she said, 'you serve *me*.'

The auric projection of the child had by then been ravelled back into the baby. Guri, ashamed of his prowess, had absconded. He was off over a hundred miles of snow, running after deer and singing.

Vuldir's daughter smiled. Taking her child, she climbed another ladder to the mattress room and crawled inside. Below, it was Nabnish who wept.

At last Saphay questioned nothing. She threw down to her first defeated enemy only one last word. *'Forcutcher.'*

Through the white architecture of the snow-forest flies moving colour. The forest knows it, has grown used to it: it *lives* here.

The running figure is that of a child, but it changes – how fast it changes. Now about three years old, now about six, now taller and leaner, more shaped and sure, no *longer* a child – twelve years, fifteen, eighteen . . .

How quickly they grow. One moment there is a babe-in-arms, next month it seems – toddling, striding, gaining opinions – an infant alters to a youth . . .

To a man.

It is a man running through the forest of fossilized snow. He is tall, strong and spare – straight as a new sword drawn for battle. He is also impossibly tanned. His hair is red as a banner and his eyes blue-black. There is none like him in these parts.

The village-city of Ranjalla has been given a great deal to ponder. They will tell you this demonic male has matured two years for every one he has lived – they watched it happen. In ten years he has become a man of almost twenty. Look at his mother, no Ranjallan sibulla, yet she can summon and organize spirits. She has subdued an important village man and uses him now as a slave. Beware of that woman and that house! They warn off their girls who turn their heads at the glimpse of red hair by the snow-chimney houses. 'He's got no name, he. He demon's get. Stay away, or whacked you'll be.'

What does *he* think of this? It is old news to him – just as it is that he has no name. Though, like a riddle, he *does* have one. The Ranjallans cannot get their mouths around the Rukarian to articulate it, but have their own version. In Rukarian or Ranjallan or Jafn, the unname Saphay attached to her son at his first birthday was, and is, *Nameless*.

Nameless then, who matured in ten years to be nearly twenty, resides in a snow-house at the periphery of the village-city, surrounded by the ruins of other collapsing snow-houses which have long been deserted. All the neighbouring Ranjallans had quickly moved off along the forest, to give this weird family a wide space. But also they take care never to offend them. Nameless has grown up noting offerings of food and wood laid at the door.

Otherwise, his home comprises a stove, a blonde mother like a queen, his periodically present ghost uncle, a feline, and a house-slave called Bit-Nabnish, who whines and cringes and is always attacked. That is actually Nabnish's function, more than to assist with the domestic arrangements. He is there to be the recipient of cruelties, Saphay's the most inventive. But Nameless is not immune to the ritual. One enters the house, greets one's mother, strokes the cat, and kicks Bit-Nabnish.

Meanwhile, aside from all of this, what truly is he, the red-haired man? He himself does not know.

Through the white architecture . . .

Nameless raced down an ice aisle and straight up a flight of steps, cut themselves from ice. Every step was roughened and set with shards to prevent slippage, but really he seemed not to need this precaution. At the top he slid, graceful and controlled, to a flawless standstill.

There stood Ranjal herself, the goddess of wood. Many statues of her were to be found in these parts – all alike. Her two arms each ended in several pairs of long-fingered hands, resembling branches or antlers.

Before her Nameless tossed blue flowers of the weed-of-light.

Three of the old women, the sibullas who guarded the statue, had come out of their hut.

Nameless smiled at them. It was the smile of a man, also of a wolf-like child, a beautiful feral smile, and it went unanswered.

Then the goddess opened her wooden lips and spoke. 'Is forest empty?'

'Fat-full of emptiness, lady,' assented Nameless.

'Pleased I.'

The old sibullas exchanged narrow glances. They had all heard the goddess speak before; they themselves could induce her to do so. But this one, this man-thing, he also could cause Ranjal to speak. He had been doing it since the dawn of adolescence.

They were jealous.

One said, 'If the forest's empty, where him get they flowers?'

Another said, 'He looks red-hot enough to burn you.'

The one in the doorway said, in a hiss, 'See *there*.'

They knew where to turn their eyes. Behind the colourful young man, an extra set of footprints was briefly to be seen, scored in the snow. No one visible had made them.

'His familiar.'

'Why does our own lady speak him, if he with his demon?'

'Go in. We go in. Let *he* alone.'

The sibullas crowded back into their hut.

'Ranjal,' said the young man, 'I want something, for the flowers.'

'Ask.' Her voice was like ice-wasps scratching in a frozen pine.

Behind him another cursed.

'Hush, Guri.'

'You take risks. This thing is a *god*.'

'No, Guri, it is a chunk of stonewood, ancient and warped, that one makes talk by will-power. That's how the witch-sibullas do it. Don't be credulous.'

He had learned his method of speaking from his mother. He did not, though partially he used the Ranjallan language, sound like any man of theirs.

Guri jumped two hundred feet up a tree. He sat in its cemented branches, observing his nephew far below connive with the statue for vast riches, three wives of surpassing loveliness, an army fully armed, and so on. She had told him stories, too, his mother; Guri had himself liked these. Now Nameless made a goddess do it.

He was sophisticated beyond his years but also *young*, this young man.

Guri sometimes felt the weariness of the adult who always companioned such a *young* person.

He sealed his ghost eyes, dozed if that was what he did, and was in a hall where amorous maidens fed him feasts on plates of jewels – the 'tween-world at its most alluring. It burst.

Guri unsealed his eyes again and found Nameless seated by him in the tree. Nameless had not jumped here. No, he had calmly *walked*.

He was the son of a god, you forgot. Well, you forgot your own abilities and strangeness, too, thought the philosophical ghost.

'You sleep more than the cat, Uncle.'

'Ah?'

'I'm bored with this place,' said Nameless, turning his handsome face up towards the unseen sky.

'I see you are. Come on, let's have a joke with the village.'

But Nameless did not respond. Only one year ago he would already have been bounding down the tree again, bough to bough. They would have dashed through the huddle of the village-city, Nameless laughing and Guri pinching bottoms and upturning pails.

A man who was a child, a child who was a man; how did you entertain such a one? It had been so much more simple last year, last month, when he was still mostly a *child*.

'I want to leave the forest, Uncle.'

Guri had thought about this, too. Somehow they had outwitted the god who hated them all. But they were hidden here. It was more than physical: these snow walls, these snowed-in minds. Outside the barricades, scurrying on the ice plains, they must be spotted as clearly as fleeing deer.

And she, she dreamed of *that one* still, and would then wake screaming, choking. At other times, Guri thought she dreamed of the dead Jafn, Athluan – but he was not sure.

'Well?' said Guri.

'No matter,' said Nameless. 'Rest yourself, Uncle. I'll see you at supper.'

Guri watched him spring down through the tree. No longer in auric form, the body-locked Nameless was yet phenomenal. Not one mortal man could do this. He landed neat as a lion on the ice beneath, and sprinted away, fire-haired, into the labyrinth of snow.

Saphay was sitting on the lip of one of her higher rooms, gazing down the ladders at Nabnish, refuelling the stove. She had thrown a stone at him, previously plucked from the wall, but her mind was not really on that.

She smoothed the cat in her lap. It was warm and purring, heavy with sleep and food. It saw to the rats that crept heroically about the empty houses, but, more than this, was her pet.

Saphay recalled how she had sat with the baby – next the infant – sleeping in her lap or on her breast. She adjusted the sleeping cat, and lay backwards.

In ten years, Saphay had not aged perceptibly. She was twenty-seven, healthy and in her prime. There was a crimson flower twined in her hair, which her son had brought her. When *he* picked flowers from the vines, they lasted, from his touch, several Endhlefons before they faded.

Sometimes in the evenings, he would still lie against her, humorous and telling her tales of the forest. It was then as if a thousand candles had been lit.

In an hour the dark would begin to come. Then she would get up and go, the cat maybe prowling at her heels, to the cook-place.

The village women, peering under their eyelids, would hand her dishes of the best food. Only once, at the very beginning, had something unnourishing been added. Guri had sussed the whiff of poison immediately and, going back with him, Saphay had screamed invective at the wives and bits, slapping their faces, while Guri distracted everyone by putting out the cooking fire and bringing other flames wastefully alive in the woodpile. After that the proffered dinners were always wholesome.

She had not noticed Guri today. Normally now she could see him, if only in a vague or distorted manner. Now and then, too, he flashed on her sight, fleshed-in and bright yellow as a lemon.

Her son would return for the evening meal. That was what Saphay looked forward to. She would be aware of his approach long before he undid the door. It seemed to her she was aware of him always. Although her intense connection to him – her sense of dislocation whenever she had had to let him go – had drained away during his first year, even now she felt some limitless and flexive rope uniting them. Even if they had been worlds apart, she would have felt it still.

There was a sound at the door. Saphay sat up. The cat, securely fastened to the shoulder of her dress by its claws, looked round. Nabnish squirmed and squealed by the stove.

'Who's there?' Saphay called in her Rukarian queen-tones. No one replied. 'Open the door,' said Saphay. Sometimes there were these infringements, safely settled. But when Bit-Nabnish hastily obeyed her, the door swung wide, and only the gloaming forest filled the doorway. Nothing, no one, was there.

'Close it.'

Nabnish closed the door. He gibbered.

The cat's ears, too, lay flat to its head; it growled and lashed its tail. Saphay felt only something like dust falling on her head. She spoke a charm she had learned among the Jafn, to see off unwanted unnatural visitants.

She had thought it was one of the Ranjallans. Occasionally they lurked about the door, patting at it. One shout was enough to make them run. Her son too had had many of the village's girls, despite village-parental warnings. These paramours would haunt the vicinity. They were wan and abstracted, hungry still for his favours. Yet none of them had ever conceived, through the four years of his sexual activities.

But this evening something else had been there, it

seemed. Saphay would ask Guri to search about, when he evolved.

In the snow-dusk an hour later, the cat refused Saphay its company. Alone she walked between the deserted houses to the cooking-place and, as she did so, suddenly knew another was behind her.

Extended close contact with the paranormal had only made her more pragmatic. She stopped and boldly turned.

No one was there. However someone *was* there. As she stood waiting, he – the presence was masculine – drew near. He passed her like a silky wind, caressing her hair, tart-cold on her cheek. She glimpsed, unseen, a face she did not know, dark and remote, and mocking. She heard the words he spoke without a voice.

'A fine Winter we are having, Saphay.'

Second Volume

THE STARS ARE DOGS

Ask the snow what it is, ask ice, wind, sea and sky,
Ask also the whale, the crait, the bear and the wolf,
Ask wisely, not one will not tell you name and self . . .
But what am I?

Urrowiy song: Northland Gech

ONE

The Gargolem stood at the top of the Stair in Ru Karismi, looking down towards the River Palest. From here the river was slender as a silver necklace in the midday sun. Other objects, these truly of metal, shone throughout the city, and the metallic Gargolem itself shone golden-bronze.

If such a creature, mechanical and beast-headed, could be said to think, now it did so.

Behind it the high walls of the palaces of the kings, which it guarded, had been put from its mind. Instead the consciousness of the Gargolem delved deep into the river. Below the Palest's frozen surface lay the Insularia of the Magikoy, a complex older than the city. Itself made long ago by their Order, the guardian was privy to the craft of these mages, and its brain now mentally transposed itself into the areas below the ice.

The Insularia was vast. Reached by several occult entrances, usable only by the Magikoy, it stretched under the river and away on either side. The precise dimensions of it were publicly unknown. Some said the Insularia occupied as much room underground as the city did above, or more. Others believed the Insularia was of quite modest size – no larger, say, than the Great Markets or the temple-town of the Ruk's army of gods.

Otherwise the Insularia was not understood. Popular

theory said it was, besides being a meeting-place of mages, a secret arsenal of immense terrors.

As the Gargolem's thought skimmed through the stone passageways which approached the centre of the complex, it encountered the Magician Thryfe.

Thryfe was riding in one of the transports which moved through the Insularia. This one was a kind of sledge of brass, elongated and able to carry up to twenty men at once, although only Thryfe now occupied it. A sail of thinnest red vitreous powered the sledge, blown along by one of the conjured winds that could be called in these tunnels. The vehicle travelled quite fast: it was airborne, though only two or three feet clear of the passage floor. There was no light as yet, except for the lamp burning on its mast. This lit the magician's face, as he glanced aside and into the Gargolem's inner eye.

'You're here too, Gargo.'

'I am here, Highness Thryfe.'

'That doesn't surprise me. You are aware of the weight of today's business?'

'I am.'

Tall Thryfe, lean and graven, had added ten sober years to his face and lost nothing in doing so. He was an eagle still.

The Gargolem watched as Thryfe's transport sailed away down the dark tunnel and, as the guardian took its watchfulness elsewhere, it noted the courteous farewell of Thryfe's lifted hand.

Beyond this tunnel, as the mage continued, the passage widened further. An amethyst radiance began, which lit the walls of dressed stone and the high-arching roof. Ahead a vast chamber appeared. It was carved with things of stone, in whose heads cool eyes now turned, gazing down. The sledge sailed into the chamber, through it, and on into another tunnel. Here the lilac light intensified. A stone mound rose abruptly from the floor in the transport's path, like a small mountain getting to its feet, but the sledge only lifted itself higher, and blew by over the mountain's head. After which the mound sank away again.

A chamber opened next which was full of liquid – or seemed to be. It was more a kind of liquid air. This it was which apparently coloured the light. Thryfe sailed across, composed and silent, as the purplish fluid washed over and through him, and was gone.

A pair of gates, high as the high roof, made of some metal that perhaps was orichalcum, now barred the way. The sledge came to a stop as the conjured wind dropped flat.

In the blink of an eye, the Gargolem of the Gate grew upwards out of it. It was made of the same metal, and in shape it was like a gigantic worm. Its eyes were cold as water.

'Who comes?' asked the Worm of the Gate.

'I. Read me and let me by.'

'I read you, Highness, and let you by.'

The gates clashed open like two mailed pages in a book. The Nonagesmian Chamber lay before Thryfe, large indeed as a market, lighted by an unflickering glow as bright as sunshine.

Nor did any outsider know the number of the mages belonging to the Order of the Magikoy. There were guesses made, particularly concerning the female members, of whom, as a rule, there were few at any time.

All of the Order, however, had gathered in the Nonagesmian.

One by one, they ascended the central rostrum and spoke.

Thryfe sat in his place, his chin on his hand, listening, observing, till it should be his turn. He did not miss a word, although all the speeches were substantially the same. Each of them had beheld the same matter, even if presented in differing, obscure symbols. Each had looked – then lost the sight as a mist veiled the mirrors.

He knew, Thryfe, all these faces, few younger than his own. He knew all the names. Here and there at the chamber's upper walls, the furthest from the rostrum, groups of the greatest of the apprentices waited, pale and biting their lips. They would not have to speak. Their time had not yet come. Perhaps now it never could.

A Magikoy, an old man whose fine white hair fell below his waist, stepped from the rostrum and glided, invisibly aided by uncanny attendants, to his seat.

Thryfe stood up. It was now his moment to address the chamber.

He had done this more times than even he could recollect, but never had he done it at such an hour, at such a fearsome pass.

The eagle which was his otherwise hidden and personal aura flared its stormy wings as he walked down to the rostrum. He felt its claws sink through his heart, then it was still.

'Every one of us,' said Thryfe, 'has the same story. What did we anticipate? Every one of us *knows*. We foresaw the arrival of this thing, and were unable to prevent it. Then and now, it throws a fog around itself. Fate is in league with it. Yet I can tell you what it is.'

Of them all, he was the first to say this.

They stared hard-eyed, not doubting him, rather *certain*, for here no man – even of the Magikoy – could do anything save speak the truth.

'I have seen those signs and images which have plagued us these past ten years. I too have tried to trace their origin and met the obscurity which clouds over every oculum, in this single instance. For me, three nights back, for one second the screen broke wide. It cracked like a plate thrown on the floor. *Why?* That I don't know. I'm neither the wisest nor by any means the best of this company. Perhaps for this very reason, then, an irony to inform a man of the middle ranks, neither new nor fully accomplished. Or else it was some accident.'

They waited.

Thryfe said, 'There are three gods – I was shown them. No, they were never clear to me, yet I know them, for I'd long known of the woman who, at her birth, was given to their notice. It was that girl Vuldir sent to the Jafn people, and meant to have killed on the road. That girl the Jafn themselves told us, a few months after, died in giving birth to the child of a Chaiord killed in battle. We know they lied. They cast her out into the ice waste because one of them, Rothger, is a murderer. The kings here know it too, through us, and broke the treaty. But there are other Jafn peoples they can make friends with instead, and they don't want to go to war over a woman's death.

'Of course,' said Thryfe, 'she didn't die, Saphay, Vuldir's daughter. They were her gods I saw. One was dimly

155

present, Ddir, rearranging the clusters of the stars. One was a greyish hound slinking through the snow – Yyrot, Winter's Lover. The other was Zeth Zezeth, the Wolf of Fire. He it is who has begotten a child in this world, and that child is the clue to the horror which is now rising. He is the Firefex, the Flame-Bringer: mad, invincible, amoral – pitiless.'

The chamber shuddered. In the false daylight, faces like death gazed back at Thryfe.

Thryfe said, 'Still young, this boy: at ten years he is a man of twenty. But he stirs. He is a baby which can hurl lightning, and like a great snow he thunders towards us, fascinated, and sharpening his teeth for the world's blood. We must resist – but how? He is the son of a god and of a mortal, with the strengths and wickedness of both. His destiny can only be death – or power everlasting.'

He had been a lamherd's son. At two years old he had staggered screaming after his mother, trying to hold her back as she went out one morning to break ice for the family water jars. But she pushed him aside, and his father was already gone to tend the lamasceps. Thirty paces from the house, where the cedars stood loaded with ice like prisms, a wolf came from the shadow and tore Thryfe's mother apart. He had always hated wolves since – worse maybe because at two years old he had already seen, floating there in his drink of milk, the exact prediction – tree, wolf, death – as vividly as he had next seen happening thirty paces away and in reality.

Later there were other things: things he foresaw and that he could do. At the age of twelve, up on the snow-hills, with the herd grazing in warm channels of dormant grass, he could call eagles, three of them, to come down to him. Ebony and bronze, they fell from the skies. His arms were soon fabulously scarred from the grip of their talons. They helped him guard the herd from the lone black wolves which haunted the hills and killed lamasceps and women gathering ice.

When he was fifteen, the eagles lifted Thryfe and flew with him. Witnessed by the herder village, this event was the end of his stay there. Afraid of Thryfe by then, his superstitious father could not wait to send him to the nearest town for examination. The envious and adversarial village witch was also keen as a blade to see him go.

He had the gift of sorcery. The first town knew enough to know that too, and sent him on, via a chain of other towns, towards the cities.

The process of learning and refining was arduous, and left nothing much of him for anything else. There were ordeals and tests most human things, if they had ever heard of them – though they did not, for they were secret – would have quailed at and fled. Some apprentices did run away, but not Thryfe. He remained and was scorched, melted and remade in the crucible, until he might enter the Order of the Magikoy. After which, presently, the warden-ship of the court of Ru Karismi, City of the Kings, was given him. This job, that of instructing nobles and lords, was not among the highest posts, of course. The greatest of the Magikoy worked among ordinary men, sometimes even in remote areas. To serve mankind meant, for the Magikoy, to serve man not king. Nevertheless, Thryfe's task was exacting.

He had a life but it was not a *life* as such – although, for all the Magikoy, male and female, it was like that too.

As he walked to his under-river lodging, across one of the great obsidian bridges of the Insularia, Thryfe reviewed his situation, but distantly – as though he himself did not *belong* to him. And he did not, naturally: he was the servant of the people of the Ruk, selected for his role by gods before his birth. Curiously, then, a sentimental stranger, he recalled those snow-hills, the eagles, the long-necked sheep heavy with their wool.

Sallusdon, King Paramount of Ruk Kar Is, lay dying.

On every side, the Death-Priests chorused out their chanting to his personal gods, asking that they assist him in the crossing of that vast divide which lay between the physical world and the realms of Paradise.

But Sallusdon paid little heed; he did not want to die. He wished instead his gods would grant him a reprieve.

Nearby stood his two queens: Azbeyd, old and colourless with familiarity and distress; and beside her the other, the one he had taken only last year on the advice of Vuldir, King Accessorate.

Jemhara was lovely and so young, her dark hair, wound with golden ornaments, falling along her back and over her round breasts, which the silk covered deliciously.

But Sallusdon felt no twinge of desire. He was only terrified. If he had been able to exchange Jemhara, giving her up to some awful fate, to human sacrifice as in antique times, he might have done it to ensure his survival. Luckily she could not be, this young queen, aware of Sallusdon's inner thoughts.

Sallusdon turned his head to prove to himself he was yet in his body. And saw, to his chagrin and fright, his third god, Preht, standing between the bed and the Priesthood of Death.

'Are you ready yet?' enquired Preht.

'Let me live!' shouted Sallusdon – but not aloud.

'Impossible,' said Preht. 'See there – that woman has made certain, on the orders of Vuldir, that you die.'

'What do you mean?'

Preht, who was thin as wire, yet glamorous as only a god could be, laughed cruelly. He was in his second aspect, unpleasant and vindictive.

'Look at the slut. How often have you fondled that black hair while her lips were on your body? Was she worth your old man's joys?'

'Jemhara . . .' whispered Sallusdon. This time he articulated, and the girl threw up her hands to her face, weeping glittering perfect tears which, a moment earlier, had seemed not to be in her. One of the Death-Priests restrained her from advancing to the bed. She was only second queen, it was not now her place.

'Remember how sometimes she has made you able to enter her body. Listen well, old fool. First she put a venom into herself – yes, even there, her choicest part. It did her no harm, for she had taken the antidote. But you it ruined. One whole year she has been at work. Vuldir had grown weary of waiting for your natural expiry.'

Sallusdon cried out. It was vocal now.

The priests started at the vociferous horror in his voice. They thought he had seen his gods, and that they were predicting for him punishments in the other world. Such a thing must be, from sheer politeness, ignored – for any king had *always* lived virtuously.

The haggard Queen Azbeyd, however, stole forward slowly. She took Sallusdon's wrinkled hand, but he did not see his loving queen, only the *un*loving one and Preht sneering in the corner, and the night-darkness of death flooding towards him like a *Summer*-broken sea.

A few minutes later, Vuldir, King Accessorate, glanced up. Shut in his shrine room alone, ostensibly to offer prayers for the King Paramount, Vuldir had been at other work. No one could enter here unless they knew the magical combination of the door lock. Only he and his mage did so.

Now, though, someone *had* come in. Of course, she had not used the door – did not need to. She had arrived, but not in her *flesh*: it was her physical spirit, exactly like her in every detail, which currently appeared on the mosaic floor.

'Are you not attending the king?' asked Vuldir, laconic.

'Yes, Majesty Vuldir. I am lying in a dead faint by his death-couch.'

Vuldir smiled. Jemhara had her own wit, which was not entirely unlike his own. She was one of the few women he had ever come across who could, now and then, amuse him.

'So he's gone.'

'Howling and pleading to remain – still he must leave.'

'The Ruk mourns.'

'My tears,' added Jemhara, 'flow like a river.'

'But the rivers are frozen over, Jemhara.'

'Just so.'

'You're too clever, my dove.'

'Too clever for some. You know I can cry and weep whenever it's required of me, just as I can unfreeze streams to flow.'

'I know you're a witch of the backlands near Sofora, who has learned the manners of the court.'

Jemhara lowered gilded eyelids. She understood well enough when to be silent. It was a fact, she had come from nothing. She possessed mage-skills, but had mostly concealed them under her cream skin, for she did not wish a legitimate career, but rather to further her ambitions through deceit. Coming to Vuldir's notice by these arts, she was now his servant and instrument. Occasionally they would engage in sexual intercourse, which she did not disenjoy, but also she was wary of him for he, like herself, was a vicious and cold-blooded creature.

'Come here,' said Vuldir.

Jemhara's spirit-body wafted to him. Vuldir showed her, lying on the shrine before his gods, a large black-red ruby. 'This is for you. I'll send it you before sundown.'

'You're most generous, my lord. Won't your gods miss the jewel?'

'Who?' asked Vuldir. He offered the altar one flick of a look. He did not believe in gods.

But Jemhara gazed under her lids at the three beings in the shrine. Two of them she did not recognize, for there were a million and more gods common to the Ruk, and men need only concentrate on those which were their personal deities. Yet one Jemhara did identify, for he had once been made known to her during her magics. And it was to him, Zeth Zezeth, Wolf of the Sun, that Jemhara's spirit surreptitiously bowed, before she faded away from Vuldir's room.

By then, the palaces were ringing with the dirge for Sallusdon.

Cold miles off, in a lodge of wood and ice blocks by the fields of ice hemming the sea, the Chaiord of the Jafn Klow sat drinking with his warriors and favourites. Among the latter was numbered the Chaiord of the Kree. Elderly Lokinda was ten years dead, he had died in the same season that saw off Athluan of the Klow. Now Lokinda's big-eared son, Lokesh, raised the passing cup to his lips.

The cup was formed from a skull, cleanly scraped, and decorated with hammered silver and white gems. It had eyes made of opals. It was the skull of Athluan, kept by the Klow to honour his memory and his death in battle. The Chaiord alone might drink from it or, at his invitation, his closest comrades.

Rothger and Lokesh were close comrades. Only they knew how close and interdependent in their plans and kingship – they, and one other. She now sat in the women's room, up the ladder and over the lodge joyhall.

The men had been drinking some while, and Lokesh felt inclined to refer to her.

'How's your lady, Roth?'

'My *what*? Oh, you mean Taeb, my witch-woman? She's well, upstairs, combing her long hair with green dye.'

Lokesh leaned near. He whispered loudly and wet, moistening Rothger's cheek. 'How's she – at the *other* thing?'

'Which thing is that?'

'You know what I speak of, Roth.'

'Do I?'

Lokesh drew back. He wiped his mouth and returned the skull-cup to Rothger, Chaiord of the Klow.

'I meant no harm, Roth.'

Rothger smiled.

The years *had* altered Rothger. He had grown heavy and fat. Except when raiders came in from the sea and Rothger rode to intercept them, or if he went hunting as he had today, more often than not he spent his time with drink and food. He was content with what he had won for himself that decade back. But, too, he had secret delights that were spoken of even less than his lack of a wife. They said he coupled with the green witch, Taeb. Certainly he accompanied her to obscure areas to practise unknown rites – but Rothger had always had a knack for magecraft.

Those that came to the Klow House now remarked on the number of amiable sprites and lesser elementals which hung about there. They were generally quite docile, for Rothger had tamed them. Only once or twice there was some mischief. Mostly you had the feeling of always being *watched*.

Rothger was respected – or he was feared.

In war he would fight, then be lost to view. Sometimes, when he returned, he seemed wounded in the face, for he dripped with fresh blood. But it was never his.

Rothger glanced around the lodge hall. The seef was about. He could feel it hovering. It was troublesome, tickling up his lust for blood. Rothger looked sidelong at Lokesh, and wondered sportively how much blood was in this burly blockhead.

All the other men here were drunk by now. They sprawled around, clanking their cups on the tables, spluttering drunkard songs or jokes. The sun had set an hour ago.

'They say the old king's dead in Karismi,' observed Lokesh.

'We've had no sending.'

'Would they send to you now? They broke the marriage treaty when they heard Athluan's Ruk wife was dead.'

'They've had no fight on their hands,' said Rothger idly. 'They're sunk in peace.'

'That may change. Then they'll call on you, broken treaty or not.'

'True – and I shall be deaf.'

Lokesh said, solemn and inebriated, 'Have you never thought, Rothger, of those south-west-over lands? If all Jafn allied with Jafn, we might make a war force – Gulla-hammer – give the Rukar a slice of bother. All they ever fought in the past was city with city. Now not even that. They're soft. Ripe enough maybe for plucking.'

'Oh,' said Rothger, as if they spoke of nothing, 'do it if you want. I'm content at home.'

There was a glint in Rothger's lazy soulless eyes. Lax as a pillow, still he got smartly up. Lokesh watched him narrowly, the hair rising a little along his scalp. Something came for Rothger at such times, and led him away to his pleasure. No one would follow.

Outside in the snow, Rothger slit his forearm open, and licked up the blood greedily, with the seef panting at his side, mewing and flushing rose-pink. From a narrow window up in the lodge wall, Taeb the witch stared down at this. Sometimes Rothger would signal to her, here or at the House, then she must fetch him something, some animal from the wastes. He loved the aftermath of battle, corpses everywhere. Tonight it seemed his own blood satisfied Rothger. Overhead, in the black, moonless sky, the eyes of stars also stared down, colder than Taeb's, perhaps less kind.

TWO

By the door of the house, a dog was lying, at ease on the snow. Dark was coming down but with, as yet, no moons.

The young man paused, regarding the dog. None of the hounds of the Ranjallans were at all like this, but shaggy maned beasts. This one was smooth, long-nosed, its ears up-pointed like the firm petals of certain flowers.

Nameless called, wordlessly yet encouragingly, to the grey velvet dog – which got up as if to come to him, then vanished in a coil of smoke.

'Good evening, Mother. There was a dog at our door.'

She gave him her hand, a lady – and he kissed her cheek. Saphay was much shorter in height than her son.

'Did you chase it off?'

'It disappeared. A vrix, perhaps?'

'Don't talk in Jafn.'

'A corrit, then?'

'I said, don't . . . Can you see such things?'

'I can see all things, Mother, but nothing so well as you.'

His flattery, transparent and flirtatious as it was, always charmed her. It was a game they played.

The cat sprang to Nameless's shoulder and clung there, purring. Stroking the cat with his right hand, Nameless strode into the house and slapped, in passing, the face of Bit-Nabnish.

Saphay continued at her chosen task, moving about the ground floor of the snow-house, lighting candles on the shelves and ledges. From the stove issued a warm red light, and dishes of food stood under covers on its roof.

Nameless gazed around him, plainly happy with the homely scene.

Saphay said, 'There has been a thing about for some days – for two Endhlefons. I've counted the times I've seen something. Once it spoke—'

'A dog which spoke.'

'No, then it wasn't a dog.'

For a fraction of a second, Nameless checked. You saw, in this fragment of time, how seldom it was that he lost his flying fearless balance in the world. For his face, taking on this abstraction and unease, ceased – for just that second – to be his. Then the look was gone. He said easily, 'Was it *him*?'

'Never,' she said. She put down her taper and slid her hand over her lips. Then she said, 'That one has never found us here. The dog *is* a vrix, if we must speak Jafn.'

'Guri believes the ignorance of the people here rubs off on the trees, and hides us.'

'Perhaps it does.'

Saphay resumed her household activities. She began to take the dishes off the stove. The cat jumped from Nameless to the floor, in order to note this procedure carefully.

'Mother, stop that a moment. Sit with me.'

They sat down on the rugs before the stove.

Nabnish had slunk away behind the ladders to the dankest dimmest cubby of the house. Saphay stared at her son. He seemed, in the firelight, *made* of golden fire, and red fire, and his eyes were blue coals.

'Yes,' she said, quiescent.

'I mean to leave this place, Mother.'

'Of course,' she said, 'one day. How could you stay?'

'I mean to leave this place tonight.'

'Tonight?' Her face was the whitest thing in the house of snow. 'Then I—'

'Guri will go with me. He's off now, the way he goes, running after deer, catching stars . . . Soon he'll be back, then I mean to set out. You can't dissuade me. When I'm ready, I'll send for you.'

At that she lifted her chin. 'Oh, so kingly you are. My *thanks*.'

'When I've found my road, then—'

'What road? You know what you are.' Her voice was rough.

'No, I don't know what I am. Of all things, that I don't know.'

'Must I write it out for you on the floor? A god's son – and *mine*.'

'Yes, yours—'

'How shall I live,' she cried, 'if you leave me—' and heard in horror the whining of her old nurse, forgotten these ten years, left behind in Ru Karismi on the night of departure for the Jafn east.

And Nameless, anyway, seemed to take no notice. He only said, 'You're safe here now, but Guri will visit you often. You know how he can be anywhere he wants in a blink. He's given me something to give you that you can employ, a magic token, to call to him or to me, if—'

'If what? If I'm attacked? If I am *bored* – you and your

ghost, this cutch of the undead Olchibe scum who caused it all, or so he confessed to me when I failed to recollect that part – caused it by chasing me . . . the whale and the ice . . . and then that death in the blackness and *he* came – *he*—'

Nameless rose. He turned his back on her. He was angry, and she saw it, and it no longer mattered. As a child sometimes, when she went against him, he had scorched her with a look. It burnt through her like a sword, then and now, but she was accustomed. He was so schooled in getting his own way.

'Mother, I'm going now. No supper, thanks. I'll eat as I travel.'

'*How* will you travel?' she said, snarling. 'On Guri's shoulders, as you did in childhood?'

'You've seen what I can do. I can run all night fast as a lion, and never stop for breath.'

'Go then. What are you to me – half mortal, not even that? To leave me here . . .'

Then he turned after all and came back. He kneeled beside her and held her as she wept the bitter tears of her coming loneliness and rage. He stayed so long, stroking her hair, telling her gentle things, that she thought she had won from him at least this one night remaining. But she had not.

And all this while, Guri was kicking his heels on the snows outside. And the cat, inside, having nosed the lid off a dish, was eating the meal no other wanted.

Presently Nameless left the snow-house. A moon had risen, and the shut forest had begun its eerie glow. Nameless again looked about him. He did not mean to return.

'She fell asleep.'

'I warned you. If you're honest about it, they make a

fuss. Only a Crarrow knows how to use a man, then let him go. The Crarrowin are like men in that.'

'Guri, she is my mother, not my whore.'

'You've had plenty of those here too. In this it's all the same.'

They walked through the trees, by the derelict houses, along the avenues of snow, away from the village-city.

'There was a grey dog – either vrix or corrit. It can be like a man, it seems, too.'

'Some bloody Ranjallan leftover – some lost thing, like me.' Guri chuckled. He did not consider himself lost. He knew where he was and what his function was. The boy was Leader, Guri his second.

The path was descending now, the trees lifting off higher and higher, and in spots great rents appeared which let in the moon and the black shadows. Although they walked, no two *human* men could have made such speed with so little effort. In a handful of minutes they were already many miles from the village. And from Saphay.

Guri had already – mostly unseen and definitely not understood – covered Saphay's snow-house with safe-guards. Ever since he became such a magus, he found these actions simple. Also he had frightened Bit-Nabnish in his sleep, making sure he would keep to his cowardice. Probably Saphay would kill the slave in her fury, anyway.

Guri felt sorry for her – a little. She was so strong and had been so brave, but she was only a woman. She could not come on this journey; it was for men. Later there would be time again for her.

The notion of the grey dog did worry him briefly, but these things were always at large, and Saphay had been sensitized to seeing them – even though her Rukar brain clamped down on her with its blindfolds. Some slippage from the 'tween-world, that was what the dog was; or some vrix she herself could see off with spells learned from her husband.

They reached the end of the forest suddenly. Guri – who had gone this way not infrequently – was surprised. A subsidence in the snow had come about, and the edges of the forest dropped into it. Nameless and he stood on the brink, and scanned out to the moonlit ice plains half a mile beyond. Then together they leapt, spanned the gulf, and hurtled away down the night.

Over palisades of frozen larch and palm blew the banners of the Snow-Ox. In terraces, the torch-fluttering Kreean-garth climbed to its House. It was the Festival of the Five Nights, indigenous to the Kree. Though the wind poured low and slanting across the land, the Chaiord had come out to make the offering to Great God, walking, armed, sun-wise round the palisade, with only the House Mage and nine picked men to escort him.

This being the Fifth Night, traditionally one of the Chaiord's sons would ritually question him later as to the purpose of the Festival and its acts. Lokesh – as had Lokinda before him, when Lokesh himself had been the questioner – would explain. Long ago a monster had emerged from the ice waste. It had stolen up from the white darkness, entered the Kreean-garth, and killed hundreds. The Festival now had sorcerous significance. If observed, it must prevent a recurrence of such mayhem.

Lokesh walked on. He was sullen and in a bad mood, chilled to the bone and fasting for a drink.

On these or similar nights, when he must be both lord and priest to his people, Lokesh became uncomfortable. He would recall how, with the help of sottish evil Rothger, he had seen an irritant half-brother slain, and had presently murdered his own father. Kree and Klow were staunch allies still, knit by the spilt blood of Lokinda and Athluan.

Ritual nights too were thick with spirits and seefs. They gathered to spy, masking themselves in driving snow or sidelong winds, such as that which blew now.

At the two gates of the garth, and at the points of guard, where long ago animals, or men, had been sacrificed to secure the palisade, Lokesh made offerings of beer, wine and meat. Before morning, fleers or other scavengers might well turn up to accept these snacks on behalf of God. The Mage brought fire. It was magenta for the occasion, a colour of power and protection.

The wind moaned.

Lokesh heard in it the voice of his father. 'Here you are then, my cunning son, Chaiord in my place, eh? Is it good?' But this had happened before. Nothing more ever came of the voice.

The Mage spoke. 'Wait, Lokesh.'

'What is it?'

'Look.'

They looked.

Across the leaden sheet of snow under three dull crescent moons, something was blowing like the wind itself. Like the wind also it had a sound – not a lament, a rumble.

'The ice is shifting!' exclaimed one of the nine warriors.

'Or the snow—' another added.

Each man stared towards the horizon, and then a fourth

moon, more luminous and golden than the the other three, began to rise.

The Mage gestured at this glow, but it did not falter. He stepped out in front of them, and called a glinting shield of air up across the men, the walls, the garth.

The fourth moon went on rising. It rose.

'Face of God!'

Over the rim of the earth roared a gleaming cloud, like fire from the mouth of a dragon. It gushed forward, skimming the snow, reflecting in it as if in a mirror, lighting up the night. Above, it was flame; below, it was a shadow which seemed to have a hundred parts.

One by one they grew conscious of what it must be, of what it comprised.

A herd of . . . *deer*, wild deer, which rushed across the snow, silent and in fearful unison, but winged with a conflagration bright as a moon . . .

'Make no move,' instructed the Mage. He was stern and composed. 'A sorcerer is at work here.'

'The Shaiy,' said one of the men, who were jabbering together.

'No, they're quiet – some rubbish of the Irhon.'

'Are they *alight*?'

'No, look – no burning and no smoke. They'd be dead if they burned in that way.'

'Are they *real* or an illusion?'

'Sirs, hold your noise,' said the Mage. He said to the Chaiord, 'Lokesh, you and I will go to meet this thing.'

Lokesh was ashamed. It was he who should have told the Mage that. Blustering, he said, 'Yes, yes, I say we must.'

The Mage strode out, piercing through and abandoning the air-shield. He was older than Lokesh, but looked vital.

He stretched his staff forward as he went, towards the brilliant deer, and the tip of the staff started to crackle, as if dipped into fire. When the air-shield fell behind him, Lokesh felt his bones tingle.

All the snow, from the uncanny herd to the walls behind, was now reflectively blazing, and the shadows of the deer striped weirdly black across it.

'They're slowing up, Mage.'

'So it seems.'

Behind them, high on the platforms of the garth, people had run out to watch. There was some disturbance back there, but not here. The deer were coming to a standstill. They now were motionless. Only some forty paces separated them from Lokesh and his Mage . . . less with every stride.

How still they were, at last, the deer. Calmly they stood there. And then . . . their moon-bright light went suddenly out.

The Mage himself now halted. Lokesh, brazen with his inadequacy, stalked forward and the Mage checked him – again with the caution: 'Wait.'

They waited then; they had halved the distance. Twenty paces off, the deer herd abruptly cantered about and dashed away, bounding back to the horizon and the invisibility of night – all but two of them. These two animals remained, sombre finally on the snow, and from between them shone the light once more, but now it was slim and slotted upright and of reduced intensity. It was not a light at all. It was a man, young and tall, his clothes of outlandish un-Jafn leathers and furs, catching some description from the opaque moons – some luminosity they

174

had not previously seemed to have – mostly on his hair and face.

Lokesh found he did not wish to speak. The Mage too said nothing. He had lowered his staff, and frowned with some inner effort.

The man who stood between the two deer bowed low in a courtly way not found among the Jafn, but seen more often in the purlieus of city palaces. Then he turned his back, fearless, arrogant, on the gaping warrior-king and his magician. Quietly the stranger touched each of the two deer between its eyes.

Himself bemused, Lokesh saw the animals grow sleepy. Their eyes closed. They lay down without hesitation.

The stranger leant across one deer and slit its throat, precisely, almost with a sort of tenderness. Turning to the second deer he did the same. Their blood unfolded, black on white. Kneeling, the stranger kept one hand on each of the deer, gently caressing them as, without distress, asleep, they died.

Then he got up. He sheathed the blade – some uncouth implement from some other land. He walked across the snow and stood in front of the Chaiord and his Mage.

'The Kree feast tonight, don't you? Please accept my offering of meat for dinner. Fresh-slaughtered, it should be tasty. Probably you don't know, but kindly killed, the flesh is sweeter and more succulent.'

Lokesh opened his mouth. It was the Mage who spoke.

'*Who are you?*'

'I am Nameless. My father died before he could either claim or name me. I'm Athluan's son. Good evening to you both.'

*

175

'Why is it, Chaiord, that on these five nights you and your Mage and your men march round our walls, and offer to God?'

The ritual question came from the ten-year-old son of the king at the correct moment, lifting through the torchlit joyhall where so many widened eyes now caught the flames.

Lokesh cleared his throat. He was better for the wine; he was used to it – it had cheered him up.

'In those days of our fathers, a creature burst out of the snows . . .'

Everyone knew the story, save perhaps the very young, hearing it for the first. It seemed even the stranger, the son of Athluan, whom Athluan had not had time to name, even he knew it, although he was Klow not Kree.

Telling the old tale, blushed with the strong black wine, Lokesh heard his own voice ring against the rafters, where the hawks ruffled their feathers. Beside his chair lay his best lion, and all around him all was *his*. He was vain tonight, vain of what he had got for himself. Lokesh, oddly, wanted to boast and to show off before the stranger who, like the stranger's Uncle Rothger it seemed, was such a clever mage.

'Four nights this thing came into the Kree House. No one could keep it out. It took men at their meal. It ripped them limb from limb. When the House Mage rose against it, before his craft could be of any use, the thing snapped off his head.'

Lokesh described what the monster was like: its hide like armour and its gigantic size, its fangs that were green with filth, polished only by blood.

'Four nights in a row it came. Hardly any were left alive.

The mages and the Chaiord and half the warriors were dead. The women and the children had fled to safety over the ice.'

Lokesh lost his place in the tale. He fumbled up his cup and drank, as if thirsty – though he was. And, as he did that, he recalled drinking, some Endhlefons since, from the cup that was Athluan's skull. As the wine snagged in Lokesh's throat, he coughed and beheld the peculiar eyes of Athluan's son, if so he really was, fixed on him.

Nameless reached across, and with no ceremony, royal to royal, thumped the Chaiord on the back.

The hall of people stared at the Nameless one. Many had seen from the garth how he had arrived. They had seen what he could do with the deer before he killed them. Only the greatest of the mages could do that, for any animal would sense its death in those moments, and resist. And he had not *stunned* them with his sorcery, but *charmed* them peaceably asleep. They said the Magikoy had this talent. But Nameless was Jafn, in his way. He spoke their languages and in the proper manner. He knew their customs. As they had stood in their streets while he climbed the garth to the Kree House, some had seen how his blue eyes, catching the lights from various angles, now and then shone for an instant with smoky crimson.

'Lokesh,' said Nameless, when the choking was benignly concluded, 'I'm a guest in the House. Will you grant me the happiness of telling the rest of this important story?'

A murmuring crossed the joyhall – then it died.

It was the Mage who spoke, as before. 'It is the business of the Chaiord to tell this tale on this fifth night.'

'So it is,' agreed the young man nicely. 'Then I'm content, sir.'

But when Lokesh tried to resume the tale, his voice was hoarse. He looked across at Nameless – and Nameless smiled at him. They were old friends, or might become old friends; all this Lokesh saw now in Nameless's curious face. Athluan had been a just man, but slow and naive. Rothger, that Lokesh had relied on, was a pervert and a sot who grew more trustless every hour. This boy had the best of both of them, however: Athluan's good looks and generosity, Rothger's psychic ability and brains.

Lokesh cleared his throat again. He sounded better now, but never mind that.

'Yes, for Athluan's sake, I'm glad to let his son speak for me. The hero who saved the Kree in those far days is current in Klow legend, too.'

There was a lacuna. Nameless looked around. His magnetic beauty unsettled, yet contrastingly soothed. He was something special in the firelight – like the heroes of the past indeed, some of whom had been very strange to look at yet blessed and powerful.

No one had objected to Lokesh's words. It was in a Chaiord's gift to lend his task – like his bow or his wine cup – to any he chose. It honoured them very much, and Nameless was plainly honoured. He got up and saluted Lokesh in the Jafn way, his right fist to his left shoulder above the heart.

Lokesh had told them all Nameless was Athluan's son. Probably Nameless had given him, in private, proofs of that. The hall accepted this, and sat back for the rest of the tale of the Five Nights.

'On the fifth night, at sundown,' said Nameless, 'the

scatter of men left watching for the Kreean-garth saw a fearsome image in the sky. Piece by piece a shape formed there. No cloud nor other ordinary thing, it went on shining long after the sun had fallen. The warriors called to each other, *Don't attend to that – as soon as the dark comes so will the creature out of the ice.* But nevertheless they marked the shining shape in the sky. There, on the dusk, they saw it was nothing but a vast and supernatural hand, which gradually turned itself and pointed down its fingers at the snow.'

Nameless told the tale as Saphay had once told it to him; he had all of it from her. She had learned so quickly in the Klow House, learned more than she thought as, leaden with pregnancy, she lay in her chair in the hall, listening to the legends of the Jafn. Maybe, too, *he* had listened, as he drifted, anchored by her and his physical self in her womb.

He rendered the story simply, without histrionics, and he employed the antique words. Standing there, he seemed to speak to each man and woman individually, his eyes looking into theirs very often. Most felt he had singled them out particularly. He made them see the pictures in their heads, so they knew him for a mighty bard as well as a genius among mages.

The hand which pointed at the snows was the Hand of God. It had presently fashioned, *from* the snows themselves, a man of snow, tall and muscular, with all his mail and armour upon him. Then came a wind, perhaps the Breath of God. It blew, and blew away, and the man of snow had come alive – but he was not white, but black as jet – his skin, his hair, his eyes. Only the balls of his eyes were white, and his teeth; and in his mouth and under his nails and in the palms of his hands it was just possible to see the coral colour of his blood within the darkness.

Of course, in changing so utterly to its opposite from something inert, frozen and unhuman, the snow had also changed colour to its opposite. This was easy to comprehend. White must be black. Nameless mentioned this fact of the myth with such humour and sense, the hall laughed and nodded. Perhaps that was when they began to see a hero might be of another shade, his skin and hair and eyes.

The Hand of the Great God withdrew. The hero Star Black remained poised alone on the snow. The brave Kree warriors were clamouring to go down and join him in the fight, but Star Black shook his head. And then, anyway, the *thing* came shouldering up out of the ice.

'At that,' said Nameless casually, skilfully, 'what do you know? The invincible God-made hero turned and ran from it.'

The Kree guards were shocked. They watched in dismay as the jet-black man raced away around the walls of the garth. The monster, bellowing and slavering, rushed after him. It was twice his size, though Star Black was tall and strongly made. But a coward?

Round and round the walls of the Kree garth pelted Star Black, with the hell creature in pursuit. The Kree on the walls fell quiet and began to pray.

'Round the walls, once round, and twice round, and three times round, ran Star Black. He ran fast, faster than any mortal man, so fast the monster could not gain on him, though it stayed only the length of two shields behind him. Three times round, and four times round, and then five times round the walls. On the fifth circuit, as he was coming back level with the main gate of the garth, Star

Black, losing neither balance nor momentum, spun about. In each of his hands was a great sword of blackest metal that gleamed like suns and, raising them up, the hero threw himself for the first – and last – against the creature from the ice. By now hypnotized from the circling and tired from the race, and too witless to anticipate a snare, the monster dashed, straight as a spear, on to both swords. One snapped in two at the impact. The other clove up through belly and ribs, and broke the stenchful heart of it.'

As Nameless stood there, cheers sprang from the Kree joyhall, and on the rafters the hawks flared their wings. How many years was it, how many decades, since old Lokinda had been able to rouse them up with this elder story?

'That was the end then,' said Nameless, after the cheering fell, 'of that thing which so afflicted the Kree.'

And the child, Lokesh's son, spoke on his cue, not to his father, but to the young man who burned before him.

'What then was the fate of Star Black?'

Nameless answered gravely, as if never before had any asked such a question, and never before had it been answered.

'Why, they made him king for his valour, a Chaiord of the Kree. He was adopted – and had adoptive uncles and brothers among them. But he ruled for a hundred years. And every year, on the Five Nights, he and nine of his men would circle the walls, not running, but at their leisure now, and make libations to thank the Great God who had so cared for his people. But,' said Nameless, 'after the hundred years, God took Star Black home again, into the Other Place. And lying on his bed of death, while his adopted family wailed, he was humble and he said this:

Even the stars are dogs – only dogs – in the hand of night. He submitted to God, as must all men, but they say that, under his black skin, his bones were white as snow.'

In the silence now, Lokesh got up. He went to Nameless and embraced him as his brother.

Chaiord Lokesh was in love, but he did not know this of himself. How could he? It was not like any love he had ever felt before.

The whole House was beglamoured.

Could they have said quite how it happened – *why* it had? Their visitor was handsome and could tell stories like a bard, and he was an accomplished magician. Yet he seemed, if not exactly modest, then civil and, in his fashion, discreet.

The warriors toasted him, and when he – Jafn Klow and Athluan's son as he had announced – kept blithely awake in their company all night, they were as pleased with him as if they had found him for themselves. The women, elderly or young, looked at him with another sense of acquisition.

But the Kree House Mage drew Lokesh aside.

'Lokesh, you know I must examine this man.'

'Surely, Mage, of course.'

'He has come from nowhere, out of the wastes.'

'He's told me how, in his infancy, he and his mother were thrust into the waste by the Klow.'

'Has he told you why?'

This dialogue took place in the morning, as preparation was going on for a hunt, and the Nameless one was preparing to go with the rest, easy as if he had always been among them.

'He said to me . . .' Lokesh appeared confused for a

second. After all, Rothger had never told Lokesh anything of the expulsion of Athluan's widow and son. Or if he had – could it be that he *had*? – Lokesh had paid no heed to it. 'Athluan's son,' said Lokesh more firmly, 'has said to me that there was bad feeling in the Klow for his mother, a woman of the Rukar. Athluan himself was just then only freshly killed in battle.' Lokesh did not stumble over *this* sentence. He had talked about Athluan's death times without number, just as he had needed to with the death of his own father, Lokinda.

Lokinda had taken too long to quit the world. Lokesh had been almost Athluan's own age of thirty, and still no sign of the old fellow setting off. No people could flourish with a decaying tree at their head. Lokesh had cut Lokinda down with an uncanny weapon given him from Rothger's bounty – a weapon that left no mark.

'It seems there's more to it than that,' said the Mage. He meant more than any Klow bad feeling in the matter of driving a woman and infant out on the snows. But Lokesh winced as if something, if only very small, had stabbed into him.

'This man is my guest, for Athluan's sake,' said Lokesh. He thought of how Athluan had died, slain in full sight by witchery and malice. He thought of Rothger and quailed, but it did not show.

'I shall examine him tonight,' said the Mage, 'when you come in from your hunting.'

Turning then, the Mage squinted down the length of the room. Many had seen an oddity of the young man's eyes: how, in certain passes of light, the black centres of their unusual blueness seemed changed to garnet. But there was another thing. *There*, suddenly the Mage saw it again – saw it, lost it. His *shadow*?

He himself was an old man, the House Mage of the Kree. Three days before the Festival of the Five Nights, he had beheld his own death painted before him in a dream. He did not have long. He had known all these years – from a similar source, his craft – of Lokesh's villainy. But the Mage had said nothing, for he had seen the ruination of the Kree lie there, either way, whatever was done, And, even ten years before, the Mage had not wanted to hurry an apocalypse.

There were fewer under-mages among the Kree. Only six others came in to sit about the Thaumary, their eyes on the House Mage, on Lokesh and on the visitor who called himself Nameless. They were none of them as wary as the House Mage. Younger men, they too had been excited by Nameless's advent. He had come among them like a new hero – perhaps he might be. Although they must now help effect the examination of any penetrating outsider, they had not got rid of an overriding interest and partiality.

'You acknowledge,' said the House Mage to the guest, 'we're bound to make sure of you.'

'I'm Jafn, respected Mage. My mother educated me in the proper customs.'

'But *are* you Jafn?'

The candid eyes met his; there was no guile in them. They were flawlessly clear and still. 'Yes.'

He lies, the Mage thought.

'And you *are* the son of the Chaiord Athluan?'

'Yes.'

'Your proofs of this?'

Nameless sat at the room's centre, graceful and unaggressive.

'I've none at all, sir – nothing. My father's enemies were mine and my mother's too, not surprisingly. They threw us out like their garbage, on the snow. We were meant to die, and they gave us nothing of my father's, doubtless not wanting to waste it on us.'

'You haven't any look of Athluan.'

Then Nameless smiled. It appeared always wonderful, that smile of his. But not to the House Mage of the Kree.

'My mother might remark differently, sir. Perhaps she knew him more thoroughly. She was his wife.'

'And I am Mage of the Kree House. Do you think *I'm* blind?'

Nameless replied, 'Isn't it the Magikoy who say the clearest sight will sometimes miss what a cloudy eye makes out?'

'They may say so. You'd know about the Magikoy from your mother.'

'So I do. And that being established, maybe you see she's the Rukarian princess, Saphay, that all Klow's allies know was married to Athluan.'

The Mage said, with no emphasis, 'I don't doubt she's your dam. But I've heard a little rumour that, nevertheless, her husband did not sire you.'

A hissing gasp went up around the Thaumary. Lokesh led that gasp. To impugn bastardy, particularly on hearsay, was grounds for feud, and a Mage might choose his words more politely.

Lokesh started, 'This—'

'Let *him* answer,' rapped the Mage.

Lokesh lapsed back. Nameless seemed neither enraged nor distressed. Rather, he looked entertained.

'Wrong,' was all he said.

'Today,' said the Mage, 'you hunted with the Kree along the ice. You rode in the chariot of the Chaiord Lokesh. You can slaughter deer by mesmerizing them, yet you elected to use a bow and arrows in the hunt.'

'The preference of my hosts.' Nameless bowed to Lokesh.

'At which he excelled,' exclaimed Lokesh instantly.

'Very possibly,' said the Mage, 'yet it was a bow this young man had in his possession. And it's not Jafn work – more like the male bows of Olchibe. And how it was put to use, that too was in the Olchibe style.'

'There was an Olchibe man in the snows who befriended us in my childhood. He was kind to us,' said Nameless, conversational.

'Perhaps kinder to your mother – and that nine or so months before you were born. You are, by my reckoning – whether from that seed or the seed of Athluan – not eleven years old. You've grown fast. Only magic can explain it. You said this Olchibe helped you in the snows. Was he a sorcerer? If so, how should I compare the facts of that and your swift growing?'

'I see,' said Nameless. He glanced down, not put out of countenance, only musing. Then his eyes lifted up again. 'Actually, the Olchibe was not a sorcerer, nor was he my father. For my age, as with my powers which it seems you think someone taught me, God gave me both, perhaps in recompense for the ill-treatment I had received from men. Otherwise, what you have said is very like the lies Rothger spread: his reason for evicting us from the Klowan-garth –

and preferably into the Other Place for safe keeping. Do I seem, besides, like an Olchibe to you?'

'You seem like no man of these countries.'

'From the Ruk, then. Are there none like me *there*?'

'I don't know enough about them to speak of that.'

'Then, sir,' said Nameless, 'put your vast skills to work, and look.'

No one made a sound at this pure insolence. The Mage did not falter, neither did Nameless. Glaring in the red-blue guileless eyes, the old man beheld the razor's edge: it was there, blatant as a shark in the sea. Yet you could not fish it out, nor come at it to get rid of.

'Listen to me,' said the Mage. 'Only I and you grasp what you are.' It seemed to him they were now alone there in that room of magic and of drawn pictures of spells and rites, alone in the Kree House – or in the whole wide Winter land.

Nameless looked into the Mage's eyes and, sliding there on the gleaming razor, the Mage saw a terrible pity – a *compassion*. And he thought of how Nameless had killed the two deer with his quiet touch and accurate knife.

'*What* am I, then?' Nameless asked him. 'Tell me. For, of the many things I know, *that* I never have.'

No other can hear this, or see. The Mage trembled. *We are locked in a moment frozen solid as any ice. And yes I know, and no I do not know, what he is.*

'I've no knowledge of what you are.'

'Then I must learn for myself.'

'Must you sharpen yourself on *us*?'

'On everything, perhaps.' Regretful, mild, Nameless rose.

The Mage sank back in his chair. And then the

187

Thaumary was vacant of all of them save Lokesh, who stood there grinning, his bat-wing ears flushed with good humour and alcohol. 'You see, Mage, I said he'd show us he was worthy.'

What had gone on, some further hallucination or trick? The Mage thought: *He showed nothing.* Had Nameless altered sight and hearing, time itself? The rest believed the examination had been drawn to a more than satisfactory conclusion. *Only I sense this, and what can I do? Where . . . where does his power begin, or end?*

In Hell, the Mage thought. *In Hell.*

Outside the shut door of the snow-house, where she had thrust him at sunfall, Saphay could hear Bit-Nabnish howling and pawing at the timbers. There were no windows here, as there would be in the Ruk or even among the Jafn, or she would have tossed hot charcoal down on him from the stove. Or maybe not, for that might have kept him warm.

I am cruel, she thought, caught between self-approval and astonishment. Had she never debated on that before?

Later she would let him in, before he froze to death. But she did not want the slave to hear her weeping as now she did, sobbing and spasming, turning inside out with grief on her mattress above the ladder.

Cruel? She was not cruel. Her son was cruel. Let him cruelly suffer then, among the detritus of humanity he preferred to her.

Or no, *let him be safe.*

She had given him no gods, had never dared. To every child born in the cities of Ruk Kar Is were awarded three gods, two from the father or paternal side, one from the mother. Vuldir, Saphay's father, had given her Zezeth. Who should she then have awarded to her son? With cause, she had come to fear them all.

She would now let in the moronic slave. That should be her offering to the gods, largesse to the wretched 'bit'.

As she descended the ladder in the stove-lit gloaming, she heard a frightful outcry go up beyond the house, worse than any of the servant's howls.

She sprang off the ladder and ran to fling open the door.

'Why are you shrieking like that, you fool, as if you're being torn apart by fleer-wolves?'

Bit-Nabnish lurked cowering and shivering before her, foul and repulsive as ever.

'Come in, then. Get to your undeserved hole in the corner.'

The slave slouched, gibbering, into the snow-house, obeying her.

Saphay did not notice the spark in his eye. She did not know that Nabnish had actually finally been put down under the snow, and that what now scuttled away across the the floor of her house was *not* Bit-Nabnish any longer.

THREE

Guri sat cross-legged on the ground, facing his nephew called Nameless, sitting also cross-legged on the other side of the fire one or other of them had summoned.

'And now you can manage their cat chariots,' said Guri. 'You learn fast, as I remember. I recall your first bow which I made you. You mastered it at four years – and in five minutes.'

'The old Mage was troubled by my Olchibe bow. Lokesh himself instructed me in handling the chariot. Lokesh is dross. Rothger's the one I want.'

They brooded on their fire. Nameless made provocative girls appear to dance among the flames, shaking their unbraided hair. Guri cackled, then, seated here about a mile from the Kreean-garth, they returned into mutual noise-lessness.

Nameless had lived among the Kree for two Endhlefons, twenty-two days. They were now his: the men, the women for that matter, even the mages. Even the old Mage in some way, for he had taken to his bed with a racking cough. Lokesh, around twenty years the young man's senior, hung on him like an enamoured friend of his own age. None thought less of the Chaiord for that, since they themselves were also besotted. They smelled the god in his blood. Guri smelled it too; it made him uneasy now sometimes. For *he* knew which god it was – that fiend under the sea.

Guri had helped herd the fire-glimmered deer towards the Kreean-garth. And long ago he had lessoned Nameless in those masculine accomplishments so necessary to everyday human survival: how to hunt, to fish, to kill and skin and cook a beast, the making of bows and other weapons. He had even tutored Nameless in the correct riding of a mammoth. But all this had gone on under the lid of the snow-forest; and to it, almost at once, Nameless had added the knack of a sorcerer.

Proud of him, yet feeling shut out in some form, Guri recollected he had not been able to teach him sleekars or chariots, as they were beneath the attention of an Olchibe; he was ignorant of them.

Nameless also stared on into the fire, from which the dancing harlots had departed. He seemed composed, as usually.

Nameless knew what Rothger had done, all of it. Or at least he knew Rothger had murdered Athluan. The deduction was facile enough, given all the circumstances. Lokesh too, Nameless could sense, had lent his clumsy aid to Athluan's destruction. But Nameless did not hate Lokesh, only despised him. And, anyway, Athluan was *not* the father of Nameless.

The boy and his mother had already sufficient grudge of their own.

There had been girls in the Kree House. There were apparently always nooks in a garth where you could take a girl – a byre, a shed, a little orchard of iced trees where apples grew under ice-glass. The girls were so thrilled, swiftly his caresses brought them to readiness. Their helpless cries of delirium cracked the ice. Apples snowed down. One evening he had called an ugly ageing woman away from the House pots. He had had her, too. He did not mind her: her body was much better than her riven face. Nameless had done this almost from desperation. It had been, so far, all too easy, while, conversely, the other thing, the thing which haunted and filled him with terror – *that* thing, the *god* – was beyond his scope, his will, even beyond his ability to live. Nameless could not bear it. He pushed it far away – Zeth, Zeth Zezeth, his true father.

Guri was now asleep. Once this occurred, he would gradually vanish. In childhood Nameless had disliked this. He would fly to his uncle and punch and claw at him – or the space he had mostly left – to bring him back. And Guri always returned for him. Now, despondent, Nameless let Guri go.

Nameless sat thinking of himself. He did this as if he pondered on another man, one alien to himself. He had no urge, this alien being, to sleep. As a rule, he never felt the need of it – which stood him in good stead with the Jafn. And yet when he decided on it, he could fall asleep instantly, like a cat. Did he dream? Now and then. Nameless did not want to think of his dreams.

Eventually, sitting here, he began to contemplate Saphay. His face grew by turns sad and adamantine; perhaps he did not even realize this. He knew, as he said, so little of himself.

Dawn undid the pale dark. The forest, packed with snow and chimney-houses, dulled then rekindled, and the five sibullas came out of their hut, along the ice-platform, to honour their lady Ranjal, goddess of wood.

There were many statues of her through the trees, but this one was the guardian of the village-city. Or it had been.

'Where she?' screeched the sibullas.

'Stolen she is . . . stealed away . . .'

The platform was empty. The goddess with antler hands and a badger's pelt no longer posed there for their adoration.

Given over to her at the age of six or seven, the decrepit sibullas were bereft and frantic, ancient children abandoned by their mother.

They skidded and squawked along the ice, peering over and down the ice-steps into the forest, which had only the normal things in it. Ranjal was not to be seen.

By then they were crying. Wizened babies, they clung to each other; but then let go, knowing they could not help each other. Only the goddess could help them.

Then one rasped, '*He* tooken her . . . went away, he . . . *he*, that fire-hair . . . tooken her away.'

Their mottled skin seared from grey and fawn through to a drained and deadly pallor. They ceased to move.

Another said, 'None know where he go. She that were with him . . . never come back.'

'Never, never,' they keened, standing alone on the platform, clad in tears.

Blue light dripping on her eyelids had made Saphay incoherently think in a dream of her son. She woke with anger.

Getting up from the bed, she drew the tattered fur coverlet around her, and crawled to the ladder's head.

There was no smell to the house this morning. Though the holy scent of the other person was gone, there should have been others – aromas of broth heating, with grain in it, for breakfast; the accustomed tang of the snow-walls giving way to indoor heat.

Today the house was not even warm.

Her slave had let the stove go out.

Saphay slid down the ladder and discovered Nabnish curled up in his corner.

'You gop ninny!'

Leaning over him like the viper she had become, Saphay raised her hand, her small clenched fist hard as bones could make it, and still with Jafn rings on it to render the blow more telling.

Nabnish uncoiled, also snake-like. Amazing her, he rolled upright and caught her wrist, all before the blow fell.

A warning sparkled in her mind. She thought of the talisman Guri had left her, whereby to call for assistance. Meanwhile she kicked Nabnish on the shin. She had put on her boots before descending, and it should have hurt.

But Bit-Nabnish laughed, waving at her her own hand still in his clutch. 'That's enough now, madam.'

Truly astounded, Saphay gaped in his face. Nabnish had spoken in the language of the Ruk, in the most genteel of the accents prevalant at the court of Ru Karismi.

Making no sense of this, she could only wait. Nabnish allowed this, looking at her solemnly, without either the fear she had grown used to from him or the sluggish malevolence he had offered her in the beginning.

Then he changed. It was as if he had shrugged off a

garment. But what Bit-Nabnish shrugged off was his own head and body, which crumpled and fell untidily on to the floor. There they faded away, but Saphay did not see that. She was transfixed by what had now emerged.

'Do you know me?' he enquired at last.

'You are . . . the one . . . who spoke to me – in the snow.'

'And the dog at which your cat spits.'

'I – I don't . . . *know* you.'

'Uneducated woman. You knew the other one, and named him. Name me now or I shall be aggrieved.'

Saphay shook. Merciless, the figure still held her wrist and observed her shaking. He was the colour of a poreless grey twilight, and his eyes were black as the outer sea. Black hair coursed over his head, down to his shoulders. The hair, even his lashes, was rimed with a kind of silvery frost. And he was dressed in a mail of ice-plates.

He was, too, very icy to the touch – her wrist was already numb. She shivered not only with fright but impending hypothermia.

'You are . . .'

'Yes?'

'You are he that . . .'

'He that?'

'Winter's Lover – Yyrot. You're a god. The second god I was given to.' Saphay threw back her head and stared with dread and fury at him. 'More abuse then, more injustice . . .' There in his grip she screamed at him in a sort of mania: 'Kill me *now*! Do what you *want*! How can I *prevent* you – you and your *kind*?'

He let her go. He turned impossibly, like a spun coin, and was across the room, seated on a ladder. But Saphay had seen her son do such things, and Guri too, whenever she could make him out. She wondered if Guri's psychic talisman would have any effect, then decided Guri too would be disempowered before this apparition. While to her son, Yyrot might prove as dangerous as the other – Zezeth.

Her legs gave way and she slipped down on to the rugs. Yyrot had put out the stove. He liked coldness, of course.

Should she try to placate him? What did he want?

The cat, which had been hunting, entered through a loose slat in the door. It had a dead rat in its jaws, bringing the feast inside to devour in comfort. Seeing Yyrot, though, the cat let the rat go. Belly lowered, the cat bared its teeth.

'Woof, woof,' said Yyrot flatly.

The cat ran away behind the ladders and chill pipes, with its tail three times its general size.

Saphay glanced at the rat, uneasily. As she had suspected, it was starting to come alive again, shaking off its terminal wounds, just as Yyrot had shaken off the simulacrum of Nabnish. Fully restored, it sidled to the door and darted out by the loose slat left there for the cat.

Conversely, the god probably meant to kill Saphay slowly, through freezing, for there was no guarantee this was his beneficent aspect. She sat on the floor, shuddering.

'What must I do?'

'I have not decided,' said Yyrot. 'The disturbance in the fabric of this physical plane, which your son has caused – that brought me here. I suppose I have a reason.'

'My son has been alive for *years*. Why did you wait so long?' Saphay snapped, startling herself.

But the cold god only replied, 'They were not years for me. My time is not like yours. Meanwhile,' he added, 'you do nothing correctly. You should at least make me an offering.'

'So I have, in the past.'

'The past is past.'

Saphay pushed herself upright. She reached into a cubby in the wall and pulled out a jar of the root beer brewed in Ranjalla. Already it was partly congealed. She dragged it over to Yyrot, still seated on the ladder, and spilled it wantonly at his ice-shod feet.

Then, straightening up, she glared at him. He too was icing over. It was like looking at a man trapped in a mirror. He sighed and white mist, burning with coldness, laved over her.

'I am too warm here. I have noted your offering.'

Something shifted the room. One moment she saw him, then the space he had occupied was bare – only a few flickers of ice falling down, and the puddle of frozen beer on the floor.

Every safeguard left on the snow-house had withered. The signalling talisman – a smooth stone with a hole in it through which Guri had told Saphay she must call – lay in pieces. She found it there and knew that Yyrot, doubtless not even intending to, had done this damage. He was like a hurricane, his passage fraught with mindless incidental destruction.

So here she was then, deserted and alone, stalked by another god, the stove out, no wood or food to hand, her slave – the original Nabnish – also presumably destroyed in passing.

Saphay had dressed. She now put on her Jafn cloak of

fur. She opened the door and noted the cat came after her, sure indication Yyrot was no longer about. They walked through the snow lanes, into the village.

Not a door was ajar, not a light showed, though the day was dusky. No one was on the streets or by the woodpiles.

Something else was no longer there. A tiny crudely made statue of the goddess Ranjal, kept by the largest of the woodpiles – that too was gone.

Some gloom or doom seemed evident. Saphay had no patience with the village's stupid little jinxes. She struck a door with her fist.

Nobody came to see, the door was not undone. None had reacted to the knock, even with an oath. She tried other doors, each the same as the first. By then she had noticed that the second statue of Ranjal, kept near the cook-place, whose fire was out, had, like the other, disappeared. There was also nothing cooked or cooking.

Had Yyrot, weirdly jealous of such a provincial and non-actual deity as Ranjal, obliterated her effigies and put out the fires in envy?

The cold depressed Saphay. No warmth seemed to lift from the usually muggy village.

She thought of her former eviction by the Jafn into the snows, trudging through ice and torrents of wind, and of dying, and Guri, and of the child at her breast . . .

Damn him, to leave me here to this.

Saphay did not refer to Guri.

The cat yowled mournfully. Then, suddenly flattening down, it shook its haunches, watching something at work in the woodpile.

Saphay spoke to the cat. 'Bring any rats you find to the house. I'll share them with you.' She turned back the way she had come and, going by, grabbed some wood off the pile, as she had not been forced to do for ten years.

It was not until she re-entered the house that Saphay realized one further item. Though the village fires were hidden or put out, her stove along with them, she had herself no means to create fire. To Guri, or her son, it had been easy. She had lost the habit therefore of self-reliance, and was no mageia. She dropped the wood, and sat down in the cold with iron eyes, waiting for her cat and their raw rat dinner to come in.

The ice oasis lay on Kree lands, but they did not claim it.

Being what it was, any might shelter there. It had come into existence only seven years before, during a time of lethal thaws, when ice cracked everywhere and snow heaps tumbled for miles around.

'Have you seen such a place ever?' Lokesh asked vain-gloriously.

'Never,' said Nameless, 'in this world.' It was a fact. In dreams, perhaps, he had glimpsed such things, but *then* there was always another matter on his mind.

Hot springs had erupted from miles down inside the frigid earth. From cliffs of ice, thinned transparent as glass, they fell in clouds of steam to form three long, bean-shaped ponds. The edges of these ponds were a ripe, unlikely green. Live grass had come up there, tall as a man, though it maintained itself only a foot or so before turning a rich black. The black grass then extended outwards for the length of ten shields – about fifty feet. The most bizarre trees rose from this grass, and out of the pools, also cara-paced in black, exploding into high-coloured coronas, rose rust-red willows, palms dark as malachite. On branches, fruit grew with skins thick as an ox's hide, but the flesh was honeyed and firm when once the shells were cut open – apples, damsons, limes, dates and nectarines.

The Kree chariots rode round the snow-packed outer rim of the oasis, while the lions sneezed and growled in the steam. The air was heavy, perfumed; the water had a fermenting odour, as if to swim there might make one drunk.

The House Mage was dead. His fever had burned him up, and the interminable coughing burst his heart. The funeral rites of such a personage were prolonged – and arduous for a Chaiord. Afterwards, a new House Mage having been promoted into authority, Lokesh and some of the men had ridden away to visit the oasis.

'My father Lokinda used to talk of another such spot. It happened when he was a child, but over on Shaiy land, and they were churlish with it, wouldn't share. It survived only ten months – God's reproval of them, he said.'

Lokesh spoke openly, and many had noticed how he referred far more often to the former Chaiord, his father, since Nameless had come here, as if something in Nameless inclined him to do so.

Nameless swung out of the chariot which he had been driving, acting as the Chaiord's charioteer and therefore brother. He had a look of Athluan about him as he did this, some thought.

Where the others hung back a little, almost wary at first of the oasis, Nameless strode into it. He was its match for colours.

Beneath a mulberry tree, thick purple with its mutated, tough-skinned berries, Nameless paused a minute, glancing round. Then he walked *up* the tree. They had seen him do this before, but still watched spellbound. Climbing in this way, he was now almost horizontal, and next upright again. Reaching a broad bough, he sat there, gazing out across the breadth of the oasis, the hot steam billowing by.

Where had he learned his magecraft? He had claimed it was inherent, but also he half told them how his mother and he had met a sorcerer in the waste, along with the Olchibe man who had taught Nameless archery. His meetings, it seemed, had always been auspicious.

When the men were ready for their swim, stripped bare in the heat, Nameless rejoined them. They had seen him naked before, as with all their own, in the garth bath-house, so were not intrigued. He was entirely tan, and at his groin the hair was also a flame. His weapon was large and well made, but consistently modestly presented at such times; he seemed to have some control of it that other men lacked, but the Kree girls whispered different things, if equally complimentary.

They plunged into the water and splashed about, roaring, and later they took the lions in, and the great lean beasts swam too, for they had learned it in the bath-house with their masters.

After the dip, they threw shavings of bronze into the largest pond, as an offering of thanks to the sprite of the waters. It was clearly visible at certain times under the surface, weed-haired and sinuous. If Nameless saw it, he did not say. They assumed, as a Jafn, he did.

Above, the grey sky gave on darkness in slow waves. By then the fire was lit to broil the meat they had hunted down en route. When grilled in the fire, fruits detonated from their skins, filling the air with added fragrance. No stars appeared but then two moons came up, one dark silver, one a smoking jewel.

'I've seen an opal like that moon,' said Lokesh. He and Nameless sat slightly back from the fire. They were scooping boiling fruits out of their kernels, spreading this on their meat with knives.

'It looks,' said Nameless, 'like some witch's secret eye.'

'Or the eye of the dead.' Lokesh's face drew in on itself. Of all the confidences and hints, he had not meant to utter this.

'The eye of the dead would be rotten,' replied Nameless, naively enough, 'or, in the Other Place bright and clear again.'

'Set in a skull-cup – I meant that,' said Lokesh. He absorbed wine in gulps. 'I feel that you know what I did,' he blurted out like a boy.

'Of course I do,' said Nameless, and added softly, 'I am a friend to you. How else would I be your friend, if not knowing you?'

'I value your friendship. We swore the oath of warrior-brotherhood—'

'So we did.'

'But if I say more, it must be blood-feud between us.'

Nameless waited. Then very gently he remarked, 'But I know that and, look, my knife is only for the food.'

The other men kept their distance, seeming to take no notice. They knew Lokesh was in love with Nameless, but any one of them would gladly have changed seats with Lokesh now. Valued alliances had been constructed, and dynasties begun among the Jafn, out of such passionate male love. If the pair talked low, no one else minded it or sought to pry.

Lokesh said, 'I must tell you what I did.'

Nameless, who had said that he already knew, answered, 'Then tell me.'

'I'm afraid of it.'

Nameless reached across. He put his hand a split second on Lokesh's shoulder. That was all it required.

Lokesh then recounted, in rapid sentences, how Rothger had made a pact with him – and with a selection of demons, seefs and other brutes. Lokesh described how Rothger had arranged the supernatural slaughter of Lokesh's unwanted bastard brother during the fight with the Fazions, and had later given Lokesh an uncanny utensil with which to destroy Lokinda. Rothger also, through his demons, sent a *copy* of Lokesh – a thing so like him it convinced any who had seen it – which left the garth and went out to shoot at a mark, in full view of the men on the garth walls, while Lokesh himself attended to the business of murder.

'It – this thing – was even spoken to when it walked down through the street. It replied in my voice, but I was in the inner room with Lokinda. It was a blade of ice Roth had given me. I showed it to my father as a curiosity. Then thrust it through his guts. He died before he could even draw breath to shout. It melted in him, but left no sign – his skin was whole. And I ran and hid myself. Then, when the thing Roth had made to look like me itself came back, I took its place in the apple grove behind the yard well. By then they'd found my father's corpse.'

Nameless still waited, saying nothing.

Lokesh went on with his confession.

He detailed how Rothger had psychically killed Athluan inside a web of magic, with the aid of a witch Lokesh himself had discovered for Roth, a woman of the furthest north beyond the Northlands. She had leached Athluan's sword and spirit, and Rothger had maimed him mortally. Outside the web, his flesh-and-blood body perished openly in battle by an arrow – but that, too, was uncanny.

'I wasn't there. Athluan had let me go to conquer the Faz Mother Ship. Later Roth described what he had done, gloating as he told me. He hated him, your father. Oh, I regret *your* father more than mine. Athluan was a good man. I've drunk from the cup of his skull that has opal eyes like that moon. And I helped Roth traduce him after, told of his weakness and a hundred invented failings – and kept the Kree allied with Rothger's Klow. I am ashamed.' Water rolled down Lokesh's cheeks.

Still silent, Nameless sat by him.

Lokesh, blinded by crying, did not notice the centres of Nameless's eyes, now red as the coals.

Calmly Nameless said, 'Listen to me. It wasn't you, brother, did any of that. It was heartless Rothger, whose soul reeks like the anus of this earth, he alone who made you do it all, and left you to suffer all the guilt.'

'You're right in that. Yes, you are right in that . . .'

Concerned, the other men about the fire all stared at them now: at Nameless sitting so still, at their Chaiord weeping.

Nameless put his hand once more on the Chaiord's shoulder. He looked about at the men, holding their eyes with his, which were now indigo again as the sky around the moons.

'By your leave, we were speaking,' said Nameless, 'of our two fathers' deaths.'

The rigidity went from them. One said, 'Yes, we all owe

such men a little grief.' They drank the health of the murdered dead.

White crows beat across the night sky. A stream of ice-
moths, translucent as thinnest milk, trailed after them like
a brief disturbance of vision.

Lokesh sat beside his new brother and friend, who had
no name.

Nameless had said very little since the revelation. He
seemed merely thoughtful, as anyway he often did.

The other men were unconscious, for it was a sleep
nocturnal. Lokesh could not or would not sleep.

The two moons went down. The third one had appeared
late, also darkly pale, wandering over the sky as if searching for them.

'What . . .' faltered Lokesh, 'what will make it right?'

'Oh, that,' said Nameless pleasantly, but as if distracted
from other more urgent meditations.

'My crimes, against you, my father . . .'

'They are Rothger's crimes,' said Nameless. Now his
tone was implacable.

The other men, sleeping, lay like the dead. Lokesh
regarded them uneasily. Did he fear some ghost or higher
power would smite him if he slumbered too?

'What am I to do? In the old times they had priests to
stand between them and God – but now we dispense with
priests. We must stand before God without an inter-
mediary.'

'I believed it was my wrath you feared, not God's,' said
Nameless lightly.

'Both . . . both. What am I to do?'

'Be revenged.'

The words sounded like cool bells deep in Lokesh's wide ears.

He sat back, his face hardening, growing solid again.

'Rothger?'

'Be *revenged* on Rothger.'

'And you, my brother, what for you?'

Nameless shrugged. 'We've sworn the brotherhood vow together. I'll partner you in vengeance.'

'The Klow are strong.'

'So are the Kree.'

'But they are allied with us – and with others.'

'Smash the alliance.'

'What grounds? What excuse?'

'The truth.'

Lokesh started. 'How can I speak *that*?'

'Say this: As we sat here and your men slept, your father's spirit came out of a moon. And he told us Rothger had slain him with a poison, for some old score. And Athluan he killed too, for the obvious reasons. Rothger is feared and mistrusted—'

'With cause! I . . . I fear him.'

'You are with me now. Don't fear him, not one jot. Besides,' said Nameless, with the same tender expression Lokesh had seen him wear when he slaughtered those first two deer, 'right is with us. And I can provide omens, occurences – enough to convince your people.'

Behind Lokesh's shoulder, unseen and unseeable by any but one, Nameless beheld his Uncle Guri, fresh from a race with the wind, and grinning wide as a skull.

*

When the men woke up, scattered about the ponds, dawn was rising. Four hours had elapsed. They looked about, and saw Lokesh and Nameless had gone away somewhere, perhaps for the purposes of nature. In the customary token of return, they had each left a coloured pebble lying on the ground.

As the Kree warriors ate their breakfast at the fire, two or three spotted a snake which trickled towards the water through the grasses.

It was a white snake, very large and long, with faint smudged markings on its scales. They watched the muscle rippling below its skin. Reaching the brink of a pool, it lowered its leonine, earless head. They thought it was drinking.

Abruptly the snake jerked backwards. In its jaws was clamped, diamond bright, a thrashing fish.

There were no fish in these waters. The heat alone would have cooked them.

Tethered to the trees, the Jafn lions stared and snarled softly.

The Kree did not exclaim, knowing now they witnessed a phenomenon.

So, when the wolf sped through the grass and seized, in turn, the snake that held the fish, they were less amazed than in the grip of a prescribed awe.

This wolf was white, a beast of the snow plains, normally found only in packs – unlike the solitary black wolves of the uplands to the west and south. The snow-wolves were not unduly fierce. Generally they avoided the haunts of men, unless starving, which this one did not look to be.

Now the wolf had hold of the snake which clasped the fish.

Even with the wolf's fangs closed on it, the snake did not let go of its own prize.

As one, the men of the Jafn Kree – also their lions – raised their heads, and from the dawning light cascaded a huge bird. It too was white, with black-fringed, endless wings, perhaps a type of lammergeyer not common to those parts.

It stooped and caught the wolf between its silent talons. It swept upwards, bearing the struggling burden – a bird of prey which grasped a wolf which grasped a snake which grasped a fish.

The morning was steely and choked by cloud, which shut over the four creatures and hid them, whether they were illusory, spiritual or real.

Then the outcry started. As it did so, Lokesh and Nameless were back among the Kree.

Lokesh held up his hand. 'Whatever you saw won't startle me. In the night . . . in the night my father came out from the Other Place, to speak to us.'

During the chariot ride back to the Kreean-garth, further events happened. The atmosphere was packed with hovors, sprites, unmalign yet mischievous, tweaking the manes of the lions, pulling off mens' riding caps, dislodging riding masks, or undoing their jewellery; dancing half-seen in the air.

When they began to approach the garth, and it grew visible up on its terraces of platforms behind the palisade, these beings drifted away. Then there was a sort of vacancy in land and sky, a gap which seemed needing to be filled.

This filling happened when they reached the main gate of the Kreean-garth.

Once, years ago, Lokinda had visited the Klow. Saphay had seen him, and described him, long after, to her son: an aged man, big and bundled in his clothes, his hair grey as a sword but whitening fast. He possessed, she had said, a face like a toad's.

Now Lokinda, with his whitening hair and toad's wrinkled face, was mistily present below the gate. He stood alone, a crag of sorrow and rage.

On the walls, sentries looking down made him out, and called to God. Women gathering ice for water in a grove beyond the walls dropped their pots and themselves turned to ice.

The chariots careered and halted. The lions growled, were stilled.

Lokesh, dead white, leaned on his chariot-rail.

'Courage,' Nameless said to him, now handling the restless lion-team as if he had done so since boyhood. 'You've nothing to fear from *him*.'

When Lokinda spoke, his voice was not human at all, but like metal struck against metal. What else might you expect of one come back all this way – and from *there*?

'My son, avenge me – you are sworn to it. Murderous Rothger of the Klow, who poisoned me, and turned like a fleer on his own brother, Athluan. Remember you are blood of my blood, bone of my bone. Do not live one day or sleep one hour more before you begin, and so lay my agony to rest.'

There would be those who might ask, ingenuously, why it had taken so long for the revenant of the old Chaiord to return and make this demand.

It was Nameless who explained. 'Their time isn't like ours. Our years to them are like an afternoon, or a night spent drinking and telling stories. But also, perhaps, he waited in courtesy for me to be of a proper age and strength to play my part. Remember how quickly God allowed me to grow up. Lokesh must avenge his sire, and I *mine*.'

Later Nameless said to Guri, 'Uncle, you acted that old man Lokinda well.'

'He was Jafn,' said Guri with contempt. 'Nothing so difficult then, but I'd be hard put to it to fake a man of the Olchibe.'

Above, the sky blazed with stars.

In the House of the Klow, Rothger was tossing and grunting in the stonewood bed. Taeb, the northern witch, sat at the far side of it, observing him.

Now and then he would have her in to pass a night with him. He never wanted her body. He preferred her to conjure sexual images on the wall, some of them perverse and some repulsive, while under the quilts he pleasured himself three or four times. Then he would, for a treat, invite her to lie by him and sleep, in her northern way, at the far side of the bed.

These times were few, as the Jafn did not seek congress during a period of slumber, not even Rothger with his self-congress, and generally he would get up and go back to the joyhall when the sexual session was done. Tonight, most curiously, he had fallen asleep, although this was not a sleep nocturnal at all.

Taeb watched him. Did it enter her mind how she could discredit him if she revealed that he had slept out of turn?

Probably not, since the mind of Taeb was not much like the minds of others. Besides, she could smell the electric upheaval that circled now above, between them and the motionless stars. Only the gods of night could put out the stars. Men were simpler to deal with.

Soon Taeb slipped free of the bed. She donned her furs and went noiselessly from the room. Descending by the ladder-stair to the hall, she moved, cloaked in a spell of non-apparency, behind the benches, among the hubbub of the House evening, and through the door into the yard.

Out in the garth, the Klow were used by now to seeing the green witch gliding around. Even sometimes she would go to the gate and leave the garth behind, off about mystic witchwork in the wilderness.

Once down on the plain, Taeb walked briskly.

The snow was exemplary tonight, crisp and firm. As Saphay had once done perforce, Taeb too now went away from the Klowan-garth. Any who noted this thought, naturally, she would be coming back. But in that they were quite wrong.

FOUR

It has come and gone, the meeting at the Thing Place. The presiding ancient ship trapped to its withers in the ice, the seventeen masts that drip with cryotites. Not truce torches of green fire, but blood-red, fashioned by the new House Mage of the Kree, the designated colour for alliance-breaking. Men of the Shaiy, the Irhon, the Vantry, all standing in the ring of black spar, watching as a nameless young man speaks to them, and at his side his vow-brother, Lokesh of the Kree.

They were sold, in an hour, the property of vengeance, and the unassailable rights of Lokesh, and the one called Nameless in honour of a father dead before he could coin his son's name. They liked too, these peoples, the idea of *taking* something. Especially the Shaiy liked it, trustless and shifting as a cloud.

The alliance of four Jafn peoples with the Klow was therefore smashed before a second moon came up. That night they feasted along the shore, and Nameless told them a story of a hero of the Vantry, and one of the Shaiy, and one of the Irhon. If they did not recognize the names or the deeds of these heroes, it scarcely mattered. They were glorious, and the tales well told. Chaiords passed around the skulls of other enemies long defeated, or former lords, patched with hot jewels and full of wine.

In the morning, they swam in the freezing hiss of liquid sea, to clear their heads. Then every man went home to call out the warriors.

He was sitting, the Chaiord of the Klow, at breakfast, when the sending came.

Nor was it done politely, mage to mage, inserted into the seclusion of the Thaumary.

There in the joyhall of the Klow, as men sat about eating, readying only for another hunt, a ball of crimson fire flashed down, burst, and revealed a colossal sword – taller than a man and upright for conflict – dressed in blood. It seemed to be stuck in the floor and to quiver, as if thrown by a giant hand.

Men started to their feet. Women let out a few wild cries. Although battle-accustomed, the Klow were not used to such sudden declarations of war, flung into their midst by their own kind.

They could hardly miss who had sent the token either, for the illusory sword in the floor had been tied with four sigils – the Raven of the Vantry, the Arrow-In-Circle of the Shaiy, the Irhon's Crested Lizard, and the Snow-Ox of the Kree.

Rothger rose more slowly from behind his pile of dishes. He kept his cup in hand, and quipped stupidly: 'What's this? What are they at?' And then, as if returning to the conscious world, 'They want a fight, do they? They shall have one . . .'

Perhaps those in the joyhall looking at this dundering lump, as if for the first time, confronted at last what he had brought them to. What body could prosper, when the head was rotten? But there was no time now to brood. The former allies had been even ruder than anticipated. They had not waited. Even as the Klow ran about, gathering their weapons and their chariots, across the plains of snow, under a sky of daylight darkness, the attacking horde came bounding.

Rothger, staring from the garth walls down at the massed clutter on the snow's white cloth, shrivelled. His lip drooped like that of a bullying child unexpectedly threatened.

He knew he must go back in, find the witch Taeb that no one else could now discover, and call to his familiars, the lurking elementals of the waste – none of whom, he secretly guessed, would come.

'There are too many of them,' the warriors of the Klow said to each other. Yet they shouldered on their armours of metal and leather; they honed their axes and swords against the whetstones grimly.

Rothger, wilting in the midst of them, still wore his hunting clothes. It was as if someone must convince him that this now was real.

Men hurried to help Rothger arm himself. His previous mail was then found to be a size too small. Between the last fray and this, he had increased his girth. Rothger pushed the useless breastplate away. Abruptly he was roaring, snorting like a beast that faces fire. *Bring me this . . . Bring me that . . .* They dashed about, trying to assist him. He was their Chaiord.

Down on the plain the shadow gathered, sparkling with steel, burning with the flames of battle-standards.

Lokesh rode forward through the Kree chariots. His own vehicle was not today crewed by his vow-brother,

Nameless, but by one of Lokesh's own bastard sons, a boy of sixteen – older than Nameless, if not in appearance or skill. It was a pity this, but Nameless had said he must ride by himself, on this occasion.

Lokesh had forgotten he had ever been the close ally of Rothger. Nameless, and the Thing Meet, and the sinews of Lokesh's own unrest, had all made him forget that. Rothger had tricked him and was outcast of God, a monster. Lokesh looked about, saw the readiness of his people and the vastness of the whole force. He wished he had drunk a little more wine. But war, after all, was wine enough for a man on such a day.

He called to his warriors: 'Tonight I'll feast in the Klow House!'

Nameless occupied the chariot Lokesh had gifted him. It was well made, and the lions two of the best. Nameless had won them over at once. Nameless did what no other man there did in war, either Chaiord or warrior: he managed his chariot alone. He had knotted the reins about his waist, and drove solely by flexing his body, a procedure his lion-team seemed already perfectly to understand. Meanwhile he had armed himself, along with his Olchibe bow, with a single long-tongued Jafn sword. No one had been able to argue Nameless away from this plan. Nor had he put on any of the protective leathers or mail. His only concession had been to tie back his hair, like the incendiary tail of a comet.

'There!' Lokesh cried.

Up on the walls of the Klowan-garth, assembled mages were letting loose preparatory rays. They shot across the dull sky, reflecting on the snow.

The men of Kree and Irhon, Vantry and Shaiy laughed loud and mockingly, to let those up on the walls hear them.

'They say Rothger's lost his favourite witch,' said Lokesh, his chariot at ease by the chariot of Nameless. '*I* found her for him. She has green hair and is very clever, but word has it she ran away when her witchcraft told her what was coming – us.'

Nameless did not reply. The slightest frown passed over his face. Lokesh assumed Nameless was angry, just a touch, that the green witch, Taeb, had not returned to her former master, Lokesh himself. But Nameless – had Lokesh realized – was simply irritated by Lokesh standing there close by him in his own chariot, buzzing like a hive-bee. Nameless did not want, at that moment, to be bothered with him, but it was not quite yet the hour to say it.

A fresh ray opened the cloud, shaped like a fishbone, searing yellow. It spread not from the garth, but from the mage-positions of the allies on the plain.

Spectacular, terrifying, it curled over miles of sky and caught the Klowan-garth in a loop of incandescence.

Those below heard the cries and shouts worsen on the walls. This made the allies laugh again. But for all that, the fishbone ray, though frightful to observe, seemed to do little more than alarm. Anyway, the Klow mages soon blasted it in bits, which scattered like brightest snow.

By then, the Klow were coming out of their gate.

The mass of them was substantial, but not against the cluster of allies which awaited it. The Klow were outnumbered, and had had no space to send for assistance from any other source – if any would have responded.

Lokesh sneered, contemptuous. 'We'll crush them between us like shells under a boot.'

Just then, he saw Nameless's eyes veer round at him.

Lokesh noticed the eyes of Nameless were like the reddest rubies. They were *full* of red – and of utter, utter scorn.

Then Nameless was gone, in a rush of bronze, iron and steel – the chariot pounding forward over the plain.

Seeing him take off like a hawk in flight, the Kree chariots behind broke loose to follow him. Almost instantly, the whole force erupted and poured towards the enemy garth. Lokesh found himself swirling in their midst, for a second nearly overturned and left behind.

Surely he must have mistaken the look Nameless gave him. Nameless and he, they were the stuff of stories – brothers, lovers – and that look was only for their adversaries.

He clouted his sixteen-year-old charioteer across the spine. 'Get on, you oaf!'

They too fled forward.

The ground rumbled at the surge, as if the sea were coming in. Snow-spume rose high, like whitest smoke. Through the heart of it the metal chariots careered, pulled by the sprinting engines of their lions. Arrows began to tear over in a hail.

Rothger, if he rode at the head of his people, was not to be distinguished. For the other force, it was Nameless who plunged out across the expanse of snow, the rest of them striving to keep up with him.

Quills and arrows clattered all around him. To any that studied him from either side, he appeared to evade every shaft. Now and then, one parted the long tail of his hair, singing through it. Then he had the Olchibe bow, had primed it, and let lose three male arrows in a single cast. They dived before him as if they bore his soul, and thunked home, unspiritually conclusive. Three Klow warriors fell dead, pierced to the quick of life.

Nameless, they all saw now, was a borjiy, a berserker, one who took on the cloak of battle-madness; Lokesh was afraid his darling would, due to his own recklessness, be killed. The Chaiord scrambled his chariot through the crowd, losing control, hitting unmercifully the boy who drove him, like some hapless beast of burden. You heard that a borjiy might fight on even when dead, unaware for some while that he was so.

The red-haired man was almost up to the sprawled front rank of his foes when the left-hand lion of his team was skewered through the forehead by a Klowan dart. The cat dropped lifeless. The chariot, still at racing speed, plunged and jumped across its corpse, snapping the waist-tied reins in two before Nameless could himself do so. Tilting now, the car turning sidelong, but Nameless remained standing yet on the floor of it, horizontal, – as he managed to stay when climbing up the trunks of trees. Instantaneously he had slashed the debris of reins from his waist, and jumped forward on to the back of the remaining lion, just as the yoke-pole gave way.

Now, fully ahead of his Jafn army, still lumbering along in chariots, Nameless sped, unencumbered by any vehicle, arrow-like against the Klow. He was standing on the lion's back, as it plummeted forward, its limbs stretched to incredible length. He was standing there, his arms outheld and his beautiful head thrown back, laughing not with mockery or pleasure, but with *violence*. And the sword was switched and held, glittering, now in his right hand, now the left.

Nonplussed, the Klow banked up before him. They had one split second for their turmoil.

Then the lion sprang right upward.

Ten years ago Nameless had seen none of these men, he had been new-born, too young. Yet he had seen *all* of them, his astral awareness being at large in the Klow House, unwitnessed but witnessing.

Whether it was a physical memory or merely instinct made no odds to this fire-arrow creature standing on a lion's leaping back.

He struck the Klow like a missile, crossing over their teams, their vehicles, hitting the breast of their fleshly human wall.

His own lion was the first with them. Combat-trained, crazed with the spirit of what rode it, its claws gouged, teeth sheared through a wrist, a shoulder, a throat. Nameless too was no longer arrow, but hammer, club and cleaving steel.

In a deluge of shattering and blood, among the scream-ing carnage, single-handed he ripped open the heart of the Klow vanguard. While behind him, swiftly the Kree came sweeping on to carve out their own share, and at their heels the greedy Shaiy and Irhon, and the Vantry with their Raven wings.

Lokesh, somewhere in the tumult, saw Nameless stand-ing on his lion, raised on a welter of howling dying *death*. Even then, Lokesh, a ninny, did not grasp with *what* he had sworn brotherhood.

For the others, many were by now also battle-mad – borjiy. Among the Klow alone, true fear woke stinking. They were crumbling. They cried for rescue, for their

219

mothers and their wives, and flaked off under the chariot-runners.

Not so many saw the sequel. The one who did, half disbelieving, took his chance.

The second lion too had been slain. Nameless walked off its shuddering skin, and jumped lightly down on to the muddled floor of battle. Through the hacking of swords and axes, Nameless walked, he *strolled*. He was dyed with blood. His blood-shade hair had escaped from its ring. He was scarlet, all of him, even his eyes still, without any strange angle of light to account for it.

Strolling, he went between the riot of runners and blades, and as men blindly smote at him on every side, he felt the sting of their weapons, which did not last on him.

Then Nameless reached a chariot wedged in at the rear of the host. It was Rothger's chariot, and it was stranded, because the man who had driven it, some distant kinsman from the garth, lay dead, and its lion-team lay dead, and Rothger balanced there, looking round and looking round.

Brown Rothger, Rothger the Fat – who had once been thin and cunning, and cold of heart. He saw what was redly strolling up to him, through that whirlpool of war, swords and knives crashing all around it, and itself somehow missing each of them. Out of the side of his chariot, Rothger hauled his unused axe. He had killed things once, and enjoyed doing so. Did he recollect that now? No, he was only afraid. Yet he who had been able to shoot so ably at a mark, and pike the horsazin of the Fazions with shafts, now raised the axe in both fists and swung it over, all his lumpen strength behind the haft.

Rothger saw, and felt, the axe-head slam home into the

body of the scarlet man. He put so much into the feat that the axe left Rothger's hands.

Rothger did not know who this man was, only that he must be seen to. And Rothger experienced a moment's gushing near-infantile happiness at the impact of his blow. He was positive he had settled something.

The man in blood still stood there. The axe had entered his upper torso, at the place between neck and left shoulder. It must have met his heart. There was no way in the world a man could live, not even a borjiy, with such a wound.

'Die then,' said Rothger, his own voice soothing him. He had not done much else in the fighting, but this might well be enough. 'Go along now, fall over and finish.'

Nameless looked up at Rothger. Nameless had known *him* at once.

'Not yet,' said Nameless, 'thank you, Uncle Roth. I'm not ready to die today. It was the same last time, out on the snow where you sent me. I wasn't ready then either.'

Rothger watched how Nameless lifted the axe gently free of his own body, with just one momentary little wince, as if he had stubbed a toe not badly, or burnt his fingers on his meat.

A mage. He was a mage, even though he fought among the warriors . . . The mage in blood stepped up into Rothger's chariot, next to him.

On every side, the fighting raged on. But here these two were in an oasis of deadly calm. There had been something like this before, Rothger thought. Ah, yes, when he removed Athluan from existence, in the hollow of the ice-wind.

This mage, who was he? How had he made the illusion with the axe, so it had not harmed him but had seemed to?

'All alone,' said Nameless kindly. 'No witch, no seef, no sweet one to love you. Only unloving Nameless, who doesn't die.'

Rothger heard himself gibber. The sound shocked him, he did not know why he had made it, and then the being in his chariot punched him, only as one man will another, hard on the temple. Slumping down into the first darkness, Rothger bleated for help. No one heard. The little atrocious war was nearly done.

Wreckage, as if a ship had smashed herself on some sea-cliff of ice, lay all about the plain beneath the walls of the Klowangarth.

Ignoring it, men rushed towards one focal point. They ran from everywhere around, abandoning their chariots and teams, even their comrades and kin. They ran to the man who was Nameless and, embracing him, some of the blood that covered him rubbed off on them like glory.

He was not insane now, nor out of his skull and wandering, as often a borjiy might be in the aftermath. Under the blood he was cool yet amiable, smiling at their enthusiasm, even it seemed at his own. As if he had tried a boyish prank, and it had been successful. There was not a scratch on him.

'The Klow are no more.' The shout went round the noisy plain.

'The Klow are wiped off the earth's belly.'

They looked towards the garth, whose platform and walls they could now breach so easily, for only women and children guarded this Jafn citadel finally, and a handful of old men.

Lokesh had meanwhile arrived in his chariot. The boy who drove it was black and blue from Lokesh's blows, and had an arrow through his arm, of which he had not yet been given time to break off the flight.

'Well, my vow-brother,' said Lokesh, 'we've gained a victory. But I think if we hadn't been quick, you would have done it alone, all by yourself, and left us no work.'

The men about them – Kree, Shaiy, Vantry, Irhon – cheered. They banged sword-hilts on armour and on the metal chariot-rails. 'Nameless!' The howl rose into the air, replacing the vanished mage-lights. Four Chaiords shouted out Nameless's name. A true hero must be vaunted.

Lokesh had left his chariot. He put his possessive arm about his vow-brother's shoulders. 'The Klowan-garth is yours, brother, and everything in it now. For Rothger's dead.'

'He's not dead,' said Nameless.

They stared, expectant. What was this?

Nameless said, 'A clean death in battle is too nice for such a man.'

A different noise began suddenly to go up. Heads turned, and Nameless leapt into Lokesh's vacated chariot, to get a better view. Lokesh's driver, exhausted and in pain, drew away from Nameless and, unnoticed, fainted on to the chariot's floor.

From the Klowan-garth a procession of sorts was now coming out by one of the lesser gates.

The allied Jafn started to jeer.

'Erdif Greybeard and all the old crank-shanks, come to beg for mercy.'

Nameless had the reins of the chariot. The lion-team moved forward, and the allied ranks opened a path for their borjiy hero to drive through.

He met the old men from the garth the first, just as he had been the first meeting the garth warriors. While Lokesh, unlike the other three Chaiords, took the notion to run panting behind his own chariot, as if he were Nameless's dog.

Erdif stood on the plain, gazing up at a being of shining red silence that looked at him with two blue eyes.

Did Erdif remember the child born during his steward-ship of the Klow House? Did he remember the casting out of the child and its mother, the alien woman from the Ruk, to die?

Mentally limited, strait-laced and sour, ten years had made Erdif only harder and more brittle. He lifted his nose at the red warrior hero, whether he recalled his origins or not.

'We offer you no harm,' declared Erdif in ringing yet cracked tones. 'We're old men, too bowed to raise a sword or swing an axe. You must, for tradition and honour, pre-serve us, and also the women and children in the garth. If you desist from rape and vandalism, the better will your praises be sung.'

Whatever else he had concluded, Erdif did seem to guess who the leader really was of this allied force.

That leader now spoke. From end to end of the battle-ground, and up on the walls themselves, they heard him.

'The Klow men, both young and old, kill their true kings, as they let Athluan be killed. The Klow kill women who are mothers, as they would have killed my mother, Athluan's wife, Saphay of the Rukar. The Klow kill babies, as they would have killed me, Athluan's son, when I was but a few days born.'

Erdif's greybearded jaw fell. Aghast he stood there.

Nameless said, 'I am more compassionate than the Klow, however – but not by very much. I will let your children, up to the age of twelve, live. Your women who are mothers of children below the age of twelve, I will let live also, to care for them. To serve their needs I will let your beasts live. The rest of you shall die, and I will burn your bloody garth. And your cutch of a Klow House I will cave in as if thunder had struck it. Do you hear me, old man? Good, I see you do. Take my words with you to the Other Place.'

As, in the war-sending, a giant hand had flung a sword, now the hand of Nameless flung the sword with which he had slaughtered the vanguard of the Klow.

Before Erdif could protest, or even scream, the sword went straight through him, and, such was the might of the hit, through two elderly others standing bemused behind him. All three collapsed to the snow, already stone dead, and their blood spread from them like an opening rose.

Not a sound now on the earth. Even the wind, they later said, held its breath in wonder and awe.

Then the warriors hurtled out of their trance. They did what Nameless had decreed, without a word of argument. They slew the old men on the plain. They rode headlong up the ramps and crashed in the gates and doors of the garth.

By dusk that evening, the place was peopled mostly by the dead, and it was burning. No Klow men were left alive, a minority only of the women. The mages, who had barricaded themselves in the Thaumary of the House, Nameless himself had gone in to, once the barricade was down. There followed lightnings and shrieks, then Nameless came out from there, but no other.

After this, with the garth and its dwellings and its icon posts in flames around them, Nameless and a chosen few went on into the Klow House, which alone had been left standing.

Five Chaiords were present in the joyhall: the Chaiords of the Shaiy, the Vantry and the Irhon, Lokesh the Chaiord of the Kree, and Rothger who had made himself a Chaiord once, and now sat in iron shackles on the ground.

The dead Klow mages had also been brought in and strewn about. The House Mage, whose neck was crushed, had been propped on a bench. The allies had mocked him, too, seeing how easily their hero had dispatched him and his magic. Right – the right of God – was on a true hero's side. It was what made him sorcerous, and great.

Nameless did not sit in the Chaiord's chair – he had offered it to Lokesh. When Lokesh would not accept, Nameless reminded him, 'You vowed to feast tonight in this Klow House.'

'So I did.'

'Sit in the chair, then.'

'But it must be yours.'

'I want,' said Nameless, 'nothing from the Klow. My friends assembled here, you must keep the Jafn women and children taken today as slaves, and all their goods.'

At this generosity they again demurred, now all four of them, even the Shaiy, exclaiming that Nameless must have most, some, *something*.

'So I will have. I will have that one's death.'

Every eye then fixed on Rothger.

He was awake again, after the concussing punch. He crouched in a venomous frightened shape, biting his flabby mouth. Now he spoke, his tongue still had an edge.

'What, pray, have I done to earn all this flattering attention?'

No one replied. They knew, for Nameless son of Athluan, and Lokesh, Lokinda's son, had told them what Rothger had done.

Rothger plucked at the chains. His edged tongue changed its tack. 'I am not,' he said, 'anyway alone, do you think, in being culpable. Ask Lokesh there. Ask *him*.'

'Ask Lokesh what?' demanded the Chaiord of the Vantry, who was tired of this now, wanting to finish up the punishments and get on to the celebration, wherever it was to be.

Outside the high-up windows, fires flicked their manes at the night-falling sky. The smell of smoke was intense.

'*Lokesh*,' insisted Rothger. 'If I'm accused of anything, then question Lokesh too.'

Lokesh huddled on his bench, appearing smaller than he had been. He glanced at Nameless, seeking a sign. Had he never thought . . .?

And Nameless simply turned to him two wide eyes, blue as an evening sky that had no fire in it at all. 'What does he mean, Lokesh?' Nameless enquired.

Lokesh gaped. He looked as Erdif had, on hearing his death sentence out on the snow – his world had gone mad. 'I . . . you know that I . . .'

Nameless, who had not sat down, moved slowly along the benches where living Chaiords and dead mages rested.

'My father,' said Nameless, 'Athluan . . .' He hesitated

227

and stared across at Rothger. 'What has Lokesh to do with any of that?'

Rothger felt something pulling at his brain, which it had been doing for some little while, coercing it into giving up its store. He was like a man who must vomit, and out it came.

'Lokesh assisted me in getting rid of Athluan. He lied to help me, and brought me a witch-woman whose spell was more effective than any poison. And in return . . . well, I enabled Lokesh to see off his own old father, Lokinda. I aided Lokesh so marvellously, I can tell you, that I doubt Lokinda even knew he was dead.'

Nameless had paused by one of the painted hall pillars. Perhaps he recalled this hall, seen while still unborn and also in his baby form, all those ten, eleven years ago; recalled Saphay stranded here, on trial without redress. He did not bother to look at Lokesh gabbling and terrified, or at the other Chaiords growing startled and angry. Nor did he look at Rothger. On Nameless a fierce impatience had come down. He must curb it in order to reach the necessary end. But just as the Vantry chief wanted his supper and cup, Nameless craved the climax of this game. Men were so sluggish, their desires – even their hatreds – so slow to bring to the boil. Yes, even though their lives were short as a sigh.

Behind him, he heard them blustering at each other now, like winds.

Nameless thought, *But my life will linger. I am invulnerable. Their weapons go into me and do nothing. I can't die. Not here, not through mankind.*

It seemed to him he had not quite known that before. But he must have known it, too.

Then Lokesh was kneeling, blubbering, on the floor at Nameless's feet. The abrupt finale to the action surprised Nameless slightly, for he had become bored, thinking they would never get to this point – at least not for a vast while.

'Brother . . . Nameless, my friend, you told me . . .'

Nameless turned from Lokesh and spoke across his prostration at the others. 'There was an omen – you've heard the Kree speak of it. A snake seized a fish, a wolf seized the snake, a crait or other great bird lit on all three of them and bore them off. Now I see,' said Nameless quietly, 'that Rothger is the snake who seized Lokesh the wriggling fish, and made him his dupe and accomplice. But we, you and I, we are the wolf that grasps the snake and the fish together.'

'And the great bird,' said the Irhon Chaiord, 'what is that?'

'That is God,' said Nameless, 'in whose Grip we are.' He kicked Lokesh aside and went back to the others. 'Fetch in the Kree. Let them judge him, this Lokesh. I can't do it. How could I do it?'

The Kree came. They judged. Rothger spoke slyly on and on. Lokesh jabbered, weeping, and as wet with sweat as if he had been bathing.

Outside the red flames sank till the sky was black.

When they had decided, they asked Nameless to choose a fate for Rothger and for Lokesh, both.

'Your father died through these men.'

'Yes,' Nameless said. Some wine had been brought by then. He drank, and threw away the cup of black jade, which had once been Athluan's, and which Rothger had soiled with his lips. It shattered.

*

Only three now, alone together in the deserted Klow House: Rothger, Lokesh, Nameless.

Lokesh suddenly laughed. Both the others, Rothger and even Nameless, glanced at him, arrested.

'It's your joke with me, brother,' said Lokesh to Nameless. 'I see it now: you won't kill me.'

'No,' said Nameless, 'not I.'

Lokesh stopped laughing. He had ceased to be a total fool. He stared at the floor where his own Kree warriors had thrown him, kicking him in the guts, the ribs, and pissing on him. 'I loved you,' he said to Nameless.

Then it was Rothger who barked out a tiny laugh. 'Love?' said Rothger. 'He gets plenty of that. His kind are used to it.'

Lokesh spoke his curse. 'Let love ruin him, then,' he said.

But Nameless paid no attention. He was putting out the last of the lamps left in the joyhall. He had no need of lights – could see, it seemed, in the dark.

That done, he got hold of Lokesh, who was partly broken, and lifted him with ease and dumped him next to Rothger. Also, to where Rothger might reach it, Nameless kicked one of the shards of Athluan's wine cup.

'You know my Uncle Roth is a vampire?' Nameless asked. 'Yes, for you and many of his men have seen him at it. Well, Uncle Roth' – and his *voice* when he spoke the word 'Uncle' – 'here's a present for you. Your seef will come, or if it won't, the mages will make sure that other seefs *do* come in. Seefs and sihpps of all sorts, the blood-drinkers by proxy. Even like this, they'll want you to do it, Uncle Roth. Perhaps they'll even promise to set you at liberty if you fill them full. Rest assured, I will make certain also that they can't. But you, you'll have to drink this one's blood. You'll drink him dry. And that, Lokesh, is your feasting here – to be feasted *on*.'

Lokesh made the smallest sound, as he had when his snapped ribs grated. Then he lay back and turned his head from both these terrors.

Rothger, incredibly, attended to hear what came next. Seeing that, Nameless obliged him.

'When Lokesh is drained, there'll be no one left to consume but yourself.'

Over Rothger's swollen face ran, hand in hand together, a look of sheer blind horror and a look of irresistible desire.

No, he would not be able to refuse.

All would be as Nameless said.

'This garbage heap can stand,' said Nameless, 'till you're done. Then some mage or other can call a couple of winds to knock it down. Not one brick on another.'

As he walked, unseen in darkness, from the hall, Rothger and even Lokesh, whose head stayed turned away, watched him somehow.

Only night was now in that place – and waiting. But for them neither night nor wait continued very long.

Behind the festive Jafn camp, Guri met his adoptive nephew, Nameless, in the hour before sunrise.

'So you didn't need me, not once,' said Guri. 'I'm good only for impersonating old dead Chaiords, or upsetting buckets.'

Astonished, Nameless gazed at him. 'But—'

'No, I was glad of a bit of peace. I'm not complaining.' Guri sat by Nameless on a snow-bank and squinted at the bright torches and fires below. He despaired over the profligacy of the fire, so unlike the abstemious war camps of Olchibe. He believed he had not minded being left out of the action, though possibly ten mortal years ago he would have done. Nameless must take his own way; Nameless was the Leader.

Nameless—

'One thing,' said Guri. 'One or two.'

'Which are?'

'Where next for you?'

'Oh,' said Nameless, 'the remainder of the Jafn, all those other clans, I'll call them in, get hold of them.'

'Yes, that's right. That's the way.'

'Gech, too,' said Nameless, bragging now, how strangely, a boy to his uncle – *bragging, he*. 'And Olchibe, Uncle, what do you think? Will Olchibe and Gech have me, too?'

'Maybe,' said Guri seriously, 'but not as you are now.'

Affronted – you could see it – Nameless glared.

Guri put back his braids and chortled. 'I mean, not by *that* name.'

'Which name?'

'*Nameless.*'

'What else do I have?'

'Poor lad. No dada to title you. Listen, I'm your uncle, ah? Shall *I* name you then?' Guri got up. He raised his hands as high as his shoulders, palms out-turned, as he had sometimes seen Peb do when he was being the priest of his band. 'The Great Gods anyway prepared a name for you. Amen. I even part-called you by it, not understanding, once or twice when you were a kiddle. Don't you recall? No, you wouldn't now.'

Nameless looked at Guri with all his eyes.

A child, a child with a new toy—

Well, he had spared all the children, up to twelve years, as Peb Yuve would have done.

'There was an omen, when we were out in the snows, you and your mother and me. Do you remember that? No? You were a baby, and the fey-sight you'd had was fading.'

'What was the name?'

'Gently, it's your old uncle you're talking to. There's a legend in Gech: a wolf that mates with a lion. It makes a creature that's holy yet profane, a beast of destiny and magic power.'

Guri had lowered his hands. His charge stared at him.

'Is that what I am?'

'Great Gods know, amen, what you are. You're a fine man – but your father was a Rukar deity. You know he was, a filth-god full of wickedness and spite.'

'Guri, he might—'

'Hear me? No, he doesn't hear. Believe me, I think now that I'd know. Why he doesn't is a mystery. After all, even with his faults, he is a *god*. He shone and glowed with superlativeness. Let him hear me say *that*. And you are half of him and half your mother, who is a human woman. That night we were all out on the waste, I saw the lion mating in the sky with the wolf. Her, she saw it too – Saphay. She caused the image to come; she'd thrown some mage-coal in the fire. I found it after. See, here it is.'

Guri put the ancient coal, dehydrated and meaningless as a fossilized turd, into his nephew's grasp. The young man sat staring at it. 'I never heard that legend,' said the unlessoned son of the god. Time hovered, till eventually he remarked, 'We should think about Saphay. I should send to her in some way or other.'

'If you like. But first—'

'First the name. *What?*'

'What you'd suppose,' said Guri, shrugging.

Nameless said nothing. Guri said nothing.

Overhead, the stars, about to be helplessly snuffed out by dawn, spangled defiance for a moment on the arc of sky.

Below in the camp the Jafn sang, and bellowed occasionally for their beloved brother and Borjiy, who had vanished from their midst.

'I'll be king,' the young man said, 'over them all.' He spoke now remotely, lost in himself. He added, 'I am *Lionwolf.*'

FIVE

Fearful, the dream.

Worse, because it went on even after her eyes were open. Now she saw it reflected in the floor.

An oval of night sky was held in a rim of faintest flame. Across the upper blackness curled long pale tendrils. She saw into them as, while still asleep, she had also done. Figures writhed and mouthed in the whiteness. She did not know, never having seen them in her waking or sleeping life before, what they were, and yet she suspected they were elemental demons of the Jafn. Athluan had once described several of these minor fiends to her. Seefs – they were seefs.

Through the high windows of some tall building they flowed like rivers of dirty milk.

It was the Klow House from which she had been exiled, and all around it the Klowan-garth lay in burnt-out rubble, like a used-up fireplace.

The vision faded without prelude.

Saphay pushed herself into a sitting position.

She was abysmally cold, for here all the heating was gone – and had been for some while. She did not know how she had survived, eating the little raw shared dinners her cat provided, both of them huddled in their furs.

The rest of the village-city of Ranjalla was deserted. On

her forays up and down, she had found no one there. The houses were icy, only the ice kept them in repair. Saphay believed that similarly only her hardiness, learned from her former trek across the snow waste, kept *her* in repair now. Additionally, she had once come back from icy death, so perhaps she always could.

But this *cold* was omnipresent and dire. It made her sluggish, and brought on a sort of muddled depression in which thoughts seldom stirred – and no dreams until now.

Saphay saw that where she had beheld the dream in the floor was exactly the spot where the god Yyrot had received the frozen solid puddle of offering beer. Sometimes since she had chipped pieces out with a knife, to suck and cheer herself, but it failed to work now. It had no taste or alcoholic worth. How long had she been here? She could not make up her mind.

The cat lay in her lap for warmth. Saphay stroked the cat. A sudden enchanting heat seemed to come up from its coat. Saphay put both her hands on it, but then she felt the heat blooming also at her back.

Some miracle. The stove must have relit itself by magical means. Had Guri at last deigned to call on her, or her heartless, abandoning son?

Saphay uncoiled and rose, the cat on one arm, ready to slap either of these two precious men across the face.

However, it was neither of them. Her spirits evaporated. 'You again,' she said.

She stood her ground, insolent with the derangement of near cryoanaesthesia.

Yyrot, Winter's Lover, had evolved at the other side of the snow-house room. He was not, today, clad in ice-mail. Sparks came and went in his black hair. His face was darker, wind-burned, it looked, as Athluan's had done when he had been out hunting. The grey eyes of the god were cloudy. He seemed slightly drunk.

Slurring his words, he told her the facts. 'This is my angry side, Saphay.'

Despite everything, Saphay jumped backwards. She had been shown the angry side of a god already – Zezeth. And that had been enough.

Yyrot stood there, indolently shaking his sleeves, and waves of warmth flew off them, smelling of pine resin and balsam.

The cat stared from Saphay's shoulder, where it had climbed. Eyes shining with approval, it purred.

Then – cold Yyrot's angry side had brought rescue? It made him *hot*.

Saphay began to giggle. She was hysterical. The cat launched itself from her and landed at Yyrot's feet, which were sheathed in boots of, or like, soft leather. There the animal rolled about in delight.

'Why are you . . . *angry*? Your lovely, comforting anger – why?' Saphay quavered, stretching her body into this miniature *Summer*. The snow was shimmering and cascading in released water down the walls. The house would melt, but she did not care.

'Oh, sometimes I lose my temper.' The god Yyrot let out an abrupt yack of laughter. He caught up the cat in long warm fingers, caressing it. The cat was ecstatic. Saphay, jealous, watched her feline revel in so much extra warmth.

He, this god, must also be amenable – when angry? The cat, which had been afraid of and hated him, seemed now to believe Yyrot was a friend.

Saphay said, 'The beer froze but, look, it's come back.'

She knelt and with her hand scooped liquid from the small pond of beer, forgetful of the seef-dream that had reflected in it. Now the alcohol went straight to her head, its potence restored.

After a while, she looked up. Yyrot had disappeared, and the cat, too, but the snow-house went on beaming with heat, and whole chunks were showering off the walls. Two or three ladders leant at precarious angles. One fell suddenly, with a splash.

Outside, she heard Yyrot laugh again, and then a dog barked.

Saphay undid the door.

The snow beyond the house, solid for decades, maybe for centuries, was a sea of quaggy mud out of which fast-growing mosses, weeds and salads were already thrusting, thin and yellow-green with newness. Ice-irises starred the vegetation, black flowers with veins of purplish blue.

There, on this carpet, Saphay's cat was coupling with the dog, which had pinned it, apparently quite willingly, to the earth. The dog was Yyrot-as-a-dog, grey and slender, exactly as Saphay and the once-disapproving cat had seen him before.

That was like something else Saphay had seen too: some vision of lights in the sky, a wolf which mated with a lion . . .

Transfixed, Saphay the voyeuse spied on this latest peculiar union. She felt her own loins tingle. Animal amorousness had never moved her before, but she had been so long without congress, and this dog was also a deity who took the persona of a youngish man.

They concluded, the cat squalling. As the dog Yyrot pulled away, the cat turned on him, as cats do with their ordinary mates, and slashed him across the muzzle with her claws. Dog-Yyrot suffered the attack stoically.

Saphay, inebriated and daft, wandered about picking the salad and the irises from the mud.

'I shall wake properly soon. Then all this will be as it was.'

But when she ambled back into the subsiding house, she thought better of it and moved out again. She sat under a tree whose black trunk had emerged steaming, carved like a pillar and garlanded with red buds. Here she started to nibble the fresh salad. She put the irises into her long and unwashed hair.

Presently she saw Yyrot again in his man-form, seated across from her on the back of what she took to be a black obsidian frog of unusual size.

'Will you kill me now?' asked beer-and-warmth feisty Saphay.

Yyrot considered. 'I think,' he said, 'I shall make you what he made you – or began to.'

'What did *he* . . .?' She did not need to question, he meant the other one, Zeth. 'What did *he* begin to make of me?'

'One of his own kind,' said Yyrot. He sighed, and a wild apricot vine sprayed out a bough of tawny ripening fruits. Before things could alter, Saphay snatched several and crammed them in her mouth. She had become properly opportunistic.

For that reason, too, she did not remonstrate with Yyrot.

All the gods of Ruk Kar Is were insane – one knew this from childhood. Had she ever believed in them, until forced to?

Yyrot said, 'I mean one of *his* kind, one of *my* kind.'

'A god.' No shyness was in her voice.

'By what he did to you,' said Yyrot, ominously frowning now, so the apricots on the vine went black, and she was glad to have seized and eaten those she had. 'By that, it started in you. Your son is something else of another sort. But *you*, you are damaged enough by your rapist's divine intervention to be remade in our image.'

Men evaded, or promised things, and normally lied. Saphay thought of her father Vuldir, of Athluan. The god Zezeth had raped her certainly. She was changed.

She sat on the warm mud under the trees, put back her head and fell asleep.

There was a body lying on the plains, spoiling the snow's pristine quality. It had been, before fleers found it, the cadaver of an old woman. She had not had the stamina to complete her journey as, with suitable etheric help, a younger woman might have. But neither had that sort of help occurred.

When living, she had been a sibulla of Ranjal, goddess of wood. Her name, when she had had a name, had been Narnifa. She alone, of her group of priestesses in Ranjalla, was prepared to set out in pursuit of her vanished goddess, whom she had served nearly since infancy. Ranjal had run off after the horrid Red-Hair boy called Nameless. The sibulla had felt it her duty – and her only recourse – to run after Ranjal.

Her sisters had tried to dissuade her. She had tried to persuade *them* to go with her. They would not, knowing their limitations. Even the village-city's witch had arrived, saying she had seen in her house-stove fire the hopelessness of any such endeavour. But Narnifa did not pay attention. She could think of nothing else to do save die at once.

She did not foresee that, anyway, the desertion of the village-city by its goddess would destroy Ranjalla's equilibrium. If she had only waited, there might have been other deserters to go with her on her quest. But she did not wait.

Old and worn down, Narnifa was not the stuff of epic heroines. Yet from her psychic ability she knew which direction to take. Off she went, hobbling on the white waste, now and then mouthing up gruel from a bottle, never acknowledging the onslaught of the cold.

One night, after she had been travelling incredibly many days and the gruel was frozen, and she had slept here and there as she trudged, Narnifa had seen Ranjal, flying above and ahead of her, on a moon-luminous dusk, like a swarm of hornets that comprised all the different Ranjal-statues from the village.

When had the goddess learned to fly? Perhaps she had learned it from watching Nameless walk up trees and then bound from one bough to another. Or it was inherent, and only just realized.

Narnifa perceived why the goddess had abandoned her worshippers, oh yes. *Nothing* was what Ranjal demanded. So Ranjalla had offered her gifts of nothing, measured out in handfuls and, on certain festival days, carried to her shrines in large empty vessels. But he, Nameless, he had given her *things*. He had corrupted her. Seduced, the goddess had fallen in love with him and left her people behind.

When she saw the swarm of Ranjals flying ahead of her, Narnifa had burst into a gallop. It was this which killed her. Her worn-out body, already scaled with frostbite on its serpentine mottles, got only a negligible distance before she toppled. She felt no pain, but then no pain could have been worse to her than losing her god.

That night, as Narnifa's dead body lay in the snow, wolves approached and, later, fleers. In the air nearby any Jafn would have noted that a pair of sihpps hung, feeding on the feeding.

Narnifa, being dead, had no say in that. The Ranjals anyway were already far off. On the very evening that Nameless received from his adoptive Uncle Guri the name of Lionwolf, all the statues were swarming in over the last lap of the sky, their long-nailed many-handed arms outstretched. The subsequent meeting, Narnifa was spared from seeing. At least she had never heard the abhorred Nameless remark that her goddess herself was only a lump of wood.

As Lionwolf, who had been Nameless, rode along the coast, his supernatural Uncle Guri rode behind him in the chariot. The Jafn did not *see* Guri, but they sensed him. And now and then they saw things he *did* – a windless ruffling of a tent-side, a single footprint artistically planted in the snow.

The weather had put on another garment. The skies were clear, a sheer silvery blue. The men and their vehicles moved under the face of the sun by day, and at night beneath three clean moons of varying sizes and forms, and clouds only of corruscating stars of many colours.

They tended westerly. Wherever a Thing Place stood, they made a camp, and the mages of the allied Jafn sent to those others whose holdings lay inland along the route. Not one of the warriors who had fought against the Klow and razed the Klowan-garth went home to his own stronghold. Instead, more of those who had remained behind were called out to join this ride beside the sea's edge.

During blue days, they heard the ice floes that elongated the shore cracking sometimes. Channels opened, frequently very deep. These they bridged with trees felled at the brink of the handy ice-forests which also edged the shoreline of the land. Men ran across whooping, chariots were driven over behind the impervious, leaping lion-teams. He, Nameless – the one they were now coming to name Lionwolf – careered his own chariot across, silent and careless – the beasts, the car, himself, all in equipoise, like some athletic work in bronze.

The Things – where meetings were made with other peoples of the Jafn – were as curious as the antique, seventeen-masted ship where four Jafn peoples had allied already against Rothger's Klow. One Thing was a mammoth which had frozen in a foundered berg of glass-green ice; another was a mystic pole of petrified wood that rose to a height of a hundred feet, twenty shield-lengths or more.

At one of the first of these stops, the Kree had chosen for themselves their new Chaiord in dead foul Lokesh's stead. Once elected, this chieftain had gone over to Lionwolf. Lionwolf had embraced him like the brother he had lost when Lokesh was found culpable. The Kree shouted their approval – but it was more than affection or manners. Lionwolf's embrace of the new Kree Chaiord had given him Lionwolf's approval, which was that of a hero, and would soon be that of an overlord. Not a man who did not guess or know this, not one who felt inclined to protest.

He, the red-haired Borjiy, held them in the palm of his hand, as he had held the mage-coal that demonstrated his destiny – and had rendered him his proper name.

Lionwolf. They took to the name, too. It was right for him. They liked it.

He had by then acquired his own standard. They had already offered him the Lion banner of the Jafn Klow. He had reminded them the Klow were gone, their identity expunged from the world. In the end, after he had told them his other name, he chose for himself a standard. It had a look of Olchibe, slightly. It had a look of nothing quite like that which had been used in the west, east or north.

Village women from the forests made it, and a smith attached to the march.

The bulk of the Jafn horde, his allied army under all its own banners, swelled. Informal in some ways, yet they had their own methods of establishing hierarchy – and that was beyond the titles 'Chaiord' or 'Borjiy'. By shooting at marks, wrestling, fighting with swords, jumping obstacles, racing man against man, chariot against chariot – these playful recreations indulged in when another nation would have snatched a few hours' sleep – lit up for them who was best among them.

They began to say that this era had been especially forged by God. And *for* this era, He had, in the furnace of His ineffable Consciousness, also coined Lionwolf.

There had been a notion, a future-myth, time out of mind, that one among them might unify the Jafn as a single body, and lead them on to conquer the earth.

And though they did not ceremoniously make Lionwolf their king, though they had, each clan, their own leader, though they called this marching now an *adventure* not a war, and addressed Lionwolf *only* by his name. Yet . . .

Yet he was lord, by then, of all.

And yet, too, they were hungry for conquest. Their numbers were now vast. At every Thing Meet these increased, and after too, as never-ending crowds of men came coursing in, in chariots and on the backs of riding-hnowas. With them they brought also their war mages, their best witches; and from the fisher huts and steads, too, men took off like bolting foxes to add themselves to this onrush. Those left behind to guard the garths and villages had been picked by lot, unwillingly. No one wished to stay home.

Seen from above, as sun, moon and stars – as their God – saw them, the host was now seemingly beyond measure. A shadow tipped with points of metal, and by night of fire, it crept forward with a deceptive slowness, turned the corner of the shore, and crawled on into the Marginal Land, towards Olchibe, Gech, and the furthest North.

Having regarded the mammoth in the ice, dead obviously and only preserved by cold – not as Saphay had been, living, in her berg – Guri was unsettled.

An invisible presence, he whirled about the march and the camps, vaguely troubling to them, like a sort of mild psychic indigestion in the army's viscera.

Though Guri would still absent himself in his unearthly, vanishing sleeps, awake he took no time for himself. He left the 'tween-world alone. It seemed to him his nephew emotionally needed him. This had not, of course, been the case with his former leader, Peb Yuve. But, then, this boy was in some ways so young, still ten or eleven. You forgot that. Then, again, Peb had been only seventeen or so when Guri, a boy himself of ten, had aspired to add himself to Peb's vandal band.

It was not that Lionwolf was unconfident – rather the reverse. However, Guri stayed about.

Also it was the idea of Olchibe.

As they neared the Marginal Land, something in Guri – some type of heart – beat rapidly.

That evening he was standing up on an escarpment of snow, pushed into a curved shape by the recent tepid days. From there he looked towards the north.

For miles spread curded ice-jungle. The sea now was distant on the right hand, opalescent black under two thin moons.

Guri glanced at the sky. This was when he saw the squadron of Ranjals coming in on the twilight.

Guri recognized them as the wooden images from the village-city. Even so, to be sure, he dived upward, peered, slewed and zoomed away.

The Jafn had lighted their fires and put up tents for the night, since it was a sleep nocturnal. Lionwolf's tent was the same as all the rest, but set to one side, up the escarpment, where snow-oaks, three-quarters buried in the drifts, lifted their daggered crowns.

Not looking about, Lionwolf spoke to Guri the instant he arrived.

'What makes the gods of the Ruk mad?'

Often such questions, out of nowhere.

'Being a god's enough to send any of us mad,' said Guri.

'You mean me?'

'No, not you. You're half mortal. But there's something outside, flying in—'

Beyond the tent, men had begun yelling. A concerted rumble of lions came like thunder, and to this was added the shocking sizzle of bowstrings and released spears.

'Useless,' said Guri. 'What do they think *that* can do?'

Lionwolf sprang from the tent. They stood together, as spectators.

Personally, Guri had been surprised for some time that Saphay had not signalled either her son or Guri himself. It was always a woman's way to go after or call out to you when you were busy. That Saphay had not done so was rather odd, but this now was just what Guri expected of females. Although the statues were a goddess, she was a female too. Rather than call after Lionwolf, she had *pursued* him.

Spears, arrows, a thrown knife or two flashed unavailingly around the swarm, which now was flying in very low. Men threw themselves flat.

The several shes landed in a bundle on the slope above the camp, below Lionwolf's tent.

The Jafn were mewling all kinds of stuff: prayers, imprecations.

Mages were emerging from the camp, shaking up threatening fires.

'Good evening, lady,' said Lionwolf.

Below, all that was visible of the great Jafn assembly gawped up at him, fire-bright under closing darkness.

The Ranjals did not now move.

There were, you thought, about fifteen or so of them. Some were the height of a tall man, and some a woman's height, some were a child's height. Yet others were small, some as little as a squirrel, and these sheltered there among the bigger ones in a way that was ridiculous, nearly touching – if they had not also looked so macabre, like a thicket full of broomsticks and talons.

Lionwolf strode down the slope. He stopped by the Ranjals and bowed, careless and graceful, rather as he had been when crossing the tree-bridges over chasms.

He indicated the camp. 'These are my Jafn kindred, lady,' he said to the Ranjals, 'my warriors.' Then he glanced down the escarpment to the men, seeming as usual to look – for all of them that could see him – a moment in their eyes. 'This is the goddess of my boyhood, sirs. Under God there are many such deities.'

Uncertain, the Jafn host regarded the thicket on the slope. Then some far back, not having heard, not seeing fully what went on but sensing as ever Lionwolf could do no wrong, began to call and bang sword and knife hilts on chariot-rails and armour. The rollicking cheer spread up through the lines in waves.

All the mages had stalled, letting their mage-fires soften and drift, or go out.

Lionwolf – when Nameless – had claimed it was he made Ranjal talk. But it appeared she had learned from that, for now she independently addressed him – and in fifteen or so combined voices.

'No emptiness, this?'

'None, lady. Full of men and war.'

'What will have you of me?'

Lionwolf smiled. Though so young, being equipped

physically and mentally as a grown male, he had gained early many knacks for pleasing women.

'Your presence here, lady, is enough.'

Turning, he broke a bough from one of the sunken oaks, and tattled off the ice. Sombre green-brazen leaves, like fine-spun metal, gleamed in firelight. Lionwolf placed the green bough at the feet of the taller Ranjals.

Guri sat cross-legged on the snow, looking on. None of them could detect him, even the Ranjals could not; they never had in the past.

The Ranjals began to murmur. It was like twigs scratching at a window.

'For the leaves, want you be tell story?' asked the Ranjal voices.

Lionwolf must have nodded. Without delay, the statues began to unfold the tale Lionwolf, in play, had long ago invented for them to tell him – one of Saphay's stories adapted. The Ranjals promised to Lionwolf, as always in his childhood and later too, the same vast riches, the three wives of surpassing loveliness, the army fully armed, the world at his feet.

These twiggy whisperings smoked down the slope; they sank into the camp. Everywhere they were heard, or partly heard, and repeated. They sprinkled men's faces like a light sweat.

'Amen,' said Guri under his breath, seeing that something deeply supernormal, if absurd, had once more taken place.

That night, the Ranjals stood before the tent of Lionwolf as he slept two hours of the allotted nocturnal. When everyone was awake again, the goddess-entity joined the march into the north.

The Ranjals had become inert again, having achieved their goal. Accordingly they were mounted on a cart with runners, pulled by three rainbow-caparisoned hnowas. They travelled among the pole-raised Jafn icons.

Every morning, Lionwolf was seen to offer the Ranjals titbits: flowers if found, such things.

Sometimes they spoke again.

They would actually speak to any man who addressed them courteously by their name. They would tell fortunes, always glamorous and encouraging. But they would accept no offering from any save Lionwolf. 'Ask nothing, I,' they said. Some of the men got in the way of it, setting a handful of nothing carefully before the Ranjal thicket in its cart, in return for a blessing or a tale of joys to come.

The weather continued smooth and blue.

A cobalt pre-dawn filled the sky, and Guri, who had been sleeping in the Otherwhere, woke with dim vestigial memories, to note an old woman prowling about. Women, even prostitutes or witches, were rare among Jafn on campaign. So the old woman bothered him instantly.

It had not been a sleep night for anyone else, and the warriors, including their Chaiords and Lionwolf, were some way off along the sheet-ice, wrestling. Hunting parties were coming in and breakfasts being cooked. None saw the old woman, except Guri.

But, then, much about her – for example, how the burgeoning glow of dawn showed through her rags, her hair, her *back* – indicated something else. She was like Guri himself: she was not alive.

Guri blew down to where she had parked herself. This was beside the cart with the rainbow-fringed hnowas snoring in the shafts. The Ranjals were there in it, and a couple

250

of men idling with them, listening to the predictable jolly news the Ranjals always gave. Nearby was posted Lionwolf's standard.

The old woman wailed.

The petitioning men did not hear.

Guri saw now her face was mottled, snake-like, even though partially translucent.

He stood behind her and uttered loudly, for her ears only: 'What?'

She heard him, of course. She looked over her fragile old shoulder at him, her face puckered with unhappiness and rage.

'She . . . she . . . why she here? She mine. Want her.'

'You can't have her, old girl. You're one of the *sibulls* from the snow-village, aren't you, ah? You must have died of loss, when this one left you.'

'Died? Never died. Hold your tongue.'

'You hold yours, you silly old crone.' Guri startled himself with his vehemence. He was furious to be so spoken to by a woman, neither Olchibe mother nor Crarrow. Then he checked himself, realizing she riled him mostly because she was one of his own kind now.

He stood there scowling fearsomely at her, ignored. He was at a loss. Then the sun rose, and with a despairing squeak she faded out like one of the stars. A feeble ghost, after all. Even so, he must look out for her, for even her sort could sometimes cause trouble, if legend was to be believed.

By the end of that day, the host had penetrated the Marginal Land.

Guri was prickly with anticipation. Soon he would be

among his own. And his peoples must be won, or annexed bloodily, to the general scheme. Which?

'Stir up the fire.'

    'Cast in the blood.'

    'Bear claw and wolf tongue . . .'

    'Bitter honey, sour wine . . .'

Four in total, the deadliest and most fervent number of power in the North, the Crarrowin circled their bonfire, which was yellow as the eye of a cat, and less yellow than their skins.

Night had been drawn like a curtain in that spot, the stars like spangles stitched on, meaningless.

Round and round the women went.

    'Crushed bone from a battle . . .'

    'Cracked bone from a foe . . .'

    'Whale tusk and fish-hide . . .'

    'Spices, amber, and plucked-out hair.'

As with all such covens, the four general ages and states of a woman were represented. One was a child still, about nine years; one a virgin girl of fourteen; the third was a woman capable of child-bearing who had borne, and indeed from the look of her she was now pregnant again. The fourth Crarrow, their Crax, was past reproduction, though in this case not yet old.

Circling, they stared into the flames.

All around, the huge night was not silent. Jungle forests massed in every direction. From these, things sometimes warbled, eerie accompaniment to the slush-slush of women's feet, the chanting.

Then motion and voices ceased. The four Crarrowin

grouped about the fire. Nothing else happened. In the flames no shape occurred. Slowly the women turned their backs, and looked away to the world's four corners: north towards Gech, south and west towards Rukar lands, east towards the Jafn.

It was the youngest one who faced that way. She said, 'From there.'

'But also from here,' said the pregnant woman who gazed southwards.

'From this way, too,' said the virgin girl, pointing a slender, butter-coloured finger at the west.

The Crax stepped out of their cornered circle. She raised her left arm towards the sky and, with her right hand held low, indicated the earth as well. 'Above – and beneath.'

The fire, which had done apparently nothing save eat what had been tossed into it, rippled and furled up into the night, in a ball. It hung over the Crarrowin a moment, like a blazing canopy. Then you saw what the fire had been, for it separated into four streams, and oozed slowly back in at each woman's abdomen, even that of the woman whose belly was swollen with child. The Crarrowin received the fire once again without agitation or comment. It was their personal incendiary, which they could draw out of their bodies at any juncture, to warm themselves or others.

'We must go and tell the Great One,' said the Crax.

She awarded him that title as she considered him to be worthy among the several leaders of the Olchibe. Under his jurisdiction ran thirteen vandal bands, all told some five thousand men.

The women pulled folds of their loose, black fur mantles up over their heads. Their faces shrank behind the fur. Gliding on foot across the snow, they resembled four black pillars, and all a similar height – for Olchibe young grew quickly, and full-grown examples of Olchibe women were seldom tall.

Down from the upper ground of the clearing they went, and moved off into the jungle below. Here there was a narrow track made of cut logs, which they followed for most of an hour. At the end of the track lay the sluhtin of Peb Yuve.

This community was impressive in its size and standing. The individual sluhts clotted one against another, dispersed through many clearings, covering a stretch of three or four miles. The communal roof, multi-layered of wood, leather, feathers, ice and other materials, rose and fell geographically. Out of it poked countless chimneys. Above, the frozen arches of figs and pineapple stems were stained red and orange from years of sluhtin smokes.

Men standing watch let the four Crarrowin through without a word. They were anyway expected.

Beyond the entrance, the air fogged over. It was humid, and odorous too, from the blond mammoths which moved, phantasmal in shadow, at their indoor pickets, slowly champing from bins of dormant grass and grain. They were peaceful when at home. They shuffled hugely and softly out of the way of the coven, rather as the men had done outside.

The sluhtin opened out. It was in reality a kind of enormous indoor camp, and everywhere throughout the clustered halls the fires burned in their clay ovens. The floor was mud, thawed from much continuous warmth, and here children played, rolling and hilarious. At the Crarrowin they only stared, too young yet to be properly impressed. But the women at the fires, and the stalking men, made gestures of respect.

Yuve was in one of the central halls. He sat on a heap of pelts, involved in a game that used teeth knocked out of assorted enemy skulls, and decoratively painted. His favourite seconds, thirty warriors, crouched around, drinking, and ready to assist the game moves, when called on.

But now that the Crarrowin were there, all that ended.

Peb Yuve stood up. He touched his right fist to his forehead, and gestured about him, offering everything to the Crax, if she would take it. The formalities over, the Crax spoke.

'He's coming, Great One – almost here. He brings a large force with him: Jafn peoples, as we've heard. But it's more than that, as we suspected, for he's unhuman.'

'Unhuman? How?'

'Half god.'

'Only half?' said Yuve. His braids had greyed, but he was hale and strong. He looked at his seconds, and grinned his own healthy, painted teeth. 'It's one of the mad gods of the Rukar got him, so you say. There is only one order of Great Gods. Our own.'

'Amen,' chorused the seconds.

'So,' said Yuve, 'this half-god. So.'

'He will win you,' said the Crax.

'How? In a fight?'

'In love,' said the Crax.

No other man, let alone woman, could have told Peb Yuve such a thing. But the Crarrowin did as they must.

Peb drew his brows together. He said, 'I don't give my love to any living thing without it's earned.'

The Crax put back the fold of fur from her head. Peb

looked at her levelly. She was one of his wives. It had not been etiquette to allow recognition of that before.

'I know it,' she said.

'You know, but still you tell me I'll be won. Is it then written somewhere, Wife?'

'Yes,' said Peb's wife. 'Written by a blue sun on a page of burning snow.'

Before he entered the tent, Guri paused. He looked up at the stars. A strange nostalgia was on him, and he thought it was only for the past – and for his people. He had beheld them tonight, springing towards them through snow and landscape, space and time. For a brief instant that was also a day and a night, he had patrolled the border of their lives. Never till now had he gone back to Olchibe. It was as he recalled: the sluhtins, the contained starlike fires.

On a bare hill of ice above jungles of basalt and chiming rime, Crarrowin had made, fed and reabsorbed their personal flames. Guri had offered to them the appropriate show of respect, even though it seemed he was invisible and it no longer mattered that he trespassed on their rite. They had not, evidently, sensed him. Or maybe the Crax alone had, somewhat. He had once known her as a coven woman of thirty – she had allowed Guri, then, to give her the first of her kiddlings. This time he had not gone close.

Guri dropped the memory, like a cloak on the ice, and walked in through the tent wall.

'Now you need me,' Guri said.

Lionwolf, who had been preparing his bow for a night hunt, looked up at him. He neither accepted nor denied the statement. Guri thought Lionwolf was beginning to learn magnificently well the gambit of lordly silence.

Guri glanced sidelong. Over the lighted tent spread Lionwolf's shadow. It seemed only mundane. And then Guri caught the ruby wink, tiny glints like eyes, little creatures hidden in the shadow's folds.

'I'll tell you exactly what you must do among the Olchibe,' said Guri. He stood very upright, clothed in pride; this was a mighty gift he gave the young man. To no other, ever, would Guri have given it. 'The greatest leader among them now will be Peb Yuve, that I served when I *lived*. He's gathered in many bands over these years, just as you have, now. It was only to be reckoned on – he's a master among men.'

'Yes?'

Something shook itself in Guri's a-physical blood. He said bluntly, 'In only a few months you've changed your whistling. Do you scorn the Olchibe now? Is that your Jafn piss-idiot side, or your shit-idiot Rukar side? Ah?'

Lionwolf came across to Guri. He put both hands on Guri's shoulders, as few else would be able to. 'Wait, Uncle, I only said *Yes*.' His hands were warm, affectionate and consoling.

Guri considered. He was not immune to Lionwolf's exercise of charisma. Who was, or could be? Yet something in Guri moved aside now, glaring, angry. He reviewed in that moment how he had not informed Lionwolf about the old sibull who haunted the Ranjals.

Guri knew that he was about to betray his former leader, Peb, whom Guri had called Great One – betray him to this Lionwolf that Guri had only just named.

However, only women resorted to sullenness at such

times. Guri straightened out his mind, and rendered his nephew the lessons he would need before the hunt began.

Across the packed undulations of snow, from a backdrop of ice-jungle and in the dark of the moons, something roved that glowed pale in starlight.

From the other direction ran something else, in a fizzing of snow-spritzed wheels and lion claws.

Seated on the high back of his mount, Peb Yuve glowered at the horizon. 'What's there.' It was not a question but an affirmation.

The fifty mammoths trod to a halt.

They stood like marble under the stars. As what came towards them came on.

Lionwolf drove his own chariot. His sole visible companion in the car was the standard he had chosen for himself. It was hammered into the chariot floor, and fastened to its side by pins of steel. It had been thought no impediment to the hunting, not tonight, for they had known, all of them – from the precognitives among their mages – what they would meet.

As he saw the bulk of the mammoths appear like other hills over the snowline, Lionwolf suddenly remembered a toy Guri had given him as a child.

Judicially, Lionwolf compared the vast mound of each beast to that toy. He dismissed the toy.

He was strongly excited but serene: this was often his dual condition. It happened like that because everything was still so *new*, yet he so confident and able – *self-possessed*.

That was Peb Yuve, then, that man on the foremost mammoth. Like Guri, but *unlike*, Yuve had gone on ageing. The spray of braids was full of grey and white. On the dark ochre cheeks spun tattoos of authority.

Lionwolf drove his chariot straight at the hillock of Yuve's mammoth, and veered across the animal's front, showering up at it the riven snow. The mammoth did not react: it towered, arrogant, above him.

Lionwolf, with the mildest twitch of the reins, brought his team to stasis.

'Greetings, Great One,' Lionwolf called to the leader on the monstrously enlarged toy. 'A lucky night for hunting – no moons. Let me entreat you, will you add your hunter's cunning to our task? We're strangers here.'

He spoke in Olchibe. It was flawless – Guri had taught him long ago. It was *choice* to employ the language, to see this ageing man crease his already age-pleated brow and stare down at him, and all his attendant warriors likewise.

'Who are you?' Peb Yuve said at last.

'Myself.'

The Olchibe men glanced from one to another. They saw that this 'stranger' grasped the value of the Riddle, and the secret thing.

Peb Yuve nodded. 'I was warned you were on your way.'

'They warned me too,' said Lionwolf, impeccable, 'that a hero and leader waited on the road before me.'

'What is it, your standard? What,' said Peb Yuve, 'does it mean? I've never seen the like of it.'

'My Jafn father died before I was born,' said Lionwolf. 'For that reason the emblem is impossible.'

'A blue sun of hammered metal,' said Peb Yuve, 'and rent silks fluttering below – fluttering red and yellow, like flames.'

'My thanks to you, Great One, for noticing the rag.'

Peb Yuve said, 'There is a multitude of Jafn over the hills, but you ride out here with only twenty men?'

'What use are twenty million men,' said Lionwolf, 'if the Great Gods desert them?'

'You know our ways.'

'I know some of your ways.'

'How do you know them?'

'My life was saved, when I was a child, by a warrior of the Olchibe.'

'Yes, if you were a child, he would have saved you. His name?'

'He let me call him *Uncle*.'

'But what was his name?'

'That of a brave man, father of many, killer of more.'

'How was he known to other men?'

Lionwolf showed obedience in the Olchibe fashion – fist to head, but head unbowed.

'The Great One isn't to be put off. He is, my Olchibe uncle, known as Guri.'

Peb Yuve blinked once, that was all.

He said, slow and quietly, 'It's a name not uncommon among the sluhtins. Do you have its meaning?'

'Star Dog.'

'Yes.'

A slim white wind came spiralling along the top-snow.

To the twenty Jafn the wind was crowded with sprites. To Peb Yuve the wind was the breath of Gods.

Lionwolf, despite any form or illusion, thought of the wind as a wind, with ice on it.

'We'll hunt then,' said Peb Yuve. 'Do you know how we hunt, we Olchibe bands?'

Lionwolf unslung the Olchibe bow from his back. 'Perhaps you will decide if I do or not.'

The Olchibe men ululated. Their mammoths were unlocked, all at once, into a prolonged sprint. The Jafn had heard of this, some had seen it before. To Lionwolf, of course, such mobility had long ago been described in detail.

He set his chariot to keep pace, the reins around his waist.

Peb beheld below, from the gallery of his mammoth's back, a flame of man and chariot, keeping pace and next outstripping him.

They surged northward. The Olchibe, who had already come out this way, had started up game en route. Now deer dashed from the frozen thickets before the hunters.

Peb Yuve saw how the one charioteer ahead of him loosed three arrows, sometimes four, every time all at once from his bow. Each found a target, and cleanly. The Olchibe leader could not see quite how it was done. He had never known any man, himself included, who could release and successfully guide more than two shafts together, while riding.

Soon they let the remainder of the deer go, having taken enough. The hunt had been hard, lucky, and extremely short.

They dismounted, Peb Yuve waiting until his beast had

kneeled. He went over to the young man who now, amid the sea of death and meat on the blood-smoking snow, attended to his own kills – there were twenty-three of them. No other single man, Jafn or Olchibe, had felled so many.

'I ask again, who are you?' said Peb Yuve.

Lionwolf smiled at him. Was ever any creature so beautiful? Even women were not, even Olchibe women of fifteen years, with their hair unbound and rubbed with spice. But it was less simple in that way, too, for Peb did not fancy this man.

Disgusted at himself, at his own wonderment which this out-tribe foreigner had kindled so very fast, Peb Yuve knew enough to be staid. He judged swiftly, judged himself, then put the judgement aside.

He had been told, after all. There was still much in reserve.

'I don't know, Great One,' said Lionwolf, 'I don't know what I am.'

'Still the Riddle?'

'No, the truth.'

Peb Yuve blinked again. He stared. Then, not turning his head, he ordered some of his own warriors forward to gut and blood Lionwolf's deer. 'There are white bear near our sluhtin,' he said. 'Have you hunted bear?'

'Now and then.'

'Our wise-women value the bear, so we let them alone. However,' said Peb Yuve, 'one's been annoying us, going after our kiddles, mauling our animals and leaving them useless to us.'

Lionwolf stood quickly to wipe his hands clean on the snow. Peb noted they were callused, workmanlike, but also, in shape, the hands of a prince. Yes, he had Rukar blood, he was god-gotten – even if the god was worthless and cracked, and he lied about it. The god-gotten one straightened. Peb said, 'If you wish, ride the mammoth there. My second will allow you.'

Lionwolf glanced across. The second had already dismounted. He was grinning, waiting for this paragon to make a fool of himself in front of them all.

'You honour me too much,' said Lionwolf.

He went over to the mammoth, which had now stood up to its full towering height. He did not attempt to order it to kneel, although Guri had taught him how. Instead, as was his habit with heights, hills, trees, Lionwolf walked calmly up the beast's hairy side. The Jafn, who had observed this before, watched in reverence. The Olchibe watched too, but with faces of iron.

At the top of the mammoth, Lionwolf swung easily into its curious saddle-seat. He scratched firmly over the animal's head, through its greasy hair, and above the trunk and tusks. Enjoying this, the mammoth snorted softly.

Leaving the Jafn to their butcher business, the Olchibe and the Stranger, who knew some of their ways, went on after bears.

Peb's wife, the Crax, had said to him, 'To kill the bear is a true test. If he makes a mess of it, he'll rouse up the wrath of the forests. If he fails to complete the task, whatever else he is he's no warrior and is worthless.'

But when the red-haired man was shown the place of the lair, high up in a shelf of snow, among the crystalline branches of the fig trees, again he performed magic.

He called to the bear, gentle like a lover – a mother. And the bear came shambling from its cave. It was old and black-toothed, and that was why it had gone for the babies and the lamasceps. Nevertheless, its coat was like the driven snow.

The red magician climbed up towards the old, malevo-lent bear. He did this without any sign of nervousness or even caution. Reaching the bear, he softly touched it on the side, and it lay down before him. That was all.

Peb and his nearest seconds had dismounted, and stood around in a semicircle below the snow-cave. They looked in silence. When the magician called to them, they climbed up, too, to see. The bear was dead, as if it slept. There was not a wound on it, the pelt unmarked.

'Tell me your name now,' said Peb Yuve. 'You've shown you're the mage-kind. You'll have no fear in being known.'

'Lionwolf.'

Through the jungle something passed. No wind now; perhaps it was the departing life-force of the dead bear.

'Who named you with such a name?'

'I,' said a man whom Peb Yuve saw, only in that moment, positioned by Lionwolf's shoulder.

He was Olchibe, and young enough, about thirty years of age. His hair had been elaborately braided for this social event, that of meeting his leader after eleven years of death.

'What are *you*?' said Peb.

'I was yours,' said Guri. He was rigid with emotion – with the anguish of this excrutiating scene of refinding.

Did Peb remember Guri?

Guri thought he did not. Why would he? A leader's warriors came and went, lived and died, just like bears.

No other man could make out Guri. They could see only the footprints he had let them see, appearing without him in the snow.

'If you were ever mine,' said Peb Yuve, 'now you're his.

You're the one he calls "Uncle". You taught him Olchibe customs?'

The vandal band heard Peb talking to another that was not to be seen, above those disembodied footprints.

Jafn magic.

Guri said to his leader, who *had* forgotten him, 'Great One, as your wife, who is a Crax, foretold you, this man, though son-by-law to a Chaiord, is in fact the son of a god through a mortal woman. Her name's Saphay. Do you recollect a princess of the Rukar you meant to steal? That was her. You sent me to fetch her, but I failed.'

'You *speak* like a Rukar,' said Peb Yuve.

Guri was taken aback. He felt ashamed, aware that was possible. He had spent a long while with Saphay, and with this nephew.

He only said, 'If you remember the woman, you'll know you might have kept her. She was young and good-looking and strong of mind, spirit and body. She would have borne you sons. One of them might have been *this* one.'

Peb Yuve looked away from the revenant of his warrior. He looked again at Lionwolf, who had collected the name of a mystic hybrid of Gech, and a blue sun standard. Gazing back at him, over the white bear, Lionwolf was not humble, nor vainglorious.

You, Peb thought stonily, *you, Wife, you have done this. By telling me he would win me, you put it on me. Now I can only be won.*

'Since you woo we Olchibe, what do you want of us?'

'To make war pact with you. All Jafn is here already.'

'The Jafn despise Olchibe. Olchibe has contempt for Jafn.'

'That can be put aside. Mutual tolerance will advance mutual benefit.'

'Why?'

'Gech will come over to us. Do you want to miss what Gech can have?'

'Which is?'

'Let us grow great enough, and we ride south together against the Ruk. Though Olchibe scorns the Jafn, the Ruk you hate.'

'Yes, that's true. We hate them. In the long ago, the Rukar disembowelled our land. They had our kind as slaves, and burned the sluht-city of Sham, which is now a dunghill.'

'Well, then. You've taken little bites off the Ruk for centuries. Don't you have a taste now for the whole dish? We'll rend the Rukar all in shreds, Peb Yuve,' said Lionwolf, using the leader's name, as fellow leader, or magician, either, might do. 'The spoils of their cities shall be ours and yours, to redress the sorrow of Sham. They shall cover us in liquid gold and pearl, give us their women to breed on, and their gardens to feed on, for a thousand years.'

'Your mother is Rukar, so your shadow-uncle says.'

'My mother,' said Lionwolf, 'will mount the flat ruins of Ru Karismi and *dance*.'

His attempt to bring Saphay to Peb Yuve had cost Guri his earthly life. Peb Yuve perhaps somewhat remembered Saphay, Guri he mislaid.

And Guri had now betrayed Peb Yuve anyway, acting as

Lionwolf's second, setting himself before Peb as the ally of another – doing all he had promised Lionwolf he would.

This seethed inside Guri like a fermenting bane. His birthrights were gone for ever.

So, he ran, he *flew*, as he had so often and often, over the ice floes, along the crinkled black edges of the sea, inland through forests of turquoise and caverns of night.

Returning to the snow-forest and the village-city of Ranjal, Guri saw none of his journey. He had not been concentrating on that.

The Olchibe, as he departed, were at a meal, eating the bear meat of Lionwolf's kill, the faultless pelt having been presented to the Crax, Peb's wife. All this had . . . offended Guri.

So, it was the chat about the woman that he kept hold of – Saphay. They had left her there; Lionwolf had left her. Now she was for her son just a symbol, it seemed, dancing on the wreck of a city. Lionwolf – worse than Peb – *forgot*, he forgot his mother, forgot his goddess there in the bloody cart, which was haunted by an intermittent old woman. He forgot Guri.

He was a child, the Lionwolf, but without a child's affectionate need or awareness of fair play, however harsh. His situation had developed: he had more to occupy him now.

Guri landed in the snow-forest, cursing and bristling. It was almost sun-up. He must make sure of Saphay.

Presently he noticed the lanes of packed ice and snow were melted everywhere, like candles, into grotesque shapes. Sky thrust through, embarrassed and flushing with dawn.

When Guri came to the village, it was over. Everything

had thawed and gone down. Metal pipes and other objects, pieces of wood and purposeless implements, lay everywhere. Trees sprang acid green among the debris. Berries drooped, arrested, bleeding.

Nabnish's house was also a thing of the past. Yet Guri discovered the decomposing corpse of Nabnish himself nearby. Of Saphay no trace remained, though, kicking through the snowy rubble, Guri saw a woman's combs, a Jafn ring, bits of clothing with black irises growing up about them. Where had she gone?

The holed stone for calling, which he had given her, Guri located. It too was broken.

Even her cat was not to be summoned.

Guri crouched on the melted floor, looking up through the space where the snow walls had formed their chimney. The sky was peach-pink. Into that, Guri deduced, she had been carried.

Ghosts and gods did such things. Yes, it was a god, again, who had her – the second. She was a slut. *One* god had not been enough for her.

Second Intervolumen

Since no mortal man can be, save he grows in a woman's womb, God first created Woman.

Truism of the Crarrowin: Olchibe

Among all the changes that occupy a sky, how could you detect one image that moves constantly, yet never alters?

Clouds – they were clouds where he lived. Perhaps they *were* clouds, of a kind.

Pale, neutral, assuming shades of sunrise and set, sometimes hardly to be seen at all. Catching sun or moon, a piled cumulus with a bulging upper storey, heavy yet weightless, gossamer that was granite.

Ddir, Placer of Stars, sailed slowly over the air. He was quite mindless. His genius, since he was a god, did not require a mind. He looked down often at the iceball of the world. More often he looked *up* into the vistas of the sky. He did not really place stars. Stars had their places already. In his unmind, though, Ddir *did* place the stars, and so, despite making no physical impression on the constellations, yet he did. Now and then mages, even ordinary men, had seen what Ddir had done. How among the stars the form of an animal, or an object, suddenly became evident in the heavens, clear as if drawn on in diamonds. Tonight, Ddir had designed a formation in the night sky like a huge toad. It had been noticed, by the observant or trained, in many lands, glittering. Only those in the Ruk who knew his name knew who was responsible.

*

Beyond Sham, sacked city of rambling markets and mud, lay the Copper Gate, whose metal-plated archway led to Gech. Ice swamps formed the landscape of Gech. Netted by frozen willows and mangrove, it teemed with striped wolverine, apes whose dun fur trailed to the ground, and tree-nesting wolves. Here mankind constructed beehive houses of coldest sludge. Cousin to Olchibe, Gech was different – a people older, more obscure and occult.

Behind the swamps, Northland Gech opened a wilderness. Huge boulders scattered the earth, which seemed to have been flung bad-temperedly from the sky to break. Next mountains pushed through, blind-white with snows. Up there, far above, a plateau spread itself, prehistoric, colossal, uncharted. This region was the Great Uaarb, the ice desert of the North.

The Uaarb was a barren spot. The expanse of it was dry and bone-hard, yet covered by a deluge of white sand, like spillages of salt. This sand was itself made of *volatile* ice. The grains were tiny, and cruel as splinters. Out of their dunes sometimes ice mesas rose, through which daylight gleamed, or the moons.

Those that lived there were nomadic, their skins pitted and darkened by ice-burn, their habits harsh. Like sensnails, they carried their houses and temples with them.

During that afternoon, there had been some banks of cloud. One of these never moved.

That night, across the table of the Uaarb, nomadic astrologers discerned a Toad picked out among the stars.

Presently the invented constellation itself began to change.

After a while it was no longer a Toad but the sparkling

outline of a Hand, fingers pointing down towards the world.

Ddir, nondescript in his garments coloured like dust, descended, walking down the night as if it were a flight of stairs.

Any who had seen – not what he did, but what he appeared to be – would not have given him a first glance, let alone a second.

In the desert of the Uaarb, small winds, ice-devils, twirled and played about Ddir. He walked barefoot among them. With his unmind, the god was thinking.

There had been Zezeth, scintillant and lethal, who had possessed a human woman in the sea under the ice, and so created, apparently unwillingly, a child. Then there was Yyrot, stimulated perversely by this act of Zezeth's, its consequences, and the being who resulted. Yyrot had taken on his canine persona and coupled with a cat. Beings – of a sort – must result also from this. Ddir, pottering about in his cloud, had somehow been alerted; an artisan of great talent, he too now wanted to *make*. Nor would a mere constellation any more satisfy him.

These gods, three of the millions known in the Ruk, themselves knew men. They had grown up amongst mankind, literally, for men had established such gods in their own image. No wonder they went mad.

Having been given to Saphay had linked these three. It was a tenuous enough bond to begin with, for elsewhere they had been split up and awarded, in different trios, to other mortals. Again, it was the act beneath the ice which had so peculiarly fused Zezeth with Yyrot and Ddir. But even that act of lust, rape and insemination, had not been random. For it, too, there must have been some reason . . .

This even the Magikoy had not fathomed. Perhaps they had not looked from that particular angle. As for the gods, they never bothered to find out.

The snow from the northerly mountains had slipped into a shallow valley of the plateau beneath.

White, so white the snow against the swarthier white of the surrounding Uaarb.

Down on to the snow floated Ddir.

He stood looking at it, this blank canvas.

Then he began.

Whiteness parted. It was like a child blowing through thin cloth. Pieces were raised, then folded and blown back. A new slope began to form between, out of the virgin snow.

Only the night and Ddir's stars watched.

They saw the shape in the snow become *swiftly* that of a woman. Her body was long and slender, perfect in proportion, initially featureless in all ways. Then the mound of the sex, the two breasts, lifted irresistibly upward, and upon the soft roundness of the breasts two budded nipples were expressed. At the same moment, from the smooth egg-shell mask of face, two deep-lidded eyes spontaneously sculpted, and two lips, full and flowering; a nose, cheekbones, ears exquisitely arrived. From the modelled forehead, out across the snow, rivers of hair began to gush like steady liquid water from some inner dam. There were narrow flexive hands and feet. There were bodily curves of a slim voluptuousness, like that of some curved knife sheathed in velvet.

Ddir paused assessingly. He, like the dark and the stars, watched carefully now. When at last the shifting planes of the snow finished their work, he walked round the woman, all about her sheer whiteness – this incredibleness he had made.

Then, like some elderly nurse, Ddir clicked his tongue. He was chiding his own oversight. Equipped with limbs, breasts, loins and mouth, lashed eyes and a mantle of hair, unseen organs and teeth, yet this masterpiece had not, of course, been born. She therefore lacked one attribute to make her acceptable to men. Leaning over, he stuck his finger quickly into her level snowy belly, to print the fault-less indent of a navel.

Night, which had been attending patiently, believed now its own instant had come.

The snow must grow living and warm. It must reverse its nature. Ddir opened his artisanic hands, and night poured down through them, and turned the wonderful woman in the snow as black as the blackest jet.

Either Ddir had heard legends outside the Ruk, or many gods simply did these things – and the former legends were true.

A hirdiy of nomads had drawn up at the foot of three mesas. The night had gained an elastic clarity that often came before an ice storm. They had duly tethered the traces of their dog-teams to the ground with spikes, and tied pro-tective bags around the animals' eyes, ears and genitals. Most of the dogs were used to this procedure. Only one young one caused a little bother. The men, women and children got into the hide tents and shut the tent-flaps with metal stays. Four men sat out by the fire to keep watch, their own protection ready.

As yet the weather was glassy, but the moons were up and each had a blurred brownish halo.

'This night for something,' said one of the four watchers. His name was Ipeyek. Though no magician, sometimes he knew things. Lacking either mage or Crarrow, his hirdiy listened to him.

When he said nothing further, another man said, 'More than storm then?'

'Maybe not storm. Only something else.'

That second there was the wind. It started from nothing, nowhere; it rushed over the plateau of the Uaarb. Though not the spinning stinging whirlwind of ice storm, laced with killing ice-grain needles, yet it made the tents tremble. Even the mesas of solid ice seemed to shake.

Then the wind had passed. It had come and it was gone. It did not come again.

The men lifted their heads. Their fire had been blown out.

Ipeyek said, 'Like single breath.'

'God's breath,' they said.

The four men got up and looked in the four directions of the world, to see what would approach next. But it was Ipeyek's ninth son who saw it first.

Only the youngest of the kiddles whimpered when the great wind blew over – like the inexperienced young dog, they had not yet learned you must take precautions, but complaint was valueless. Ipeyek's ninth son, at three years old, was well versed in the lesson. As his two mothers comforted the babies, the child, hearing before the others did that the wind was gone, and curious, poked his head out of a slit in the tent.

So he saw her.

Even the night now was not so dark. It was, however, as if actual Night walked naked over the plateau, clad only in a waterfall of hair. And her eyes were stars.

They *called* her Night. That was their name for her. In the subtext of nomadic language, which avoided both verbs and similarly redundant words such as *a* or *the*, Night meant also coldness, and beauty, and a bell-like sound which was composed of silence, distance and eternity. Their word for Night was *Chillel*.

She lived in the hirdiy temple. The temple was the house not of God – for they believed the sky and the earth were all one house to God – but of their ancestors' bones. It was a kind of hard tent, made of lacquered hide, with carven pillar-ribs of fossilized wood. The temple rode on a cart drawn by a team of six dogs, just as the home-tents all did, while other dogs ran alongside carrying packs and utensils, as everywhere among the hirdiy.

By day, she would leave the temple door-flap open as they journeyed. The nomads could see her, Night, sitting among the lacquer caskets of skeletons.

She said nothing. She had never spoken to them, or made any noise. They did not know if she had a voice. Perhaps, then, neither did she.

Yet the faintest music came from her. There was the rustle of her long hair, which was smoky black, and curling like the finest wool of a lamascep, and fell to her feet; there was the silken rasp of her skin, mirror-smooth, against itself, or against her hair, or presently against the garments they gave her. Also she breathed, in and out – but they knew her first breath had come from the lips and nostrils of God.

Night – Chillel – was impervious to cold. She had been fashioned out of snow – it was the fireside she avoided, standing far off, or staying poised in the mouth of the temple.

Seeing she had come from God, the hirdiy did half expect her to tell them something. When she did not speak, they thought she would instruct them by example. They watched her for signals.

The garments they brought her were those they would have given a Crarrow, if ever one had offered to join them. Most hirdiys kept such clothing by. The long shift was lined with spun dormant grass bartered for from the swampland further south, and top-covered by black-striped wolverine fur from the same area. The mantle was of woven black wool with eye-like patterns of marigold, azure and mauve braided in. They gave her hairpins of antique whaletooth to control her hair, earrings of gold, and a necklet of silver-washed brass, all from some place they could no longer identify.

Chillel dressed herself, having been shown by the women how to do so. Like the nomads, she never thereafter removed her garments, nor washed her body. This was common enough. In her case, rather than the bready, self-muting staleness of mankind, Chillel's scent was cool and not of flesh.

Although she did take a token amount of food, they thought she had no bodily functions. At night, if they had stopped, she would leave the temple and pace slowly about the camp's edges. One dusk then Ipeyek glimpsed Chillel squatting like any ordinary woman behind a dune.

Urine trickled along the ground, but it was as silvery as her necklet, caused no heat, and smelled of fresh snow.

She did *not* teach them, even by example. She had no facial expressions, not even of bewilderment or animosity. Her features were very still, her body also. Yet her eyes looked about, she blinked and could shut them. Her coordinated movements were sublime.

Just as the balls of her eyes were white, and her teeth – perhaps her bones, too – they had noted that the palms of her hands and the soles of her feet were slightly paler and rosier than the rest of her skin, and that inside her mouth a human colour existed. Her blood – if she had blood – would be red, then, even though she was made by God out of night.

Ipeyek told none of them about the personal thing he had seen.

The hirdiy did not know the Jafn legend of Star Black, the warrior hero formed from snow. They had nothing to guide them but religious esteem.

All this time, the nomads were not specifically travelling anywhere. They always went up and down the Uaarb, though seldom to its brinks: of mountains in the north, or the sea. Sometimes even they travelled in circles. They were like Magikoy clockwork. Once set in motion, they persisted in it – but for them it had no purpose save itself.

Then came a night of triple moonrise.

That was when they would take the bones out of the temple, and ask them questions.

The ritual was explained to Chillel. She did not so much as nod, but they had come to think she now understood their speech. She had. She left the temple with its door-flap wide, and stood by, far off from the fires.

The hirdiy brought out the caskets, and slid the bones down in the square which emphasized all four directions. Offerings were made to the bones.

Above, the three moons hung like three white stares. It was as bright as midday.

Occasionally, the hirdiy bones would answer.

Tonight the bones got up. They made a palisade. Filmy lights squirmed among them. Then they began to swim counter-sunwise, along the unseen line that described a square.

The hirdiy observed, awe-stricken. Such an event had not happened in living memory. But more was to come. The eddying bones shot suddenly from the square. They dashed upward and rained down like spears, unmistakably making now a fence. It lay between the hirdiy and the woman they had named Chillel.

Stuck upright in this fence, the bones were again stationary. Crackling voices filtered into the air.

'Out,' they prattled, 'out – away. She – no. Out of Uaarb. Out *she* – off *she*.'

Behind the abrupt partition of bones, the hirdiy stood dumb. But the other voices nagged on, growing ever more shrill and ghastly.

Ipeyek, corralled with his people, murmured, 'But to *us*, she—'

At that the bones spat off a stuff like fiery phlegm.

Some of the nomads pushed Ipeyek to the earth. They stuffed ice in his mouth to shut him up, his mage credentials set aside.

As the bones spat and screamed, the hirdiy turned in frenzy, and picking up clods of cold-baked ice-sand, hurled them over the bone-fence at the woman they had clothed and roomed in their temple.

They drove Chillel out, as they had taken her in, as they would take in anything useful and drive out anything inimical. Though God had constructed her, the ancestors would not have her. At least no one imagined she would run from them. She did not. She only paced further and further away from the flung clods, until she vanished over the dunes.

Her face had shown nothing. Her eyes were open wide, yet relaxed. She did not look back. Only Ipeyek noted that she moved towards the south, and recalled she had been going that way to begin with, since it was from the north she came to them.

Days later, he was following her, or the trail of her narrow, high-arched feet, across the dunes.

Ipeyek had left his family of two wives and dozen children, left his tent-house and cart, his dog-team, and three burden-carrying dogs. He took only his fight-and-hunting weapons, and the clothes he always wore. No one remonstrated, though the wives were solemn and some of the youngest children cried. It was the way of the Northland, generally, not to debate.

Why did he go after the woman called Chillel?

The simplest cause: he had fallen in love with her. And he had done this sufficiently to be able to give up everything else.

Most often, his quarry was herself out of sight. Sometimes he saw her in the distance, but she moved on too, after sunset.

In Gech lands, to sleep by night was the norm, but Ipeyek rationed sleep now.

He hunted as he went across the ice desert. Game was scarce, yet he had grown up with the scarcity and the country, and knew their secrets. The infrequent hares fell to his sling. Once he saw the tracks of a tattarope, found its hole in the dunes, and dragged the snake out. He ate all food raw, as he walked after Chillel, and for drink chipped ice off the mesas with a razor-like flint knife.

Chillel, he thought, ate nothing. Possibly she had only accepted small portions of the hirdiy food from a bizarre courtesy – because eating was one more thing that humans seemed to do?

Ipeyek wondered, startled, if she had only urinated for the same reason.

He did not ever attempt to catch up. Not even when he could see her there a long way ahead of him, like a solitary black finger moving over the bleached sand, writing something on the sky he could not read.

Ipeyek did not measure time as he crossed the Uaarb. Presumably neither did Chillel.

One morning, after he had been striding monotonously for hours, Ipeyek grew aware that he approached the plateau's end.

Here the external mountains became involved again with the flat terrain. The land dipped, crumbled. As it gave way more and more, Ipeyek came to see the slopes reeling off below, down to the lower sweeps of the northern Gech wilderness. He had never been so many miles towards the south.

All that day he never saw Chillel, and the rockier

ground hid her footprints. Persistent, single-minded, he kept doggedly on.

That evening he made, unmagically, a fire in the lee of a rock, striking up sparks from his flint. Darkness came, and only emptiness was there – but night and unsound were also Chillel.

Next day he found her. She was about twenty feet from him. She had halted confronting the massive final drop, as the plateau plunged over towards the wilderness far, far below. He did not think it was fear that had stayed her. She was perplexed.

'I and you down mountain,' he said. 'I able. You easy with me.'

She could not fly. That was odd, but fortunate, or else he might then not have caught up to her at all.

He had scaled and descended mountain outcrops along the Uaarb, even the slippery mesas of ice. Ipeyek therefore went first, picking the safest path. Without a protest or query, now she followed him.

They were two days on the mountainside, getting down. The second night, with the lower wilderness quite near enough to reach tomorrow, Ipeyek sling-shot a wild grey rat-pig. He peeled it of its fur, cut it up, and grilled the meat. When he offered some to Chillel, she accepted a mouthful, as she had among the hirdiy. Afterwards, he lay down by her, then put his head into her lap. She did not deny this.

Her smell was still fragrant and remote. He supposed she never slept; he had never seen it. There were other races like that. He put up a quiet hand and cupped one of her delicious breasts inside the shift. Nor did Chillel deny him that.

'I on you?' Ipeyek asked her. Among the nomads, that was enough of a request. He pondered if she comprehended. It appeared that she did.

Expressionless, unresisting, she spread herself back against the slope.

Ipeyek embraced her, sliding his hands inside the shift, burying his face in her breasts, her hair, her loins. Her centre was glamorous. When he penetrated it, she seemed cooler than any woman he had ever known, yet firm and lush. She was not a virgin. Ipeyek did not know the god who made her had dispensed with all such silly impediments – or had forgotten, as he had almost forgotten her navel.

'No hurt,' Ipeyek whispered in a while. 'Wife.'

They were married.

The hirdiy of the Uaarb evolved no word for happiness. He slept against her, holding her to him – *his*.

Man and wife then, Ipeyek and Chillel journeyed over the wilderness, going south towards the swamps of Gech. He assumed she still wished to go that way, and if she changed her mind would somehow indicate as much.

Every night, once or twice, he would copulate with her. She never refused, nor did she show any enjoyment – yet there was nothing off-putting or angering in her lack of participation. It seemed in fact she *did* participate, offering her body so immediately, in all its loveliness. Her black and shining unshut eyes transported him to ever sharper pleasures. Fertile, he considered if he would make her pregnant. He decided it was unlikely. He was correct.

The opaque neutrality of the weather ceased as they neared south Gech.

Swamp began, leaden mud under cracked glazings of

ice. The hideous spidered mangroves frostily enclosed them, with boles and tentacles. Overhead the sky tore to storm and uncanny lightning in wheels and bolts.

They forged on across the swamps. Under semi-transparent ice channels, things lay imprisoned: big saurians that in other parts had escaped and scuttled over the land. They were armoured, these beasts, with heads that nearly split on fangs, but almost sightless. Ipeyek, who had heard of south Gech, ushered Chillel up into the safety of palm trees by climbing rungs of ice. There were apes, too, several of which intended to assault them, but Ipeyek killed three with his sling and, uttering bellowing screams, the others fled.

Leeches fastened on Ipeyek whenever they moved through the softer mud. He rubbed ice on them to dislodge them. They did not attach themselves ever to Chillel.

Going further south, they arrived among the haunts of men. In villages of beehive houses, the doors remained closed. No one would come out. Once a lone Crarrow emerged. She asked Ipeyek, in another language of Gech, what he did there. When he could not grasp her meaning, the Crarrow shook her head. Her hair was dyed green. Demonstrating no craft, she slunk back into her house. Chillel she had strictly ignored.

They saw no wolves. The storms abated.

Ipeyek spoke to his wife of the Copper Gate that marked the termination of all Gech lands. This was like the ends of the earth to Ipeyek, even though he had always known about it.

They saw the Gate at last, through heavy mist and frozen willows, over a wide expanse of mud and active saurians. It was soon after dawn. Formerly the Gate had been wide and high – twenty chariots might have passed through together. Now, though its size was still impressive, much was fallen, and the shining copper plates of history had changed to a sickly verdigris.

Beyond the Gate stretched more mud, right to the shambles of Sham.

The city's walls were gone. Its architecture was centuries down and sunk in the frigid mud. On top of and out of this muck-heap, like insects, men had put up buildings of a kind. Sham was a warren of alleys and fighting arenas, slave markets, brothels, dens of ethnic vice.

The out-city Olchibe bands still talked of Sham. They brought to Sham any Rukar slaves they kept alive, as offerings to its disgrace.

Today life stirred quite busily in its sink. Smokes hung on it in a rich pall.

Ipeyek and Chillel went through the Gate, listening to the grunting of the swamp alligators, gradually hearing another sound which rang round and round. Ipeyek of course did not know Sham was not always this vocal, smoky, or full of life.

So very far they had come. To a nomad, the travel in itself was nothing, but Ipeyek had left his world behind. He tied Chillel to him by a protective leash before they went into the city.

This had been well advised, though ultimately not effective.

In the alleys almost instantly they were among crowds. Most gaped at Chillel – there were no black skins in any of these regions. Ipeyek caught the title *Crarrow*, as he thrust to get them through.

It was bad enough among the Olchibe and the Gech who were in Sham, and who did not necessarily know the myth of Star Black. However, now there were Jafn peoples present too, a thing that had seldom occurred. The first of these white-skinned warriors Ipeyek had ever actually seen came milling along over the hills of sunken buildings in their chariots. Olchibe stepped mildly out of their road, for Olchibe at this time tolerated, indeed made friends with, Jafn.

That in itself surprised Ipeyek. Then several chariots had hemmed him in, and lions.

Chillel stood at the end of her leash, which Ipeyek had fastened round her waist. She might have been a slave, but made of jet. Ipeyek had deduced she wished to go into Sham. He had never tried to learn why.

He waited, sling in hand, for what might come. He knew about the Jafn, they were warlike and irascible.

But the men in the chariots stared – they *stared* at Chillel. Some made signs over their bodies to things in the air Ipeyek could not make out.

Then a Jafn started to speak to Ipeyek himself.

Ipeyek spoke back.

Neither understood the other.

Out of the press of people slipped a wiry one-eyed man covered in scars. He was a Gech, a fighter of alligators in the pits here. But he knew both the tongue of the Uaarb and a little Jafn. Electing himself their interpreter, he soon informed Ipeyek that though she might be his wife, the black woman must go with the Jafn now. They wished to take her to their Special One – so the Gech translated – who would be interested to see her.

'No. She with me,' cried Ipeyek, fruitlessly, as white-haired Jafn left their chariots, held Ipeyek still, gave him to the alligator-fighter to hold, slashed the tether from Chillel, and led her up the mud-hills and away.

The skies cleared again and were a dense concrete violet. A few clouds loitered, one of which never moved at all, or altered its shape.

Was Ddir responsible for what went on below? Was it only an inevitable result of colliding legend and reality?

Among the cloud mass, no creature was active.

Having set so much in motion, had Ddir lost interest?

Where Sham subsided back towards the south, an ice road of sorts remained. It was here that the mass of the allied force, All-Jafn and much of Olchibe, had settled. The army, and its tents, were like a hawkery: bustling and savage. To this, Gech was adding itself. Parties of men had stridden from the swamp-lands under totem banners prettied for battles: mummified animal heads and skulls – saurian, wolfish, wolverine, ape – Gech, unlike Olchibe, did not often raise the heads of men on sticks. Gech and Olchibe both exuded volunteers from Sham. There were beast-fighters, thieves, absconding captives who had somehow bribed someone, and would rather fight the Rukar than die aboard a Vorm or Fazion Mother Ship shackled to an oar.

Ipeyek might not have been remarked upon, if he had not brought the supernal with him on a lead.

The camp was loud with singing and hammering, the snort, roar and trample of mammoths, lions and dogs mingling. Men play-fought, practising for more serious affairs. The atmosphere also twanged to the note of bow-strings and the zing of mark-flung spears.

As the Jafn warriors carried her up through the encampment, heads were turned. Smith after smith hesitated between one moulding blow and another, the sword or knife cooling on the anvil. Olchibe after Olchibe, cooking something at his portable oven, let go chunks of meat into the fire.

Outside story, there had been none like her. She walked like royalty, a royalty they had, none of them, ever known yet *recognized* at once. Black as night, fair as the sun.

If the Jafn warriors thought themselves her jailers, by her mere *presence* she had made them her bodyguards as she had made Ipeyek not husband but slave.

Gradually a hush spread about her progress.

They saw how she held herself, how her hair brushed her footsteps, saw her eyes, and they grew immobile.

He was among the mammoths now. He had a trick, which was to go up on to the back of the mammoth Peb Yuve had given him, with the two lions from his Jafn chariot. They were all up there now, he and the lions on the mammoth's back. Because it was what he wanted, he had charmed the mammoth not to mind; the lions seemed also glad enough, sunning themselves high in the icy brilliant daylight, kneading the mammoth's tangle of hair with their paws, as cats do when content.

It was one of Peb's men who came running, Olchibe, young.

'Hey! Hey!'

None of them addressed Lionwolf as a king or leader – they put all that into his name.

'Lionwolf, look what your whitehaireds found for you!'

Lionwolf looked down the mile of the mammoth's back, and saw Chillel, created of snow and night, walking towards him through the war camp.

Like a liquid, curving river . . . like the flight of a bird out of the heart.

Her beauty was not of the earth, though she had been made from what lay upon the ground.

In the Olchibe tongue, Lionwolf said quietly, 'What's there.' Not a question: an affirmation.

With a series of bounds, his feet weightlessly striking off its side, he dropped from the mammoth, leaving the purring lions in possession. Anticipating the manoeuvre, the assembled army nodded. They had seen this often. They accepted that he, the Lionwolf, was a god – yes, for the mortal half of him had become to them slowly irrelevant.

And the woman, what could *she* be but god-created? The Jafn accepted too that the Great God had made her, for she was like Star Black, the hero of Jafn Klow and Kree.

So they had brought her to *their* hero.

He and she.

It was a foregone conclusion.

Heaven had sent her here, for *him*. But did *he* think that?

What did he think? Only half god, despite Jafn amnesia, Lionwolf had a mind; he thought like a man – if sometimes like a boy. He beheld the beauty of Chillel, as familiar to him as his own, just a fact.

For the camp, those that watched, this was how they were: Lionwolf was a statue of amber, red hair burning over his head and shoulders and back, as if the rising or setting sun bloomed secretly in his skull. And his blue eyes – that were like eyes never seen in Gech, in Olchibe, and rarely among the Jafn peoples – were sapphire.

They had remarked and received much proof of his vitality, magecraft and warlike abilities. He did not even *smell* as other men did. He had the scent of light and *newness*, never unclean.

And to this she, the woman, was the counterpoise. Though they had seen black eyes, yet none like hers; black hair – the same. Her skin was midnight, the perfume that hung on her – as his was – heaven sent.

How could she be for any, then, save for him?

How could even he, with his erratic mercurial brain, think otherwise?

'Who are you?' Lionwolf said to the black woman, conversational there in the middle of his warrior host.

It was what many had said to himself, on meeting.

Lionwolf did not know this woman had never spoken before in her short, short life – nor that she was even younger than he, and had had even less of an infancy.

When she answered him, none of them were amazed. Only Ipeyek would have been, and his hirdiy, but they were not present. Her voice was soft as distance, clear as silence.

'I Chillel,' said the woman. She used the syntax of the Northland.

But Lionwolf, who had spoken to her only in Shamish

Olchibe, did not baulk that she understood him, while he himself knew by now all the languages of Gech. They had long said, you had only to speak a couple of words of any tongue to him for him to become fluent.

So he said to her now attentively, in Northlandish, 'You Chillel. Why here?'

None of them knew either she had never smiled, till then. She did it beautifully. It was not feasible for Chillel, after all, to do anything in any ugly way. Even her urination had been a deed of fastidious flair.

When she smiled, they noticed Lionwolf smiled back at her.

'Here as wife,' said Chillel.

'Whose?' he said.

She might have answered, *Ipeyek*. Chillel did not.

'Now I choose,' said Chillel.

This was not modest. How could she, though, goddess as she was, be modest?

Those hundreds of men grouped there, close enough to see and hear, did not expect modesty. Only the Northland Gech among them were offended, for she had employed a *verb*.

Lionwolf must have noted that too. He changed to *southern* Gech, to see what she would do with that. 'You'll choose? Well, look about. Who will you have?'

No, she had no difficulty with a switch of language. She gazed smiling into the face of Lionwolf which, smiling back at her, was shadowy sun to her sunlit shadow.

As if eventually willing to be modest, Chillel lowered her eyes. She turned her head, and next her body, and pointed straight away towards the tallest of the four white-haired Jafn who had arrested her.

'That man,' said Chillel. 'I choose that man as husband. His name is Arok.'

The wheat flamed golden.

Saphay stood gazing at it, puzzled and dejected. It was not what she had ever known before.

In the end, she walked forward through the wheat. She had done this before. Stalk on stalk bent with a dancer's sway away from her, and sprang back when she had passed. The tasselled heads were taller than her own, though in colour not unlike her hair.

Beyond the wheat field lay an apple grove. Red fruit glowed as gaudily as the ruby windows of Ru Karismi.

She reached an area where there was nothing, and sat down in relief on a blunt spur of ice.

Looking up, she saw the tapering ceiling of the iceberg, itself colourless and deathly – familiar. It was high as sky.

These pyramids were Yyrot's. There were three or four of them. One led into another by large cave-like doorways in the ice. They were full of forests, fields, vineyards – but not of the type that Saphay was comfortable with, for every blade of grass or grain, every bough and frond and fruit, had come alive, woken by the heat of Yyrot's persisting malign side.

Here the god had put Saphay. She had come to under green leaves and, stretching out her hand, touched a grapevine with beads of jade. At first she had been thrilled at this land of plenty. Crops and vegetables were never of this sort – or at least she had never seen them. In the magnificent farming regions about Ruk cities, all was dormant, held in tight husk or vitreous stem, or sealed in cryogenic globules.

This pyramidal bounty palled after she had made herself puke on purple plums and dates.

She was also lonely. It was the loneliness of the prisoner, worse than that of the free.

Wandering about in the pyramids of ice, in the shining pearly twilight that was there by day or night, now and then Saphay saw Yyrot himself. *He* was in dog mode, and sporting always with Saphay's feline.

Saphay thought in fury that she had been cheated sexually. Her lovers turned on her as murderers, or selfishly got themselves slain, and now this one, who might have been a lover, preferred to be a hound and fornicate with her *cat*.

The craziness of having such annoyances too, that upset her nerves.

Once or twice, she had come up against the inner walls of the icebergs. She was generally unable to peer out through them. Only one time did she, having climbed some species of ramp, seem to see through a semi-transparent patch like a frosted window pane. It was the night sky before her then. The stars were very bright out in the world, and in the veils of them she believed she detected a constellation shaped like a huge toad.

Yyrot had sat on a toad for a chair, before he brought her here. He was fond of animals? Not of her, certainly – though she was a sort of mother-by-law to him, since his liaison with the cat.

Sitting on the ice-spur, Saphay felt again the tugging ache under her heart. That was for the other faithless one, her son. Had she dreamed of him? She thought she had.

She had been jealous in the dream of some other woman to whom he paid attention, despite never before being affected by any of his numerous erotic exploits. This female, however, in the dream – an unrecollected alien – had filled Saphay with envy and an added sense of power-lessness.

Thinking of dreaming, Saphay's eyelids drooped. The environ made her sleepy.

Someone stood in front of her.

Yyrot as a man? No, not he. It was . . . it was her son, Nameless.

No.

Saphay tried to wake up. So long since this had happened – eleven years – her guard had slipped. Too late now.

He was with her – Zeth Zezeth, who in her girlhood shrine had had his name written in Rukarian characters only as *Zzth*. The same noise a dagger made, slicing cloth.

'What,' he said, 'did you suppose I was done with you? Your punishment I keep for you in a box of agate. At last we shall savour it, you and I.'

'When?' she whispered.

Laval silver, his hair; his breathtaking face was masked in indigo. With this ignition of vitriol she had lain in ecstasy.

'There is none like you,' she said.

She feared him still. There was no fear left on earth for her, after she had known his wrath. He had toughened her, and cured her of true terror over any but himself.

She thought he smiled, but it was the mouthing of a feeding wolf before its teeth meet.

'None,' he agreed.

Vain – he was still that.

Saphay kneeled down on the ice before him.

She wondered dizzily why he had not manifested to her through all this time, and why he did so now.

'Your son,' said Zeth Zezeth.

'What do you mean?'

'Ask me in a while. Ask me when I bring the agate box and flay your skin off your soul's blood with the agonies I keep for you. Into eternity I will take you, Saphay, shrieking. It is owed.'

Saphay raised her head. Ashamed, she murmured, 'Is there nothing else possible? Why . . . why . . .?'

Yyrot stood in front of her, and not the other one. She was not kneeling, but slumped on the spur. The cat sat nearby, sleek, her belly heavy with Yyrot's young. But Yyrot was back to his insane benign side, a sullen man garbed in icicles. The wheat was already shrivelling. Cold griped in Saphay as the plums had done in her intestines.

Without a word to Yyrot, Saphay rose, contemptuous, and went away. Presently the cat, aware of some unwanted change in her paramour, went trotting after her.

Saphay walked now, weeping. Despite all things, she had come to see what love was worth. She had come to see why she had loved her son so much, and Athluan not at all. That was not virtue; it was because she had loved *him*, the monstrous one who would have killed her and would do it yet. Him, Zezeth.

'She's sobbing, poor thing, look, crying in her dream. Best leave her be. God knows what I should do.'

The woman, whose village lay along the east-north

shore, in the land of the Jafn Holas, had trouble enough. Her man had recently gone off to join the alliance of armies – up towards Olchibe, they said, and next back and away into the foreign south and west.

She talked to herself, the village fishwife. There was no one else to chatter to. The poor deranged woman, who had been dragged ashore that day – eleven years back – out of the liquid sea and reefs of ice, had grown a little older but not more lucid.

She had been, this wreck, good-looking once, or so the fishwife thought: a girl then with garish yellow hair, like hot-house wine.

There had never been a life story she could get out of the girl. Even the village witch could not, though the witch had seemed not to like being here in the hut, once the girl was there.

Fishermen had found her. She had got snagged in their nets. Sometimes the Holas woman wished the men had then borne their catch further along, to some other house. Maybe even they should have left her to die, as the fisher-husband had said. He had never been keen on their enforced guest. Perhaps, now off to a war, he would not come back, instead take up with some Olchibe bitch or Rukar bitch . . .

Then the only company the fishwife would ever have was the rescued woman. And she ate very little.

'Nameless!' cried the demented one from her heap of rags.

She often cried out this un-name – sometimes quite angrily. She used Jafn speech by now, though in the beginning had rambled in some outland tongue. The fishwife believed the woman had somehow learned Jafn through hearing talk in the hut. But now, just as frequently, the other stranger words came out – Yyr-something, and something else that sounded like a knife slicing through cloth. Her own name they had never been sure of, *Saffi* being the nearest they could reckon.

Saphay, weeping far off on Yyrot's dead wheat, did not know her body lay also here. She did not know that, on the day Athluan had released her from one ice pyramid, part of herself *had also come out of the sea at another spot*. Which then was the real Saphay? She that had been Athluan's consort and borne the son of a god, who had trekked over the ice waste, sat in the snow-house? Or this one, this wretched bundle, ageing before its time, in the fisher-hut – as if Saphay's dress had also taken on her life in that fatal hour of Zezeth's undersea lovemaking, and subsequently been washed up here, knowing no better.

Third Volume

IN THE HAND OF NIGHT

It is sometimes possible to outwit one's Fate, but in doing so the Fates of others in proximity may also be fatally disturbed – as fire blackens the hearth it burns on.

Magikoy saying: Ruk Kar Is

ONE

Funeral rites for Sallusdon, King Paramount, had continued for months, as was customary. During the first twenty days, the cities of Ruk Kar Is, especially the capital Ru Karismi, came to a standstill. Death alone moved along the ice river called Palest, robed and mailed in black and blackest crimson. After this, with the embalmed corpse buried in the Place of Sepulchres at the Palest's end, though the rituals did not cease, yet they diminished. The streets and markets lost their immobility. On the fiftieth day, at noon, the new King Paramount, clad in mourning clothes, walked up the steps to his throne, high above the city: Vuldir the arch-conniver. One King Accessorate stood at the throne's foot, and that was Bhorth the fool.

There had been no problem over Vuldir's ascension; he had been elected by due process. Ru Karismi rang with bells and paeans of loyalty. Vuldir sat on the marble seat, looking on, garments impeccable, demeanour calm.

That evening Thryfe the magician left the city for his southern house.

It was a moonless night. Emerging from the glassy woods, he saw the windows of his mansion, still far off, flashing at him vivid white, for danger. Thryfe spoke to the lashdeer of his sleekar. In a blur of speed, he reached the house in minutes.

Many gargolem servants stood sentinel out on the snow. 'What has happened?'

One of the servants answered in its slow mechanical voice, 'We are not knowing, Highness. Something is about.'

Thryfe gave the chariot to the non-human grooms. He waited a while out on the snow, staring miles across the countryside. Eagle-sighted was Thryfe, but he could detect nothing. Nevertheless there was a slight electric tremor in the air, more than the cold or the sheer darkness. Aware of his return, the windows were fading down, and lamps lit inside.

Presently Thryfe turned and went into the mansion, leaving the half circle of gargolem guards to their watch.

That Vuldir became King Paramount held no surprise for Thryfe. Even before Sallusdon had died, Vuldir would have been busy seeing to this. The destiny of kings had little interest for any of the Magikoy. Centuries past, a king was also the High Priest of his people, their leader and – if necessary – interceding sacrifice. But no longer. Now royalty remained, a greedy parasite that was tolerated, and by many revered because it gave the nation of the Ruk its figurehead. For that reason too, all rituals were closely observed. No sign of respect was ever omitted. For to lapse was to display the lords of the land as hollow toys, unimportant, and so lessen their only value.

With Thryfe such people barely counted – only sometimes what they did, or caused.

He sat in the towery of the South House, gazing at his own thoughts, which had not even touched on Vuldir.

For several months he had lodged under the city in the

Insularia, among his fellow Magikoy. Rumours circulated above that they prepared down there some special show or artefact meant to benefit the Ruk. In a way that was true. It was about the Ruk that the Magikoy debated and laboured and grew incensed with each other, there in the complex underworld below the ice.

Rumours also sank down to them, below. There were wars among the Jafn barbarians to the east. This had happened before, and was always happening. But it meant little to Ru Karismi. Later another news broadcast started. The Jafn had themselves elected some sort of petty king – how risible – and were now at war with the sub-human Olchibe and Gech. The sophisticated city was even quite tickled at this idea, that the Jafn might mop up such scum and so incidentally safeguard those Ruk caravans which still moved eastwards or north.

By the Magikoy, however, these distant war games were scrutinized with horror. The Magikoy knew what smouldered at their core.

The creature, half human, half god, they had now – several of them – been shown in the spheres of oculums: as a Firefex, as a lion, or a wolf made of fire. Thryfe had seen something else. He had been shown the standard the creature had adopted, a smoking blue sun over a flag of flames. But *none* of them had been able – not even the greatest among them – ever to behold the creature's actual *face* or *body*. Such was his power, and inimicality, magic could reveal him only in symbols.

Yet the symbols demonstrated plainly enough what he could do. He could win and take whoever, *whatever* he desired. Armed with so vast a legion as he was now gathering, what other goal would he have than the Ruk itself? It was merely a matter of time before the avalanche of this savage and genius-inspired horde swept round into the west and south.

The Rukarian lands must be defended. Not one of the Magikoy did not know this: against such odds, it would only be possible by supernatural means.

Though many in above-ground Ru Karismi recalled the ancient sorcerous weapons reputedly stored there at the heart of the Insularia, they did not grasp their significance. To the Magikoy themselves, these weapons of ultimate retaliation were unthinkable things. But now perhaps they were the only chance of deflecting the fate of the Ruk – the world's fate, even.

The arsenal's awakening was therefore debated, in an atmosphere of depression and terror.

Thryfe had stood before them all in the Nonagesmian Chamber. 'No,' he had said. '*No*, are we mad that we consider it at all?'

'These thaumaturgicals have never been tried,' said another. 'They may not be quite as we've been told.'

'Worse,' said Thryfe. 'They're worse. Human imagination can't encompass what they are. Who hasn't read the writing which tells us *that*?'

Others too again spoke *against* the weapons. And others spoke again *for* them, as unavoidable.

The argument raged. The breath of horror swelled and choked the room, so its fakery of sunlight turned to murk.

The armament was not anything like the mage rays and arrowing lights any battle might engender. It was itself as terrible as the events continuing in the east. Or more so – much more.

Recent generations of Magikoy had never seen the

weapons. Secretly formed, they crouched there in the underworld's heart, unemployed, disarmed – waiting.

Appallingly, in the very moments of protesting for or against them, every one of the Magikoy, male or female, master or apprentice, *guessed* that the time of the weapons had come, the season of their unleashing. The creature from the east had given licence for their use. By no other method could they resist him.

The debates ended. A dreadful quiet covered the labyrinth of the Insularia. Several Magikoy meanwhile crossed back over the bridges and sought an interval of peace in their mansions. Thryfe was one of these. As he rode away, the election of a villainous king meant nothing to him. The *world* was tumbling from the brink.

Crystals hung from the roof of the shrine, and tinkled as the woman walked by below.

In her black-blood gown, hair cascading with jewels, one saw she was a royal woman of the court. Some wondered why she had come to the temple-town with such a slight escort. Others recognized her as the younger of the two Queen-Widows. She must be pious, here to make an offering to the gods of dead Sallusdon: Preht, Yuvis and Zezeth.

A shrine guardian bowed to the Queen-Widow Jemhara.

'Why,' said Jemhara, 'is the god not in his niche?'

'Which god, exalted lady?'

Jemhara pointed. The guardian squinted among the array of little god-statues, each ensconced in a gilded recess. One recess was empty.

'Particularly,' said Jemhara, 'I wished to appease Zeth Zezeth.'

'That's unusual. He is a very spiteful god, when in malign mode.'

'Where then do I find him?'

'The statue has been taken out for some purpose. Perhaps to clean it. Or a patron of the shrine wished to borrow it.'

'Am I not now a patron of the shrine? Am I not always the widow of Sallusdon, dead King Paramount?'

'Lady, excuse me. I'll go directly and ask where the statue is.'

Jemhara stayed by the altar table, looking under her lids at the gods. This was the third shrine where she had failed to discover an image of Zezeth Sun Wolf – while in Vuldir's personal shrine, they said, the statue had been dropped and broken. The slave who had been so careless had died a slow and grisly death, screaming to the end that the statue was never dropped, but *came apart* when he touched it.

Elsewhere, too, Jemhara had heard of the icons of Zeth developing black stains. There was one she herself had come across, at the corner of a small side court in the palace, that had gradually cracked and darkened like a rotting fruit.

She had once glimpsed the god, his kind side, during a magical conjuration long ago. She was then hardly more than a child, but she knew enough to kiss the ground at his feet. Later, those few she told informed her she lied, or had been mistaken. Zezeth would hardly have honoured her immature spell with his visitation; he was not an elemental or demon. Despite that, ever since, she had been fascinated by this god. *Why* had he come before her? And why now did he withdraw from the city – for it seemed to her that was what he did.

A shrine priest approached. He said, 'Lady, the statue of the Sun Wolf went a month ago.'

'How could that be – was it stolen?'

'It dissolved.'

'*Dissolved!*' Jemhara's eyes sprang wide. For a second you saw right into them, but only a short way; their lovely floor was shallow.

The priest shook his head. 'The shrine lets in cold air. There are faults in the roof. These conditions are unfavourable—' He left off his whining as the Queen-Widow turned in a cloudy swell of mantle and hair. Her attendants ran after her as she swirled on out of the shrine.

Jemhara got into her litter. Her slaves carried her through the temple-town, past all the other painted shrines, and next up ramps towards the palace.

Returned into her rooms – new ones and less grand, no longer those of a second reigning queen – Jemhara took her scrying mirror from its box. She stared into the milky surface, and saw nothing. Then Vuldir was there, tiny and far off, with the great gold crown of paramouncy perched on his head.

'Is it you?' he said. 'How long you take to answer me.'

'I was away in the city, Mightiness.'

The crown was a cipher. He was not actually wearing it; it was for state occasions, and heavy. But the mirror showed her his mood. He was preening, at his kingship. And he wanted something from her, she thought. Was it sex? She believed not.

'I have an hour when you may visit me,' he said. 'Attend in person, in your flesh.'

He no longer liked her appearing before him in her spirit form, seeping through walls and doors without needing a key. Had he stopped trusting her? She had better be wary, for she had helped Vuldir destroy Sallusdon, and the ones who helped Vuldir, quite often – the same as the ones who hindered – he rid himself of.

She went up to those apartments where he saw courtiers of more minor eminence – lower princes and Widow-Queens.

When Jemhara entered, Vuldir was alone.

'I have a piece of work for you,' said Vuldir. She bowed. 'Your sister-Queen-Widow has withdrawn herself, very properly, from the city. She's no longer seen at court. Now your turn for modesty has come.'

Jemhara lowered her eyes to hide her displeasure. She must never seem to go against him. 'Mightiest lord, whatever you wish.'

'Go south to the village of Stones.'

Despite all self-training, Jemhara's head darted up.

'Where?'

'Yes, dear dove. A village, a pigsty, and with all the appurtenances of a sty. But the Stones stand there. You may like those.'

Aghast, she looked at him.

'Your eyes have become quite round,' he observed. At that she lidded them over in the normal way. 'That's better. Don't you know who has one of his houses near the Stones?'

Jemhara lifted her head more slowly now.

'Thryfe, the Magikoy lord.'

'Just so, Thryfe. No sooner did I assume my office than he sped off there. I think he has always tried to frustrate my plans. I don't trust him. I wish him gone from my life, and therefore from his own. And you have your skills, don't you, Jemhara?'

'But he is Magikoy.'

'He is a man.'

Jemhara trembled. Like a cat, she stared at nothing. Her hair crackled with neurotic galvanism.

'He has no interest in women.'

'Make him find one. Sallusdon hadn't performed as a man for twenty years till you got your kitten claws into him. Look where that led.'

'But he is *Magikoy.*'

'Are you a gargolem? You sound mechanical, repetitive, unclever. A pity, that.'

Jemhara put her hands together under her chin. If this was all the chance she had, she had better take it.

'If you require it, my lord, I shall try my best.'

'Oh, improve on that. *Succeed* or I'll be annoyed.'

Thryfe had gone down from the towery. Outside, in moonlessness, he struck off across the higher land beyond his house. It was an hour's journey.

He was thinking deeply, deciding how it must be done, the dissuasion of the Magikoy from the use of their thaumaturgical weapons. It would, if they acted soon, be plausible to construct another armament, strong and efficient, actually *usable*. That was, sorcery which killed cleanly, and left some hope behind.

The land opened. An island of ice-forest curled over the dully starlit snow. In that direction was the sprawl of a village, now unseen. Nearer, about a hundred paces off, rose the Stones.

It was because of the Stones that Thryfe had had this house built here. Initially, when at home, he had gone to visit them every day or night, but then he ceased to do so. Their inexplicable beauty, their unsolvable enigma, eventually made him forget them.

As he drew closer, he began to see their light. One was not always able to make them out. Chameleon-like they would mimic the colours of day or evening, shining aquamarine at dusk or blush at sunrise, or, on nights of triple moons, a brilliant white. Tonight, though, in the dark, they had chosen – and maybe they *had* chosen, for they might be sentient, no one knew – the hot blue of turquoise.

They stood in their ring, ahead of him. In number they were fifty, or some said fifty-one, but Thryfe had counted them. Perhaps one Stone had disappeared before he came there. They were tall, twelve or thirteen feet, smooth and wan. Their light commenced deep inside them, like the glow in a lamp. One shone up, then a second, then the light spread in variable order into all. They pulsed, now quickly, now with melting imperceptibility. The flame bloomed, expanded, died, revived.

All around, the snow and ice reflected and became turquoise.

Thryfe stopped where he was, seeing them as if for the first.

Was the unhuman energy that motivated the flame in the Stones like the power which had formed the secret weapons of the Insularia? Magic was everywhere, ready to be used by any with the talent and schooling to do so. But these things here were not of that type. They were beyond the scope even of the highest mages. They must be left alone.

Something cracked through the air like a whip.

Thryfe altered. He was no longer motionless – even though he did not move at all.

He realized fully it was not any noise he had heard, or anything he had seen, that sudden whiplash. Something psychic, separate from himself, and probably separate from the Stones, had entered the scene.

Against the sea of light, on the blue snow, Thryfe spotted it quickly enough.

It was a hare, long and slender, its ears upraised. Unlike most of its kind, it was not white but black, and on the lit ground as easy to notice as a bit of spilled night. It sprang about, playing with nothing, seeming entertained – and complacent.

Thryfe watched the hare. No, it was *not* a hare. A shape-changer was here.

An element, long controlled and unutilized, shifted within the psyche of Thryfe. Not many had witnessed his smile. Just as well: the smile was not humorous, not amiable. It carved his features to a ruthless line. Then it – and he – were gone.

His alter-self – Eagle – soared up into the sky. Over the playing hare fell a great, still shadow.

It had been, she thought, an arduous expedition to the village. Jemhara had hated every moment. And it was all the more vile because she understood that, once installed, not only her slee but also most of her travelling luxuries would be withdrawn.

She had grown up in just such a frozen midden. That had been a stead to the west, outside the minor Ruk city of Sofora. The farming people there had meant Jemhara – then known as Jema – to grow to a life of honest toil. Learning that, at the age of five, she could do extraordinary things, such as turning, through will, a jug of thick chipped ice to *water* in a matter of seconds, they apprenticed her to the steading witch. The old woman was impatient, and sarcastic. Additionally she abused Jema, both by beating her and sexually. The child knew no other way; even so, she did not like her treatment. When she was eight, she led her old tutor on to the ice of a river, and magically melted out an aperture under the witch's feet. The witch went in without the space even to yell, and Jema healed the ice over instantly. Perhaps no one suspected her. Ice did occasionally give way. In any case they needed her by then, having no other mageia. At nine years, Jema gained authority over the whole stead. She received the best food for her assistance, and blackmailed steaders besides over events she glimpsed in her scrying mirror – which was at that time a shard of broken bottle.

When she was fourteen, Jema deserted the stead. She went with a seller of pelts to the capital. Tiring of the man and impressed by Ru Karismi, Jema – who now called herself Jemhara – began to worm into the bottom levels of the court.

She was fly, and heartless, and lovely. She was also only sixteen when Vuldir first took note of her, eighteen when, with Vuldir's connivance, she wedded Sallusdon, King Paramount.

She had come a long way, and did not like to go back to her gross beginnings now.

The village of Stones was awful to her. The dwellings were built of tree-trunks and ice-brick. A fog of choking and unwarming smother hung on it from its fires. Jemhara lodged in an empty guest-house with her two servants. She offered no magical help to the struggling village. She was a fine lady now.

As for Thryfe – Jemhara had not yet formulated any plan. She credited her own skills, but knew she was no match for a Magikoy master. Had Vuldir only sent her here to have Thryfe destroy her? Vuldir was prone to callous yet random plots.

Boredom seized on her after a day and a night in the village. Respectful of her status, the villagers had brought her kindling and provisions, and not intruded. The two servants sat dejected in the back room.

A curious latent hunger for the open air followed boredom into Jemhara's mind. It occurred to her she might go and spy on the house of Thryfe – which of course, being governed by Magikoy sorcery, her mirror could not show.

She had been capable of shape-changing since she began to menstruate at eleven.

The night was one of no moons, and Jemhara preferred the dark for her changes. The servants thought she slept, and her door was bolted on the inside. A black hare bounded from the low window hole and away across the ice.

Though a witch of more than ordinary gifts, Jemhara had never properly exercised dominion over them. When she became an animal, something of her was intellectually lost. For her that made the state more enjoyable.

Yet, in that condition, having found the Stones and the

blue light tidally coming and going, Jemhara-as-hare gave in to the urge to play.

Thus she missed any signal in the atmosphere that might have warned her some *other* was present.

Not until the shadow fell did she halfway see her predicament.

Then she sat up on the snow, hare-like, her eyes discs of fear.

Human, she would have reasoned eagles and craits were rare in this area, tending to the uplands or the coast. Animal, she merely saw death with a wingspan broad as the sky, stooping on her.

Her trance shattered. She fled away, leaping down the slope towards the cover of the ice-forest.

Two shapes now, one small and racing, one soaring *gently* overhead.

As the glow of the Stones was left behind, only starlight illuminated the chase.

The hare pelted forward. All thought was over. Panic ruled her – she had become only a little hunted beast.

The eagle sailed on its wings, drifting. He looked weightless as a cobweb. Then, the tremendous pinions flared and closed—

He dropped, no longer cobweb but a hammer of basalt. The night parted, *tore*, to let him through.

At the edge of the forest, up against its first glacial columns, the eagle met his quarry. His talons, like hooks of bronze, pierced into her back.

She screamed. Blood spurted in darkness.

A vapour seemed to cloud and clear, and Jemhara lay

pinned to the earth, naked on the snow but for a ruby on her hand, and her cloak of hair. Thryfe stood above her, residue of nightmare. His face was still that of the eagle, though the blade of beak and bitumen feathers were sloughed. His eyes assessed Jemhara. They were incendiary and – worse than insane – quite *sane*.

Sensing the change in her adversary, as in herself, her humanness returning, the woman pushed herself up on her elbows. The cold ground seared her, but no more fearsomely than the bloody wounds that glared in her back.

She knew who he was. Who else *could* he be? She had seen him too, now and then, at the court, striding about there clad in his scorn. When she angled her head to look at him now, prudently she did not meet his eyes.

Thryfe, though, had never properly noticed her.

'Why have you hurt me?' she whispered. Even in this situation, she was nearly flirtatious.

'To teach you a lesson,' he said.

'I am taught.'

'No. Next time, if an eagle hunts you, girl, take on again your human shape before he strikes. Have you learned that now?'

'Yes. Please let me up, or I'll be burnt.'

Thryfe stepped away. He watched her get herself to her feet. The front of her body was flushed from snow-burn, but not badly. Her attractions, which like this were very obvious, would not be spoiled. Her back might be another matter.

Could she heal herself of the scars his talons had undoubtedly made? Who was she anyway? From her ring alone, he could tell she was some city woman – but a witch. It came to him then: he recalled who she was, and that she

315

belonged not to the dead Sallusdon, but to the living Vuldir.

'Good night, madam,' said Thryfe. He turned and began to move away.

He was not astonished to hear the whimper she gave, or next the soft sound as she collapsed to the snow. She had surely not fainted; it was her ploy to gain his aid.

He paused. Would he give it? When he looked back, she lay there sidelong on the ground, and over her velvet body, black hair and black blood dripped. If she did now pretend, it demanded stamina in her, to lie so still again on the freezing earth.

Thryfe walked over and picked her up in his arms. It was many years since he had held a woman. Her eyes flicked open. For an instant put out, Thryfe saw that she had not pretended at all, but had been unconscious. And looking down into her eyes then, Thryfe met their shallow floor, and beheld that, behind the shallowness, they possessed a depth which went on for miles. Her eyes were like an oculum: you might see eternity in them.

'I'd better remedy your scratches,' he said. She sighed as he carried her over the snow towards his house.

At some point, Thryfe drew off his cloak and wrapped her in it. The blood pressed on through the heavy cloth. It was already on his hands, his own clothes.

Strangely, moving through the blank of night, her blood seemed to him to have a scent, unlike the expensive perfumes of her body and hair. It was like the smell of pure, liquid water.

He was completely aware that, as the eagle, he had wished to scatter this blood, and rip chunks of her body off her bones. He had not hunted anything in that manner in over twenty years, about the same margin as his celibacy.

When he reached the house, the gargolem guards had returned inside. Whatever weirdness had been abroad in the night, then, was now extinguished. Thryfe supposed, anyway, that he held it in his arms.

She was senseless and icy. She might have been dead, though her blood went on streaming from her.

But she would live.

More than most, the Magikoy, who had studied the ancient texts of the Ruk, and reports from all the known world, comprehended the knack of human survival. When first the age of ice had fastened on these lands, a great heart had been stilled. Man and beast, and flora of all kinds, were cauterized by the cold. To begin with, it was only possible to go on by huddling in fastnesses. Perhaps they had prayed, but the cold did not relent. It was Winter – and Winter had come to stay.

Once Winter ruled, however, the arts of a vibrant mage-craft were born among mankind. From desperation or from blind faith, magic matured, and became the limitless technology by which mankind could persist. But also humankind was itself adapting. A century or more had passed, and cut away with it the weakest among man, animal and plant. A new race arose from the embers of the old one. These were peoples and creatures who could withstand the negative temperatures, and whose blood did not congeal on the sub-zero plains. As for the vegetation, it had clearly learned how to outwit the cold. Palm trees wrapped themselves in steel, grapevines clustered the ice in protective cryogenic pods; fruit and grain slept, awaiting only the kiss of warmth.

Therefore, now, Thryfe could stride back for an hour over the frozen waste, a naked bleeding woman in his grip. And she would live.

He healed her wounds swiftly, in the subtor chamber deep below the house. Then he restored her blood. All this Thryfe did by his craft. For one of his order, it was not difficult.

He left her to sleep in the care of a jinnan, a mild spirit of the house which was adept at seeing to such things.

Up in the towery, Thryfe resumed his inner debate on the weapons of the Insularia. His mind would not stay on this, since Jemhara still glinted at the border of perception. To her, his thoughts returned. She was like a silver splinter under his skin.

The night went by, and the next day. In the oculum, Thryfe scanned the city of Ru Karismi, loud with banners, glad after its mourning. Olchibe and Gech too he visited through the sphere. Like ants, the armies of the north and east teemed together now. Among them something blazed.

Thryfe knew he must decide, and go back to the capital.

On the second night, he went into the room where he ate – when he did eat – and found two places set at his table. The jinnan housekeepers had done this, maybe because the girl had asked them to, though he had not proscribed it. He questioned himself why he had not.

Then Jemhara entered the room. They had given her a dress from some pattern kept here for visitors – as if there were ever such beings as visitors, or as if they would ever have needed spare clothing. Her hands were free of gems, her face of make-up. She was like a pretty child – but he had seen into her eyes.

None but Thryfe, or some similarly acute mage, could

ever have seen what her eyes truly contained. And who among such persons would ever have looked? If he stared now at her spiritual heart, he could see the same. Heartless, yet the heart-bud was there, a miniature atom. It had begun to swell and grow, bursting the calyx.

Jemhara stood gazing at Thryfe. Her *eyes* – they overwhelmed him, filled him with vertigo. He had not lived, and here life was. He could never have predicted this moment, nor any other foreseen it for him. Yet it was inevitable as sunrise. Be the night long as twenty-eight years, still dawn must arrive.

As for her, she could not take her eyes from his. She, who hid everything, hid nothing. He had seen her soul. She had one: it was now undeniable. She wanted only to be seen – by him.

She fell on her knees to him. This was neither fright nor deception.

'You must go back to the court,' Thryfe said.

While he spoke, he thought, *What rubbish am I saying?*

Jemhara said, 'Don't send me away. Vuldir forced me to come to you. He wants you dead. I can tell you all he's done – and I have done for him.'

'Vuldir?' Thryfe hesitated, between amusement at the absurd idea, and agony at *this*. 'Get up,' he said.

Jemhara spread her body on the floor at his feet.

She was a witch, and had talents. Thryfe could see those as well, through her physical casing, like jewels frozen in water.

He leant down and lifted her upright, on to her feet.

Her eyes were so near now, he saw the triumph in them. Why had he never noticed her, this woman? He had, he thought, not dared to.

But she *had* seen him. Her lies to herself had been much greater.

The triumph in her eyes was sexual. *He* wanted to cast her out – kill her even.

Instead he held her there.

Jemhara had no terror – except that these minutes might end.

Unlike the mage, a love-life had been predicted for her. Her mother back in the stead had saccharinely promised it, and the old witch-sadist had threatened it would be *removed* if eight-year-old Jema did not obey her. But heartless, made deliberately so, Jemhara was as ill-educated as Thryfe. Although her heart, like her eyes, would soon have achieved a depth not normal among mankind. Jemhara after all could melt ice. She had melted his – and her own.

Braver than he by far, she flung herself against him and took hold of his neck. Her claws bit into him like eagle talons.

'Vuldir gave me a ruby ring. I've crushed it to bits. I will kill Vuldir for you. Let *me* die for you,' she said. 'Kill me, if you like.'

'Tomorrow,' he said. 'There's time enough.'

Mouth to mouth, breast to breast, flesh to flesh, words were uninvented. The sky crashed and world spun into the abyss. New lovers always think so.

TWO

In the tent of Arok, warrior of the Jafn Holas, a night-black woman sat in silence, braiding beads into her hair.

They were a present brought her by a man, a warrior of the Jafn Shaiy, and they were gold.

Arok lay on the tent floor, a pillow under his head. It was a sleep night, but he could not sleep.

'Chillel?'

She did not answer. Her silences nevertheless were sometimes like dialogue.

'Chillel – come here. Lie down with me.'

Chillel put aside the beads and went to her husband, whom she had wed by Jafn ritual, a cord tied round her right hand and his left hand.

Arok now made love to Chillel, although this was not the practice of a sleep nocturnal. As ever she was welcoming, blissful – totally uninvolved.

Arok hit her, a slap across the face. It did not seem to affect her at all. He had done it before, and there was never a mark. He had originally anticipated she would bruise *white* on her darkness.

The Gullahammer, the force of allied Jafn, Olchibe and Gech, had turned and now was riding and parading back, down the northern outcrop of the land, into the south.

It moved, as ever, slowly, trundling chariots and carts,

mammoths, lions and men, like a sleepy inrush of thawed sea. They had reached the Marginal. From the ice-forests still men came out to join them. Elsewhere villages lay deserted, either in fear or unable to sustain themselves, their male population all gone.

A month back, Fazions had ridden into the war camp, on their demon horsazin fish-horses. This was some way inland from the coast, yet they had made the trip.

Several of the Jafn spoke their gabbling tongue; he, the Lionwolf, had of course learned it. Then he and some of the Chaiords, Peb Yuve the Olchibe leader, and three wizards from Gech, sat down with the Fazions. Their blued faces and the standard of the blue sun were lit up together by Jafn truce torches of green fire.

Arok had been there also. He was not unknown to the Lionwolf, who had graced the wedding ritual as Arok wed Chillel, and afterwards feasted among the wedding guests. Arok, as custom dictated, did not speak to his wife until they were alone. The custom derived from Star Black, and could not have been more uncannily suitable.

The Fazions, however, had come to ally themselves with the Gullahammer. They foresaw nice pickings, and offered their ten Mother Ships, and ten jalees of thirteen vessels each, in service to Lionwolf's cause.

Arok, who had himself a smattering of Fazion speech, overheard them muttering to each other. 'He is a god,' they said of Lionwolf. They had been quicker than most to dispense with excuses.

Their shamans soon performed a sending, to fetch in others, and some Vormish allies of the Fazions too.

The Jafn regarded the Faz shamans with critical distaste – filthy stenchful men draped in the reeking fishy skins and horns of dead horsazin, they pranced about shaking rattles, and shrieking like girls in sex or childbed. Yet the sending was a success. More Faz rode in, together with the Vorms, whose faces were striped with carmine. Each Vormish horsaz had been striped similarly.

Arok lay trying to think about this recruitment, and how the camp of the Gullahammer now stank of fish. Meanwhile his exquisite wife, who had chosen him, yet whom all men had wanted . . . well, now most of them had had her, too, he believed.

Because she was reckoned supernatural, no one had denied her other choices, nor had Arok challenged any of them. He had not known what to do; for the first time in his adult life, no proper code applied.

He had gone to the Ranjal-goddesses in the cart, told them his predicament.

They answered that he need only enjoy Chillel, and no harm would come.

'But if she conceives a son how will I know if it's *mine*?'

With unusual coherence, the Ranjals said, '*Be* yours, if you husband her.'

God had made Chillel, made her directly – without recourse to anything human. Against this you could not go. And so – though a woman – she held Arok helpless in her hand.

When he hit her, he was afraid. Since he was afraid, he did it now quite regularly, facing up to it. It made no impression on her. But nor did God smite Arok for his blasphemy.* *What did God want?*

'To make a fool of me,' said Arok, aloud.

She had now left the bed and gone back to her beads.

Arok got up. He crossed the tent and smashed the beads in all directions.

'Cutch-whore, take yourself out of my tent. Go to one of your three thousand others, and stay with him – you bitch.'

Without a word, Chillel rose. She had that slight enchanting smile on her lips he first saw when she chose him. He wanted to break her neck – but was too cowardly to try.

When she had left the tent, he stood in the opening, watching her move away through the firelit dark of the huge camp.

On the horizon, almost, above the sleeping Jafn tents, Arok saw a Faz warrior appear – keeping barbarically sleepless for seven nights, as always.

Arok's proud blood froze. Before, she had gone among the Jafn, even maybe among the *leaders* of Olchibe vandal bands – but not with such as *this*.

The Faz had put out his hand, and Chillel took it.

Arok retched. He hawked and spat on the snow. While doing that, he missed the last sight of her going down the slope to the hearth of her current mate.

Peb Yuve sat across from Lionwolf in the Jafn tent. Lionwolf's chariot lions, in their indoor golden collars, lay at the men's feet. Peb had become accustomed to the lions, just as had Lionwolf's mammoth.

Peb and Lionwolf played a Jafn war game, with a painted board and little carved figures. Lionwolf was letting Peb win, and Peb knew this, accepting the courtesy. Having surrendered after Lionwolf slew the white bear, Peb Yuve had offered the young man-god the formal

Olchibe kindnesses of a father to a grown son – exactly as the Olchibe ghost, Guri, had suggested he might.

Peb Yuve had only seen the ghost once – and did not see him tonight, though he was sitting up on a small table at Peb's back. The lions sometimes did see Guri, but were tolerant of him – even if, now and then, he would pull their manes and they would snap.

Lionwolf could see him too, over Peb's shoulder.

Guri sat there scowling at the floor and retying his braids, on and on. He had not been about for a season.

'Your chieftain is dead,' said Peb, removing the figure and winning the game.

'So he is. Well managed, sir.'

They conversed in Olchibe, but Peb by now was also used to turns of Jafn and Rukar phrases, titles.

'You let me win.'

'*I?*' Lionwolf's eyes widened. He had the charm not of a man but of what he was – something between king, animal and elemental, tinged always with deity and strangeness.

Over Peb's shoulder, Guri swore, tore a knot out of his hair, rebraided viciously.

'The black woman,' said Peb Yuve, 'they say she's left her Jafn match. She's off among the Blue-Faces.'

'The Faz? Why not?' Lionwolf seemed indifferent.

'She's caused some trouble between your Jafn warriors,' said Peb. 'Some skirmish for her.'

'Soon they'll have more important work to do.'

'Not a man that stood by, thought she'd come there for any but you.'

'Then she must have been confused,' said Lionwolf. 'Maybe the sun was in her eyes. Why, Peb Yuve, are we talking about women?'

'You think she is a sacred being, like your hero down east, Star Black. She's a harlot – and a good thing you never took her to yourself.'

'Oh, if *I'd* had her, do you think she'd have gone off with any other?' The young magician had bridled.

On his table Guri wriggled. A cup set there made a knocking sound.

Not looking about, Peb said, 'Is he here, your shadow-uncle?'

'Yes.'

'Greeting, Guri,' said Peb Yuve. He was always polite to Lionwolf's familiar. Guri shook his head. 'Did he hear me?'

'He's embarrassed to be a ghost, Peb Yuve. He'd have liked to fight with you, under your banner, as before.'

'He would have been welcome. I thank you, Guri.'

'Did I never say,' said Lionwolf, 'you sent him to his death?'

Like a cat silkily unsheathing its claws.

Both Peb Yuve and ghost Guri sat up. Then Yuve said, 'If he was part of my vandal bands, I may have done. In a raid or fight, was it?'

'It was when you sent him to fetch back my escaping mother. He told you he failed. That was because he had died.'

Peb thought. His eyes cunning, he looked at Lionwolf and said, 'Yes, I remember that man – a brave man. I must have his name written on my banner staff: Guri.'

Lionwolf replied, 'Perhaps he'd care for that. There now – he's vanished suddenly. Self-conscious, as I explained.'

Later, as Peb went to his own tents to sleep, he glanced cautiously about him. The three or four seconds who accompanied him wondered at this, for no man of the alliance was presently hostile to them. Peb himself, one eye out for the invisible ghost, realized this other game Lionwolf had been playing was that of a son with his father. Olchibe history was full of such jests and mental tests that could wrong-foot you. So it did not worry Peb, he expected nothing else, and it was always wise to take care with the dead.

Guri though, now depressed, was down by the Ranjal cart. Here, whenever he was in the camp of the Gullahammer, he would patrol. Often he found her there too, the old sibulla. She was there tonight, sitting on the floor of the cart, miserable as an old boot.

'What are you at?'

She did not look at him. 'With lady,' said Narnifa.

Guri knew her name, for *she* knew it. Undead telepathy. He had come to know much about her, not wanting to, like that, and trusted he was, to her, far more opaque.

'Why don't you go off to your grave, you silly old cow?'

'Want here.'

'Want, then.'

Morning always removed her, or it always had done. Guri had not been by to check for a while.

He noted Peb Yuve was now far from the Lionwolf tent. Guri winked out of one spot, and reappeared on the table.

The lamp had been doused. The lions lay across the doorway, and Lionwolf himself lay on the floor pillows. His eyes were wide open. Guri caught their red flash as they turned to him. How bright his shadow had been, too, this evening, for any who could perceive such things, like a dark phosphorescence on the tent wall. Lionwolf was stronger than ever, and less predictable.

'You've been off two months or more,' said Lionwolf. 'Were you in a pleasurable place?'

'Sometimes.'

Guri had run away after Lionwolf had met Peb Yuve. Once only had he returned, to inform Lionwolf that Saphay was now again missing. That time, Lionwolf had looked long at him, with eyes blue in daylight. Lionwolf had said, 'She's found some other protector.' In his tone had been stubborn uninterest but also condemnation – prudish as Guri's own response – worst of all, *jealousy*. As Guri knew, you must always recall that Lionwolf was eleven or twelve now, though a man of twenty-one years. Among the Olchibe, boy-men did not cleave to their mothers in this way, but then they grew up amongst men and learnt the ways of men. What males had this boy seen? A dead step-father and a fiend of a step-uncle, a rancid bit-slave, other Ranjallan oafs, and a god from hell. There had been Guri, too, and Guri had done his best with him. But Guri was – undead.

So, Guri had been bounding about the ice-wastes, flying up and trying to touch stars – which he never reached. Sometimes he slid perversely away once more into the 'tween-world, slew phantom foes, ate banquets. He had had intercourse there with a mera, grappling her mermaid tail in spasms of delight. She had bitten him and promised she would lay his egg – but all such matters grew vague when he came back into this sorry, totally physical world.

It was a fact: Guri was ashamed. Of not making a better job of Lionwolf's upbringing, of teaching him so much of Olchibe ways that Peb was in thrall to him. Ashamed of having died.

'Soon,' said Lionwolf, after a lapse of a half hour, 'we'll

cross into Ruk lands.' One of the lions raised its head at his voice, then lowered it again. He preferred a chariot in battle, and already one pair of lions had died. These new ones, who also slept in his tent and fed from his hands, often lay up on the mammoth he rode only for recreation.

'Into the Ruk, yes.'

'Then we will take them, the villages, the cities, Ru Karismi itself. I'm sorry my mother won't be there to see that. Perhaps she'll suddenly arrive from wherever it is she's gone. Do you know, Guri, my father . . . I mean my *father*, that one—'

'Yes?'

'I think he too – he's gone away. He must have done, or wouldn't I have seen him? Not even any more in a dream.'

'*Do* you dream, Lionwolf? Your lions sleep, but you don't.'

'No, but I can if I wish.'

'What about the woman coloured like ebony?' asked Guri. He had been absent when the army was in Sham, but here and now the camp was rife with talk of her. He had glimpsed her, and goggled in disbelief. Nothing living should be so black. Her beauty was so extreme, to Guri she had seemed ugly. Despite that, he sensed, as no other quite did, Lionwolf's vast lust for her. He had always had women as and when he liked. But this one he had not approached.

'Who's that?' said Lionwolf.

Coy? Guri got up and stamped impatiently, as if his feet were cold, which now they never were.

'You want her. Why not have her?'

'She's the Gullahammer chariot. Two-thirds of the warriors have ridden her.'

Guri laughed. 'But she's God-made, isn't she? In her case, whoring won't change her.'

'Perhaps *he* made her, that one,' said Lionwolf, 'to trap me after all.'

Guri considered this. It might be true. Zeth Zezeth – who could guess what he was at, his laval hand hidden. Something flickered oddly through Guri's spirit-brain. His mind saw an especially fine constellation he had once rushed at – and missed. It had been shaped like a frog or a toad.

The young man lay there, looking unblinkingly at nothing now. An abrupt sympathy of long association led Guri over to squat beside him.

'Go to sleep,' said Guri. 'Go on. I'll watch.'

'I'm not afraid to—'

'Of course not. But sleep. Your old uncle's here.'

'Guri, I can do *anything* – or not, I don't know. But this road I'm on is made of flames. Sometimes I look back and see the distance I've come. Or forward, and I see a light as if the earth burned. And sometimes I wonder what choice I have.'

'No choice. Your kind – none.'

'Great Gods,' said Lionwolf softly, in the Olchibe tongue. 'Amen.' He turned on his side. Guri sat back, whistling, hearing the boy crying. Then the crying stopped. The young god slept.

Chillel stood before a Faz bivouac, her neck and wrists garlanded with rings and necklaces of eyes – Fazion war-jewellery. A few feet away, three Fazions had set about killing each other for her sake.

Her face was sober, neither distraught nor glad. It was

anyway rather hard to be sure of her expressions; her darkness and her beauty hid them to a great extent.

Other Faz circled the duelling ground. At their pickets, horsazin whinnied shrilly for the lost sea.

THREE

The Gullahammer flowed south – a south, that was, which tended west, for there lay the vital centres of the Ruk, the larger villages, the minor cities – ultimately Ru Karismi itself.

The top of the continent, as map makers had partly recorded, was in the shape of a bloated and unwieldy sword. The Northlands formed its hand grip; to the east the land shelved away until The Spear provided a pathetically whittled end-piece of hilt. Westward, the other portion of the hilt, curving back as if to protect the giant fist that might hold it, cupped in the Rukarian cities of Thase Jyr and Kandexa. To these, the bulk of the ships and jalees of the Fazions and Vorms, some twelve thousand men, had set off, hauling their vessels overland by means of wooden runners, axed trees, and sorcery. Others sailed north to west, and lugged the ships inland there, across the frozen sea that filled in the coastline.

Thase had had some warning – her mages had intercepted sendings between the sea peoples and the rest of the Gullahammer. Also the Magikoy had sent to alert the west. But of those Magikoy who had personally held wardenships in western regions, none went back there. For a fact, all physical routes westward were fast closing to Rukarian traffic. It was the Faz overland advance which shut them.

Additionally, Olchibe and Gech vandal bands, split off from the main thrust of the Gullahammer, quartered the snows searching for Rukar prey. On anything they found, they dropped like lammergeyers. Strayed caravans and small garrisons and villages were erased. No slaves now were taken. Pillars of smoke erected colonnades across the waste.

They said in Thase, and in Kandexa too as it received the bad news, that the Magikoy alone of all men might have braved the enemy blockade, but had abandoned the west to its fate. All Magikoy power had been concentrated in the capital. The rest might burn, or sink in hell.

And Thase Jyr did burn. Sallusdon had kept a palace there, and mage-coined defences existed. The dozen psychic cannon that had been activated on the walls wounded the landed armada of Fazions and Vorms with peeled-off rays. But more and more of the invaders poured in to brim the gap, like melting water. The cannon, improperly manned, proving too much for soldier and local mage alike, exploded. Balls of light engulfed areas of the city. Fires started in an ignition of screaming. The gates went down.

Kandexa capitulated without a blow. Thinking itself sensible, it let the sea-reivers in at once, tried to welcome them. But Kandexa was battered, raped and murdered. Only her stones remained, with over-eaten Vorms vomiting and urinating on them, and crows standing sentinel.

These cities were small, and the force from the sea substantial. Yet never before would any reiver have dared to come against a metropolis of Ruk Kar Is. In itself, this daring was enough to fill the Ruk with terror. Besides, their own soldiery had been properly untried for half a century.

None had thought the whole of the east and north, plus the peoples of the northern sea, would ally.

By now the main body of the Gullahammer stretched over the landscape.

The larger Rukarian villages were swallowed. No mercy was ever shown, and no adult slaves taken. Only the children were spared, in the Olchibe way, up to the age of twelve. Even then not always, for to the Jafn, as to Faz and Vorm, enemy children had the dangerous potential of growing up to make a blood-feud. Lionwolf himself had been the intended victim of just such a theme.

Lionwolf.

There on the back of the mammoth given him by Peb Yuve, one of so many of his adoptive fathers, or in the lion chariot, he was an icon of bronze and fire. On cloudy days, he shone for them like the sun.

He needed to do so little. He walked among the warriors, or sat with them. He joined in their games of skill, their archery contests, their feasts, drank with them by the side of the war road. He told them stories around the fires, as only the best of bards could do, wondrous tales never before heard – or dreamed of – of heroes, of battle and honour and the winning of wives and riches. Which made them recall, too, the prophecy of the Ranjals on his behalf. He himself had that knack the ancient lays of bards described: the ability to be one with men and lose nothing of his kingliness, his godhead.

Sometimes there was magic. He performed a miracle – he changed an iron bracelet into a gold one, a jug of Jafn wine into fierce Fazion spirit. Once, a man on a litter asked the Lionwolf to cure his broken leg. Lionwolf frowned, as if thinking. Then he touched the leg, below the knee. The warrior – a Gech – said he felt scorching heat. Then he got up on both legs, and raced about. The crowd of men cheered. Later, the Gech toppled down; the bone had given way again, it seemed. He blamed himself – he had been too previous in his gymnastics.

Every one of them felt that he had spoken to the Lionwolf, knew him, was known, was bonded to him by brotherhood.

They vaunted him, admired him, and were reverently in awe – afraid. But he was pitiless solely to their foes; for his people of the north and east, he wanted only victories and rewards. Seeing him, *knowing* him so well, they never doubted that, by following his blue sun, they would get their heart's desire. They had been subjected, and of little worth, for centuries.

And so the spilling march ran on, and cities burned.

'How is it their mounts survive out of the ocean? I thought they rode fish.'

Vuldir's facetiousness was ignored.

'Horsazin. The reivers carry barrels of sea water, and wash the beasts down from time to time.'

'I understand! But the second question persists. How have they achieved this much?'

'They're inspired.'

'By what?'

'By what you have already been told of, Vuldir.'

'Thryfe's nonsense, this god-king – surely only some berserk Jafn princelet?'

Vuldir plainly did not know he spoke of Saphay's son, his own grandson.

335

The Magikoy who addressed him, an older man, grey-haired, did not enlighten him. This mage master had been warden to a village of the western shore – but no longer.

'Ru Karismi,' said the Magikoy, 'must ready herself.'

'Not quite. That's your task.' The Magikoy turned and began to walk out of the room. 'Wait,' commanded Vuldir. The Magikoy took no notice. At the door, two guards moved from his way. No man blocked the path of a Magikoy, unless he was crazed.

For a moment, Vuldir seemed angry. Then he put that from him. He was not alarmed. He knew this rabble from the outlands could do nothing here. Only the idiocy of Thase and Kandexa had let it do anything *there*. Meanwhile, Thryfe had not come to tell him of the sending from the west, but this fellow. Thryfe, it would seem, was otherwise engaged. How fascinating that such a tiny morsel as Jemhara could tackle such a mage as Thryfe. But to Vuldir all men were fallible. Not himself, perhaps.

Servant-apprentices of the Magikoy rode westward and southward of the city, to Thryfe's two known houses. At the quintul house, all was quiet and empty. The windows shone blue: nothing had happened there. The South House, nearer to Ru Karismi and where it had been thought Thryfe had retired, was harder to discover. Only the Magikoy-trained could ever have found it.

They stood in their sleekars on the snow, looking up at it in dismay.

Thryfe had given his pledge to return to the capital inside five days. He had by now been gone sixteen.

'But he never stayed *here*,' the senior apprentice remarked. 'He must have seen this and gone elsewhere.'

'No one said the house was in bad repair,' murmured another. 'Something's occurred.'

'What? What could *occur* – to Thryfe? He's one of the foremost magicians, though modestly he never admits as much.'

Above them, the house loomed against twilight. The ground below had subsided slightly, as if the snow had thawed at some unknown heat – dropped, then locked again as abruptly.

None of the minor gargolems were in evidence. No spirit-attendant appeared. It was not possible, here, to see the colour the windows might, or might not, have been, to show either threat or uneventfulness. They were closed over by *ice*. The entire house had been sealed in it. Though the building's shape was discernible, for the ice had followed its every contour, the barrier of it was yards thick, and cloudy.

'The Stones that give off lights, they lie up there,' they said. 'No one knows what the Stones truly are. Could *they* have done this to the house of a Magikoy?'

They left their chariots, the lashdeer shaking their heads, ill at ease. No less concerned, the senior apprentice made a circuit of the mansion.

It was impenetrable, unless some blasting magic were applied. The senior apprentice, though able enough, had neither the jurisdiction nor the confidence – probably not the power – to try it.

Thin winds veered along the snow plains.

One of the party spoke. 'If Highness Thryfe isn't here, and isn't in the west . . . then where?'

No one answered.

As they edged down from the mansion, one or two glanced back. They had the impression the imprisoned building was cladding itself ever more thickly in the ice, becoming solid all through.

Above, a moon rose. In the forests below, opal spiders spun their wicked webs.

Between the Gullahammer and the core of the Ruk lay next the south-west city of Sofora. Like the coastal cities, it should have proved harder to consume than a village.

It was possible, but not prudent, to bypass Sofora. Sofora had troops, who must surely pursue and attack the Gullahammer from the rear, should the Gullahammer fail to lay siege. Sofora had been so ordered by sendings from the capital.

She marched out her soldiers in any case, to meet the barbarians on the icescape under her walls.

From a tower on a high point of the city, non-Magikoy mages sent to the capital a vision of the alien army. And the words, *They are too many*.

Further on, a second imaged message entered Ru Karismi. It displayed a bluish fire devouring the snow, the walls, all Sofora – and words cried over and over, never being completed: *There is ONE among them . . .*

He rode into the battle under Sofora, as he had done against the Jafn Klow, in a lion chariot.

Elsewhere he *had* sometimes ridden the mammoth, but perhaps he risked it less, valuing it as the gift of Peb Yuve. He had certainly lost many of his lion-teams to arrows, knives and clubs – but there were always more lions brought to him, the best the Jafn kept by as battle spares. It was not he did not love all the lions. He fed them by hand, they slept in his tent. None drew any comparison: that those he loved he used, then lost, and then forgot.

Only one magical cannon was retained at Sofora. It turned out that, lacking Magikoy, they did not dare to start it, having heard of the effect at Thase Jyr. The sorcerous gun peered out through the walls, a green dragon-head with open jaws, yet unarmed. By sunset, the men of the Gullahammer had pushed it off its perch and let it smash in harmless pieces on the ice plain beneath.

Lionwolf had led them into the city, driving straight through Ruk soldiery and straight at the gate, taking invulnerably blows on every side, for once his chariot-team being also unscathed. He killed personally so many men in the gateway that they provided a barricade – but not for very long. Then he left the chariot, impatient as always. He flung himself, running, into the city, the colossal riot of an army roistering after him.

He killed there, too. Those that witnessed it had always said he slaughtered women as simply as men. It was as if he saw no difference. Only the young he spared – his Olchibe indoctrination.

Under his blue sun banner, soon Sofora was put physically to the torch.

In the mage tower, the last remaining mage cast off his sending of the horrible scene below. This done, like the solitary unused cannon, he dashed himself from the height, and died on the stones in blood, fire and darkness.

After Sofora, Or Tash, the one city now left standing between the Gullahammer and the capital, sent to the King Paramount for aid.

Vuldir shook his head at this. 'They must go without our help,' he said. 'It seems this business is serious. We will keep all our soldiery here.'

Bhorth, the foolish weak King Accessorate, pounced round on his heel and left the noiseless chamber. Descending from the palaces, he took his guard, rode at once for his nearest estate, and called up every able-bodied male. Furnished with two thousand men, armoured, and in fighting-sleekars from Bhorth's royal possession, they sheered northward and west towards Or Tash. No Magikoy accompanied them. At a small deserted town a blizzard began, and shored them up for days and nights. Not one sending percolated through the sheeting snow. When eventually they could get on, and reached Or Tash, the Gullahammer had already taken it, and done so as the wolf or leopard took a deer.

As if by magecraft then, too, Bhorth and his appalled makeshift troops, were themselves surrounded by the horde.

Bhorth, wielding his war-axe and engraved sword, beheld men of the Jafn shoulder to shoulder with Olchibe and the blue-faced rabble of the outer seas. If he had not had to keep his wits, his mouth would have fallen open.

Then he himself was felled.

Reviving, he learned that they knew him. This was not hard, for he had put on the traditional steel helm of a lesser king, circled with its golden crown. They let Bhorth retain just three of his guard, all hurt. The barbarians conducted them over the smoking hem of Or Tash, where men, chariots, deer and lions waded through a river of slowly freezing blood.

Bhorth pig-headedly thought they meant to make a

death-spectacle also of him. He glowered on them all. He was a king.

However, they were taking him instead to meet their own leader.

The tent, pitched by the city's ruin, was nothing. Ruk splendours these savages only destroyed. Outside it, though, the weird standard added to Bhorth's foreboding. And he noticed as well, down the slope, some kind of dishevelled cart full of wooden things like broomsticks, which seemed to be speaking supernaturally to a crowd of laughing, blood-drunk warriors.

Bhorth, King Accessorate, was ushered into the tent itself.

He saw a mixed group of men like those who had fought, white-haired Jafn and yellow-skinned Gech or Olchibe. A Vormish reiver, with purple-striped cheeks, had come out as Bhorth entered. Bhorth had thought all the reivers off at the coast, bouncing on the rubble of Thase.

Then something happened. It was the way a wind changed direction over the ice fields.

Bhorth was staring suddenly between or through all the men in the tent, to one man standing washing his hands and face in a basin of snow. The man shook back his hair, and wiped his face with a towel one of the Jafn handed him.

Bhorth had heard the dislocated rumours of red hair, and not credited them. Here it was.

He was not, Bhorth, a man who had sexual or romantic feelings for men. Nor was he at all aesthetic in his appreciation. But once, when a boy, he had seen a sunset, heart-red jointed with gold, and never mislaid its marvel. This man – this *creature* – was like that, a phenomenon. It might not be overlooked – or only at one's peril. And this thought came from Bhorth, reckoned to be a fool.

The phenomenon walked towards him. A lion padded dog-like at the phenomenon's heels – there was blood in its grey mane.

'Good evening, sir,' said Lionwolf in impeccable aristocratic Rukarian. 'I expect you don't know, but we are related.'

Bhorth's mouth did as it wished, it dropped open. He spoke after several moments. 'How's that?'

'My mother is Saphay, daughter to Vuldir, King Paramount. Since you're my grandfather Vuldir's brother, I greet you as my great-uncle.'

'I remember no daughter of that name.'

'You must trust me to know my own birth-line,' said Lionwolf. He held out his hand. It had been cleaned of blood, like his extraordinary face. The rest of him was still dyed with it, though he had no smell of that, and his skin was not Olchibe yellow, as Bhorth had first thought, but a clear brown. Though there were Jafn about, and Fazions, with bluish eyes, they were not his blue. The eyes of this one matched the sun of his standard. *There is ONE among them . . .*

'What are you?' said Bhorth, not grasping Lionwolf's proffered hand. But Lionwolf held out his hand still, unabashed, composed, only waiting. To take that hand must be inevitable. Bhorth shivered under his fat. He was tired, and a captive, yet still he had asked his question. He was not aware of how many had already asked it.

'What am I? Like you, my lord Bhorth, a king.'

Maybe it was the first time the Lionwolf had ever called

himself that, but no man in the tent protested. Oh, he was king – King Forever – over all.

'You're a barbarian,' said Bhorth, 'that's what you are.'

Lionwolf smiled at him.

'Am I? Perhaps, sir, before God and gods, we are all barbarians. But won't you accept my hand? I won't burn you.'

'I will not,' said Bhorth.

'Ah, then,' said the Lionwolf softly, 'I must take yours.'

Just as a mother did, gentle with a child, before Bhorth knew what would happen, the young man's hand, strong and warm, had taken Bhorth's hand, which was battered from the haft of the axe, knuckles bruised from the hilt of the sword. The strong warm hand was itself callused but not battle-marked – yet he fought like a fiend, they said. His flesh, it seemed, accepted only those scars which would be helpful.

Bhorth did not want to let go the hand of the Lionwolf, who was King Forever Over All. In a dislodged world, this hand alone was likely to hold him up.

'You're courageous, Great-Uncle,' said the king. 'You, and no other prince, to come out against us.'

'I and my men.'

'I regret your men. But I offer no harm to *you*. You shall be honoured.' Swansdown could not be as delicate: 'When Vuldir and his capital are in shreds, you, Bhorth, can live.'

Hours after, Bhorth felt himself ashamed of this conversation. By then he was in another tent. His wounds, and those of his three guards, had been washed by some witch with herbals. Bhorth was sitting on the ground, and they had brought him black Jafn wine and some food. If he was a prisoner he did not know or care. Anyway, it would not matter. He was done for, like all of them.

When Vuldir and his capital are in shreds . . .

Somewhere in Bhorth's brain memory nagged, reminding him both he and Vuldir had been warned of all this long ago. And now it was too late.

Shouting filled the one upright dwelling left in Or Tash. It was Lionwolf's habit sometimes to keep a single building whole, and celebrate with his captains inside it. Somehow this had been begun at the Klowan-garth, where he had given Lokesh and Rothger over to their hideous feast. The building chosen in Or Tash was a rough-hewn palace on a platform, where royalty had never stayed.

The feast-fire pranced high. Jafn mages had filled it with gyrating shapes of lions and bears, and women. No other woman, of whom anyway there were few about the war camp, came to these junketings.

All the chieftains and leaders were present. The most favoured sat nearest to Lionwolf – Peb Yuve and some of his seconds, three or four other Olchibe commanders, and Gech premiers from the swamps. The chiefs of all the Jafn clans, their sons and kin had their correct places. No one tried for precedence – formerly feuds had started over much less. The two jalee captains of the Fazions, those not still at Thase and Kandexa, sat on the fur-piled wooden benches. There were beasts besides. Jafn brought their best lions to a feast, and now the three Vorm ship-lords wished to bring in their horsazin. This Lionwolf allowed, despite Jafn complaints that the dinners now tasted always of fish.

Tonight the third Vorm entered late with his son, and with his horse – a horned fish out of water, painted stem to stern in magenta stripes. Behind the men and the horsaz, walked the Vorm's woman.

Every other man in the room stared, for the Vorm's woman this evening was black Chillel.

She wore by now a fortune in trinkets and baubles, spangling on her darkness, given her by her endless succession of lovers.

Only Arok of the Jafn Holas turned his look instantly aside. He was at the feast because he was kin to the Holas Chaiord, and had divorced Chillel by now, in her absence, by the swift Jafn method. Not all men who had once had her fretted when she was gone. But, then, she had publicly chosen Arok, and he had wed her; that was different.

If Lionwolf looked with the rest, he also looked away soon enough. He seemed to pay no special attention to Chillel, yet no man there, if he had had her or not, seemed quite able to ignore her. She was like a subtle sound vibrating in the air. Always in your ear, you grew used to its being there.

The shouts rose again, the rafters of the hall rang. Outside, the flattened city showed its corpse to a couple of high, narrow moons.

Peb Yuve leaned over to Lionwolf. 'That woman should not live.'

Lionwolf glanced at him. 'Which woman?'

Stonily, Peb said, 'I wish I had my Crarrow wife with me. She'd tell you.'

'A Crarrow, yes – but what is there to fear from an ordinary *woman*, sir?'

Just then the third Vorm ship-lord stood up and clouted his own son across the head. The younger man went down.

The Vorm did not sit. His face, paint-striped like his horse, was hard to read, but every man there read his action. The son too had had Chillel, it appeared.

To Lionwolf, the Vorm bowed, banging his head down on his fists in the Vormish way. In the language and syntax of the north sea, he muttered, 'Pardon this me that struck out by your eating-hearth. Shall I go die, young father?'

Lionwolf laughed. 'No, sit down. Make it up with your son. He's a fine warrior, nearly as fine as you are.'

'You are faultless in judgement, young father.'

The Vorm bent over his son – knocked out by the hefty paternal smack – and began to soothe him.

Peb Yuve said to Lionwolf, '*He'll* kill her now.'

'Who will he kill?'

'The Night-Woman.'

'Doesn't he know she lies down with any man who asks . . .' As Lionwolf paused, his lips formed silently, in Rukarian, the words, 'Excepting myself.'

Vormish father and son were now sitting back on their bench. Chillel, who had been sitting by them on a low stool, the Vorm ship-lord now kicked, with a sudden movement, away on to the floor.

All sound ended in the hall, apart from the eternal whisper of Chillel's own music of *presence*. That did not alter.

It was the oddest thing. However graceful, how could any woman maintain her grace when kicked away like that?

To Lionwolf himself, Chillel's kicking-away and fall were as if a swathe of liquid water had sprung outwards, changing but not letting go its form – and then, as immediately, recoiled. With amazement, he gazed at her. She was already standing up, unharmed, unmarred, as if nothing had been done to her.

Was she like this during lovemaking? Yes, it must be so.

Lionwolf got to his feet.

The other men stared rapt – now at the woman, now at their man-god.

Everything was briefly as it had been on the ice road by Sham, when Chillel was first brought to them.

'Come and sit here,' said Lionwolf to Chillel.

With miraculous normalcy, she obeyed.

Peb Yuve now stood, and moved away as she approached. His seconds followed him. The nearest Jafn chieftains shifted. Lionwolf pointed to the bench beside him. Chillel, without a word, sat there. Then Lionwolf resumed his seat.

He spoke to her low, but others heard him: 'You'd better stay by me a while.'

Chillel regarded him with uncluttered acceptance.

Was she now another plaything to him – one more untried, intriguing item? He did not know, but he desired her. That was what he was most conscious of, the organ of his sex, over which he could exercise great control, striving against his will, so finally he allowed it to expand and crane as it wished.

He said to her, again very low, 'What will you do for *me*?'

'Nothing.'

'Ah, like last time, then.'

Both of them looked back at the hall. No one overhearing believed either her rejection or his wooing. How could two things like he and she deal in such ordinary currency?

He gave her wine to drink. She drank it. Lionwolf drank, like all his men, copiously, though was never drunk. But she did not drink much, always putting the cup down after a sip. She was the same with the food.

The rest – even the Olchibe men apart from Peb Yuve – became hot and high as the moons. They began to vie and wrestle with each other, then the story-telling commenced.

All through this, the two of them sat there like two statues made of amber and jet.

Night crossed towards morning. At dawn, the Gullahammer would be on its war road again, flowing towards Ru Karismi.

His captains, who might soon die for Lionwolf, banged cups on the benches and called for a story from him.

Lionwolf looked over his shoulder, seeing no one was there. Guri was seldom with him, now. He had, obviously, offended Guri – and the living Peb Yuve too. But Lionwolf could charm them back. 'What story shall it be?'

Peb Yuve said across the feast-fire to him, 'Let the woman tell a story.'

Lionwolf shrugged. Among Jafn and Northlanders alike women did not tell tales in hall, not even the Crarrowin.

'Do you know a story?' Lionwolf enquired of Chillel.

On the other bench, the Vorm who had struck his son lowered his face in anger like a bull, but kept still.

Chillel had risen, as the storyteller must. One supposed she had seen others recite bardic lays.

Peb Yuve's face was granite.

Chillel picked up the cup she had been drinking from.

It was three-quarters full. Leaving Lionwolf, she went unhurriedly about between the benches and the fire. She offered the cup to every man she came to, whether chief or second or their kin. Most drank from the cup.

This was not servile, it was a mystic, priestly act. And those who refused – not actually the Vorm or his son, but Arok, Peb, two or three more – she passed away from like a moon-moved shadow.

After this, she came back to the spot below Lionwolf's bench.

The feast-fire was low now. As she spoke across it, her quiet voice filled the last hall in Or Tash, as clear as a chime.

'I am this cup. If you will drink, you will drink. If you will not drink, I will not be drunk by you.'

Not a man there did not feel the hairs crawl on his neck and scalp. Even Peb Yuve felt it, and thought: *She's Crarrow, after all. Then let her be, Great Gods witness me.*

Chillel spoke: 'From nothing I was made – from night and snow. I am the vessel of what made me, who are three gods, or one god that has three persons. For this, and to be this, I was created and am. He that sits there in the king's place, he was made also by a god, who is three, though in another way. Once,' said Chillel, 'it was *Summer* in the world. The sun dropped down into the sea one night, and never rose any more. Only the ghost of the sun rose, and gave no heat. Winter slunk into the world.'

Peb Yuve thought, *She speaks good Olchibe.*

Jafn – even wretched Arok – thought, *She speaks the Jafn tongue. I taught her well.*

Lionwolf knew Chillel could, as could he, speak any language she must, and simultaneously if needed.

He wanted to end her words. She talked about gods: the gods of his mother Saphay, and so of *him* – about Zeth Zezeth.

'Be quiet, Chillel,' said Lionwolf. He had heard the name bandied around very often. '*This* isn't a story.'

Chillel ceased to speak.

Lionwolf said, 'Enough of this. Let's go and cool our heads outside. There are marks set up on the wreck of the city for shooting at.'

Men ran whooping out into the snow. Others, Gech and Olchibe, saluted Lionwolf and left the hall to snatch some sleep.

As he walked by Chillel towards the open doors, Lionwolf took the cup from her hand to drink. It was empty.

'Later, I'll come in again to see you.'

Chillel said, 'I am not for you. You have no need of me.'

'Yes, I'll fuck you, girl. In here, at sunrise, before my army leaves.'

What language did they use now? All they had ever heard, perhaps some they had not.

But still she replied, 'No, I am not for you.'

Lionwolf gave her back the cup. He bent to kiss her forehead, but somehow he did not reach her skin. She smelled fragrant and cold, just as he smelled clean and flame-like.

Outside, the Lionwolf shot through the sticks and broke them, as he had broken Or Tash and Sofora. He did not bother to go to see if the woman had waited. She had not.

*

Sunset lit Ru Karismi of the Kings. So often the city had glowed in this same light. Now it resembled something burning.

A glittering fever of fear held the streets. People hurried beetle-like about. Conversely doors slammed, windows were shut and barred.

No one had run away. There was nowhere to go save the snow waste, or to uncouth and scarcely explored southern lands.

Provisions had been made, stores were being brought in, also grain, cattle and people from the surrounding steads and ice fields. Soldiery had put up makeshift wooden conning towers along the ice road of Kings Mile. Just north of the walls, bulwarks of frozen snow had been raised, and also surmounted with towers. From the highest points of the city, sentries kept watch day and night.

'What is to become of us?' said the whisper.

Other whispers added, 'Long ago this should have been stopped.'

Some declared, 'We have our High Mages – the Magikoy. They can protect us. No one can go against their magic. There are weapons here superior to anything.'

In the palaces on the highest heights, Vuldir, King Paramount, passed his evenings dining with music, even though his brother, that fool Bhorth, was a captive of the enemy.

God-statues were stolen in quantities from the temple-town. Every man wanted his own three personal deities with him, and in the most sacred form available. People fought for them there, and in the Great Markets they fought each other too for siege stores. Then soldiers came down the ramps from the upper city and dispersed the crowds with swords, and with sorcerous rays provided by magicians.

Sunset faded on Ru Karismi. Her lamps showed less in the darkness because she was hoarding oil along with all other necessities. So the light went out on her.

From the dusk, a man had come and climbed the thousand-stepped staircase of marble known as the Stair. Diagonally placed, its steel figures stood impervious. He examined only one of these, the one he usually looked at when he paused to take breath on the seven hundredth or seven hundred and first step up. It was a swordsman, with head slightly tilted and blade lowered in repose.

When the man reached the Stair top, the Gargolem came from its alcove in the high door.

'Greetings and welcome, Highness Wundest.'

'Good evening, Gargo. But I'm not here for the kings. It's you, Gargo,' said Magikoy Wundest, 'that I wish to talk with.'

The Gargolem attended. Its metallic face, that of an unknown beast, looked down at Wundest, of course expressionless.

'How may I assist you?'

'You know about the advance of war, and what we have come to – and what we approach?'

'I do.'

'Do you know that Thryfe, who might have been of help here, has vanished?'

'I am aware of it.'

'Gargo,' said the Magikoy Wundest, 'by most ancient decree, all Magikoy must assist the capital, for it is the heart of the Ruk. This you know, but do you also know where Thryfe is?'

'Yes, Highness.'

The Magikoy braced himself. 'I've been sent to ask you. Answer then, is he dead?'

'Not dead. He is in his southern house.'

'Behind walls of impenetrable ice, which not even our oculums can see through. What's happened there, Gargo?'

The Gargolem spoke through the great quietness of the city and the palaces. 'I can see in, a little, with my inner eye. The ice has also blocked up every room, every aperture. But it is not, Highness Wundest, ice.'

'Then *what*?'

'Time.'

Wundest drew back. He stared around him as if never before had he seen Ru Karismi. In fact he did not see it at all.

'Time has ceased in the South House,' elaborated the Gargolem, 'and it is therefore the passage into a second dimension, unconnected to this one, which forms an impression of freezing.'

'Did Thryfe do that? *Why*? Has he reneged on his duty to the people of the Ruk? Buried himself alive?'

'That I cannot answer, Highness.'

'He might have done something here,' said Wundest, to the city. 'He might have devised some other course.'

The Gargolem kept politely on the Stair until Wundest went away down the steps. The magician walked more hesitantly while descending, and paused three or four times. By the moment he reached the bottom, the Gargolem had gone back into its alcove.

Did it care anything for the fate of men? Sorcerously

built to serve them, yet it was indifferent – just and reason-able only through programming. Returned into its obscure corner, presumably it went on with its own thoughts.

Much further down, along the River Palest, that night other lesser gargolems had emerged. They stationed them-selves to guard parts of the solid river, in the ice of which strange symmetrical cracks had appeared. Some citizens perhaps even attributed the cracks to a change of weather.

But yet further down below the ice-sheet, seven Magikoy, of whom Wundest was not one, of whom Thryfe *should* have been – journeyed over the obsidian bridges of the Insularia and along the slopes of rock to an area beneath all the rest.

These seven had been chosen from the Order for a specific task.

The way to it was itself guarded by several gargolems. The seven Magikoy, primed as were no other men with the correct responses, soon passed through every check.

Lastly they entered, through seven separate complex gates, the central shaft.

It was a well of black glass plunging to an unknown depth. The seven, balanced on air, dropped swiftly together, by means of the shaft's own mechanism, to the place below, the Telumultuan Chamber.

To each of them then, these powerful ones, it seemed he had fallen into a tiny cubicle barely big enough to contain him, made of stone and blind of windows or any door. No others of the Magikoy with whom he had fallen were now still with him. He was alone.

For a while there was nothing else. Each Magikoy must wait in patience and calm. Well trained, each did so.

Then, from the walls, the Gargolem of the Chamber spoke. 'What are you doing here?'

Each Magikoy replied, 'There is true peril. I am here to defend from it the Rukarian people.'

'Do you know the price?'

'I know it.'

'Will you pay?'

'I will pay.'

'Pay then.'

From each of the seven sets of four close walls, a sword snaked out. They were unlike the swords of fighting men. Whippy and extended and dancing, they sliced into the bodies of the Magikoy, hurting them. The magicians must stay, under this onslaught, still as the stones. Otherwise they would die. Their blood dripped.

Presently the swords withdrew.

Trembling – not one of them did not, less from pain than physical shock – the Magikoy remained in all other ways motionless.

The walls, having analysed their intention and worth from their blood, began slowly to expand.

Seven Magikoy beheld seven narrow doors, each filled by a cold light. They walked into it, it healed their wounds. And beyond lay the Chamber of the Telumultuan, which no living thing had entered through countless centuries, except in nightmares.

The space was both high and far. It disappeared on all sides into mists of dimness and perspective. It was featureless aside from the things which stood here.

Dwarfed by these, the Magikoy gazed up and up at them.

They knew they would never, afterwards, be permitted

to speak of what they had seen, but even to themselves they would never quite be able to *describe* what they saw.

Like a forest they rose, the indescribable things, uncountable but many.

Faintly they glimmered, like a grey dawn on platinum. Their shape was, maybe, most like that of fearsome trees which had been shorn of ice and snow, and also every leaf and bough – and which had thrived on such cruelty, and become stronger. So high up they went, you could not be sure where they ended, nor if any were taller than others, and yet everyone of them was different, and everyone identical.

They were the ultimate thaumaturgical weapons the Order of the Magikoy had made, in a time so long before, it was another world.

Not one man now present still asked if it must come to this. It had *come* to it. All debate was over.

They sat down, the seven, on the floor, which seemed to be of a sort of polished granite.

They must wait until the signal reached them from the Chamber's Guardian. That was all. And it was *everything*.

None of the steadings they went by now had a man left on them, nor any animal.

The citywards fleeing Rukar had emptied the byres and barns, the growing-channels and smoke-houses and towers of brewing. Hothouses and orchards had been stripped and burnt. Nothing was willingly abandoned to assist the invader.

But these peoples of the north and east, they were used to surviving – and now their blood was up. They knew also tricks of the waste. Inventive and accurate hunters, they took meat from every patch of glacial woodland, birds from the sky, and found pockets of dormant fruit under the ice.

These lands were fabulously fertile and rich. How had they been so daft as not to come here before?

That morning, shamans of the Fazions and Vorms entered the tent of the king-leader, Lionwolf. They told him they could smell the city now. It was near, less than two whole days' march. Its size and opulence made it reek for them of plenty and luxury and overripeness. They smacked their lips.

Wizards of the Gech took auguries. The Olchibe, who never included their Crarrowin in a war march or vandal band, sat on their mammoths, smiling. They knew the city was near, right enough, and they would get there. Among the Jafn, though, the mages worked in circles of blood-red torches, preparing stews of magic to distress Ru Karismi.

'They have a few weapons there, Magikoy stuff,' said the Jafn warriors, 'past their best from lack of use.' They laughed at the weapons, having legends enough of their own, and very few of Ruk Kar Is.

Later, when they had halted again, the camp held chariot races along the ice. Lionwolf joined in. He perched on the chariot-rail, and the lions seemed to run along the air. He won; he always would – a race, a city.

When full night set in, while telling stories at the fires, they glanced up to find Lionwolf walking among them, as he often did. He told them stories also, and his stories were always of the finest. When he went to make his friendly offerings at the Ranjal cart, hundreds of his men went with him to watch. The Ranjals were the Gullahammer's talisman, and God was God – or Gods – but the Lionwolf was their own god, here and now.

'After we've taken the Rukar, what?' they asked each other. They grinned and answered, 'Perhaps the earth?'

They were on an incandescent wheel which rolled downhill, while in the imagined valley below lay Ru Karismi, small and pitiful with distance.

It was a sleep night, for tomorrow they would be against the walls.

Lionwolf retired late. He let the tent-flap drop behind him, against the mage-flames and sentry torches and dying cookfires. He fed the two lions titbits, and they lay down by the tent's entrance. Lionwolf sat on the ground.

'Guri?' he enquired of the tent. But Guri was not there. Guri now was more frequently elsewhere.

As a child it would have enraged Lionwolf, the absconding of any he wanted about him. *He* might dismiss, or absent himself – never others.

Now, he felt only loneliness. Of course, he was not unused to that: even from the first he had been placed apart. Once ejected from his mother's womb, he had been alone. It never occurred to him this was the case for everyone.

He had spotted Chillel tonight. She stood out like a black moon amid the virtually womanless camp. She was currently with an Olchibe man, not even the leader of a vandal band. He treated her respectfully, for it seemed Olchibe had come to the conclusion Chillel was some type of Crarrow. But she had told them in her tale-telling: she was directly made by the gods.

Lionwolf did not understand women. They had been too easy for him; they always worshipped him, gave in.

Even if they railed against his faithlessness, as only one or two had – Saphay one of these – they did not do it in a way that taught him anything about them.

He would have Chillel, he decided, after this battle under the Ruk capital. When all the rest was done, destroyed. To the battle he looked forward, not knowing this was his childishness, but thinking it the war-greed of a man.

Would he sleep tonight? No, he would not bother.

Something touched Lionwolf. It was like the brush of a feather along his neck. He turned frowning – and found, startled, that he *was* asleep and dreaming.

He knew this dream. It was what he avoided. Guri knew it too – should Lionwolf shout now for Guri?

A shadow was there before Lionwolf. For a second he hoped it was his own, that luminous shadow with its sparks.

The shadow addressed him. *'You make me wait.'*

It was *not* his own shadow.

Lionwolf had no terror of men; he was invulnerable to them and their implements of violence. But this was not a mortal man.

He, whose name was spelled by Rukarian scribes *Zzth*, stood there forming *in* the shadow. His hair was silver hot from a furnace. His eyes were sun-discs of gold. His face, however, was not painted indigo.

By his side was a great wolf, bluish-white. He stroked its head idly, just as Lionwolf caressed the heads of lions.

'I say, you keep me waiting, boy.'

Lionwolf glared back at him. 'What do you want from me?'

'One day, you will know.'

'You'd kill me? I am strong. You can't.'

'Oh, can I not? We shall see, when the hour breaks. Kiss the city for me tomorrow. I have shrines there.'

Lionwolf spun into the vortex of the dream and leapt for its exit-point. With a cry heard only in his head, he burst free.

Awake, he lay there on the ground. Why did he dream again of the god? The god was returning to attack and ruin him? That could never happen: Lionwolf was grown, his vitality supreme—

The human part of Lionwolf pushed inside him, humorously informing him, *It was only a dream.*

As men do, he listened to that. How else is it possible to survive?

Jemhara and Thryfe were pressed body to body. Rukarians, they had no awkwardness with sleep – which for the Jafn had become so deeply associated with dying and the state of death. Even the stars were only dogs in the hand of night, the Jafn said. Night put out the stars, just as dogs died in the service of men. Until then, *resist.*

But Thryfe and Jemhara slept, exhausted by lovemaking and sexual appetite. They had been unknowingly parched for lust and culmination; now they could not have enough. Soon they would wake to each other again. Skin and hair, limbs and hands, would slide in circling delirium, until he and she could fit themselves together in the most flawless completion. Neither had desired this or expected this. It seemed *this* had desired and expected *them.* They had therefore no autonomy. They became two parts of one whole being which yearned only to regain itself. *She* had not wanted those minutes to end, and he – he had no time for anything save her. Magicians of such power, the minutes could *not* end for her; for him time, otherwise, was redundant.

FOUR

Like a relentless hand, something had kept pulling Guri away – from the Gullahammer riding march, from Lionwolf whom he had adopted; and from, it began to seem to Guri, the physical world. He found himself *irked* by the deeds of mankind. Yes, even by the deeds – the capitulation – of Peb Yuve. Guri himself had assisted in Peb's motivation towards a war with the south. Then, Guri had brooded to see his former commander as one of the captains of – this boy. Even though, formerly, Guri had called the *boy* his leader.

He had the manners of a Rukar prince, the Lionwolf, but, Guri thought now, the *bad* manners.

The 'tween-world drew Guri off like the head from beer. He exploded into there, lay with mermaids and got them with egg, played at Olchibe battles with mammoths and comrades, and adversaries either unharmable or illusory. He squatted too, whole nights and days, on heights of the earthly landscape, staring at heaven and stars.

That was what his name meant: 'Star Dog', 'Dog Star'. Guri, so used to his name, had forgotten, until it was spoken by Lionwolf to Peb.

It was the stars Guri ached for, although mostly he refused to see this. The stars and what was behind them . . . behind the whole sorry scheme.

The day the Gullahammer swept down on to the ice fields just north of Ru Karismi, Guri had gone to the seaside. He stood on the far ice, staring at liquid black water running to an iron horizon. He was there hours or minutes, searching for something – not knowing what. A voice seemed to call to him from under the sea, under the icy extension of the shore – a mera maybe, one who had got through properly on to the mortal plane.

Disconsolate, Guri felt old. If he had lived, he would by now have reached his late thirties. Olchibe, though tough and often long-lived, greyed and lined early. He would have looked his age, as Peb did.

Better go back, see how it went. One more city smashed and eaten alive. One more triumph. Guri too had heard the boasts in the camp: the Ruk tomorrow, next the world. Preferable, then, to leave such a world. The trouble was, Guri had mislaid the means – it was finally less *when* than *how*?

When he returned into existence on the Rukar ice fields, Guri saw he had popped up by the travelling Ranjal cart, and was not best pleased. Perhaps he had been aiming for Lionwolf's standard, but now it was not here.

Instead, the deceased sibulla sat there on the cart, frustrated as uncommitted sin.

'Get off with you, you old bat,' snarled Guri.

He saw she was crying bitter tears of loss.

Both of them alive, she would have been nothing to him. He would have killed her at once, she being too elderly for rape. But now, like an Olchibe woman, Narnifa was one of his own kind.

Reluctant, Guri sat down beside her.

'Listen, silly, there's other places to go. Don't you know that?'

'Want lady,' she snivelled.

'Your lady moved about a bit, but that was some magical twitch. She's only a lump of wood. Most of these gods, that's all they are. Only the Rukar gods seem to be real – and the Great Gods too, amen. Look,' said Guri. He did a thing to the air as he could do now, and it undrew like a curtain.

Despite her grief, the sibulla glanced inside. It was a glimpse of the 'tween-world, and Guri wanted her to see something nice. She might go off after it then, not lurk here.

'You could find your Ranjal lady there,' said Guri. He recalled that he had thought Ranjal was a real god himself, once or twice. You made these mistakes.

Then he noticed what Narnifa could see through the curtain. It was a sort of foggy nothingness.

'Me not go,' she said stubbornly. He did not blame her. Guri wondered why she had seen *that* instead of what was actually there. Did she believe after death nothing was all there was? Yet here she sat.

Guri lost interest in her abruptly. He shut the air curtain, stood up and took in the overview of everything else.

They had come to Vuldir and asked him if he wished to go up to a higher room of the palace, to regard the horde covering the ice fields below the city. Vuldir had said he had no concern with garbage; that was the job of others.

When the three Magikoy arrived, one was the older

man, Wundest, who had attended Vuldir before in place of Thryfe.

'Where's Thryfe?' said Vuldir. He pulled a playful face. 'Too thoughtless of him. He is warden to my court. He should, shouldn't he, be here on such a day?'

'Thryfe is unable to attend you, Vuldir. But we are Magikoy, and that is enough for you.'

'Is it? So high-handed always, your Order. But look at the predicament of the city. What have you been at?'

'Preparation for the city's defence,' said Wundest.

'Oh, good.'

'It is not good, Vuldir. Magikoy law has held the Order here, but you yourself should have deployed troops. Your lesser cities might have been defended, saved. You have lost them all – Thase Jyr, Kandexa, Sofora . . .'

'Yes, I remember their names.'

'. . . Or Tash,' finished Wundest. His voice, unusual in a Magikoy, carried a fierce emotion – reined-in anger.

But Vuldir paid no heed. Vuldir's universe had always been minuscule. His cleverness seemed profound to others, and to himself, only in such a little confine. However, things had changed.

'It appears,' said Vuldir, 'there are a lot of these barbarians.'

'We believe over thirty thousand men.'

Even Vuldir was, for a second, astonished. Only for a second. 'Rabble.'

'Vuldir,' said Wundest, 'you yourself, through your ambition and villainous plots, your idiocy, your self-obsessive laziness and lack of care, have brought Ru Karismi and the Ruk to this. Only the highest gods now

know what outcome is written in Fate's book. But if any of
the Magikoy survive, you will answer to us.'

'I?'

'You. What are *you*? Less than the lowest of your
subjects who carries out excrement, or corpses for burial.
These men earn their keep. Even he that lies always drunk,
and dreams, is worth more, Vuldir, than you are, for he
causes no injury by what he does to another. But you,
you, you batten on your people, taking everything and
giving nothing back. Only this you've given them – their
death.'

Vuldir had nothing to say. Then he spoke: 'But no one
will die inside Ru Karismi. I'm king here. I've been told of
the sorcerous armament beneath the river—'

Wundest turned from Vuldir, King Paramount. The two
other Magikoy turned about with him.

They left Vuldir standing there, in his elegant and
artistic room that could not even show him the enemy
smothering the plains outside, and inside his little rotten
personal world.

But otherwise, on every high terrace or tower or roof, Ru
Karismi had come out to see.

What they saw was lit darkness, a shadow which
sparkled, spilling down and down over the white scroll of
the snow and ice towards them.

It was like the avalanches of the mountains, or the tides
of the liquid outer sea.

The watchers watched, and their hearts turned like
milk.

From the conning towers and makeshift out-wall forts,

the soldiery was speeding back along the ice road, and over the barricades of snow. Back to the walls of the city they hurried, and were taken in. Manpower alone could never hold off this streaming ocean of enemy darkness, bright with weapons and banners. Rukarian soldiers would man the walls from within: no more could or would be asked of them.

It was a fact, if these battalions had been sent earlier to the Ruk's western cities, they could not have saved them against such odds. Perhaps, on the other hand, if there had been Magikoy left in those cities, all four *might* have been saved. Wundest had spoken to the king illogically, hating Vuldir's insouciance and his corruption. The Order of the Magikoy knew all this was Vuldir's fault – it had come from his plot to have killed his own daughter Saphay, rather than allow her use in a treaty, which act had thrown her in the way of a god, and so led to the birth of the Lionwolf. Yet the Magikoy too were guilty. They had failed to pierce the veil and foretell sufficiently and in time. And this they also knew.

As the huge gates south and north of Ru Karismi were shut and their giant bolts thrust home, the south-flowing horde began to puddle and bulge at its head. The bulge then opened out to either side, a great distance, before rolling forward once more in two severed streams. The intention of the manoeuvre was instantly apparent. The two terrible arms opened from the body of the horde kept extending and extending to encircle the city and hold it tight.

Until now it had been, this horde, a *creature* in its own right, less or more horrible for that. But as it came ever nearer, now the watchers saw at last what made it up. They saw the numberless chariots, the leaping of lions, the flaxen bulk of mammoths, the fish-horses with forehead horns plated by glass and bronze. Banners they saw, highly coloured rags and tags of scarlet and blue and yellow and white, and skulls and icons on poles. The weak sun flared on metal wheels and shieldings, armouring, blades, lances. But nevertheless the shadow, so bright and spangling, stayed for the city as dark as night. And how near night was – they were afraid.

By now through Ru Karismi stalked the lesser gargolems of the Magikoy. Citizens turned to see these, too, in fear. The gargolems spoke gently to them: 'Hear this from the Magikoy. Go in now. Go in and close all your doors and your windows, and every opening of the house. Keep your children by you. Bind their eyes, and yours, with cloth. Lie flat on your faces on the floor. Whatever occurs, do not look to see. Pray to your gods.' Over and over, this message uttered. 'What—' the citizens cried, 'what does it mean?' The gargolems did not explain, but moved on to tell all others. People milled, veered away. The Magikoy must be obeyed. Most, as they ran, grasped after all what the instruction meant – the legendary arsenal was to be utilized. The city was to be rescued.

Down by the River Palest, those running saw the ice-sheets appallingly split. Vast slots appeared, but under them there was no thaw of water, only impossible depths. The Insularia lay below – they needed to see no more.

The soldiers and guards were being withdrawn from the walls. Some went protesting, for already spears, arrows and burning missiles were being shot upwards from forming enemy emplacements below. What the enemy did looked to the professional soldiers of the Ruk capricious and careless. Yet, given the sheer numbers of the foe, even these haphazard actions were overpoweringly threatening.

'It is with the Magikoy now,' the soldiery was told.

They saw Wundest the magician walking along the walltop. Two others of the Order were with him. He told the remaining soldiers on the north wall to go down.

'What of you, sir?'

Wundest did not answer.

The soldiery went towards their protecting barracks. Here they were told to bind their eyes, and lie down on the floor.

Below, random barbarian shooting went on, for the most part missing its target, for the walltops were high and the city built up behind them. Now and then something would land, crackle and splutter out in the cold.

It seemed none of this fire had yet been mage-charged. The enemy was not yet being entirely serious.

Wundest gazed out to the north. It was dark with the horde, for miles on miles.

'He is there,' he said.

The other Magikoy nodded.

They could sense him, the god-demon-man called Lionwolf, just as the hungry Faz shamans had *smelled* the city.

The second Magikoy said to Wundest, 'Is that his name – Vashdran?'

'Yes, in the Rukarian tongue, *Vashdran*. It means Lion-who-is-wolf and Wolf-who-is-lion. That's what he is to them. Some fabled beast of the Northlands.'

They stopped talking, looking out towards the

war-thousands of the one called Vashdran, thinking of a death so close they could hear the silence of its heart.

He rode his mammoth along the lines of his men.

He had chosen it for its height, so they could all see him. Next, as he normally did, he would take to his lion chariot. That would be once he went to break a gate, or if any came out to fight them.

So far nothing stirred from the city.

The introductory slight activity – Ruk soldiers running away, a slinging of lodged flame-arrows off the walls – all that had stopped and nothing else begun.

This city disappointed Lionwolf. He had anticipated much more of it. It looked as if it were only carved from snow, and was not as large as Saphay had led him to believe.

Would the battle also disappoint?

Surely the Rukarians were readying themselves?

The Jafn warriors, arranged in rows in their chariots, their lions restless and eagerly snarling and mage-fires carried about among them, were jeering at the Rukar city. 'What, are they *asleep*, these sleep-lovers?' This mocking chant had soon caught on. They were bellowing towards the vacancy of the high walls, *'Wake up! Your friends are here!'*

Lionwolf smiled, to show his Jafn he appreciated their bravery and wit.

Over on the left flank of the Gullahammer, Peb Yuve's mammoth towered among other mammoth towers. Lionwolf raised his hand, and Yuve's yellow banner, with its fresh decaying head, was shaken back at him.

Lionwolf's own blue sun and fire flag had been bolted already into his chariot.

Gech battle lines lay over behind the Olchibe. Their leaders had tossed a painted counter to decide which nation should have the honour of the front place – Olchibe won. From the left flank, Olchibe had constructed the left city-encircling arm, but Gech had pounded with them too, despite losing the toss.

The right arm was crammed with Jafn, Vorms and Faz, mingled in ravening harmony. Lionwolf had promised the Fazions – who had worked so vigorously at Thase and Kandexa, and raced back overland to join him here – the south gate.

Lionwolf nodded to the Faz shaman, trotting yards down by the mammoth's feet. The shaman erected his skinny arm and sent a coppery ball of light whirling away over the pack of warriors, who yelled. It was the signal to the right arm that it might begin to *hammer*.

Gullahammer – *hammer of a million heads*, that was what the antique word meant. It was a pun – the heads were those of the allies who comprised it, who were it seemed a million strong – also the heads of those enemies they would stave in.

As this enormous ripple of motion flexed across the horde, Lionwolf watched a moment, a fascinated spectator.

He spoke to the men around him, who were craning for his every utterance. 'No need to fight them if they're too tired to meet us. We can *push* their bloody city over.'

Laughter yowled along the lines. 'What did he say? Did he say *that* – yes! Push over the city of the sleepers.'

Lionwolf swung from the mammoth's back, walked off down its side.

His chariot was there for him. He ran round and gripped the manes of the two lions, kissing their lipless mouths. 'Live long, my brothers. Kill a multitude.'

He sprang into the chariot and waved again, up at the pale mammoth, as if bidding his favourite girl goodbye – but only for an hour or two. The mammoth trumpeted.

From the Gullahammer's left arm, the trumpeting of other mammoths rose miles higher than their own height.

The atmosphere, which had been quiescent save for the waiting noises of beasts and metal and the chants of derision, rang now like brazen bells. It was full of thunder, wheels and thudding, footfalling progression, jangle of weapons, armour, carapaces, the clacking storm-wrack of banners, the battle-screams of men.

A new upcast rain of fire-arrows and spears was launched at the walls.

Lionwolf drove straight at the north gate called Northgate. It was his, he had claimed it. His army made way for him, widening an avenue, then pouring in to fill the flaming comet's tail of his chariot's passage.

On every side, rainbow rays and upward-falling stars of mage-fire crossed each other as they flew at Ru Karismi.

Lionwolf rode with his head back. He too was in flight.

That was when, through the galvanic thrust of speed, he saw abruptly, and too clearly, that three men did stand there up on the northern wall.

Only three – and so well defined. They must be magicians of the city, the famous Magikoy.

Lionwolf laughed to note them. It came to him that the gate would burst open and no one could stand against him, and that he, a god, could run directly up the city's colossal wall, and seize these three Magikoy and hurl them off, under the churning wheels of those who would follow him, charging into the resistless city—

As his Jafn warriors were doing, Lionwolf let out a bellowing shout of victory and bloodlust. His mind was uncluttered as a shard of glass. He saw reflected there this world he would have, and that he was invincible.

High above him, the Magician Wundest and his two companions looked down.

'*Now*,' said Wundest. 'It is *now*. Gods pardon us for this, and take in payment our three lives, here given willingly to atone.'

Like the Gullahammer, like the Lionwolf, Wundest flung his voice upward in a scream. It was for loss, for rage and terror, and for the agony to come.

Northgate was splintering. All around, walls rocked to the crash of iron and wood rams and incendiary blasts. Mage-fires danced along the walltops. The sky was ribboned by rays. Southgate also staggered. Horsazin, shod with steel, kicked shrieking at undefended timbers.

Ru Karismi lay blindfolded on its face. Tears and urine soaked the floors. Do not look – do not *look*.

Under the ice of the Palest River, a hiss. Then a rush, like enormous wings.

It was anyway not possible to see what emerged from the slots in the ice, out of the Insularia below, from the bowel of the Telumultuan Chamber. A glimmer in the air, like softest lightning – that was all.

But, oh, the *sound*.

A great throat had come undone. Neither men nor mages nor mammoths could forge such a tumult. It outdid the storming of the horde of the Gullahammer. It even quenched that. It was so loud, then it passed away into a silence. The silence was *white* – noise had become silence and silence white.

White *was* on the plains beneath Ru Karismi. There was an impact; it was silent. The impact was whiter than the whitest snow. It was beyond whiteness. It was crimson and then black. It was night. It was the night that ends all days.

One second, there had been movement, war, violence, *life*—

A second more, a second of white that was black, and sound that was white that was black—

A third second began. In the third second, there was no longer movement. No violence, no noise, not even a noise that was silent and white. The white died.

The sky had sagged to a stale dark green. From it fluttered a kind of transparent sleet.

This dropped mildly to the ice fields, and to the city of Ru Karismi.

The third second, however, persisted. Nothing altered. Nothing *moved*.

Ah, something after all – from the northern wall, three pillars like blocks of congealed salt, formless, unidentifiable, toppling slowly off.

Down through the green air they spun. Reaching the ground, they shattered into pieces. And, in shattering, shattered what had been there – the other things of salt, some lumpen, some almost – *almost* – to be recognized.

A weird glimmering, like a translucent forest of stalks, lingered over the flat, colourless plains, then faded.

Still nothing moved. At last a wind whistled by, a thoughtless wind.

A man stood up in a cage of salt that had been – had it? – a chariot. The wind combed back his red hair. He was naked. His clothes had become salt, his standard of sun and fire also. He stood looking at the lions of his chariot team, each a perfect leaping statue, changed to stone. But, oh, the wind came, thoughtless, and breathed on them. They crumbled, and with the wind, their salt-dust blew away.

FIVE

If you had not seen this place, you could not know it, now.

Yet, even so, nor *could* you ever know it. Unknowable.

Guri picked his way, like a man of flesh and blood, between the pillars, stacks and mounds of fused, partly eroded salt. Always the wind came whistling, and scoured off more of the salty dust. Chariot wheels, lances, standards, men and beasts, skin, hair and bones – *eyes*, *hearts* – blew odourless, colourless on the wind.

Guri leant over and threw up. Or he thought he did. It was what one must do here, spew or sob. Or lie down and die, and Guri did not have that option.

Here, where he had come, had been parked the baggage carts, the dray or riding hnowas, spare weapons and vehicles, spare lion teams, young mammoths kept back to learn at a distance. Here too had been sent the few witches and women. None of this would you ever guess.

Guri cried.

Then he stood still and said aloud what he had witnessed: 'Like a lightning flash that *stayed*—' and then, 'I saw the spirits of men and animals go up in clouds, all together, like smoke. They went into another sky, behind the stars.'

Guri cried like a boy, knuckling his eyes, wiping his nose on his braids.

Peb Yuve was dead. Olchibe – all Olchibe – dead. Gech. Jafn. Half the sons of Vormland and Faz.

Guri did not look for the Lionwolf. To see the Lionwolf would have made Guri very sick again. No, he had come to discover what had happened to the old sibull who haunted the Ranjal cart.

But where was the cart? She was not a goddess, Ranjal – not a real goddess. Even though she had once taken wing like a hornet, she would have been struck to stone and salt like everything else.

Something poked Guri hard in the back ribs.

He jumped round.

He almost sat down, fell over, from surprise.

One Ranjal was standing in the salt desert, on the sour, discoloured ice. She was no longer wooden or inanimate. As he recollected from her images, her untidy rough hair streamed down her back like a badger's pelt. Multi-handed, her fingers and nails were branch-like claws, with one of which she had stabbed at his back. Her eyes were black and brilliant.

'Ranjal-Narnifa, I,' she said. She had a young voice now. 'Bow me, man-ghost.'

What had slain so many things of every type had done with the sibull and her goddess something else. Neither had been fleshly-living. They had become an amalgam, and alive.

Guri wanted to kick her, this two-in-one undeserving refugee. But he was sensible. Who knew now what she was capable of? He bowed and put at her feet, with a fawning word, several handfuls of nothing.

*

Over Ru Karismi, true night had passed. The new day was sunny, but the blue sky curiously and unevenly shaded, as if stained.

They looked at it in fear, now the blindfolds were off.

The following day, the sky showed clean again. This, however, was the day on which illness and dying began.

A child sank down on a street by the Great Markets, where some effort at commerce was again being made. Picking the child up, its mother learned it was already dead. As the sun went over, others sank and perished. The malaise was swift – a tiredness, a pallor, a state between fainting and slumber. The weakest were swept up in minutes; the very strong lasted between one and seven days.

Some were immune, apparently. Again, occasionally some, rather than sicken went mad, and dashed howling through the city, striking out, biting and wailing gibberish. There seemed no logic to these ailments. Often the frail did not sicken, and instead the young and healthy were dispatched.

They said a plague had been brought to the city with the enemy horde. Only the medicinal weapons of the Magikoy had disinfected it, if not quite in time.

Naturally, though, it was those same weapons which had seeded the plague. Gradually some became aware of that.

Those inside the city had seldom glanced beyond it – what had ever been outside to intrigue them? Now, forbidden for safety's sake to leave the metropolis for the salt-yard outside, claustrophobia erupted among the people. Riots ensued: they were put down harshly, and at once, by the surviving soldiery and guards.

The shrines of the temple-town grew full to over-flowing, then drained to emptiness.

Above, the beautiful clarity of the skies went on, washed and burnished by the hands of heartless gods.

Many of the Magikoy were also dead. Intent on helping the citizens, they had come out from the fastness of their Insularia inside an hour, and so were also exposed to the creeping death.

Now, of the formerly unknown number of these magicians, only eleven men and two women remained in Ru Karismi.

They stood in a half circle and gazed at Vuldir, King Paramount, seated on his carved chair.

'Tonight, Vuldir, you will die.'

Vuldir, who had been allowed to keep his elegant garments and jewels, but not the crown of king, did not deign to reply.

That evening, under a triple moonrise of searing brightness, Vuldir was burned alive at the foot of the great Stair.

This the city watched in voiceless malice, and dread. He had not tried to escape, did not beg for mercy, excuse himself, rant or even cry out as the flames ate him. It was said he had been given an opiate to spare him the pain of the fire.

Later, crowds roamed the thoroughfares, climbed the thousand steps to gaze transfixed at the palace walls. There were no longer guards. Anyone who wanted entered the citadel of their kings, and wandered around unlit palaces and pavilions, beneath sculptures of ice and marble.

Law and the everyday rituals were finished.

The Magikoy called the Gargolem, but it never came. It had not even come out when the crowds climbed up the Stair.

Winds blew soft. Colourless dust coated the city. The citizens were now accustomed to it. Ashes rested in the hair and on the lips of those wandering in the gardens of kings, tasting of *white*.

'No other way. There was no other way to defend ourselves. Lives will be lost, now and through the coming months; perhaps one-third of those inside the walls will sicken and die. But if the barbarians of the north and east had got in, *all* of us would have died. We saw *their* mercy, that god-driven mob, at Or Tash—'

Bhorth turned on his bed, troubled by the voice he heard. Then he thought it was his own voice, lecturing in his brain.

He sat upright. He was not on a pallet in the enemy tent, but lying on the ground. Yes, lying on the salt-dust – which was corpses.

Bhorth got up. He brushed himself off, spat. He was naked – his clothes had gone with everything else in the white second. Oddly, what had heatlessly scorched them from him had not harmed a hair of his head or body. He did not feel cold.

He remembered now, back before the world ended, he had been in the tent after the woman was gone. That was a funny business. Had the Lionwolf-king sent her to him as some sort of treat or trial? She was black all over – Bhorth had never seen such a woman, so beautiful, perfect. She had offered herself without preamble, and Bhorth accepted.

The tent having been pitched for him among the baggage and stores, his three guards went off with two of the witchgirls, Gech creatures with green-dyed hair. Neither these girls nor Bhorth had been, though captive, shackled or restrained in any way.

Bhorth had known the city was just along the ice fields, but he was by then one man alone, without an army. He had done his best. After the black woman left him, he lay there listening grumpily to the noises of battle, cursing. He would not go out to see. What point? Then whiteness came, and sound that was without sound.

For a scatter of days since, Bhorth, once King Accessorate, had been blundering about the salty heaps, looking for his past – or some reason. The city was hidden from him now by a kind of haze, which shone by day and in moonlight – the fog of the death-dust catching light. Bhorth could not make himself go towards the hidden city.

He asked himself what he meant to do, and could not answer himself. He kept forgetting anyway what had happened, dropping asleep, then waking and freshly remembering. He knew this was what he did. What he had said to himself just now, that too he had said before. He, as a minor king, had known about the ultimate weapons under the city. He had thought they were a lie. But lies, it seemed, coming true were more forceful than mere truth. Probably the Magikoy had said what Bhorth kept on repeating to himself. Somehow he had heard it blown to him on the wind of aftermath, only rephrasing it in his own words.

Going around a chunk of salt-death, Bhorth stopped. A

man was there – another man like himself, if of a different race. Yellow-skinned, he too was naked, but kept his hair on body and head.

Bhorth was madly happy to find him. He bounded forward and grabbed the man and hugged him close as a long-lost son.

The man hugged him back. In some outlandish tongue he murmured to Bhorth.

Bhorth thought perhaps he could understand it – Gech, yes it was Gech, from the furthest North.

'Name – give me your name,' demanded Bhorth, wanting to know everything, rationing himself.

'Ipeyek.'

Bhorth was thankful his grasp of the Gech language was so much better than he recalled.

'I am Bhorth—' About to say something of kingship, Bhorth grunted. 'Are there others – like us?'

'Yes,' said the man called Ipeyek. 'Some alive.'

'Only the gods know how. The blast must have missed us—'

He and Ipeyek stepped apart.

Ipeyek said seriously, 'No, but protection on us.'

Bhorth thought of this. He was a king, but apparently he had not been elected to survive through that, for here was this Gech nomad – had he said he was a nomad? – but he too. It seemed to Bhorth he himself spoke Rukarian after all, yet the Gech followed, as he, Bhorth, followed the Gech tongue the nomad spoke.

'*What* protection?'

'Through wife,' said Ipeyek.

'Whose?'

'Wife of me.'

'Your wife then is a mageia? She must have vast powers. Have I *met* your wife?'

Ipeyek modestly lowered his eyes. There was dust thick on his lashes.

The wind blew. When it lay down, both men spat filth from their mouths.

It was then that Bhorth saw two other live ones, Jafn tribals from their white hair, aimlessly meandering along maybe half a mile away, between the stacks of salt.

'See!' Bhorth shouted. Waving his arms, he began to gallop towards these further fellow survivors, wanting to hug them, love them, where a dozen days back he would have spitted them on a sword.

Thirty men sat together on the ground. They were all unarmed, naked, their bodies clad only in hair. They did not seem to feel the cold, even in the pith of night.

Sometimes they talked. Now one would say this, now another would say it, or something very similar. They were in agreement, and could each understand exactly what every man there said, though the languages were several, and the dialects diverse. A band of brothers, now and then they would put a hand on another man's shoulder, or jokingly cuff him.

Only Arok stood outside the fellowship, morose and bereft.

It was not that he could not also fathom the languages, or make himself clear. It was not that he was unwelcomed.

At the start he had been, like all of them, wild with joy at the prospect of company. But slowly, going about in the dust with them, sitting down with them in an untidy circle as if about an unlit invisible hearth, Arok had seen, he believed, his difference.

He was in fact not even the first with her – with Chillel. Ipeyek had been first. *Then* there was Arok. *Then* all the others, only some of whom were represented here tonight. It would seem, however, the rest of the others must be *somewhere* about. For whoever Chillel had cutched, he had lived through the Magikoy weapon-death. *They* had not changed to pillars of salt, which the wind whittled away.

None of them could rationalize it. She had not even selected them, but allowed them to select her. If they had been in doubt, her anecdote about the cup of drink – which tale had travelled the war camp after Or Tash – made so much obvious. Arok, though, she *had* chosen.

Why had she *chosen* Arok?

Perturbed, he moved around the edges of the circle, his bare feet scuffing the dust. His own insidious importance riled him, and the unawareness of it among the twenty-nine other men. He had never had much authority, Arok. Kin to the Holas Chaiord, he had had no prospects of more than kinship. He lived in hall with the other Holas warriors, took women when they were available, and fought when his chief said so.

It nagged at Arok, now, that there was something he must do.

'She chose me,' he said to the circle.

None of them registered his words.

Arok realized he had not spoken them aloud.

Turning, he gazed away through night towards the area where the Rukar city went on standing. It should have been rubble, but was not. Also, by night, in dust-fog without moonlight, it vanished.

Arok considered going off that way. That man over there, he was one of the lower kings of the city – either this had been told to Arok, or Arok had guessed it, in the way they correctly guessed each other's languages. But this man, Bhorth, showed no sign of going back to his city.

Arok decided *he* would go.

'Farewell,' he said.

No one heard him. Obviously, his individuality had shut him from their notice.

As he set out, loping through the dust, Arok pondered if Chillel herself had lived. Perhaps she was not anyway real – simply some antidote God made for men to take against the Magikoy weapons. Of the fate of the Lionwolf, Arok did not think. Not one of them had. It was as if he, the being who had caused all this, had been erased from memory.

The night was very dark. Arok did not judge it properly. The way the ice was now, hard as a petrified drum, and the dust . . . they misled him, too.

He was running in the wrong direction, not south, but east. He was running back towards Jafn lands. His body did maybe know this, even if the compass of his mind was out.

Presently he smelled something other than the white smell of the powdered dead. It was the scent of ice and snow stretching away and away, and even conceivably the frigid tang of the sea. Running yet, Arok assessed these aromas and knew he went the wrong – or right – way.

Two or three hours after, moons rose in the east in front of him. By then he was well into his stride. He loped on, steady as a wolf, towards the moons.

Third Intervolumen

God forgive me for ever having lived.

Bardic Lay of the Hero Kind Heart: Jafn

Vashdran . . . Lionwolf . . . Nameless.

If birds had been in the sky – and there were none – they would have seen him. He was a solitary figure, mythic in its incongruity, a naked man walking southwards. His head was down: he looked, it seemed, only at the waste of the snow, as if it were chancy here to take a step. The ice road, Kings Mile, had vanished but anyway, by now, he had left it far behind. The landscape was featureless. Above was a wan sky and a pastel sun that seemed hooded in its own smoke. Probably he had been walking for many days, also during many nights. There was no living thing there but for himself. Once there was an ice-forest to the west – or to the east. It gleamed, that was all. Later it too was left behind.

No birds then to see this. Perhaps therefore only the sun could see, being so much higher, what came walking *after* the naked red-haired man, maybe half a day at his back. This second walker was like . . . his *shadow*.

The land went upwards. Still peering at his feet, the man climbed unerringly up with it, taking no notice of it or of anything.

Somehow – in fact quite easily, for the waste was wide – he had passed no familiar landmark, nothing he had ever been told of, either by his Rukarian mother or by earth-bounding Uncle Guri. If he had seen anything like that, recognizable, might it have slowed him or focused his thoughts in a new way? If he had seen the *Shadow*, would he have noted *that*?

Really, it could not be his shadow at all. His shadow was full of lights, and this one coal-black. Also, its shape was not masculine but distinctly female.

When the long slope of the land had gone up for centuries into the sky, and another night came, the man dropped on his face without any warning, even to himself. Flat on the ice, he appeared to sleep, his head turned across one arm. Hour on hour he slept, as he had not done since babyhood. And so, in the dusk of dawn, she, Chillel, at last caught up with him.

He woke to find her seated by him. She was a figure of supreme remoteness, and naked as he apart from her long, long hair. She turned and gazed at him. She said, 'Now I am yours.'

Lionwolf took no notice of this. Yet, perhaps he did, for he turned his head the other way from her.

While he returned to sleep, Chillel sat beside him. She seemed comfortable in the snow, where he had only seemed enduring. Of course, snow was her mother.

The sun rose. The sky blued.

Then he woke up again. Lionwolf pulled himself to his feet. He acted awkwardly a moment, like a boy of ten or eleven, then haughtily he moved off a short space and urinated, side on to Chillel, sitting unconcerned down the hill. She watched in silence.

Lionwolf came back. He sat next to her.

'I've no use for you now.'

She said nothing.

After an hour, Lionwolf got up again without glancing

at the woman, and walked off along the snow-ridge southwards.

Chillel also got up. She followed him as before, but now keeping only a Jafn spear-length behind him.

Below the ridge lay more of the white desert, with nothing on it but frozen ridges and runnels, some quite large.

The lands south of the borders of the Ruk had been reckoned savage by all and sundry. For incalculable distances they were vacant, even their forests virtually unpopulated. Eventually there began ice-locked rocky crags. Hollow tunnels, maybe natural, led through, among emerald caves, to a region the Magikoy and other sages had sparsely written of, Kraagparia – the country of the Kraag. Who or what these people were had been a matter of uninterested debate in the Ruk, of indifference only to other races north and east. Saphay, and therefore Lionwolf, knew nothing of them, though she and he had heard their name.

If Chillel knew anything of them – or of anything at all – only the god who made her could say.

Lionwolf walked, and Chillel walked behind him. The sun walked over above and, when dark came back, the moons.

Near the last quarter of the night, again Lionwolf stopped. Now he did not drop down to sleep. He stood looking up at the stars – the moons had sunk by then.

In the end, he spoke to her once more.

'What do you want?'

'What you will give me.'

'What's that?'

'I must wait and see.'

'I told you what I'd give you, and you wouldn't take it

then. Now, though you're naked as a knife, I couldn't care less for you. Don't you know, woman, something *happened* – back where the city was, and the battle. Don't you know?'

She did not speak.

Lionwolf said, 'Where do I go to talk of this? I call Guri – he doesn't answer. Is it possible he *too* . . . Where am I to go?'

Chillel said, 'You walk southwards.'

'I don't know why. Away – that's all. I walk *away* from *that*.' He hunkered down on the ground, as Guri had done. Lionwolf said, 'What must I do?'

Did he ask *her*?

Chillel did not answer. Nothing did.

Like a child, Lionwolf thought, *Let me forget all this*. Like a man, he thought, *I can never be free of this, what I did and caused*. He had no one to pray to, no friend to consult. His own self he did not know except as an alluring stranger.

He sprang up and now he ran, coordinated and light as an animal or a machine, leaping over the runnels of snow – southwards still southwards. Chillel walked after him. When he was a mile off, due to the now downward slope of the terrain she continued to see him without difficulty.

Very close to sunrise, a white icenvel broke from its burrow under the snow and bolted across Lionwolf's path. Stooping even as he ran, without loss of momentum, Lionwolf pulled a shard out of the top-snow. He shaped it in seconds, and flung it, and brought the thick-furred, rat-like creature down, dead with the blow.

Then he halted. He stood over the icenvel, marvelling at how sudden death always was. He had had some vague idea that he had killed it for food, but he had now no wish or need to eat. He had done this out of fear of what he *could* do. The pointless slaughter of the icenvel thrilled him to a terror beyond thought. It ranked level for him, in its own minor, total way, with the death of thirty or forty thousand human things.

Chillel reached him when the sun was lifting over the horizon, for he had stayed there, staring at the icenvel.

Then she performed a peculiar act. He believed it peculiar, turning to watch her.

She buried the icenvel under the ice and snow, using her hands to make the little grave. Then she fashioned, from the same snow, three flower-like shapes, letting them perch there on the mound.

'Is that,' he asked her, 'some custom of Gech?'

Chillel smiled her mysterious smile, and shook her head.

Lionwolf moved off again, only striding now, not running.

For a minute, Chillel did not yet follow. She paused to observe the rays of the sun melting the glassy edges of the flowers she had made. The unusual phenomenon seemed to involve her, but it was hard to tell.

The land stumbled down into an ice-lake. It was broad, almost to the sky's edge. When they too descended and began to cross its surface, they were able to see big slaty fish imprisoned under and in its mirror. A day was necessary in crossing the lake.

On its south shore, a band of primitive hutters lived, the first live creatures – aside from Chillel, and the icenvel – that Lionwolf had beheld since Ru Karismi.

The hutters were not afraid, nor benign. They rushed out of their low thin ice-huts, brandishing ice-spears, the grips bound in fish-skin. A low thin people, to match their huts, they scudded along the shore, ululating.

Lionwolf said, 'What shall I do? Shall I kill them too?'

Chillel said nothing.

Lionwolf growled and spat on the lake. Then he plunged forward. Meeting the first three men, he smashed their spears, and next their skulls, with his fists. The rest separated into two groups, one of which stayed motionless while the other swarmed in over Lionwolf.

He slew them all, breaking them in pieces. Not a cut or thrust of theirs harmed him, as usual.

The remaining group, once the others were dead, flew round and dived back shorewards and into the huts, blocking up the doors with door-shapes of ice that had been standing ready.

Lionwolf stripped the dead of their fish-skin and furs. These he threw before Chillel.

'Dress yourself,' he said, 'you whore.' Then he laughed.

Having himself donned a selection of the stinking garments, Lionwolf strode off again. Chillel, having obeyed him and also dressed, followed.

The foul smell of the improvised clothes soon dispersed, rinsed away by their two supernatural bodies.

After this meeting, they met no others. But the next day an ice-jungle appeared, spread all across the route.

Once they had reached and entered it, they found after all that game existed there. Presently, using an ice-spear retained from the huts, Lionwolf killed a deer. This he skinned, bled, jointed and ate raw, sitting on the ground.

Chillel did not eat, but she drew a single bone out of the flesh, cleaning it in the snow.

'Why do you want that?'

'I have never properly seen a bone just then taken outside the body.'

'What *are* you?' said Lionwolf.

It was again the question most often asked of him.

'I am Chillel.'

He shrugged but his eyes narrowed, watching her in the silvery jungle dimness. 'What does your name mean?'

'Cold,' she said. 'Darkness,' she said. 'The nomads named me.'

He must, with his command of language, already have known that.

'Who was your mother?'

Chillel said, 'I was not born.'

'No? How then? You spoke before about three gods.'

'I don't know.'

'You *know*.'

'Then I know but have forgotten.'

'Make *me* forget, Chillel,' he said. 'Come here.'

'Soon,' she said.

'What, are you putting me off again – after all *this*?'

They sat several feet apart while saying these things. He had not reached towards her. Even his sexual organ did not stir at the prospect of her, though the furs concealed it.

Lionwolf lay down, then he turned over on his face. He began to beat on the icy ground, and to shout and scream in the bell-like way of stags, and men.

When the seizure of his anguish, which he did not

grasp, and so could neither accept nor dismiss, left him, he fell asleep again.

Further along in the night, he got up and stood in the jungle clearing, calling loudly for Guri. But Guri never came.

The woman did nothing either time. She sat there all night, turning a deer-bone in her hand.

Forests, jungles met them, disbanded. Twice more they saw other beings at large in the world – once a caravan of an ungainly sort, with woolly elephants as drays; once a village, a shambles of hovels and smokes. To neither of these human manifestations was Lionwolf drawn. He had now anyway an utter basic contempt for humanity. By out-witting and charming it, by *besting* it, he had come mostly to this overpowering scorn; although by *destroying* it he had given it another power over him – but that he had not yet understood.

Once too there was what looked like a ruinous city or town marooned in the midst of the ice plain. They did not go near. Perhaps it was only a weird formation of rocks and ice.

The southern ice-crags themselves were visible by now. They climbed them, he striding up *horizontally*, as he had not done since Ru Karismi. He flaunted himself, all his glamour and cleverness, before Chillel. Perhaps he did not realize this.

At night, sitting on the ground, she would tell him stories. He had started to like them, to rely on them – a familiar consolation. Saphay had story-told in the past, and Guri, and even Ranjal, goddess of wood.

Chillel's stories he did not fathom, not quite. They were, as in the hall at Or Tash, oblique.

She spoke often of the dying of the sun. She spoke of the Age of Ice, the Winter of five centuries and more.

One time she did tell a sort of actual story. It concerned the creation of beasts out of stars, painted on the heavens and then let go to fill the earth.

Every night, he coaxed her to lie down with him and make love. 'Soon,' she said.

'Always it's soon, never now. Suppose I force you.'

Chillel said, in a voice like the faintest shimmer on the ice, 'It would be no good.'

'How do you know? Perhaps I should just try.'

But the slight heat in his eyes – red, blue – went out. He was thinking, to put him off she need only remind him of that place – the place of *salt* – of two lions made of black or white clinker that crumbled in a breeze—

'There is a tower,' said Chillel, story-telling. 'It is the sun's tower. Men know it by its windows. It was, now is not, but will be. A hero always goes to such a tower, the tower of a god, even if he is only a man and a warrior. There are others: one,' said Chillel, 'is a tower of ice, and one a tower of cloud. But this one is a tower with fiery windows.'

When she was silent, Lionwolf said to her, 'Which hero is it that *always* goes there?' He wanted to name the heroes, and their races: Jafn, Gech, Olchibe – but he could not name them. They were done.

He lay with his unabating pain a terrible while, watching moons and stars, and the south crags. He thought now it was a failing in him, because he was not human, that he could not deal with despair, agony and guilt – not knowing it was the *human* part of him which could not, and therefore how much stronger it had become.

Only sometimes did she speak in an informal way to him. She did it when they reached the first cave system tunnelling the crags. 'It's here – here we go in, don't we?'

'Why not,' he said. He had no notion where he went, or why. He had been trying to outstride horror which kept pace.

The caves were like grape-green jacinth.

'Do you know this cave?' he asked her.

'No.'

He believed she talked more now, perhaps the stories had got her used to it. Also he thought she lied more.

He did not like her. He wanted her – also more and more, the more she spoke. And he felt *alone* when with her, as he had never felt even when alone and feeling alone. As with so much, he did not comprehend what he felt.

They entered the green jacinth caves.

It was warm in there: cryotites blazed like sulphurous fangs. Even in the night, light loitered in the caves, and strange songs were sung by air or winds blowing through holes and crevices.

'We could build our house here,' he said. 'Why travel on?'

That night she made fire, not calling it out of herself as the Crarrowin had, or from the atmosphere as mages had in the Ruk or the garths of the Jafn. She simply pulled a bit of flint out of the hutter fur, rasped it on a rock, and when the flame came, shook it off on the floor. It took, and

burned. And she the one who had always avoided close-
ness to a fireside.

'Is it now, Chillel? Have we arrived at *soon*?'

Lionwolf's eyes lit red in the green caves, his shadow on
the green wall pointed with garnets.

She said, 'Soon is now, now is soon.'

'By God, you've made me wait.'

All of him stood up then, his body to its feet and his
phallic weapon to its height. Like a human man, he had
sworn by God. And she, like a human woman, hospitable,
lay back and her garments fell from her like mist.

As his mouth touched hers, and his hands her flesh, he
sensed without prologue what she must be. It was already
too late. Not only had she drawn him to her, but she had
in turn been magnetized to him.

'We're one,' he heard himself say. It was a Jafn expression. Men now and then employed it in the garths – for to
make yourself one with a woman was to her a great compliment. Athluan had apparently said this, too, to Saphay on
the first occasion.

Yet Lionwolf and Chillel – now he had pierced her,
entered her body – *were* one.

Her eyes were full of the waking flood he had glimpsed
in so many women's eyes – but with her it was not the
same.

He stared into her eyes – reflective ice, mirrors, black as
liquid seas – then bent to her lips again.

He had never had such pleasure with a woman. He had
expected that – she was supernatural, as was he. It had

always come off her anyway, the spice of a promised special sexual joy.

That he gave her fierce pleasure in return was revealed by every inch of her body, even its swimming textures – and by her eyes. She murmured to him. Her tongue wrote out curious languages in his mouth—

But—

At first he takes no time to be aware of what he has just seen in her eyes, and felt written on his own tongue. Even so, he *becomes* aware. As they couple – *couple*. Then—

And—

It is the god that Lionwolf discovers there deep down in the black mirror eyes of Chillel – Zezeth, *he* is there. Nor is he any part of her, but the mirrored reflection of Lionwolf *himself*.

Though Lionwolf has *seen*, yet this now cannot be stopped.

Not only hunger, and the victory of possession, drive them on, he and she each clinging to the other, each crying out – it is this, though never before, the foregone conclusion of Fate. For now Zezeth will retrieve what once – profligate and by this very act – he gave away.

Three in one, one in three, Yyrot, Ddir, Zezeth. So they were, or had become. Zezeth had fashioned Lionwolf, perhaps inadvertently, in the womb of a mortal woman. So then Yyrot copied him, irrelevantly through a skewed bestiality. Then Ddir created Chillel. Of all these three makings, only the first had *stolen* from its creator.

In the cave, skin ebbed over skin, flesh drove with flesh like an engine of eternity. Stars fell, burst, scattered in her eyes, in his.

For other men she had been able to perform a miracle.

She had inoculated them against thaumaturgic death. On Lionwolf she would work differently.

It is he who shouts aloud. He feels himself split, as a snake does, rearing from its skin. As the heat spears from him, the rest of the fire that has always been in him, that too erupts from every psychic pore of his body.

Lacerated and *aborted*, he feels this other fire as it births itself away from him, a coruscating sheet which for an instant flares to mountainous size, and bathes the walls of the caves with scarlet . . . It is done.

He lies on the earth, knowing nothing at all. He lies there reasonless, stricken, and at peace.

But of course such a peace will not last.

'Chillel . . .'

Chillel does not answer – so often her way.

And then Lionwolf stares over his shoulder, behind him, and looks where his shadow, more awful than he or any have ever seen it, enormously glows and *bubbles* with its fire-hearts of jewels.

The shadow no longer imitates Lionwolf. It does not now do as he does.

It is separate and *free* of him.

Meanwhile, in mockery, a *human* shadow such as any man might cast, spreads away from him on the wall instead.

Slowly Lionwolf pulls himself round, to confront what has happened, but does not digest what it is. His body, though, tells him: it twangs and cracks with rage – and sudden weaknesses. *It* – if not he – knows what it has been robbed of.

The independent bright shadow hangs there a moment

more, like a giant insect folded in gem-stitched wings. Then it dazzles entirely away. This leaves a great darkness.

Shuddering, Lionwolf tries to find Chillel. But he cannot find her. His hands meet only the hard rock and ice of the cave.

Sex between them has evicted the fire of the god – the *essence* of Zezeth from Lionwolf. She – a woman made of snow – it has *melted*.

Wandering, both physically and in his mind, the man stumbles through the green caves of ice.

He experiences the numbing cold, and the debility of malnutrition, for he has been there an age, perhaps one of months. Deprived of the essence of the god, is he now mortal? Not as any ordinary man, certainly, but still crippled in a way unknown to him, and horrible. He is frightened of himself and what has become of him, frightened of being in the labyrinth of caves. Sometimes he lies down to sleep. Distressing dreams rouse him up again. He has forgotten his name, and who he is, but after all who he is – is *no longer* who he is . . . A riddle worthy of Olchibe.

Sometimes he does sleep and does dream, but then the dreams do not wake him. He sees cities blazing and blown white dust and a woman flowing away under his body like a liquid river by night. His dreams are all of dissolutions.

One day, daylight filters through to the cave where he is wandering. It takes him several hours to clamber up the wall to it. He had attempted to *walk* up the wall, fallen, suffered from the ground's impact and been bruised.

He squeezes out through a funnel of ice. The sun is over on the right hand, low and streaked with cruel colours. He watches it, registers it is going down and, guided by that, trudges along the cragside, keeping to a southerly direction. That night, after sunset, snow comes.

Noon parasoled the deep valley, which was full of the stalks of frozen wheat. The crags which made a solid barrier to the north threw no shade there as yet. Everything glistened from the new snow, like the ringing of bells.

Four women were dancing in a wide clearing among the grain. There was a floor there of flat scored snow.

They wore white, so for a while it might have been hard to see them. But some had wine-yellow hair and some dark brown, you could spot this quickly – also the flash of the four swords in their hands as they smote them together in the dance. The sound of that rose, too: it was like metal barking.

Their eyes were masked in visors of blackish glass which gave off rainbows.

The man who had shambled down along the snows had halted, looking at this.

It seemed the women did not themselves see him.

Clack went the swords.

Nameless, who had been Lionwolf, sat down on the slope, and gradually the noon sun, cold-hot after the cave tunnel, made him sleep.

'Darhana, who is this?'

The youngest of the women, malt-haired, bent over Nameless. She considered him.

Then she turned her head to look at her companions, the other three dancers. She did this turning of the head without shifting the rest of her body about.

It was the same in the dance. At one juncture she would position herself, this Darhana, her head facing north, her body south, one foot with toes to the west, one foot toes to the east. Without changing her arms at all, she could rotate her hands. This she now did – it helped her to think.

'No enemy,' said Darhana.

'Is he dead?'

'Partly. But not all.'

'He's tall, and heavier than he looks with muscle,' said one.

'Are you able to carry him?'

Darhana nodded. She was a young girl, but she leant right over now and drew the red-haired stranger up from the snow in one solitary lift, as if he were a boneless cloth.

Then she carried him in her arms, stepping without awkwardness between the white wheat, the three others moving after.

Nameless was in Kraagparia.

Fourth Volume

TOWER OF THE SUN WITH GOLDEN EYES

Where does the sun fly, when here he dies?
Where does the sun die, when here he rise?

Graffito from the Copper Gate,
Sham: Gech

ONE

Arok had trotted like a wolf over the ice plains. That time now was blurred and alien to him. Like the collision with the White Death that changed the world, though he could not forget it he pushed it to the depths of his mind. Somewhere eventually he had come on a stead of his own people.

Old men and a crowd of women asked him for news of the Gullahammer and the Rukar war. Ashamed, he said the Borjiy Lionwolf had all the men besieging a city. Arok had been sent back, he told them, for a secret military reason. He was not by then naked. He had killed a deer, brought it down by means of a club he constructed from packed snow – a new skill, as was his durability. He said to the steaders that he had been set on and robbed by Ruk soldiers, renegades who had escaped the city, and so reduced to wearing a foul and uncured skin. There were no boys left at the stead. This depressed Arok. They too then must have died at Ru Karismi, like nine-tenths of all the Jafn peoples. The steaders let him take a hnowa from them, to finish his journey.

All along the north-eastern landboard, it was the same. Where he found a village or a stead – old men, women, now and then a sickly lad or youth who had wanted to go and fight but been kept at home. At least some male children remained, but children might die before they grew up. How long would it take to build the clans of the east again? Centuries? 'They besiege the Ruk,' declared Arok, and rode on.

He came out on to the ice fields, going more northerly now, to Holas land.

He thought of reaching the Holasan-garth, and of what then he would have to tell. For himself, Arok saw no advantage. He did not want to claim the Chaiord's chair and rule a blighted people.

So, he lingered along the shore. In the homespun clothes the first stead had also given him, he waded out on the ice edges. He fished from cracks and channels, while the hnowa, well fed with dormant grain before it began the trek, stood mildly chewing the cud. Their progress now was almost aimless.

One early evening, Arok spotted a whaler village and, stuck in the ground outside, a post with the Holas emblem of a roaring seal.

The village was quite deserted, it seemed. Everyone had gone, either with the Gullahammer or away to another village. Then, as the dusk closed in, he noticed a slip of light under one hut door. This was a fisher-hut, for a neg-lected net, stiff with ice, hung from its outer wall – as, here and there, on other huts about it.

Arok sat on his hnowa, looking at the hut. He thought he would go in. It was one more delay to keep him from the garth and bad-news-telling.

'What do you want?'

She was youngish, the fishwife, but worn and

uncomely. Nor was she civil, but by now Arok thought he probably had no look of a part-royal Jafn warrior.

He said he would like a place by the fire for the night.

She was doubtful. Then came the inevitable second question: 'Are you from the war?'

'Yes.'

'I've a man there. They all went – to follow the golden man with red hair, the Borjiy. Have you seen him?'

'Who, your husband or the Borjiy?'

'Either . . .' she faltered.

'Both,' Arok said angrily. 'Now I'm coming in.'

After he had pummelled the hnowa into the hut's rear – the only stable on offer – Arok glimpsed someone else lying on a rag-bed in the corner. 'Who?'

The woman glanced uneasily, and said nothing. Arok decided this second person was also female, and feeble, and let it go. He sat by the fire, watching the smoke go up to the roof, where ancient kippers and ice-bass had been altered by it to leaves of purest bronze. She did not starve, the fishwife, though she had lost her man. She kept a wood store too, fuelled from some forest inland. She brought him beer.

Outside the dark fell, and pooled in under the door – as the light did the other way. Arok grew heavy. He requested a kipper courteously. Without a word, the woman stretched up and pulled one from its hook. As she gave it to him, the figure on the rags stirred.

'Oh . . . he is there . . . oh, he is dying there . . .'

Startled, Arok sprung round. He glared at the rag-bed.

'No trouble, sir,' said the fishwife, 'it's only Saffi. She cries out sometimes.'

'What's she on about?'

'She sees things that others don't.'

The hair bristled on Arok's neck, even along his rough-hacked beard. *Dying*—

'Is she your witch?'

'No, fishers got her in their nets. She came up from the sea, eleven – twelve years since. Never right in her head. And she lives somewhere else in her dreams.'

Arok got up and crossed over again to the rag-bed. He lifted a brand he had taken off the fire and held it up to examine the madwoman by its light.

She was old, he thought. But, no, not so old. Her raddled face must have been fair once. Her hair was yellow as lampglow.

Now her eyes met his; they were black. For a second he remembered Chillel . . . that passed. The madwoman stared up at him.

Then she spoke clearly. 'You are Athluan.'

Arok really started now. He knew of Athluan, naturally, the Klow Chaiord who had perished in battle, or was murdered – father or guardian to *That One*.

'I'm not Athluan.'

'No,' agreed the madwoman, 'he's dead. They die. Men die. But Nameless can never die. How could he—'

'*Nameless?*'

'My son's name. But you know him too by another name – I've seen . . . I've seen all of it – Vashdran!' cried the woman. She began to speak hoarsely in the Rukarian tongue.

The fishwife said, 'She knows foreign words – or it's only nonsense.'

'Quiet!' Arok rapped. 'I understand her.' And he did. Since the White Death, he could speak and know like a native all these languages. But he shook. She was talking, this mad Saffi, of the Lionwolf. And she was talking of the city and the silent Sound, the White, the Salt—

'He lived. He lived. Now – now must he die? He's more than mortal – how *can* he die? It's not for him, death – but power and glory everlasting—'

Something caught in her throat. The madwoman choked, then dropped back. Her eyes shut. She murmured something even Arok could not hear, then slept.

'She slumbers a lot,' apologized the fishwife. 'Outland woman!'

All through the night, as the fishwife sat mending nets, Arok also sat by her fire. He could hear the sea murmur miles away. Once a piece of the ice cracked, but it was not a big crack, not urgent.

He himself had not slept for countless days and nights, and eventually he thought he should. He asked the woman if it was a sleep night for her, but it was not. 'Wake me, then, in two hours.'

It seemed to him he always dreamed now, but the instant he regained consciousness the dreams were blanked from his brain. This had been since Ru Karismi.

Not tonight, though.

Arok dreamed a black dog-thing was snuffling round the perimeter of the hut. Dreaming, he ogled it, for it was a type of dog he had never seen. Then a corrit swooped down, a Jafn demon Arok had not come across for a great while – in fact not since leaving Jafn lands. This corrit was like a vicious coil of thin rope. It whipped about the neck of the dog-beast and tried to throttle it. But the dog put up its front paw – as a cat *not a* dog would do it – hooked in claws and peeled the corrit off. The dog then ate the corrit, with a revolting noise of teeth and corritish objection.

'Wake!'

'I'm awake. Have I had my two hours?'

'*No*. Something is sniffing about outside. It's happened before, but now *you're* here.'

'I'm not your husband. I don't have to see to it.'

'You're a guest,' said the fishwife, 'and noble Jafn.'

Arok shrugged and got up. He took a fish-gutting knife off the wall. He recalled the dream-dog exactly.

Throwing open the door, there it was.

What *was* it? It was not any sprite or demon he had ever seen or heard of. It had small pointed ears, and a dog's longish muzzle. Its eyes were not dog-like. It was covered in a thick silk fur, and had a fluidly thrashing tail at its back. Still eating – something invisible – it looked round at him and hissed.

Arok flung the knife. It was not intended for throwing and turned over in the air, missing the dog, who took no notice.

A moon was up, almost full.

By its light, Arok now saw the other . . . *thing*.

'Great God.' Then the woman was there, crowding at his back. 'Get in!'

'No,' she said, disobedient – no wonder her man had preferred warring to her. 'I've seen these. Oh, wait – I have something put by for them, no trouble,' she added. 'I thought it was the bear that comes sometimes and scratches to get in, or I'd never have bothered you.'

Arok stood aside, aghast.

The fishwife came out by him, and tossed one of her

smoked fishes to the monster dog. The other monster, over along the ice, would not come near, however.

'That one's caught a fish anyway,' said the wife.

It was true. Where the second apparition rooted about on a ruffle of the ice, it had dug up and now held a fish in its jaws.

He might have thought it a brown cat if he had not got such a sure look at it. Its ears were tall and close together on its head, and though it had a cat's face, the jaw was long and jutted out. Its legs were long and shaped like those of a hound, and it had a hound's tail with a whitish tuft. The coat of it was smooth, even hairless. Dropping its fish, it barked a thin whistling bark, and Arok stepped back into the hut.

'There,' said the woman, also coming in. She shut the door. Glancing again at Arok now with motherly scorn, she said, 'They do no harm.'

Arok did not try to resume his sleep, did not want it now.

She went on moronically mending her nets, and on the bed the Rukar woman slept in silence.

When the sun came up, Arok went out and inspected the terrain.

There were padmarks in the softer snow by the hut, the dog-thing's pads, and smaller ones – the cat-thing's.

Arok patrolled the shore, brooding. Obviously the two animals were magical, perhaps sprites like those he had seen, in the Jafn manner, since childhood – and yet, after the White Death, seldom or never saw now. Something wiggled in his mind, a name. Gech, he thought, a Gech name. Dog-cat, Catdog . . . It was a kind of travesty of the other northern legend, known also in Olchibe, and perhaps among the Jafn certainly by now, of the lionwolf born from the mating of a lion and a wolf.

There were wild lions here in the east, he knew, though you did not often come across them – and wolves all over. But dogs and cats were found everywhere.

The names leapt out. He stood still and mouthed them.

'Dog-cat: Drajjerchach. Cat-dog: Chachadraj.'

And the madwoman on the rags said she was the mother of the Lionwolf. She raved, that was all, he thought.

He went hunting, running on foot inland, with the bow that the first stead had given him.

Near evening again, when he was coming back, a couple of hares over his shoulder, he reached the shore and paused to watch the sun going down. Here, where the coast turned slightly northwards, sunset splashed across most of the sea-facing ice fields, changing them to gilded brass.

Arok became aware something was moving out beyond the rim of the ice. Its darkness broke the wide gleam of the sun abruptly.

Seals perhaps were there, or a young whale strayed in too far to the ice-shelf? If it beached itself, became stranded, that would provide a few dinners.

But the dark melted back into the horizon. And, anyway, he would hardly remain here much longer – even to put off telling his news among the Holas.

Opening the hut door familiarly, Arok swore. The hares of his kill fell off on the floor. Then he had to move quickly to save them. 'Get back – get away, you devil—'

'Don't use your boots on them, sir,' said the woman.

'I'll use them on you, you scratchered bitch. What are

you at? Are *you* the witch here – if not, you've no business meddling in magic.'

The woman did not seem to fear Arok. She never had. She looked at him under her lids and went on with stirring a pot of broth over the fire.

The drajjerchach dog-cat, having given up trying to grab the hares, had withdrawn to the fire, where it sat in a dog-like position. Over in the corner, the hnowa showed no alarm, but hnowas were stupid beasts. The fishwife had found it some dormant grass, which it was champing contentedly. Then he saw the Rukar madwoman was sitting up on her rags. On her lap was the cat-dog chachadraj. She was stroking it.

'I let them in sometimes,' said the fishwife.

'Abominations.'

Her only reply was the stirring of the spoon in the broth.

Arok gave up on it. He skinned and cleaned the hares, portioned them and handed them to the fishwife to cook.

Very quickly everything seemed ordinary to him. With a little effort you could forget the two other things in the hut were anything but a dog and a cat.

After they had eaten, the woman washed her hair in heated snow-water, then sat combing it dry, across the fire from him. The scent of this made him want her.

'I'm sorry to say,' Arok announced softly, 'very many Jafn men died in the south.' She said nothing. Arok said, 'I think your man may be one of them.'

'Yes,' she said. 'He'd never have come back anyway.'

'Do you get lonely?'

She looked at him then. 'Are you asking?'

'I'm asking.'

She laughed. 'And you a fine Jafn noble?'

'No longer. There's not much of us left. We need to make new ones.'

'Is that all you want?'

'You've got pretty hair.'

Presently he said, into her hair, 'What about the Rukar over there?'

'She's asleep. Look. Both her animals are snuggled up to her. She's better when they're here.'

'I think you're a damned witch after all—'

In the morning she was still formally respectful. Arok liked that in her. He went out once more to hunt. He did not mind this life. Though he would never take to a boat to fish the open fluid sea, he believed he might learn casting methods with a net. But all this was simply a holiday, before he went on. The draj and chach had been gone by the time he had looked over again at the rag-bed.

He took a seal that day. This was great luck. Hauling it back along the shore in the afternoon, Arok believed, although he had always been strong, that he had become stronger.

He was about a mile from the village hut when the night came up in the east, out of the sea.

Astounded, Arok watched the huge curve of shining blackness rising, pouring over, going down again deep into the ocean. It was several miles out, and had only just showed, he thought, the crest of its back – a whale, one of the great horned kind, yet of extraordinary size. But it was gone now.

As Arok went on along the shore, he saw a man standing some way ahead of him, and next to him a woman, slender and vividly golden-haired. Arok checked, wondering who they were, for neither had a Jafn look. He was too far to read their faces, but their clothes, what he could see of them at that distance, looked fine. The man was dark-haired, or Arok thought so; then he was not sure, for next the man seemed blond – a sort of hot colour that was also cold. There seemed to be a blue streak over his nose and cheeks – a Faz in war-paint? Even a Faz, Arok thought, must be made much of now.

Arok began to walk on steadily, and was somehow not surprised when the two figures dissolved before his eyes. They were sprites then – glers, maybe, taking human form? Best be careful. However, he was quite glad he could see Jafn demons again.

Reaching the hut he went in, leaving the dead seal outside for skinning.

No uncanny animals called on them that night. The Rukar woman lay tossing and turning, crying out for a man she named Zeth. This disturbed Arok during his lovemaking with the fishwife, but not too badly. He had forgotten to tell her about the whale.

Further south, in the towery of Thryfe's frozen house, the oculum blazed and juddered in its web of ice, trying to alert the magician, failing to do so.

Even the local constipation of time could not stop an oculum. A magic eye, it must see; a magical viewer, it must *show* what it had found.

Over the surface of its globe, clouded by ice, shot lightnings. Something black and of a gigantic size rose within them. The oculum vibrated with frustrated power. A crack appeared, another, and another. The oculum ceased to vibrate. It disengaged from itself and flew apart in a shower of sparkling flinders.

Thryfe opened his eyes. He saw in front of him the sweet sleeping face of Jemhara, and brushed back softly trails of her hair, kissing them—

Something had disconnected the quiet of sleep. What had that been? Was the night finally over?

Thryfe listened, at first indolently then intently. The absence of all sound, other than his breathing and hers, seemed appealing, then curious – suddenly wrong.

He sat up. Jemhara stirred. 'Sleep, love,' he said to her, and the tenderness in his voice filled him all at once with astonishment, next repulsion—

What was she doing here? What had happened?

Clearly, he had spent a night with this woman. He could remember every act between them. And it had gone on here in his secret house. Himself with this cheap witch of Vuldir's court – why? Sexual appetite Thryfe had, from his adolescence, been able to control: to use its energies for more important work. Well, he had given in this once. But why to *her*? There were women among the Magikoy willing to engage in sex, some beautiful and his equal. There had been royal women too, in the past, exquisite, nor fools, who had tried to gain his interest. All these women he had put aside, never wanting them, never wanting to spoil his feast of abstinence.

Then this one – *this*.

He stood there in the chamber staring at Jemhara, who slowly also opened her eyes and gazed at him guilelessly.

Without a word, she held out her hand.

Her naked body, her breasts, her hair – these sent through him one further surge of desire. He slammed desire from him and felt it fall away down the cliff of his fury.

'You've been cunning,' he said, 'Jema.' Of course he knew her steader name.

To the insult of its use she paid no heed. 'Have I? To be in love – is that so clever, my lord?'

'Don't use court phrases to me. They stink of where you come from – of Vuldir.'

Fear, after all, started up in her face, like the hare she had been starting across blue snow.

'You have some other place to go to?' he said.

'None—'

'Then find one. Be gone from this house inside one hour, or I'll put you out. You will prefer to travel, I believe, by your own volition.'

'What have I done?'

'To earn my anger? What do you think? What you were told to do and did. Go back to Ru Karismi and boast that you fucked with a Magikoy. *That* you've merited. From me, you will keep away.'

The room was intolerably hot. Thryfe turned, staring now at it: the walls running with wet, the pools of water on the floor. A pane of ice dropped from the ceiling and smashed in front of him.

Jemhara screamed.

'In the name of nothingness,' said Thryfe, 'what's this?'

'I don't know—' Jemhara whispered. But Thryfe the magician had left the chamber.

Through the house Thryfe strode, then ran. He broke the web of the ice with his hands and feet, and with his psychic

419

power. Besides it was giving way, this entity time had formed by stopping. He did not know what had occurred. Then in the towery, finding the wreckage of the oculum, he hesitated in a deathly apprehension.

Only a blind and arrogant man would question himself at such a moment – how have I, even *I* who am impervious, been beguiled and ruined? Thryfe did not question himself, nor would he question her.

Whether she left the house or stayed in it, now he had no care. Gargolems came to him, sluggish as if, like himself, just roused from a drugged sleep.

When the sleekar and team of lashdeer were ready in the yard outside, Thryfe stepped into the chariot. With a sorcerous command that would set them racing, he turned their heads towards Ru Karismi, City of the Kings.

Just before he wakened, Arok thought he was lying by Chillel. She no longer smelled of coolness, but like an ordinary healthy shore-woman. Arok thought he had converted her; then he came to and saw the fishwife stretched beside him. She lay on her back and faintly snored.

For a moment he was aggrieved. Then a sort of kindness for her overcame him.

She had been willing and eager, enjoyable. Moreover, she still treated him with the correct courtesy, and called him *sir* when they were not in bed. Her name was Nirri.

Nevertheless Arok sat up with a curse. This was no sleep nocturnal – and he had been *asleep*.

Oh, this life, then, it was no use. It was making him sloppy, a sot. All those days and nights crossing the snow waste, he had never slept, with stamina better than a Fazion's—

Arok walked out of the hut. The sun was up, about a handspan above the ocean.

Great fissures had opened in the ice less than thirty strides from the village. They ran back towards the slender bright line of liquid sea.

Arok knew he must go out and check these channels, to see if they might threaten the stability of the ice here, or if anything edible were swimming about in them.

Before he could take a step, the whole horizon opened.

Up out of the sea, out of the ice – out of the sky itself – came thrusting, like a sword, a *tower of ivory*.

Thunders roared – a compendium of waters and breaking ice – which growled and croaked with the sound of giant bones snapping.

But a building was flying up from the sea.

The tower was contained in a palisade of lesser towers, spur-spikes in a ring large as a palace of the Rukarians. This architecture ascended, mile on mile of it, or so it seemed. Behind it came its *reason*.

The wife, Nirri, had hurried out and was standing behind Arok in the hut door. To her credit, she did not shriek, but he heard the breath go out of her as if she had been punched in the belly.

What rose from the ocean was an ice-whale.

Arok had heard of monsters among them, larger than a Faz Mother Ship, but to this animal they were what a child would be to a full-grown man—

Only landmasses, seas and skies, Arok numbly thought, were as vast as this one whale.

Its black uneven body rose on and on. Already it had

cancelled out all light from the sun. Night fell back on to the shore.

From the blowhole, which must be huge itself as the Holas House – a whole garth even – it ejected a gross ray of water. When this crashed down, the sea plunged, and a dense rain of brine thrashed over the village.

The little forearms of the ice-whale were each the size of a small whale. But they hung loosely from its body – it did not *need* their help.

How much more of it could rise? How much more could even the ocean hold?

In the thick darkness of the shore. Arok turned round to Nirri. She was hypnotized by the whale. He shook her.

'Run!' She gaped at him. 'No, wait – I'll get the hnowa. We'll go faster—'

Still she gaped. He pushed by her, back into the hut. From the fire he picked up a burning brand, then got the hnowa and pulled it from the hut. At the old mad Rukar woman Arok did not even glance, for in her state she was better dead, and now soon would be.

Nirri did not protest as he bundled her on to the hnowa. Nervous, it trampled and defecated on the snow, afraid of the dark mass still going up – *still rising* from the sea – but too brainless fully to react. The air stank of rotten fish and ocean depths.

Arok vaulted astride. He grabbed Nirri before him and, around her, the guiding reins. Then he touched the hnowa with the burning brand. It squealed in pain and galloped snorting over the ice – inland.

Behind them, the whale still rose—

Great God—

From slightly higher ground, Arok looked back once.

They had been just in time. The whale stood at last on its tail – impossible. The titanic mass of it, even from this distance, was unreal. Yet there, in the night it had created, it gleamed with a sorcerous luminescence.

In that split second, Arok saw the prodigious body begin to bend over. Its breaching done, it was commencing its dive back to the bottom of the sea—

He rammed the fire-brand into the hide of the hnowa and held it there.

As they tore away in smoke and screaming, Arok thought this would make quite a tale for the long nights – if they lived, or if any Jafn Holas were left to hear it.

On the rags, the Rukarian woman they called Saffi had also woken up. She reached out to feel if the beasts were there, her cat and her dog. They were not.

Nor was anyone in the hut.

The hut was warm, the fire crackled. There had been a noise, and this had roused her. But it was more than a noise.

She could smell a stench of burnt hair, and an overpowering reek of fish. A primeval odour overhung everything else, and a rumbling sound – and it was night.

Very seldom did she get up, and merely to answer the now only occasional purposes of nature.

Something, though, drew Saffi to the hut door which stood wide.

She had no brain either, not exactly. Her brain had died under the ice, or else – remnant or revenant that she was of the true Saffi, called Saphay – this Saffi had never had one.

She ambled to the door and looked out, and in that

moment the night sky, which was the gargantuan whale, plummeted back under the sea.

Water, which had swirled inward and down, as if into some sink-hole, was now displaced by the returning bulk of the whale.

As its black brilliance speared home, a tidal wave rose up and up in turn, approximate to the whale's stupendous girth. The water formed a spangled wall against a sun which now was almost visible. The wall was high as the roof of heaven.

Saffi screamed. It was merely a response; she had no other. She simply stood there, and the tidal wave curled, in imitation of the plunging whale, and flung itself over to cover the frozen land.

The shores of ice broke now like thinnest glass. Immense blocks of ice went whirling through the grey wind of the water.

The wave smashed forward, rushing screeching across the coast.

Everything gave before it. The village was lost in one minute, the tough black huts crushed like things of paper. All that was there was swept up by the wind-that-was-sea: wood, stones, nets, beached boats, artefacts that had been pots and pans, now abstract bits.

In this water-hurricane Saffi too was carried, her eyes wide, her hair streaming, constantly turning over, doubt-less also broken.

The wave ran in for two miles, three miles, four. It met its match against a very high snow-cliff ballasted by rock, but nevertheless left its impression there: the *shape* of its final defeat and withdrawal.

It had missed too the man and woman on the hnowa – missed by the margin of a quarter mile.

On the land, the stranded fish slapped and died. The debris of the ocean floor lay in slabs of oily weed, shells the wave had granulated, other items unrecognizable to man.

The wave crawled, tired now, back into its parent ocean. With it, it took very much of its spoils from the ice, including the woman called Saffi.

Down through the sea the dregs of the wave bore her, with the rest of its booty.

Midnight beyond all nights shut Saffi's eyes, cold beyond all Winters covered her.

Again.

The pyramids of ice were in poor repair. Gusts of air moaned through chinks in their sides. It had started to remind Saphay of her princess apartment in Ru Karismi. She mooned about from area to area, looking at the rotting black grain fields and orchards. She never found anything to eat but this, like the cold, did not seem to affect her now, except in principle. The cat too was indifferent to temperature and lack of food, though it hunted savagely among the mess.

The cat had delivered itself of kittens some time ago. Saphay had not seen them – and been glad of that – only the cat reappearing, slim again and quite self-satisfied. What could they have been, these offspring – result of cat mated with god-as-dog?

What should Saphay do? There was, as so often, little option.

Her thoughts moved, despite her will, to the other one,

to Zeth Zezeth. She had had other dreams of him since their last dream-meeting. Although these dreams were *about* the god Zeth, he was not, surely, actually in them. She dreamed of seeing him a long way off. In the dream she would run away, or sometimes ride in a runaway slee. But along with terror was the wish that he would pursue and catch her. Also she had dreamed she was on an icy shore with him, and out at sea a black whale extruded its back. The dreams were memories from her life, mingled with desires and fears. Despite her comparative youngness, Saphay seemed to herself to have lived many decades, to be old, withered and perhaps becoming senile. How would she know? She had no company, no mirror. Her hands though, when she looked at them, were young.

The cat played sturdily and nastily with an imaginary mouse among the putrid wheat.

A strange noise filled the air. It was a type of screaming, but there was a rumbling too, like thunder in the sea.

Saphay felt a tug at her body. Abruptly her head spun. She went down limply on the ground and, when the world steadied, found the cat planted on her breast, gazing in her face.

What had occurred now? Slowly, testing herself, she sat up again.

Had something happened to her son, her faithless son, who had abandoned her without a word for so long – the son that she adored and loved only because he was in the image of his evil fiend of a father? Why then this pain of distress in her heart at the idea of harm coming to her son?

They sat there on the ice, Saphay and her cat.

'Where's Yyrot, your lover?'

The cat sprang suddenly away.

'Where is *everything*?' Saphay asked the collapsing pyramids of ice.

She saw the cat then passing out through a kind of doorway in the air.

Alarmed, offended despite all that had gone on, Saphay stood up. She walked over to the aperture and looked into and through it. Nothing was there. It was like a pane of thickest ice.

Saphay put out her hand and one finger met the ice-pane. It parted.

She beheld a scorchingly golden landscape, like a picture seen in the core of a fire. Within it, trees that seemed in a foliage of flame surrounded a mountain of ripe orichalc, from whose head drifted plumes like roses.

'Not yet,' said a voice.

Saphay threw herself about to see—

No one was there.

When again she looked for the aperture into the fire, it had vanished.

Guri, sitting on an ice floe, watched uneasily as his mera suckled her new-hatched egg. It was female, and had already bitten Guri with its snaggle teeth.

The 'tween-place was dismal today, swept by long claws of winds. He could not get it to be anything else for him. And the mera, though she had allowed him to father his child on her, had not been friendly.

He had come away from the plains of death below the Rukar city, soon after making his offering to the Ranjal goddess. She in turn had flown off anyway across the sky, like a hawkish broomstick, and left him there.

A concussion went dimly through the sea below the ice. Guri glanced down. He wondered what had caused the shock, for in the 'tween-place normally such things did not penetrate, let alone factually go on.

Then he felt, worse than the vague blow beneath, a sucking drag on him. Guri resisted vigorously.

The mera, apparently noting his agitation, jumped back into the waves and was off, the merchild clutched to her breast.

The tugging stopped.

Shaken, Guri stamped about the floe. What had taken hold of him? Was it *that one* again? Almost, Guri could smell Zeth Zezeth about – or *nearly* about. He seemed to have evaded some supernatural detention, and to be at large once more.

If so, where could Guri hide? The world, and other worlds, were open to him – yet that would not be enough. No, he would need to get behind the very stars to avoid that one. And he had earned this god's hate by loyalty to the boy, the *man* because of whom—

Guri burst from the 'tween-world like a shooting star.

Slinging his feet down on the snow of the earth, he began to race the wind, running like hell to get away from the vision of Ru Karismi.

Ru Karismi, however, showed itself now to others.

The salt-dusts were growing inert, and sinking. It was feasible to see the city walls, the sculptured metropolis behind, although the parasols of crystal on the heights no longer winked at a westering sun.

Thryfe drove across the endless plain.

Nowhere did anything remain outside the city, to a distance of three or four miles. The steadings, the fields, were all gone, leaving no trace. The ice of the plains had grown *brown*. It was a disgusting colour, like something decayed, or evacuated. Here the dust had become more like sand.

As the sleekar carried him nearer to the city, he saw, against the hard, unnatural shine of the sky, narrow streams of smoke going up from every quarter.

At Southgate, hollow-eyed guards let him through grudgingly. The gate had been damaged too. He left the chariot just inside.

He soon found the explanation of the smoke. The citizens were burning their dead, having too many corpses by now to bury.

People on the sloping streets paid Thryfe no attention. Their faces were hopeless, or clenched with an angry fear.

He saw a dead man, of about twenty years, carried out of a house. Those with him did not even exclaim. They put him down on the roadway for the crematory wagon to collect, like a dead flower from the hothouse.

Another man, one of the Magikoy, met Thryfe as he was walking up the Stair of a thousand steps. The man was coming down.

'Who paid the atonement price for this?' Thryfe asked him.

'Wundest and two others. And Vuldir was burned, but alive.'

'I too must pay the price. I should have prevented it. But had the Magikoy *forgotten* the old writings that suggest to us that once – *this* was done before – weapons like these were used in the furthest north. I too must pay.'

'That's your affair. Burn yourself if you want. You'd do better to work in the city.'

'To save them? They're already lost.'

The other Magikoy walked on down the Stair.

They had, these two magicians, no time for each other. It was the same among all the Order, what was left of it. Their individual shame and regret poisoned them, as the residue of the weapons had done their colleagues.

Going on up the Stair, Thryfe did not hesitate to draw breath. But at the top he found he must lean on the wall.

The Gargolem did not emerge. None had seen it since that day.

In the palace gardens there was no one at all. Thryfe regarded the pavilions and palaces and statues.

Although – or because – the sky was so over-clear, the setting sun gave off almost no red.

He would have wept, Thryfe, but he could not be so impertinent as to weep for this catastrophe he might have turned aside, or for these people he might have shielded, or for himself who deserved not one single tear. A tall man, he felt now the tallest thing in that garden, and the slightest thing, too, and neither of these conditions was of any use.

TWO

Under an ice-cedar like moonstone lay the house of the white dancers.

In its sprawl it had four pillared doors, facing north, south, east and west, and windows which were covered by wavered glass that made everything outside resemble running water. About a hundred people lived there. They had what they called a Mother and a Father. Other than these two elected rulers, there was no authority over them.

Lionwolf sat in the small room they had given him. He sat on the floor of hard chipped wood.

Darhana came in. She had borne him up here, in her arms, from the frozen wheat fields. Several days had passed before he gave over sleeping. It was as if he had not slept enough in his life ever before.

The girl, without her snow-visor, had bright, pale-brown eyes, and she looked at him intently.

'Here's food.'

He nodded, thanked her, looked away.

She put the bowl down beside him.

The language of Kraag had been more difficult for him to learn than any other, but that was because he was changed, lessened. It had taken him five days to begin to speak it at all coherently, and perhaps he had only mastered it because some of the house people spoke a little Rukarian.

'The Father,' said Darhana, 'is inclined to talk to you. In one hour – will that be reasonable for you?'

'Yes, if he wants.'

Darhana went to Lionwolf. She stroked his forehead and down his mane of hair, quietly, kindly, once only. Then she went out.

He thought he could have had her. Maybe not. The last woman he had lain with—

Lionwolf leapt up. He kicked the bowl of grain porridge across the room and watched it shatter against the wall. He was sorry then. He sat down again.

Outside the rippled glass of the window, gemmy cedar branches melted and reformed.

The Father had a room up under the eaves, reached by a twisting stair of logs. He was a man of about thirty, and many other men in the dancer-house were older. The Mother though was an old woman, and she had not once spoken to Lionwolf.

'I will call you Vashdran.'

'Yes, if you want.'

'It isn't what I am to want. Do you prefer another name?'

'Yes, my first. I was called No-Name – Nameless.'

'Very well.'

They talked Kraag, a lilting tongue with sudden gutturals.

The Lionwolf heard every Kraag word he himself used, grasping its meaning belatedly, as if his body could speak the language and he could not. This psychological aphasia disturbed him, but so did everything now. His mental skin was pulled taut, fragile.

'You are from the northern south,' said the Father. Lionwolf – Nameless – nodded. 'Rukarian?' said the Father. Nameless did not reply. The Father said, 'We know nothing of your past. We know little of the northern south and east.'

'Splendid,' said Nameless. 'They no longer exist.'

The Father regarded Nameless attentively, yet made no comment. He said, 'To where are you travelling?'

'Not to – but away.'

'Do you know anything of the Kraag country?'

'Nothing.'

'To us,' said the Father, 'reality is not real.'

Nameless raised his head and looked at the Father properly. 'What else can reality be *but* real?'

'You mean in Rukarian philosophy, or among the east-erners?'

'Universal.'

'Ah, only a Rukarian would speak of a universe. It is the general way, besides, for men believe what's before them, and hesitate to believe what is not. For example, would you believe in other lands far off over the seas, to east and west, north and south?'

'There are the reivers' lands, northwards.'

'And many more,' said the Father, 'but few credit their existence, for no one has seen them in centuries.'

'Have you seen them?'

'Never.'

'You believe in them.'

'Yes. I believe in many things I've not yet seen. What is

called reality is very determined that we believe only in *it*. For this reason it makes itself hard as steel, and will not give way. But, too, it may be parted like liquid or blown off like smoke. Reality is malleable and can be reshaped. But the more you are able to do this, the more it will fight you. It's like a true liar found out; it can't stop its lying, becomes more inventive.'

Nameless stretched, a young man who was bored and would rather be off hunting, or with a girl. All that was in the gesture – and his royalty, this too. These had remained, for good or ill.

The Father said, 'I tell you of such things, not to educate but to prepare you. Have you heard of *Summer*?'

'Oh, *Summer*. Sometimes the Jafn remember *Summer*-thaws, the land floods and they lose cattle and people—' Nameless paused. He shrugged. None of this would concern the Jafn now – they were all lost.

'Reality is Winter,' said the Father calmly. 'We do not believe in Winter. Our men and our girls go out to dance, to call the sun back from under the sea. The unreal sun, which was once the real sun, lies there drowned. Kraag knows this true unreal sun will be reborn. We have no priests, for we say the gods are all one with us and we with them. Our dances therefore are our prayers.'

'That's quaint.'

The Father ignored this Rukarian jibe, spoken in Rukarian. He went on.

'Through us, then, there is sometimes a place of the *Summer*, here in Kraag.'

Nameless said, 'A thaw? Perhaps you'll tell me how to avoid the area and the high waters.'

'There's no flood. The land is firm and green with

plants. This unreal real Winter sun shines there with a greater heat. Flowers cover the hills.'

'An oasis with hot springs.'

'Oh no.'

'Then you report some dream, or its sorcery. The Jafn peoples saw demons and spirits everywhere; that was their knack. This *Summer*, then, is yours.'

'At the centre of the Kraag *Summer*,' said the Father imperturbably, 'stands the ruin of a high tower. It is the Sun's Tower. It was built far back in time, to call the sun as a visitor – as the dancers of Kraagparia pray to the sun through dance.'

'Very well. What's any of this to do with me?'

'You were told that a woman of sixteen years carried you here in her arms?'

'Yes, I was told.'

'Darhana can turn her head, for example, to the south, while her body faces northwards. Many of our dancers can do likewise.'

'Yes, you're mages.'

'No, something other than that. It isn't what you would call magic. Darhana too is able to pass her sword through her own heart, draw it out, and continue dancing. She could do this from the age of three. Again, many of us are thus able.'

'You?'

At the challenge, the Father laughed. 'Once, but the skill left me. It was a harsh time of my life. My handfast wife died. Some of my belief soaked into the earth with her blood.'

Lionwolf bowed his head. He murmured, with genuine contrition, 'I'm sorry for your cruel loss, sir.'

'Yes, I see you are. I give you thanks.'

They sat in silence a short while. Around them, the everyday noises of the house – drums, pipes, clack of dancers' swords, clatter of kitchen pots, and voices calling through the corridors – wove a tapestry like those that hung in such wild greens and blues on the house walls.

'I've called to your mind, Nameless, the skills of my people, so that you may partly trust us. The area of the *Summer* and the Sun-Tower are stamped on you as evidently as if you were written over with the map of that place. Some piece of you has been taken out and has run before you, into *Summer* – into the Tower.'

Inside the tan of the nameless young man's face, whiteness and horror showed themselves.

'*There?*'

'What is it you fear, Nameless?'

'Only one. Then – then *he* is there.'

'Something is.'

'He took my shadow from me,' said Nameless.

'I see your shadow, Nameless, cast plainly on the wall.'

'I had another shadow. There was fire in it. I think that he was in it, too. Now it's free of me. And he's waiting – she told me of this, the woman who was starry night and death. She said—' Nameless sat rapt in his own bleak reverie. Then he said, 'She told me I'd go to it. My fate. Guri said, my kind . . . have no choice.'

'I think,' said the Father, 'your kind are what my kind would name gods, if we thought the gods separate from men.'

'Once,' said Nameless. He smiled. 'Like you, sir, I lost

the skill. It soaked into the earth, not with blood but with ashes.'

Darhana danced with her three sisters and four brothers. The swords cracked together. The dancers spun the swords, fell back to the ground, took the points directly into their bodies, sprang up and whirled away, the honed steel sparking as they drew it out again from uncut flesh.

Two moons rose in the ice-cedar.

Darhana came from the white shadows under the window. 'The Mother says I shall guide you to the *Summer*, Nameless.'

'No.'

'She says I must. I don't mind to.'

'No, there's danger. I can find my own way.'

'The Mother says you're afraid, and so will become lost in order to avoid the way. But as you must still take the way, I must go to make sure you reach the place.'

'Speak Rukar. You speak Kraag as you dance, round and round, and then a sword strikes out.'

'I'm to be your guide,' said Darhana, whose Rukarian was excellent. 'That's that.'

'I won't take you.'

Darhana stole up to Nameless. Standing on tiptoe, for she was not tall, she kissed him delicately on the mouth.

'Don't. Something else kissed there, some god-made demon out of the darkest night.'

'It isn't catching, Lionwolf.'

'Don't call me by that name.'

'Look,' said Darhana.

He looked and saw she was not on tiptoe, but standing

on thin air about seven inches off the floor. She dropped back with a giggle. Lionwolf, or Nameless, turned from her. 'Then we'll leave now.'

'If you want.'

'It's not what I am to want,' he said, like the Father, in Kraag, 'I've no choice.'

If he had expected her to protest, even beg time for farewells, she disappointed him. She was in love with him, then, like all the others. That was why she would leave everything, including security, to serve as his guide. But she was only a girl, his mother Saphay's age when Vuldir had sent her to her death across the ice.

Beyond the outbuildings, a small cart waited, drawn by two wide-horned deer. They and it were strung with bells and colours. In this vehicle the Lionwolf and his companion began their journey before moonset.

During the first days the weather was fine. After the first night, they both slept in the cart after dark, among the furs. On the fifth night, he took her. She was willing, enjoyed herself, seemed to think the action as minor as sharing the blanket.

'What if you conceive?' he asked her.

'You can't make children.'

'What? How do you guess that?'

'Oh, you can't – not yet.'

It did not appeal to him, this statement. He had been nearly afraid he would not be able to rise to the occasion, after Chillel, after . . . all of that. To make love and find again the pleasure, for himself and this girl, had cheered him briefly. Now she wrecked it. He spoke harshly and coldly to her all the next day. Darhana was unaffected. The sixth night he kissed her. 'Since you're so sure you're safe with me—'

Later, in Rukarian, he said, 'How do you know I'm sterile?'

'I didn't say that. I said *now* you are.'

He lay thinking of this. He was unfinished and poorly made, for all his powers and all his glory.

But, in any case, Darhana had not been a virgin. He had already seen that the Kraag reckoned sex on a level with music and food, and even when bonded they held any children communally.

The deer cantered fast and well under clear skies, the bells singing on their antlers. The terrain was mostly flat, and the top-snow reliable.

About the tenth day, fresh snow began to descend. By sunfall, the sky was black already. Then the storms started.

Squalls of ice, sleet and winds flared over. Deep in the sky, thunder rolled like metal balls.

He suggested they dig into the snow. Darhana said it made no odds.

The deer leapt fleetly on through the gale and lack of visibility, only their natural blinders covering their eyes, while ice formed so thickly on their antlers he anticipated it might snap them.

The rush of passage burnt his face. What did he care about that? He tried to make Darhana sit back in the cart and shield her head. She would not. Her cheeks blazed red from the smack of the wind, that was all. Her eyes gleamed.

All night they ran. In the morning they broke out of the storm.

They were on a range of hills. Ice-forests of pine and

cedar and ice-jungles of fig, palm and terebinth crowded up the slopes. Through all this they had pounded, unable to see, and no harm had come to them.

'You're a witch,' he told her.

'No, it's what I believe, that is all.'

'That none of this is real?'

'Real in its own way – but to be altered as we need. How else was any of it ever made if it wasn't malleable?'

'God – or gods – made it,' he said.

'But again, unless malleable, how?'

Her view of this plasticine world, available for resculpting where necessary, amused him.

The day was grey as the Mother's hair. They rested in the afternoon, not sleeping but doing other things. Ice was shaken off branches and a flock of black crows with rime-silvered wings fled into the sky.

'Are they real?'

'As real as we.'

'Are *we* real?'

'As real as we make ourselves to be.'

'Riddles.'

'Answers.'

'Answers that are riddles.'

'What are riddles but answers formed from questions.'

'You,' he said, 'could argue well among the Magikoy.'

'I've heard of them,' she said. 'Are they very great?'

Nameless's face changed. It became that of the Lionwolf. Rage and sadism strode there, pain and despair.

'A while ago they were. But their weapons of war were greater.'

It had taken him all this while to be certain what had happened on the plains about Ru Karismi. He heard the words issue from his mouth now, an answer formed from a riddle of doom.

The deer cart ran on. The deer, too, seldom seemed to want rest. They craned their strong necks, and with their horns batted frozen leaves and creepers from the trees, and ate them as they bolted along, sometimes belching with fearful noises. Food had also been provided for the human travellers.

'Are there no other houses in these parts?' he asked her.

'Look there.'

He saw a distant thatched ramble of building, misty with warmth and smoke. It had appeared through the trees literally as she replied to his query. Was it real?

'Did you fashion that house out of the air, to entertain me?'

'Perhaps *you* did – or it fashioned itself. Or it was elsewhere but made itself visible here.'

Sometimes she spoke the Kraag mantra: 'What is real is unreal; what is unreal is real.'

Low cliffs evolved in front of them. The deer and cart galloped straight up, never stumbling and barely jolting.

Nameless Lionwolf thought of how he could walk horizontally up the side of things, could still do it even now – if with far less ease.

One evening on the cliffs he said, 'Don't you regret making the gods angry, by not believing in them?'

'The gods are born from mankind,' she said. 'If you want gods you need only call to them. Or else you let them be.'

'He,' said Nameless, '*he* is real.'

She looked at him as she held and guided the reins of the racing deer. 'That is the one you go to find?'

'To find? No, to *lose*. I'll kill him. It's my only chance. His foulness in me has destroyed anything I might have been.'

She said gently, 'Never believe it.'

'Belief? I believe nothing,' he said to her. 'Therefore for me *nothing* is real. Not the real, not the unreal, neither you nor I – *nothing*.'

The sun set and they stopped the cart, ate supper, and made love. Probably he did not believe in any of that either.

The next day the storms returned. A wind came like a scythe. The deer dived through it like minnows dashing through a wave of the outer sea.

Over the cliffs were valleys full of frozen grains, empty orchards podded and roped by cryogenized fruits and berries. The winds axed whole trees before they could dislodge what tenaciously grew on them.

Darhana sent the deer eastward now; the land cascaded down. On heights to the left, staircases of frozen water hung above basins of snow, rocking and booming at the storm lash. Sometimes, due to falling snow, one saw nothing. It was like the very thing he had described: a world of nothingness.

They reached an inlet of the sea. Against and through the white tumult, the water was inky blue – crinkling and liquid.

'The sea moves,' he said.

'We're near the place.'

The storm ebbed away, and a sunset stained the sky over the indigo finger of sea below.

That night she made a fire, striking it from a flint, as had Chillel.

'Can't you call it?' he mocked her.

Darhana turned her head and looked at him, the rest of

her body still facing the hearth. 'What else have I done with the flint?'

'You struck the fire in the ordinary way, girl, even if your head's on back to front.'

'A flint's magic too,' she said. 'For where does fire come from? It's like the sun, which vanishes under the earth.'

'The Gech say,' Nameless said, 'it shines then in Hell, but *there* the sun burns cold.'

The food was all gone. She heated the last of the honey ale from the dancer-house, and they drank that. The rim of the snow bled wet from the fire.

The Nameless Lionwolf thought of all he had done, and all there was to do. He would kill the god who had sired him, or the god would kill him. No longer afraid of it, he found the prospect dreary. He pondered what Guri was doing, and did not care any more. He thought of Saphay, and could scarcely recall she was his mother. Lightning flashed.

He thought of Chillel and of Ru Karismi. Like a book he must learn by heart and, even now he had learned it, must go on learning and learning, he read over the story of his life. A few years – it seemed to have been a millennium. He hated it but, despite all he had said, believed in it incorrigibly, and so it stayed entirely real.

Snow that melts in fire will refreeze.

It may even take on again its former shape.

Lionwolf dreamed – lying by Darhana above the melted sea – of a place far to the north of them.

Shepherds had climbed up the crags, taking their more agile sheep to pastures of dormant grass among the rocks.

These sheep were the long-necked, lion-faced kind that Lionwolf recollected from the village of Ranjalla. Under the white peaks, the men sat in the middle of their flock, sharing a drink about their fire. In that venue there were no storms. The stars wheeled slowly by overhead.

Then, from a cave mouth above, something came out.

The men turned and looked. They got to their feet. He heard them grunting. They raised their staves to beat it off, this night-blackness gliding down the cliffside towards their bivouac.

Chillel came walking through the flock, which was not at all nervous of her, and nuzzled her hands.

She came walking, clothed in all the beauty of the night, and fragrance hung on her, and the faint wonderful melodies of her naked skin brushed by armoured grass and her own long hair that swept the ground.

She had done her creator's will, the three-in-one Ddir, Yyrot, Zeth. She had disembowelled the astral body of Lionwolf of the essence of the god. That heat had transmuted her to transparent water. But sheer cold had brought her back again from some psychic mould, and in her own perfect image.

Lionwolf watched the shepherds, who slid from alarm to fascination, and wrapped her in a fleece, and drew her to their fire. She had, it seemed, no aversion to flames now. She sat with her new court. He guessed she would perhaps tell them a story – of the sun dying in the sea.

It seemed to him she was not evil, not a destroyer. Only in his case had she worked *against* . . . He wondered a moment, insanely in his sleep, if rather than *perfect* wrongness, she was an example of perfect thoughtless *good*. Had he not deserved punishment after all?

Dreaming, he knew he did not dream. Of course, whatever she was, Chillel could come back to life. For himself, half mortal, thieved of the wellspring of his powers, there would be no such guarantee.

Despite what Darhana had said, days and nights advanced swiftly with the cart, the inlet of sea fell behind, but no extraordinary scene of *Summer* arrived.

'We'll drive on for ever,' he said. 'That's all right. Shall I marry you, Darhana?'

'No, Kraag don't marry. We only love.'

'Do you love me?'

'Yes – and others.'

'Faithless.'

'Faith-*full*.'

No storms now, the sky was a deep blue. Ice-lakes were to be seen on all sides as they went on along the eastern brink of the land, still going south. These lakes glimmered blue from sun and sky, as if full of liquid water, but it was only an effect. The shore too, where they saw it, was now solid with ice, with only the most far-off lines of moving waves.

She had been wrong about the inlet. There must be some hotness there, under the ground and water, to keep it fluid. That had nothing to do with any episode of *Summer*.

'Tomorrow, you will see,' she said.

'Will I?'

'I must leave you here.'

He thought he could manage to reach some derelict tower in the snow without difficulty. And if the god did wait for him there, better Darhana was gone as many miles off as she could get.

They had not eaten for some days. This evening she made the fire, and next set before him a dish of roast meat with braised roots and squares of boiled salted dough. At his elbow she put a wooden cup with wine, the black wine he had downed among the Jafn. He said nothing to her. There had been no food till now, and she had not been cooking.

He ate the food. The cup, when he had drained it, each time became full again.

'If it's so easy, Darhana, why can't all mankind do this?'

'All could. And some can.'

That night birds flew over, flocks of them – winds of them. A lonely moon prettied them with gilt.

'You see,' she said, 'I'm not really here with you. Neither I nor the cart nor the deer. I made you believe I was. And so I was. We journeyed fast, didn't we? But believe I love you.'

The night felt tepid to him, like the caves where he had wandered after Chillel. When he woke, Darhana was not there. The cart and the deer were not. The snow was soft enough to take the imprint of his boots and evidence the tracks of hares and icenvels. There were no tracks of anything else. No cart runners had disturbed the surfaces. The deer, who had marked every halt with steaming dung, had left none.

As the sun began to come up he saw, across the plain below, two hills, one slightly behind the other. There was a mist on them, the mist of heat. One had a lilac sheen over it, the other bluish green. The sun slid up between these hills. On the cool still air, Lionwolf smelled grass, sweet as the body of a young girl, and flowers as if from Jafn hot-houses and indoor vines.

Then the sun lifted, and where it had left space, between the mauve hill and the green, a thing stood dark and looked at him like a beast with three golden eyes.

THREE

Purple irises grew up through the snow and ice of the first hill. Tall green grasses speared up through the second. A dipping pass divided the two hills. You looked over into a cup of land which was also green and ribbed with many other colours. A traveller on the hills might assess its diameter as several hundred miles. But the third hill, where the tower rose, was comparatively near.

Nameless stood there, looking over into the *Summer*.

It was afternoon by then; it had been a longish distance down – and then climb up – even for him.

The flowers and grass seemed real enough, and from the wide, rounded valley pulsed the rich scents of growth. He was reminded of the Faz and Vorm shamans, who had *smelled* the city. Of what did the tower smell? Great heat, perhaps.

Why pretend? He was still the Lionwolf. Changing his name backwards could not remove his repugnant guilt.

Lionwolf walked down into the cup of *Summer*, towards the third hill and the tower that, even by day, had windows that burned gold.

In the hour before the sun set, the heat of the *Summer*'s day boiled. The air shimmered, and sunlight lay like blisters, blinding and unbearable. Flowers flamed in the grasses. Even where clumps of jungle appeared in islands standing out of the plain, heat waited, wetly terrible, smoking, dripping. It lay leaden on him, gargantuan hands pushing his body towards the ground. Where he could, he kept to the shade. For he did not sweat like other men: he could not get cool. At first it made him angry, the heat of the mad *Summer* sun. Then he had nothing to spare for anger.

Approaching that final pre-sunset hour, he stopped and sat down under a massive tree. Its leaves were green – the *world* was green, green and boiling, slashed with white. The shade itself was hot-red like copper on an anvil. But Lionwolf had sat down in it, and he stared away, to where the sun seemed glancing back from the windows of the high tower. Perhaps, since the sun sank now behind him and the tree, only reflected light made the tower windows burn so brightly. Or perhaps not, for they had burned like that all day.

The tower was not, he could see quite well now, any sort of ruin but solid and many storeys high.

He had got closer to it, very close now, but in the firehaze of *Summer*, distances deceived.

Night would come soon. Then it must be cooler. Lionwolf had never encountered the agony of such a heat. He wished idly he were in Hell, where the Gech said it was even colder than the cold Winter earth.

Lionwolf fell asleep. He slept a hundred minutes. He woke cursing himself, and what he had lost, what he had destroyed.

And then he saw the serpent – the dragon – uncoiling out and out in front of him, glittering and red. He got up slowly. His eyes cleared.

No, it was not a mythical snake. That had been an optical illusion – or else Kraag laws operated again, and it had only *altered*. For what he saw now was a procession of maybe a thousand persons, covered by scarlet garments, and in their hands were fragments of the sun held up on sticks: torches. The procession wound towards the tower, beginning to ascend the third hill, vanishing there into forest, its torch fires glimpsing between the trees. Where the procession had had its origin he could not be sure.

Lionwolf breathed the deadly air as if gulping wine. Then he ran; he was still fast as a leopard.

As he did this, the hurt of heat dropped from him like a discarded mantle. It came to him that he could do more than he thought, and was still largely himself, whoever that self was.

Swiftly Lionwolf gained on, and joined the stragglers at the procession's back. Then he ceased to run.

Under their torches faces were hooded over, probably against the sun's rays. Where the hoods were cut to expose eyes, visors had been put on. Of course, they were Kraag. They were going to the tower, which, by willpower it seemed, they had put right, just as they had made *Summer* here. They were going to worship the sun.

Lionwolf strode among them now. He did not speak to them. His hair had something in it of their red, that was all. They did not either resist or acknowledge him.

The tower loomed directly ahead, craning at a strange angle above the forest's juicy foliage. The windows were like the torches, dazzling from inside. He thought of the cities which had burned, and of the Klowan-garth – but there the fire had consumed, and here it did not. Fire only *lived* in the tower.

How many storeys high was it? Certainly higher than the highest roof of Ru Karismi. The windows which ringed the top of it were immensely long, and oval in shape – three, four, five were visible, as the procession went on into the wood. Then the tower was concealed behind the boughs.

Birds sang. He had never heard this before, for in the Winter lands they only made sounds, and then not always. The birdsong disturbed him; he did not like it.

The wood soaked Lionwolf in its scalding wet shadows, its scents filled his head. He felt an unpleasant drunkenness from that, such as he had heard described, but never known.

At a glade, the tower appeared again. As before, it seemed leaning over, watching with all its eyes.

They reached a stairway carved into the hill. The steps were steep and covered in mosses, creepers, other things.

The procession climbed, spread out along a vast terrace above. It was paved, and might have been finished only yesterday. The stones were pristine.

The tower rose from the terrace. Its base was a box of columns, this alone some seventy or eighty feet in height. Dim openings led into it, unfathomable. From the centre of the box, the tower pushed up like the head of a snake.

The procession was no longer impressive, dwarfed by the building and the tower. Lionwolf decided what he saw. This was a temple, the house of a god.

Something flickered then in the dimness of the box, some energy coming alert.

Behind them all, the sun was crushed out on the horizon. Blood washed up the sky. The temple turned to cinnabar.

All of them stood, the faceless Kraag pilgrims and Lionwolf, while the sunglow faded and dusk moved up the hill. Stars split the seams of the dark.

As night approached, the energy in the lower building strengthened. It was a kind of lightning, intermittent, growing brilliant. But nothing emerged, and no one entered.

Lionwolf felt the first welcome coolness of evening. He recalled how the god had hunted him in dreams. The god was *here*, the god lived with fire in his house – Zeth Zezeth, Sun Wolf.

The highest windows continued to flash. They gave *out* no actual light, lit nothing. All *that* they kept inside.

Lionwolf went forward.

As had always happened among the Jafn, the army of the Gullahammer, the people on the terrace parted to let him go by.

Curtained in blackness, the aisles among the columns revealed little except at a lightning flare. However, Lionwolf saw in the dark: even between lightnings, he caught sight of big stone figures; then, when the flares came, he noted they were statues of the god.

Eventually he reached the place where the way opened into the tower. Here an altar – he guessed it was an altar – bulked ready for some sacrifice or apparition, or other numinous drama.

Lionwolf put his hand down flat on the stone. It was hot as a hearth. He spat on the altar. His spit sizzled, sparked, went out.

A noise like a great wing opening, spreading, folding back, hushed through the temple.

Now, when the lightning came, it showed another statue standing behind the altar, at the entry to the tower. It had not been there a moment ago.

'I made you wait,' said Lionwolf. 'My regrets.'

The lightning came again. There was no figure there at all. Instead, the way up into the tower was shown, a flight of curling steps.

Lionwolf shook off, as he had the *Summer* heat, his trepidation, his misery of terror that had now no meaning, though he had felt it so long. It dropped from him.

Hollow, he climbed the twining steps.

The light from the windows was now at the stair's head. Without shining down on the stair, where only an animal – or one like Lionwolf – could have seen, it hung ahead and above him. At first he could detect nothing in it.

Lionwolf gained the upper room of the tower after half an hour. Then the light enveloped him. It was warm but not violently so, far less than the day had been. Now inside, Lionwolf saw what else was there.

Three wolves padded to and fro. Their hides were like gold leaf, and their hair ran with crackling flames. Their eyes were jewellery, hiding everything, even their animality. In the fire too, as if underwater, objects seemed to move about, but – unlike the wolves – were not clearly visible.

The man who stood at the room's central point was Lionwolf himself. He was not one month older, not one inch taller, not one pound lighter or more heavy.

His face was Lionwolf's, and Lionwolf's face was his.

Unlike Lionwolf, only, his silvery laval mane and his eyes of gold.

Though formed himself of the precise material of the golden light, he was to be seen more definitely than anything else.

He *was* the light. The window-eyes of the tower blazed because of *him*.

The wolves padded about his feet.

'Do you walk up here armed?' Zezeth asked, in a courtly voice. He did not speak Rukarian, or any tongue Lionwolf knew, but Lionwolf knew it.

'Yes, Kraag weapons – no doubt unreal and useless.'

'Even should they be useful, they could do nothing to me. And so then how,' said Zezeth, 'will you do it?'

'Kill you? I don't know. How will you kill *me*?'

The god smiled. It was Lionwolf's smile. It charmed and enticed, and now turned the blood to ice, there in the *Summer* warmth.

Zezeth walked towards Lionwolf. It seemed the god would reach him after some twenty paces through the room. But the god took those paces and was no nearer.

Lionwolf too had started to walk towards the god. The advance was unsuppressible. He did not think they would meet for many hours, maybe not for days and nights . . . a year. But he could not turn back, could not run away. There was nowhere else to go.

For days and nights Guri had been running along the top-snow. Earth's night had fallen, and he found himself once more at the sea's edge.

He sat down on the ice, and undid his pale braids. The tiny beast skulls threaded into them were as intact as ten, twelve years ago. He looked at them with an odd wonder. Nothing had changed; everything did.

Far out within the depths of night and ocean, Guri sensed again the tug and pull of some great, separate force.

He rose and skimmed out along the ice, then along the fluid waves, squinting down at them.

He was lonely. He experienced something like a raw open wound. They were all gone, his people – like the Jafn and the rest. A few women and children were left – what would become of *them*? Probably the last of the Fazions and Kelps and Vorms, and other crazed boors of the northern seas, would sweep in on those depleted lands, in the manner the Gullahammer had already demonstrated. There could be no resistance. Even the cities of the Rukar south and west, ravaged, could hardly resist now. Although he had not gone back to that desert of salt and ash, Guri *knew*. The Rukar magicians, too, had died – the precious Magikoy. Guri could feel the news of all this as if it had been written for him on the snow.

Even the Ranjal-goddess flew off.

'And here I am,' Guri said aloud, 'looking for the doorway. Where's the door, ah?'

He meant the exit from existence.

Then he thought of the Lionwolf, and Guri spat on the sea; as Lionwolf, if Guri had known – maybe he did – spat on the altar of Zeth Zezeth.

But Guri too was a ghost haunted by other things. They had crept up on him unawares. In the 'tween-world now, when he tried it, he would meet again with villagers he had burned – and with women he had raped, who stood in groups and looked at him with baleful anguished eyes.

He had not intended to *hurt* them. Did they really mind

it so much: rape, torture and death? He had somehow never thought so. Only Olchibe had profound feelings, only children were worth saving – surely?

Guri's heart fogged over with bewildered, unwilling grief at all the pain he had personally added to the fortunes of life.

Then it came *again* – that lunge which seemed to grip his psychic roots. There, down *there*, under the moving water—

He could dive deep, and try to discover it.

'I'm feared to,' he told the night. 'Guri's afraid.'

Miles, *aeons* down, something thrummed the darkness like a harp.

Guri's mind somersaulted over itself. It landed, stared head on into the apex of the past.

Then he knew – his fear, his *connection* – why this entity *could* pull on him. It was the *whale*. It was the horned whale on whose back he had scrambled, on whose sword of horn he had died. Still his bones must lie there, knotted round those spikes. Not only the whale but his own mortal remains were *summoning* Guri.

Guri sprang up, aiming himself back at the inland shore. Too late.

'Since you ask about your death, I will tell you. I shall not see to it. It is my son who will kill *you*.'

'*I* am your son.'

'Yes, that is why you are to be punished – for daring to be my son. But I have another.'

Lionwolf, walking through gold light, fixes his eyes only on the mirror-face of the god.

'I do not mean to sully myself,' says Zeth Zezeth Zzth, 'with the bother of it – your partly human debris strewn and scattered.'

'Why then did you create me?' says Lionwolf.

'Did you not coerce me into making you?'

Lionwolf checks, but goes on walking. The god seems amiable. His face is not blue: this is his benign side.

'How could I have done anything? I wasn't even alive—'

'Oh, you were there. There in *her*, a seed already planted, waiting only for me to quicken you. Do you think a silly human woman, drowning in her yellow hair in the cold ocean, could tempt *me*? Your benighted mother – it was your power that drew me to her. Poor Zezeth, helpless in her clutches – yours.' The god grins. He is tickled by this absurdity. No doubt, too, he lies, like the compulsive lie of reality the Kraag described, worse when found out.

'I put myself into her,' says the god, grinning on. The grin is hideous, yet does not mar his beauty. 'Truly, Nameless One, I put *myself* into her. I was trapped there in her, in *you*. How else could you be made in flesh? Oh, I had better be precise, as you grew up among barbarians. Have you seen two wolves when they mate, or foxes? Sometimes the male becomes enmeshed in the female's sexual passage. I mean nothing like that. I was drawn *entire* into the body of your mother, into her womb, and so into the being you became through me. That is why your shadow had fire in it, little Nameless One. *I* was in your shadow. The red gems of my spilled and special blood. But my other selves stayed active. A woman was created from snow and called after night – your counterbalance. Others lay down with her and were improved. You she emptied, as you know, of your prisoner – myself. Sex is an ancient magic among every kind. And now, lacking me, what is there for you? Though I have made you so strong, I will have you put out like the blown flame on the candle.'

'Because I trapped you . . . in my *shadow*?'

'Just that. It is, boy, enough.'

'And your other son will kill me.'

'I took another shape once, and possessed another mortal creature of similar shape, in the sea. Supernaturals do such things, as any of your Jafn songs will tell you. *She* gave birth, this animal, but not requiring to burgle and absorb my essence. Even so, her child is half deity. It is he who will be the agent of your death. He would have killed your mother already, before ever I consorted with her. Being what he is, he was cognizant, and could foretell somewhat the events to come. He grew jealous – so, you see, he has too his own score to settle with you.'

They have approached no nearer, Lionwolf, Zzth, walking on and on, together and towards—

Something in Lionwolf kicks at him under the heart.

'Where is Saphay?' he asks.

'Are you interested? What shall I offer you? She is somewhere, waiting – not for you.'

'For you?' Lionwolf says.

'For me. It is all for me now.'

The god's hair turns the colour of *salt* and *ash*. His eyes are black. Bars of dark blue mask his face. The wolves pacing with him are black, and white fire flutters in their pelts.

This is to be the malign side, after all.

Lionwolf recalls a child, not even born, screaming for Guri. But Guri will not come to him now. That is all over.

'Then let's get on,' he says to his father. 'I never heard any man talk so much. I never knew the gods chattered.'

Zzth strikes him.

It is painless, like the condition of death. But death is to come, apparently.

Lionwolf falls through something – downwards, forwards, upwards. The gold light spins and whirls. He wishes only he had been able to kill the god, but the next best thing is obviously to die himself.

Lionwolf opened his eyes. He was neither dead nor in a room of golden light. Instead, he was seated by the brutish altar, below the stairs into the god's tower. It was night and the temple was pitch black, and not one stray flicker of lightning now moved across it. He could just perceive the statues, but they were ruinous, missing limbs and some their heads.

The temple smelled of cold stone – *cold*.

'Face of God—' The Jafn oath came out of him, taking him by surprise. He pushed himself up and away from the altar. He felt a type of exhaustion new to him.

A cold, *cold* light was beginning to trickle in along the floor from two of the doorless entries. A moon must be rising.

Lionwolf glanced towards the stairway. It was, he now saw, also mostly down, blasted by something – perhaps some blow of a peevish deity.

Had the events he had undergone been one more dream induced by Zezeth?

Why had the god spoken at such length, so elaborately,

like some old soldier determined to mull over all his former battles?

If none of this had been real, then, by Kraag statute, it was more real than anything else.

Lionwolf crossed the temple floor and reached one of the moonlit doormouths.

Summer had ended.

Beyond Zeth's temple, the snow lay in spotless white carpets. Ice-jungles glittered hard as daggers under the single winter moon.

There were peculiar shapes along the terrace, partly under the snow. They were human, and it seemed they had lain down there and wrapped the snow about themselves for warmth. Their clothing had been red, but the moon, weather and time had bleached it.

He bent over them, one by one. The visors still covered their eyes, the hoods their faces. Removing some of these, Lionwolf learned that the processional pilgrims were all dead; only the freezing of the land had kept them whole.

Moon, weather, time . . .

Time, then, had passed, days and nights, even a year, during that long fruitless walk towards the god.

As for the Kraag, believing in any rebirth of *Summer* had been, it seemed, hasty.

The valley was no longer properly like a cup; it had a different geography and, now the moon was high, from the terrace Lionwolf could see clear away to the east. The ocean was there, in its rims and shelves of shore ice.

Already he was descending the hill stair from the temple, heading off towards the sea. That was where the god intended Lionwolf to go, to meet the ordained assassin.

There was no point any more in avoidance. It gave a curious sense of freedom, this giving up.

Later, when the moon was sinking, Lionwolf looked back. The ruinous tower leant like a crooked chimney, and its windows were unlit.

He understood what it was, the vengeance Zezeth would employ. What else could it be but that first death which had seized Saphay – and Guri – had evicted them only against its will, and now longed to retrieve them. It was the horned whale.

Lionwolf ran along the snow of the valley towards the sea and the whale. He had never felt his own life so vitally. He was almost happy, eager for another fight. He would meet the whale, which the god had somehow also fathered – and indeed the Jafn songs, as well as legends of the Rukarians, were full of such antics. Having met him, he would harm this bestial half-brother, he would visit on him – on it – all the wrath that he could not bludgeon Zezeth with. The whale would kill Lionwolf anyway.

After that, Lionwolf had no concrete plans. This was probably the reason for his sensation of lightness.

The landscape channelled down. Hills mobbed up, cliffs of ice and snow. Daylight returned: the sky was blue.

He dreamed somewhere, sleeping a couple of minutes as he travelled, that the god drove over the sky in a chariot drawn by fiery wolves. In mockery, Zezeth sliced from the blue heavens a blue sun, and threw it down to Lionwolf to replace his war-standard. But where the blue sun hit the ground it smashed, while in the sky the cut-omission it had left behind bruised, and from its edges ran drops of gore. About it the rest of the sky looked poisoned.

Some days after this dream, Lionwolf stopped running.

He stayed motionless a brief time there on the snow waste. There was one cloud in the sky that did not seem to move either. Soon he resumed running.

That evening he reached the shoreline. Phosphorus sparkled on the flat breakers, and up against the shore the ice had rifted. An iceberg, transparent like a phantom, was sailing slowly along, miles off. Yes, there had been heat in this region, but not for many months.

Lionwolf stationed himself on the shore and fished in the tricky Olchibe way, tapping along the broken ice floes. He ate the fish he caught, not cooking them. All his thoughts were for other things, memories, and among them he constantly saw Saphay. He reminisced to himself about his childhood with her, and how he could make her laugh, and how they bullied Bit-Nabnish, and then Guri bounded into Lionwolf's thoughts, and even the little toy mammoth . . . and then the live mammoth Peb Yuve had given him, and the lion teams and the armies, and Lionwolf stared rigidly away from memory, out towards the sea from which violence and death would come to deliver him.

On that night, men's voices were heard cheerily calling and shouting along the shore, a small way inland. Not wanting to be disturbed. Lionwolf blended against the slopes, and witnessed a group of men in lion chariots driving along.

They were Jafn warriors, and what they were doing here was incomprehensible, for the Jafn lands lay most of a continent off, in the north and east, and anyway Jafn was gone.

A white-haired man led the others. He had an ice-hawk perched on his shoulder, as he guided the chariot. Once he had drawn closer, he turned his head and looked at Lionwolf, spotting him without delay.

Lionwolf knew this man, but had never seen him before. That was, he had never seen him after Lionwolf was born. *Those* memories, from that pre-advent era, were normally unsure and disorderly.

What was the man's name? Who was he?

The Jafn turned his chariot now. The lions were magnificent, leaping on physical strings, manes alight with ornaments.

'Greetings in peace, good evening. Do you speak the Jafn tongue?'

'Yes,' said Lionwolf.

'I am Athluan,' said the man, 'Chaiord of the Klow.'

'You're dead,' replied Lionwolf. Having said that, he blushed like an adolescent who has uttered the worst faux pas.

But Athluan said, 'So I gather. But nevertheless I'm here, and some of my warriors with me. Not my brother – Rothger I did not bring.'

'Rothger I slew for you,' said Lionwolf. He laughed all at once at his own immaturity. He was always, so far, both a man and a child.

'My thanks,' said Athluan. 'I should have done it. It was owed to me. He did his very best to *make* me do it, but I failed.'

Behind Athluan, Chaiord of the Klow, and his chariot, lions and hawk, a campfire was now burning a welcome on the snow.

'Come and dine with us,' said Athluan. Lionwolf gazed at him. 'Aren't you hungry yet? What's a pair of uncooked fish? Come on, sir, I tell you, now.'

'You tell me?'

'Why not? You owe me some obedience. I'm your father.'

The Lionwolf, child and man, widened his eyes, amazed, and stared transfixed. He said softly, 'I would, by Great God, you were.'

'Hush. Your mother was my wife. If I'd lived, no man would have troubled a hair of her head, nor of yours.'

From the glow of the fire, a warrior called merrily, 'Come eat, Chaiord. Lionwolf, come and eat.'

'They know me?'

'We're the dead, and know very much.'

'In a while, I'll be one with your company.'

'No, forgive me, Lionwolf, our paths are different.'

'Yes, I thought that might be it. Where, then, for me?'

'Whatever, it will find you. No man can be stripped of his soul, not even the son of a god. Perhaps your human spirit is greater than the fire of the god that he gave you.'

'Gave me – then snatched back.'

'Did he tell you that? Rothger was a liar, too. The god of the Ruk took back *himself*. What was yours, he couldn't take. Be conscious of this, Lionwolf. And now we go to dinner.'

There was broiled venison, and baked fish, and beer. Lionwolf thought of Darhana, who had brought cooked food from nothingness. The dead, though, could always eat well if they wanted to – so Guri had assured him.

When they had eaten they did not, of course, sleep. They shot at marks stuck in the snow – Athluan lent Lionwolf his bow. They told stories as the stars spiralled towards the morning. The stories were all ones Lionwolf already knew from his sojourn among the Jafn and from the Gullahammer. No one, however, mentioned recent war or last Endhlefon's history.

He thought, *If he had been my father, what then could I have been, myself?*

But that chance was gone. He did not even know if Athluan were one of the undead, like Guri, or a true ghost – or an illusion, a dream, a figment of belief.

He had begun to think the procession in the *Summer* valley had been something of that sort, some ghost ritual recorded on the air and made visible through the whim of the god. The corpses mummified in ice had been there since long ago – so long that even an interval of *Summer* had not thawed them.

He thought too, as he sat among the dead Jafn warriors, that conceivably he the Lionwolf had not been told a single thing by Zezeth. The god had merely, unforgivably, worked Lionwolf's own mind like a puppet to make the explanation. And when Zeth struck him, less than a reprimand, it was a scornful punctuation mark.

All this meditation dulled Lionwolf. He hid that from his uncanny hosts, used to making a fine display among men. Lionwolf too told stories, asked riddles. He splintered the marks with the bow and arrows they lent him, shooting in the Olchibe way, on which none of them now commented. There was, after the first, very little personal conversation between them. Nobody harked back to any other place – or life.

When the sun rose, all the men – and their guest – jumped into the sea, yelling at the icy water. They drank the last of the beer.

Athluan embraced Lionwolf, and Lionwolf felt pressed on his body every physical muscle, every sinew and bone of Athluan's. The white hair smelled of frosty fire-smoke, as Lionwolf had scented it on others after a hunting camp.

'I go that way,' said Athluan. He pointed inland, maybe northerly. 'Kiss your mother for me, when you see her again.'

'I may never—'

'Oh yes, my son, oh, yes. Till then.'

They parted. The chariots rode off with the springing lions and laughter of the warriors. You would have thought they were simply going home.

When they had gone from sight, unexpectedly Athluan's hawk came circling back. It stooped quickly to Lionwolf and lighted on his shoulder. He smoothed its striped feathers and, before it lifted away once more, the fierce beak pecked him and drew a fleck of blood. Watching the bird vanish again into the morning, he knew it had returned to bid him farewell.

That next night, from the upper room of the Holas House, Nirri was searching the sky beyond her window.

She had seen a meteor, and knew it was an arrow fired from behind the static constellations – out of the Other Place. This might be the token of a coming death or a coming life. It was the second, she hoped, for she was large with Arok's child: a son, the House Mage had told her.

The Holas had made Arok Chaiord in the Holasangarth, for he had been nearest kin to the slain Chaiord. There were so few grown males, Arok had, on being told Nirri carried a male, married her, though she was a fishwife from a whaler village and just possibly her lawful spouse was yet alive.

Pregnant, and a queen, Nirri grew younger and better looking. Despite the garth's being now a sad and echoing citadel, nevertheless she found it hard to mourn, for where others had lost so much, she had only gained. With her former husband, besides, she had never been able to conceive. But she had known her destiny was now assured when they escaped the whale and the wall of sea.

Below, in the joyhall, there was a faint mutter of carouse from the group of elderly men and youths. They did their utmost to make the rafters ring. But Nirri had been sent up to sleep, as she was in her eighth month. Soon enough she got into the bed, only a straw mattress here, but nicer than any she had ever known. She slept quickly; she was not uneasy, had nothing to be frightened of. These people were hers, and she had come up in the world.

Below again, deep down in the area under the hall and the House cellars, Arok was standing with the faceless, formless Jafn statue of God.

He did not pray or speak, but waited with his hands on the statue, thinking. Tonight the House Mage had approached him and drawn him aside, which was easy to do in such a barely inhabited dwelling.

'Arok, I've glimpsed your son in the belly of its mother. God cherishes us and sends us a hero. I mean no idle compliment. A great and terrific phenomenon has occurred.'

'What?' Arok demanded.

Now he poised here, digesting *what*. For his Mage had informed him that the son of Arok and Nirri was black – black as coal – as black as Chillel, though this the Mage did not mention, for he did not know of the penultimate woman Arok had cutched.

*

467

All the ice had come down.

The pyramids Yyrot built or annexed were in bits. Saphay wandered disconsolately among them, the cat – returned from some elsewhere – prowling after her, looking to see if any mice or rats might explode out of the demolition.

Saphay was aware that the cold did not reduce her and, though she had not eaten or drunk anything for a long while, she was healthy and clear-headed.

It was the disdain of her she minded the most, the indifference she had always endured.

In the east the sky was saffron, the shade of her hair. Sunrise indicated the land beyond the shallow ice-shelves where the pyramids had been anchored. But how could she bridge the rocky, unsafe ice?

Something else must happen; she did not know what. Even in the gentle dawn, the sea had a threatening aspect.

'You,' she said to the cat, 'you slut.'

The cat ignored her. One final hallucination of a rat was scurrying over the spoilt ice. The cat set off in pursuit.

That was the moment when the sea undid itself behind Saphay and, looking round, she screamed and heard her own voice like the cry of a bird in the sky, nothing to do with her at all.

A horned tower soared from the water and the ice, that was crowned with bright dawn on ivory, and also black as a shadow – its eyes small and searing, two tiny molten suns.

First Volume

BRIGHTSHADE

Even the stars are dogs – only dogs – in the Hand of Night.

Bardic Death Lay of the Hero Star Black: Jafn

ONE

This hero was unlike others.

He was a world.

Perhaps it had been fifteen years before that his mother followed her own designs beneath the blackness of the sea. Above her, that day, the ice-shelf was thin; even if it had been otherwise, she had no fear of entrapment under the ice. Needing to rise from the water every several hours to take air, her race, the whales, had long ago developed their clutching forelimbs, and a piercing unitary horn.

The female whale was of great size, forty-five or fifty feet in length, a celebrity of her people.

For a while she grazed along the ocean floor, rubbing her body there to clean it. She was in search of food, not a prospective mate, but when he came to her through the water, a leviathan greater in size even than she, he brought her, in his mouth, a feast. Three fresh-killed sharks and another, smaller, whale were laid before her, all garnished by torrents of fish.

She and he fed together. When he nudged against her she did not resist.

Clasping each other with their agile forelimbs, he possessed her and she consented to possession.

He did not stay to escort her after, though that was the

normal habit of a mating pair. Pregnant, she soon forgot him.

She carried the kalfi one year and three months before birthing it. Then she nurtured her young, a male, suckling him another whole year, teaching him, persuading him to the surface to take his own at first more frequently needed breaths.

If she was in any way aware this kalfi was the child of a god who had capriciously taken on the appearance of her kind, she never vocalized it in her songs under the ocean.

Her son grew great as she was, then great as his father, greater and more great, until he became too big to be remembered by her. By then, anyway, she had mated elsewhere and had other kalfis to replace him.

But he – he *knew* what he was. He left her without thought – yes, *thought*, for in his manner he did think almost in a human fashion. He surged away through the deeps, rising up, when he wished, to burst the ice far inshore. *Still* growing, he was already a titan among his race. He feared nothing, no predator, no destiny. He had never met his father or earned that father's disapproval.

There was a certain telepathy among the whale kind. They communicated not merely by physical sound. The kalfi of the god was not immune to these skills and, as he grew to adolescence, he too began to hear and receive information.

Some trace reached him of the thoughts of his father; some desire or – worse – compulsion.

Without knowing what it was in any absolute terms, for to a *whale* these concepts had no meaning, Zezeth's first son grasped that his own uniqueness was under threat. Like many a first-born child, he did not like the idea of the arrival of another. He grew jealous, so Zezeth had seemed to say. And so it was.

Yet this rival sibling had not at that point been conceived. It was still to happen.

Zezeth's first-born strayed inland, far in among the ice-locked channels that partitioned the Marginal north.

By his telepathy too, which in his case extended beyond genus to include the very masses of the land, the very air mankind and whalekind must breathe, the great mammal sensed and understood what came towards him, and saw how he must strike at it.

Those twelve or thirteen years before, Saphay, pursued by the Olchibe vandal band among the snow lanes, was driven towards her true executioner: the whale. And so he rose out of the ice beneath her, shattering, breaching, leaping. He slew uncaringly those animal and human things which for him had no importance. Even Guri had been one of those. It was the woman the whale meant to destroy, she alone, before she could be made the vessel of an unwanted half-brother.

He got her almost inadvertently. For the young whale god it was too simple.

Into the depths of the sea then he plunged with her. He would drown her before she could annoy. But the sea had stayed the domain of Zezeth. As in so many myths, the very deed meant to avert some chance had *caused* it.

The young whale now knew this also: he had killed Saphay – yet she *lived*. As for the rival son, *he* lived too; they were competitors.

He had a name, the whale. It had come to him through the currents of sea and thought, like most notions he received. It evolved from the vision of a shadow which held light and fire inside it. In the language of whales this name had neither characters nor sound, but it had a *shape*. The shape, in the tongues of men, was spelled *Brightshade*.

A long while – or a little while, for his judgement of time was unlike a man's – Brightshade experienced his whale life in the deeps. He hunted and fed, slept, fought and copulated. That he had produced no offspring he never knew, for like his father he never continued to escort the females he united with. Sometimes he drew near the land, playing like an animate mountain in the semi-solid white surf. Or, dancing upwards from the lowest ocean, he sank the ship-packs and jalees of men.

In the belly of the whale called Brightshade lay whole cargos, whole vessels smashed in chunks or – very few – peculiarly intact, along with skeletons of beasts and men. None of these items bothered him. He was comfortable with them inside, never felt them. However, he had picked up remnants not only inside but *out*.

Those who had seen him close – and in recent years any who had did not survive to tell the story – beheld on the back of this astronomic whale, an *environment*.

Into that, if they outlasted the initial onslaught, they were tossed or floundered – into a dank miasma of the horrifically organic, of cold stinking abysms and gulches, crags of filth bricked in by flotsam and jetsam.

Again, the landscape on his back posed no difficulty for the whale. Brightshade felt nothing of it, or nothing urgent. If it ever itched him, he rolled against something hard and scratched it off.

While he swam along the surface, men had often wandered about on the continent of the whale's back, sometimes for as much as a month, for he could breach and breathe, as with all else, an abnormal stretch of time. In the end, he would go down again. Then they were taken too.

But even his external dead victims did not always leave him. The horrorland of his back was augmented, like his guts, with bones.

For some while he had been making his way along the outlying waters of this coast. He had picked up, on his journey, various extras, but usually without any purpose. Only two acquisitions had recently pleased him. A collector in his own right, he had meant to have these two particular pieces a long while. There was a third piece he had already kept for years, waiting patiently, and now the set was complete. One further thing had come his way. Because his biology was mixed, and he approximated human thought, this one had briefly puzzled him. But he lost interest in it quickly. Brightshade was intent now on his own heroic quest.

Like his brother Lionwolf once, the gargantuan whale was hot for revenge. On this occasion, Brightshade's paramount enemy would die. He would make sure of it.

On the night he reached the place, infallibly he knew. He coasted in towards the shore, unconcerned at beaching himself. His bottomless strength was a match for any strip of land.

The night sea broke on his back, broke and ran from him.

Brightshade, who could spring minute on minute for the sun, and crash back, his ascent, his dive causing a tidal wave, eased in against the coast, subtle as a lover.

It was the hour before sunrise. The sky was paling, cruel fingers stubbing out the stars.

Something had changed. What was it?

The sea wrinkled, ebbed and flowed. The ice lay further in.

Something spread between the outer sea and the frozen inner, that was all.

The scene was peaceful.

After his other father had gone away along the shore, Lionwolf sat and watched the sea. Morning flew up, noon and afternoon went after it. The sun set at his back; two crescent moons lifted like boats on the distant liquid waterline.

Lionwolf was watching for the coming of his adversary, his father's agent sent to slaughter him. The whale.

Saphay had told her son of her escape from it, though he did not remember quite when she had. Now, therefore, he anticipated something very large and awesome, but was in ignorance, of course, of what this creature had finally become.

In the night Lionwolf slept. That was his mortal Rukarian blood, so he believed. A god would never need to sleep.

Dawn woke him. He lay gazing. The sea was no longer there. The shore had extended.

The ice ran out, then the country altered. Not ice, snow or open water, it seemed part of a landmass which had thawed overnight. Some new variant of *Summer*?

Lionwolf stood up. He looked far out and saw no sign at all of the sea. Instead, a swarthy silty terrain lay there, with tall black reed-beds; and a mile off, a sort of hill rose, not snowed in but also dark in colour. It seemed to him there was some type of palisade running along the top of this hill. It glittered murkily in the early sun.

There were tales of sunken islands that pushed up again out of the sea. Was this one of them?

Whatever it was, it had come between him and his meeting with his enemy. Lionwolf must travel over the barrier, in order once more to reach the coast.

He walked out on to the ice, towards the verges of the ugly and curious land.

At no time since the White Death at Ru Karismi had Lionwolf been entirely gathered together inside himself. Even before Chillel thieved half his soul – so he still phrased it, when he considered it – he had been diminished. Never knowing what he was, never coming to grips with his own persona, now he was only an incomplete group of fragments hitting against each other with an empty noise.

With Athluan, for a little while Lionwolf had played at being who he had been – or reckoned he was obliged to be. But now no one else was there.

He wanted the whale also for this reason. To fight against and try to kill it, even to be killed by it, gave Lionwolf back a part to act.

He walked doggedly off the ice on to the surface of the bizarre island.

The ground was abnormal. It felt both greasy and turgid and pulled at his Kraagish boots. An eerie fishy smell rose from the ground, too, that turned his stomach. But going on, after a time he grew accustomed to its stink. Nor did the smell alert him. This area had been submerged in ocean.

Presently the reed banks began. They were tall, the reeds, in many spots reaching over his head, enclosing him.

He thought they were a kind of seaweed which had mutated, grown upright and stiff as leather treated for war.

When a light cold wind blew inwards from the direction of the unseen water, the reeds rattled against each other. Things were caught in them, too: he saw other weeds and pods he recognized from marine trophies of the Vorms. Even fish had been trapped there; some had become bones, others only withered to brown husks like the dead leaves pared from orchards. Then other material came to Lionwolf's notice. He saw a rusted dagger lying there, down in the sludge that nourished the reeds, later some spears and a weighted net. Again none of this amazed him. Ships sank, and so had this island, once. Although the place was so dismal, he started almost to be interested in it.

By now he had walked about an hour, and was seeing that the land sloped always slightly upward.

Next, stepping out from the reeds, he confronted the hill he had seen from the shore.

It was high as the platform of a garth. It had, too, its own ranker stink, primal and somehow alcoholic. As he had thought, it was mostly black in colour but, seen close to, patched and gullied with other unlikely shades – reddish ochre, puce, yellow. On the top, right where the upper walls of a garth would have been, the palisade ran round.

Lionwolf climbed up the reeking mound. It was not easy to scale, even by the supernatural horizonal means he could still access. It offered hand and foot holds, but also it was in parts soft and treacherous, trying to swallow his boots, legs, all of him.

When he gained the summit, the going was more firm.

He found the palisade was made of the etched and sharpened bones of some great sea-being, which had become stranded there. They poked up at the grey sky.

He walked through them, again quite interested at their largeness, thinking of yarns of the Vorms and Fazions about sea monsters and giant whales. Perhaps this skeleton was the remains of one. It did not occur to him, even mistaken as he was, that *his* whale could ever have met such a fate.

On the far side of the bones, he found other similar hills. They mounded away to, and formed, a shut horizon. This was less interesting, for these hills were all very alike.

Lionwolf ran, putting on incredible speed. He did it only to outwit the suction of the muck, and to get over the dull hills and see what was on their other side. As he ran, he marvelled vaguely at himself, that he was still capable of such speed, or of desiring to use it.

The hills, though, went on and on. He thought he would never be shot of them.

Hours into the afternoon, he raced down the last stretch, and was in a marsh.

He had seen a little of Gech, but the ice swamps there were not like this. Here the tepid thaw persisted. Glaucous water oozed in runnels and pools between more of the reed banks. In addition, trees of sallow fungus grew here, with branching crowns.

As Lionwolf forged on through this waterland, he was stalled momentarily when flocks of weird, tattered black birds erupted from deep inside the fungus woods. They had been feeding on things rotting there, and he disturbed them, but not for long. He became accustomed to having scores of these birds whirr up ahead of him, falling back like a fractured night when he had passed. He did not know what they were. Presumably they had opportunistically flown out from some region inland, and yet he could not shake the suspicion he soon had that in fact they had evolved spontaneously out of the island – as worms did, the Jafn said, in a too-warm corpse.

When the sun set in cloud behind the island, Lionwolf grew conscious of thirst.

It was his mortal side winning over his depleted superpowers. On the mainland, thirst would have caused no problem. Ice was everywhere, and snow that might be heated or at worst sucked for moisture. Here there were only the unclean marsh pools. Lionwolf, fastidious, would not turn to those. He thrust the idea of thirst away. Soon enough, he knew, it would not matter.

Evening drew in. In the gloaming the territory reorganized itself again.

The waterways had drained off into a sort of forest. The trees now were stalks, more poles than anything, but sticky. They had snagged in their glue new articles which swung and clattered at Lionwolf's passage through them. He glimpsed metal mesh, iron chains green with barnacles and slime, and formations of loose hanging bones that, as the dark intensified, shone.

And from this forest of bones and chains, instead of birds bursting up, a man's figure suddenly materialized.

Before Lionwolf could spring at it, or away, his body faltered. His body, before his brain, exactly remembered the physique of this man. It was Guri.

Guri, too, was taken aback.

They stood there in the luminous dusk, staring at each other, astounded by their meeting.

Guri spoke first. 'Before the Great Gods, what are you at here?'

'What are *you* at here, Guri?'

'I had no choice.'

'I believed *I* was the one who had no choice – or so you told me once.'

'Yes . . . that was different. Great Gods,' said Guri again. He did not add the respectful *Amen*, nor did Lionwolf.

The bones and chains swung, creaking like gibbets.

A ghastly white moon came stalking up from the east, where the sea was, somewhere.

The men sat down, at a cleaner drier place, further into the forest, that Guri had located and it seemed made his camp for the night.

He had been foraging, he said, and found a semi-intact clay pot. In this he now put fire, which he did not summon in the original manner learned as an undead. He rubbed bits of fossilized stuff together till they took a spark. No, in all ways, Guri looked to be attempting his ordinary previous life.

They sat there then, by the potted Olchibe fire. Above, through the stalk poles and swinging things, the moon blazed. Around it too, in the diluted dark of the sky, some other strangeness seemed to be going on.

Having spoken of his reconnoitring and shopping expeditions about the local countryside, Guri ceased talking.

Lionwolf said at last, 'Where are you making for? It's not like you to stop about, once you start off.'

'Ah, isn't it? I thought it was you that likes to get on.'

'You're no longer my friend, I think, Guri – no longer my uncle.'

'No.'

'Because of Ru Karismi.'

'It wasn't your fault,' said Guri glumly. 'The bloody Rukar soint Magikoy did it. Too big for their boots to carry. They've paid for it now. Even so, it was *because* of you.'

'I know.'

'I've nothing to forgive you, Lion. But I never will forgive you.'

'No.'

The moon moved off into the higher sky. Where it had been, stars appeared, looking too bright.

'I'll share your fire tonight with thanks, Guri. I'll make on tomorrow, and let you be.'

'Let me *be*?' Shocked out of reticence and antipathy, Guri stared again. 'I'm stuck here. So are you, unless you've got godpower enough to save yourself. Probably you have, but me – well. My past's caught me up. I have to get on, too, in the morning. *That* way.' He pointed east.

Lionwolf said, 'What do you mean?'

'Don't you know where we *are*? What this place *is*?'

'Some land come up from the sea—'

'*Land!* Oh yes, land, *some* land—' Guri gave a wild laugh, slapping his hands about in his braids. 'It's *alive*, this land. It *lives*. It swims far down, and surfaces when it chooses. We met before, it and I. It was a smaller one then, but still a monster.'

Lionwolf breathed slowly out. 'The great whale.'

'Ah.'

Abruptly, Lionwolf also laughed. 'I thought I was walking out to the sea's edge to find it.'

'It's saved you a walk.'

'Perhaps. But it *killed* you, Guri. Why are you here?'

'I said, it came back for me. It breached right under me, and I was taken up with it, away through the sea, over and *under*. You think I could just project myself away – wink out of that place, be some other place. I couldn't. For a while I couldn't move at all, then I could again. But only like a living man – only *here*. It's my destiny, my doom: my span on this earth is finished. I'm not sorry, at least not much. I suppose I have to pay my own dues now, in Hell.' He shrugged mournfully.

Lionwolf said, 'It's *his*, this whale.'

'The shit-god? Yes, I thought it was. In the end, I thought so. What did he do – put on whaleness and fiddle with its mother?'

'As you say.'

'Well, that sounds like him.'

'*He* sent me to it, or it to me, so it can murder me for him. He didn't wish to soil his divinity personally.'

'It was *his* side failed you, Lion. Your mother, even if she was Rukar, was no bad woman. No – fit for Peb she would have been, but he doesn't need her now.'

The fire sank. It was not cold, but dank in the forest of bones and chains.

Miles off, something rustled dimly, some other geography combed by the wind.

'I have to keep on, you see,' said Guri, 'towards the head of it, this thing. That's where I died. My bones must be up there. Its horn tore through me, but my body will have rotted off by now, dropped away, and the skeleton will have rolled down on to the horn-spurs. That's where, when I meet my own self.'

'I would have made for the head too, Guri. I'll do what I can to damage it.'

'Do you think you can? You're not yourself, are you, not now?'

'I never was – but less now. I can still work magecraft though, certain things. I mean to try. That's all I have.'

'We'll go on together, then,' said Guri.

'Not if you don't want.' Sullen, yet resigned, adult.

'What does it matter, Lion, what *I* want? Or what *you* want now?'

Lionwolf glanced up. He said, almost in a whisper, '*Look*, three-in-one is joking again – Yyrot-Zeth-Ddir. *Making* things.'

Both of them got to their feet.

They stood staring up, through the forest on the back of the whale, at *another* whale, this one picked out in diamond stars across two-thirds of the night sky.

The next morning they went on together.

They had travelled sufficiently together in the past for each of them to find this now equally familiar and uncomfortable.

Once clear of the forest, it appeared to them the 'land' of the whale's back was rising steeply. The filth here was thick and hardened. Cliffs and deep defiles channelled out of and through it. There were caves. Here inchoate creatures seemed to be shifting about, sometimes signalling to each other in curious, scarcely-to-be-heard caterwaulings. It might all only have been a trick of the light and the wind.

'Is there other life abroad on this thing?' Lionwolf asked.

He learned it was oddly easy to return to the child's way with Guri, asking questions.

Guri nodded. 'Have you seen the bird-things? Well, there are those. Up ahead there'll be something else, something bigger. I've heard it now and then, by day and night, galloping about over the beast. Seen something, once, fly across the moon.'

'Birds?'

'Even the birds aren't birds. Great Gods know what they are – something that lives properly *under* the sea, far down. But this whale is often on the surface, and then they sprout wings. Did you see, they hadn't any eyes?'

Lionwolf was silent.

In the caves of filth, voices faintly resounded, arguing, yattering. A cry ripped up, like the scream of a hunting hawk. Nothing otherwise came out.

'They're parasites,' said Lionwolf, 'scavengers. By feeding off it, they've gained some of the whale's supernal qualities, and adapted to do better for themselves.'

'Do you have a knife, a sword?' enquired Guri judiciously.

'Both. Kraag weapons for food, or dancing with. But they'll do, providing they're *real*.'

'We'll reach the top, by the head, around sundown. I sense that: my *bones* are telling me.'

'Truly a great whale, two days of travel to cover it. Worthy of the Faz storytellers.'

'It's lifting itself, Lion. So slow we can't feel it, lifting up its head for us to find.'

'It may just dive under the water.'

'Too mediocre, don't you think, to drown or freeze you

– if that's possible even now? And me, I'm already dead. It will be some other method.'

'What?'

'How do *I* know? Maybe *it* doesn't know.'

'Maybe *all* of us know, but we forget.'

'I'm thinking that could be so.'

They took a rest at noon. Though the sky was leaden, a white sun scorched down icy-cold heat. Lionwolf coughed from thirst, and Guri recalled how this half-god had seemed about to die that time in his babyhood. Lionwolf *could* be made to die, oh yes. Guri regarded this prospect, frowning, but there was himself to consider too. He thought he *did* know how it would be for him.

The bones – *his* bones – where they still lay, that was where—

Another forest or jungle began soon after they went on. Dry seaweed creepers roped pillar-like stems that rose house-high towards the sun. It was in this region that the greater scavenger-horde of the whale attacked.

They loped on four legs, like a wolf-pack, through the tree columns. Otherwise they were not like wolves but a gelatinous mass of blackest shadow, unlit by eyes – or teeth.

It seemed these animals did not either fly or *bite*.

Then they were there, swarming with shrill shrieks. In a few seconds, Lionwolf was covered by them. Their mere weight – considerable – felled him. He lay under the stenchful hot seethe of their slippery bodies, sticking sword and knife through and through. Blackish blood splashed him, and awful other fluids. From the narrowest holes of mouths, ribbon-like tongues extruded. Where they fastened on his flesh, they *entered*, unhurtful, hungry. They were a type of leech.

Fighting them off, Lionwolf saw Guri, too, fighting. But Guri was undead – he could neither be harmed, nor could he *harm*. Yet Lionwolf beheld, through the chaos of disgusting battle, that this was no longer the case. Guri hacked and sawed, stabbed and wrenched with his Olchibe blades, with his hands, kicking with his feet. The leech-things died in vast quantities, but where they had attached to him, he streamed with wounds.

The contest ended only when the last leech perished.

Lionwolf, sloughing corpses, got up. He too streamed with blood.

He was mortal now. If he had needed proof, here it was upon him.

He knelt on the whale's back, cursing and weeping in rage, blind with the pity of self which is the right of every living creature. He cursed god – the god who was his father.

When he stood and strode on, Guri was already ahead of him by half a mile.

Before the whale, picked out in constellations, reappeared at dusk, they had reached the gulch that lay before the head of Brightshade.

There was no way to cross it unless they climbed down, then up again. There had been a time when either of them could have jumped the gulf with elegance. Maybe still they could have done that, but they had ceased to believe they could. The Kraag would have told them the lack of belief in powers preceded, and hurried, those powers' end.

Across the ravine, some way off, an extraordinary, slender, pale mountain soared upward and up from the blackness of the landscape. The horn of the whale.

The ravine, when they got down into it, was a treasure-chest.

A torrent of scummy water foamed through its very bottom, presumably coming in from the sea, miles away on one side, and departing via the miles-distant other side. In the ridges and banks that led down to the water, some ships lay broken in two or more pieces. Most were smaller vessels, carved reiver rafts, or the clinker-built boats of whalers and fishermen. One ship, which lay furthest off to the north, was of a design unknown to them. It had only three masts, but was huge, erected in galleries – so they asked each other how ever it had stayed upright on the sea.

The cargos of these craft had spilt and settled in the sludge. Here and there, already Lionwolf had noticed the glint of goldwork or a jewel, but in this spot the spoils were thick on the ground. They turned in all directions to examine them.

'Rubies. Amber. Look, Guri, chrysolites, beryls—'

'Mother-of-pearl,' added Guri grimly. 'We'll be rich. We can go and live in Sham, like kings of old.'

Gold and silver chalices, and armour and weapons chased with these metals, vied in the mud with gemstones, necklaces and hair ornaments in extravagant designs. A loose cache of pearls lay scattered like sugar.

There was, too, a vast quantity of picked bones.

'*Gnawed*, you will see,' said Guri.

'This is a scavenger that hoards bright objects, and has fangs.'

Something moved further up the gulch on its other side.

Lionwolf turned back.

Guri turned back and shouted.

They were strong mortal men again, appalled, alarmed, for a forgetful moment nearly exhilarated.

'A dragon. It's a dragon,' said Guri, deciding.

It was not, though, a dragon of the proper serpentine construct, as described in tales and lays. It heaved itself up and up from the dense mud of the bank, worm-like yet with massive foreclaws like a crab's. Its head was one with its body and, like all the other life forms of the whale's back, it had no eyes. Then the jaws reamed open, and the teeth were to be viewed. What would it need eyes for, with such teeth? It was the size of a couple of the smaller ships together, and its dentition was long, pointed and strangely clean.

Now all of it was out of the bank. It posed for them.

'It's smelling us through its open mouth,' said Lionwolf.

'Well,' said Guri, 'it's here, and we're here.'

Something else shifted at the dragon's far side, also forcing a way up from the mud.

'Another one, much smaller – the thing's young perhaps?'

'No, Guri, see, it's a woman.'

They stared in paralysis as the woman dragged herself finally upright. She was clotted in the muck, but she raised her fists in the air, and then she squealed a sort of triumph. Her captor ignored her.

'The burrow's down there. It must have taken her there to eat later. Why didn't she suffocate? Brave bitch to follow it back up here—'

'Guri, there's another one coming out.'

The second figure did not manage as well as the first,

but was also a woman, it seemed, though maybe much older and less able. The first escapee gave the second no help.

The worm-dragon closed its jaws. The clash echoed all over the gulch. Taking no notice of errant former victims from the burrow, it sprang solidly off the bank. Lionwolf and Guri then saw that it too had developed wings. They opened wide, and the last sunlight underlined them with veins of garnet. It flew straight across and down the gulf, steering itself faultlessly for the two men.

Lionwolf leapt to meet it. Two-handed, in the Jafn way, he swung the Kraagish sword and, as the creature descended to him, sheared off the front right claw.

Gore sprayed from the blow. In a black-red rain, Lionwolf fought on, Guri now cleavering at the beast from the other direction.

A wing was sliced. Losing momentum, the worm-dragon staggered into a landing. Grounded, it showed no sign of distress, however, lashing out at once with both the intact and dismembered claws.

Lionwolf felt the scald as it raked his shoulders and chest. He dropped down and moved in again, crouching, to get up under the clashing jaws.

A true mythic dragon would be armoured by scales, but this one was only tough and desensitized. The sword went in, and in.

It was Guri who darted up the tail of the legless torso and pranced on the monster's spine – if such it had. Here he drove in knives.

Lionwolf struck the worm repeatedly under the jaw. Further blood poured.

He rolled away before the teeth could have him. He quite unremembered he had probably come here to die.

Presently the worm heaved itself up and down, and Guri was dislodged. He lost a knife in this manoeuvre, which exasperated him – as, more than a decade ago, it would have done.

This thing was so witless it did not seem to know it was badly hurt, even dying perhaps.

Again and again they struck it. It and they fought on in a welter of blood and debris, jewels and gold cups splashing up from the impact of their feet and bodies.

At last the worm fell over. Its claws were by now both gone. The wings were useless. Yet, incredible and unthinkable, the jaws full of teeth clashed without pause, famished to bite human flesh.

Eventually the sun was going: the blood seemed to have got into the dying light.

As Lionwolf stepped away once more, seeing those clean and devilish fangs still blindly crashing and snapping at him from the bank, almost the only thing now of the worm which could move, a terrifying pity filled his mind.

'It won't die, Guri, it won't die.'

'It must,' said Guri.

'You must,' said Lionwolf to the worm. 'Go back, Guri. I can do this. I can't heal – once I tried, it didn't take – but I *can* kill.'

Guri stood back, his face set.

Lionwolf walked forward once more. The jaws reared to meet him, and Lionwolf drew in one long breath. Then he leant across, and merely touched the worm, a gentle touch between the places where, if it had had them, its eyes would have been.

Just as he had seen many times in the past, with deer or with bear, Guri now saw the worm grow sleepy. All its frantic activity stopped. It lowered its head calmly to the mud. Lionwolf kept his hand caressively on the blob of skull. When he was sure, he took his hand away and drove the sword in and down and through. He stroked the creature as, sleeping, it died. It might have been a hound he had loved, or a lion.

Silence filled the gulch. Then one of the women on the far bank began to screech again.

Lionwolf straightened and looked at her in anger. Only then did he realize that she was . . . that *both* of them were – his mother, Saphay.

Deep within his golden-eyed brain, Brightshade heard the beings trampling and talking, in the country of his back. Activity there seldom engaged the whale, but these people were different: he was highly conscious of them. Even the third – or fourth – addition, the undead man, had begun to impress Brightshade. The undead man seemed to have a meaning after all, though not such a telling one as the two aspects of the woman who had borne the god. As for Lionwolf, Brightshade had felt his every step like fire.

The whale did not understand any of the languages they spoke. He did not especially understand their intentions. Nevertheless, he read them like clearly written books.

He lay immobile now, enough of his head above the water for them to scale it and visit his last, and best, collection of bones. The horn, which was a mountain, or a giant's tower, ringed by spur-foothills or by an eccentric spur-palace, was catching on its tip the concluding ember of daylight.

Up on the sky, the whale zodiac was already beginning to burn.

They were not climbing to the pinnacle yet. They sat all together, but on the head side of the gulch, the men having clambered over there. The scavenger-worm's death had made no impression at all on Brightshade. Such beasts came and went. They worked better in the sea depths, cleansing the whale – his servants and unnecessary guards.

Brightshade cruised in motionless concentration. The sky darkened behind the star-whale.

Clothed in congealed blood and filth, the four of them sat watching the constellation.

Nearby, a grove of dead sailors the worm-dragon had also saved, rotted in fantastic, luminous colours. The smell had no importance among all the other effluvia.

'Only harsh words then, Mother,' said Lionwolf.

'You deserve nothing else.'

They had been like this since he reached her. There they had balanced, glaring at each other, she because she said he had wronged and deserted her, and everything therefore was his fault; he, because she said it.

Guri paid them no – or not much – attention. Saphay made him uneasy, as so often before. Now there were *two* of her, besides. The older one was demented obviously, tattered and bent, her long broken nails scrabbling over each other. She muttered to herself, calling out names sometimes in the Rukar tongue, or Jafn, usually names that Guri did not want to hear uttered.

'Can't you make her keep quiet?' he demanded of the other Saphay.

'How I wish I could. She drove me out of my wits in the hole down there.'

Did Saphay fully realize this other woman was *herself*?

The first Saphay, the Saphay Guri had known, was – under the mud – much as he recalled. Even strands of her distinctive hair were visible.

She seemed to know that Guri had, at least once, gone back to the snow-village, trying to find her. She treated *him* with chilly good manners. On her son she turned the barrage of her female rage.

Tomorrow they would all be dead, presumably. Why not be friends? But women held on to grudges. In all the worst feuds, so you heard, they were the ones who would never let go.

Now and then too, by the corpse-light, Guri saw her gazing sidelong at her son. Her eyes softened then with love, with sadness. Once she said, as if she could not contain it, 'You've grown to be a fine man, tall and strong. But I never saw that happen. It happened *away* from me. You never *let* me see it. No, I was *nothing* to you.'

And Lionwolf sat sulking, scowling. Guri asked the Great Gods if only *he*, dead Guri, had yet the sense he was born with.

They had nothing to eat or drink. Only Lionwolf seemed to miss these luxuries. Psychic impairment, now common to all of them, perhaps made the lack worse. Lionwolf had taken to sucking the hilt of the Kraag knife, though it was dirty beyond nightmares, to bring moisture into his mouth. Another man, of course, would already have collapsed or gone insane from dehydration after such physical exploits.

In the end, Guri asked Saphay how she had come to the whale. He thought she might have been compelled to it, as he had, and though what she said was evasive – icebergs, some lover she rejected, her cat, who also apparently was disloyal – what she answered did not change that thought. The monster had swum in close to shore and swept her up like a pebble under a broom.

'I remember nothing then. Sometimes, I think, we were under the water – but I survived. When I woke I was in this hell-land. At first I never knew I was on the creature's back. I still expected to die at every second.' Her face was mask-like with self-deception. Then her look grew troubled. 'It's death anyway. The death I had before, returned.' She glanced at Guri. He did not say anything. Saphay said, 'As I wandered about here, I met *her*.'

On her cue, the other oldish woman started to bleat. '*Zeth*,' she quavered. Saphay leant over and slapped her. Yes, Guri thought with tolerance, she *was* still a bitch. But it did shut the old fool up.

'*She* is called Saffi,' announced Saphay wilfully, it seemed, not attaching significance to the likeness of this name to her own. 'She told me so, in a lucid moment – as if I should have any need or wish to know.' She hesitated, then she said, 'No one else is alive here but for repulsive things that feed and fly or run about.'

'Did none of them attack you?' Guri was curious.

'Only that last one – *that* attacked. I'd come among all the jewels and the wreckage of ships, and the ground threw up that crab-worm.' Saphay shook back her mat of unspeakable hair. 'It didn't kill me. It made a sort of pet of me – and of *her*, that one.'

495

'Perhaps it loathed only men,' said Lionwolf. 'Perhaps it was female.'

Even in the weird light and under the dirt, Guri saw her cheeks flame.

'Yes, we have some cause, don't we. Oh, if you had known—' Suddenly she fell dumb. A minute passed. She sat looking at him. 'My son,' she said, 'my son.' Then she cried, and the tears washed her face. Beside her the old one began to sob too.

Guri got up. 'Well, I'm off.'

None of them made a move, the women howling, Lionwolf downcast, unable now to be charismatic and sweet to them.

Guri climbed laboriously up the slope of the whale's bulbous head, up and up until the three figures below disappeared behind ridges of polluted matter.

Higher up, though, the terrain levelled. Here the whale's architectural improvements were fewer.

Ahead, the spike of the horn showed black on the starry sky. From this point it would be, Guri imagined, an hour's stroll in the morning – that was all. The women would take longer over it. There was always that, to delay the end.

Should he simply go on alone, get it done with? Guri guessed it was no use to make the attempt. Somehow, as with leaving, he would be prevented – just as he had not drowned yet, nor she. As before, he and she had to be destroyed approximately at the same time or it could not happen. He was dead anyway – why bother about doing it over?

Beyond the headland of the whale, he thought he could make out now the sea far down, coldly tangling.

Guri stamped on the whale's head. He doubted it could feel him.

'What have you got planned for him, black whale? For me it's the spiking again, that I can tell. For her, too, the same; the cold and the water-death, under ice. But for him – for Lionwolf – what?' Up here, Guri became aware of the faintest tremor. He thought the whale was beginning at long last to move out into the wide sea. 'He's a *god*, black whale – even reduced as he is – invulnerable once, and even now his wounds heal in minutes. Throttled by thirst, he's alive, aware, can still speak, fine as bronze. *What is it to be?*'

Brightshade spoke to Guri.

Guri had not expected a reply, and fell over. He lay sprawled on the whale's headland, and heard the song Brightshade sang to him from courtesy and matchless wickedness.

And although the polite and wicked song had no words, yet Guri's mental arena was flooded by its *shape*.

When it was finished, Guri lay without moving a long while.

'I shan't tell him of it,' he said. He bit his lip, the inside of his mouth. Guri too began to cry. Near to dawn he raised his head and shouted at the sky, not in words but in *shapes*: panic, terror, the fury of thirteen years and more.

Then he went down again, and found Lionwolf asleep with his head on the knees of his young sleeping mother, and the older mother also asleep, held tight in one of his arms.

'You I forgive, Lion,' said Guri. 'It is the Great Gods I never will.'

*

497

The Lionwolf was dreaming. As nearly always, he *knew* that he was. Some clever mage stood before him, one of the Magikoy he believed, but he was unsure, for details of dress and speech were not clear, only the ritual the man performed.

It was, it seemed, a spell of unmaking. Spellbound by the periphery energies, Lionwolf watched.

Even here, he could not be sure what he was seeing. The mage subtracted amorphous elements from a vessel, and gradually a light that shone in the vessel went out.

'So it is,' said the unknown mage, 'when what has caused it to be is cancelled by precise sorcerous formulae. A magic of symbol – you will find it effective.'

Lionwolf opened his eyes. The old Saffi simpered at him. She had sat up and was combing her hair with her claws. Saphay was smoothing his own hair. He thought of Darhana, and a hundred women who had done this. But a man's mother, of course, had usually been the first.

He was glad they were reconciled. He was sorry he could not save her from this second death – Guri too. For himself he felt only the familiar bewilderment, the newly met despair.

Had the dream been intended to alert some rescuer's scheme in him? It had not done so.

Guri stood waiting as everyone got up, and the women tidied themselves in the meagre and only ways they could. Guri noted, however, that not one of them now required to exercise any bodily function.

Saphay was stern today, but collected. She helped her crone-self along as they went up to the headland. Once she called the old one 'Nurse', then clicked her tongue at the error.

Guri and Lionwolf walked in front. They did not speak.

Then, reaching the top, Lionwolf stared out. The sun was rising, and it was plain they were now at sea, the great whale coursing along, smooth as butter. It was misty but sunlight sprinkled the waves so many miles below, as they parted at the animal's astonishing progress.

'Guri—'

'No more,' said Guri. 'We've done too much in this world to talk about it. It talks loud enough for itself.'

'Agreed.'

'I'll see you in Hell, Lion,' said Guri. 'Only, my hell may not be the same as yours.'

'Great Gods grant your hell is far better than mine.'

Again, neither man said *Amen*. Guri was done with his gods. Lionwolf had yet to find some.

The women toiled on over the crest of the dirt banks, and came walking together along the head of the whale.

'A pretty morning,' said Saphay.

Her tear-sponged face was already skeletal with fear. Of them all, she was the most frightened. She had hoped for immortality, but the weight of death was on her here. She knew she would not escape one more time. But she had been trained as royal once. To Guri, haughtily she said, 'Where must we go now?'

'Up to the spurs and the horn of it.'

'Very well.'

Now Lionwolf walked between the women, with one on each arm, as if at the royal court in wasted Ru Karismi.

Guri marched behind, their bodyguard.

What a bloody day to die on. But, then, would he have liked it better if there was a gale?

The palace that was spurs became larger and more

miraculous, and the spike above too towering now to judge or analyse its size.

Saphay thought, *Perhaps nothing will happen. Perhaps it only wants this: for us to behave as if we go to die—*

They stood under the colossus of the spurs. Here the real skeletons were, festooning spears of ivory. Too excessive in numbers to seem even like a boneyard, yet Saphay glimpsed the skulls of horned lashdeer draped in a garland about a string of human bones that ended in a human skull. These were hers, she knew instantly, totally. So did her other self, old Saffi, who hid her eyes – then, absurdly, uncovered them, beamed, broke away and ran smiling *towards* the skeleton, as if to a beloved relative.

Guri also detected his skeleton at once. It was a noble effort, he thought, still whitish in bits, and the head on the right way.

The breeze of passage laced their lips with salt. He remembered the ash plain by the city. Probably Lionwolf did too.

Saphay thought, *Surely, then, this is all—*

But, before she could speak, the butter-smoothness of the ride was over.

Abruptly the whale had flung itself upward, in a kind of bound.

Lionwolf reached out to grab hold of Saphay. But she was gone. He saw her stricken face sliding away from him; and Guri lifted as if in unseen hands, yelling, snarling a war-chant—

Lionwolf, slung against the spurs, found himself pinned there, anchored and tied in place. The old woman mouthed up at him. 'Goodbye,' she said kindly.

The world of the whale cracked apart, the sea smashed like a million mirrors.

Water covered Lionwolf, beating him down flat, but trapped still by his clothing caught on the jagged edge of a spur.

He heard Saphay screaming. Guri's borjiy roar was done; he had been tossed skyward, turned over in the air. High as the sun he looked now, Guri, impaled on the razor tip of the impossible horn of the whale. He was dead again. His red blood trickled resinous down the horn-side, like honey.

Saphay had been thrown off into the ocean. Lionwolf had not seen this either, only the result – her absence. The older Saphay had vanished, too, without a protest.

Only Lionwolf now, clutched by native bone on to the back of Brightshade, the god's assassin.

And to Lionwolf came in another tide – which was one of time and measurement.

Unmaking. The god, through his votary the whale, had unmade them: the mother who had conceived and borne Lionwolf, Guri who had saved him from Zezeth's wrath. This had been committed, the unmaking, in a flawless copy of the first death of each. One to the spike, one to the water under deepest submarine ice. They were erased. History was dismantled, Zeth victorious.

Lionwolf felt the tide wash over him, that was not water.

He tried to stand against the spur, to free himself of it, of everything.

He was weak. His hands . . . were too small.

If any had seen, if Brightshade had, and perhaps he alone could, Lionwolf the man was melted down in those moments. A red-haired boy struggled against the spur, then, even the boy—

A red-haired child of four or five years clung on the back of the whale, not struggling but *shrieking* for his dead mother and for his dead uncle—

A *child*.

But then, even the *child*—

He was dissolved all away. It was a *baby* shrieking there—

And then it is only a wisp of a thing, an embryo outside a womb. A seed.

Spell of symbols. History expunged, as if . . . he had never been. Unconceived, *unborn*. Unmaking, *unmade*.

It is nothing.

Nothing.

He is nothing.

Gone—

But oh his *soul*, the soul of the Lionwolf, *that* falls on and on into the deepest sea of all, and to the Battle Gates of Hell.

TWO

Nine Vormish men witnessed her nascence on their coast. They would become her priesthood.

There had been an apocalypse of death, far far to the south. The lands of all the north sea peoples had been decimated. Such swathes of their sons had been cut down, but they had suffered not as terribly, even so, as the peoples of the continent itself, and already Vorms, Kelps and Fazions prepared to sail against the helpless landmass. They had been reivers, snatchers, for centuries. Now, despite tragedy, it was an epoch for great gain.

And thus the birth of a goddess out of the ocean was to their taste.

Jord and his brother, Majord, were with their ship under the bluff. They were organizing the scouring of the gut of the ship, and her rowers' benches.

The seven other men were drunk still from a funeral wake the previous night – the brothers, too, but they were intent on denying it. Amid the arguments and horseplay, Jord looked up and saw.

'*What is that, there, on our water?*'

Nine men left their work, their everyday lives. They grouped on the stony shore, and stared.

A long wave, green as apples, was spurling around the

coast. Up in the pleated curve of it, which never shattered, stood a snow-white woman in a second wave of topaz hair.

Sea-birthed, she rode into the harbour of the Vormish island, showing no trace of any other world, nor of her mortal royalty, nor of her double drowning in a frigid sea. No, the sea was her lover and handmaiden. It brought her gloriously to landfall.

When the wave creamed down on the beach, and the woman stepped from it as if out of a green shell, the Vormish men, knowing she was divine, dropped at her naked feet.

All of her was naked. All of her was beautiful. But, then, she was a goddess.

He had made sure of it – just as the other made sure of patterns in the stars. Whether actually an individual – or only the third aspect of the three who comprised that god fragmentedly known as Yyrot, Ddir, Zeth – Yyrot had energized and altered Saphay. By means she never noticed, he had somehow given her the godhead he warned of or promised. Zezeth wanted her dead; Yyrot took care she lived, but in the ultimate unassailable form, all mortal dross thrown away. Her second death in the sea had ensured as much.

Not only schizophrenic then, the individuals of this god-triad, but a composite of threefold personality.

Saphay did not, just then, recollect any of them.

She stepped ashore, fresh as a cucumber, delicious as a flower.

She laughed as the human men obeised themselves, and Majord, their bard, praised her.

It was only later, in the wooden hall like an upside-down boat, seated in a shrine and worshipped, that

Saphay's goddess eyes darkened. Then – and for this the Vormland would adore her – she spoke as did countless Vormish women in that year of sorrow and wars. It was in Vormish, too. She was, after all, a god, and multilingual. 'My son,' she wept. 'My son.'

. . . Unended . . .
Next

HERE IN COLD HELL
BOOK TWO OF THE LIONWOLF TRILOGY

Glossary

Bit – Human chattel: Ranjalla, and southern north-east
Borjiy – Berserker, fearless fighter: Jafn

Chaiord – Clan chieftain/king: Jafn
Concubina – Unmarried royal wife: Ruk Kar Is
Corrit – Demon-sprite: Jafn
Crait – Type of lammergeyer: Rukarian uplands
Crarrow (pl. **Crarrowin**) – Coven witches of Olchibe and
  parts of Gech
Crax – Chief witch of **Crarrowin** coven
Cutch – Fuck

Dilf – One of several forms of dormant grain and cereal:
  general, but found mostly in more fertile areas

Endhlefon – Time period of eleven days and nights: Jafn

Firefex – Phoenix: Rukarian
Fleer-wolf – A kind of wolf-like jackal, known for its
  lamenting cries: general to the snow-wastes
Flylarch – Pine-like berried plant: general to the continent
Forcutcher – Insulting variation, of obscure exact
  meaning, deriving from the word **cutch**

Gargolem – Magically activated metallic non-human servant; the greatest of these creatures guards the kings at Ru Karismi: Rukarian

Gler – Demon-sprite: Jafn

Hirdiy – Nomadic band: northern north Gech

Hnowa – Riding animal: Jafn

Horsaz (pl. **Horsazin**) – A breed of horse apparently part-bred with fish; scaled and acclimated to land and ocean: Fazion, Kelp and Vorm

Hovor – Wind-spirit: Jafn

Icenvel – Type of weaselish thick-furred rodent: general to the continent

Insularia – Sub-river complex belonging solely to, and solely accessible to, the **Magikoy**: Ru Karismi

Jalee – Fleet of war vessels, including Mother Ship, usually thirteen in number: Fazion, Kelp and Vorm

Jinan/Jinnan – Magically activated house-spirit: Rukarian – normally **Magikoy**

Kalfi – Whale calf: general

Kiddle/Kiddling – Baby or child up to twelve years: Olchibe

Lamascep – Sheep of long, thick wool: general to the north

Lashdeer – Fine-bred, highly trained chariot animals used for high-speed travel over snow and ice: Rukarian

Mageia – Female mage: Ruk Kar Is, and elsewhere in the north

Magikoy – Order of magician-scholars, established centuries in the past; possessed of extraordinary and closely guarded powers: Ruk Kar Is

Mera – Mermaid: general to the north

Oculum Magikoy – scrying glass, or magic mirror of incredible scope: Ruk Kar Is

Quintul – Five-towered: Rukarian

Scratchered – Basically, overused: Jafn

Seef – Demon, a type of vampire: Jafn

Sihpp – Similar to **seef**: Jafn

Slee – Riding ice carriage: Rukarian

Sleekar – Ice chariot: Rukarian

Sluhts – Communal tent/cave/hut dwellings: Olchibe

Sluhtins – Large city groupings of **sluhts**: Olchibe

Soint – Obscure insult, seeming to have to do with either genital or lavatorial practices (?): Jafn, but also elsewhere in the north and east, including Ruk Kar Is

Subtor – Lowest underground chambers of magician's house: **Magikoy**

Tattarope – Snake of corded, rope-like skin: Uaarb and far north

Thaumary – Thaumaturgic or sorcerous chamber attached to main hall, for use mostly by mages of a garth or House – even the chieftain does not enter here uninvited: Jafn

GLOSSARY

Towery – Complex of towers connected to each other by
walkways and/or inner passages: **Magikoy**, Ruk Kar Is

Vrix – Demon-sprite: Jafn

Weed-of-light – Forest-growing ice plant, having blue
flowers: north and east

White-kadi – Type of gull: eastern seaboard

Woman bow – Bow which can fire only one arrow at a
time (male bows can fire up to four arrows at a
time, depending on the skill of the archer): Olchibe